ANGEL

ANGEL by Alton Gansky
Published by Realms
A Strang Company
600 Rinehart Road
Lake Mary, Florida 32746

Scripture quotations are from the New American Standard Bible—Updated
Edition, Copyright © 1960, 1962, 1963, 1968, 1971, 1972, 1973, 1975, 1977,
1995 by The Lockman Foundation. Used by permission. (www.Lockman.org)

The characters portrayed in this book are fictitious unless they are historical figures explicitly named. Otherwise, any resemblance to actual people,
whether living or dead, is coincidental.

Cover Design: studiogearbox.com
Executive Design Director: Bill Johnson

ISBN 978-0-7394-8944-4

Printed in the United States of America

ANGEL

ALTON GANSKY

REALMS
A STRANG COMPANY

Prologue

Last Will and Testament of Priscilla Cloe Simms
Digital video recording from somewhere in Minnesota

M Y NAME IS PRISCILLA SIMMS. Yes, *that* Priscilla Simms. This is my last will and testament. Being of sound mind and weary body, I make this recording of my own volition and under no compulsion. Before I pass my earthly belongings on, I wish to make a statement, to give an account of what has led me to this place and what will likely lead to my death.

I'm recording this from a secret location...scratch that. By the time you see this, I'll be in another location—or dead. Probably dead. Since I can't edit this video, I'm afraid you're going to have to endure raw footage. Sorry. I wish I could do better, but things aren't ideal for me. Not anymore...

I doubt I'll be here much longer. I have to keep moving—keep hiding—but I suppose it's only a matter of time. From reporter to rebel in eighteen months seems too much to believe. Half the time I think I'm dreaming, but when I open my eyes the nightmare continues.

I know you—whoever you are—don't need me to tell you all that's happened since Aster's arrival, but you do need me to tell you what few others will: the truth.

You know some of the story—the part he wants you to know, the parts we all believed, the parts I helped broadcast to the world. There's more—much more. All the goodness you see...things aren't what they seem, and I'm not what the authorities say I am. I wish I could prove that to you—to the world—but I harbor no illusions about that. Still, I must try. This is bigger than me or my opinion. This is larger than any one person. This goes beyond this life. It extends into eternity.

I should have known better, really. Hindsight, as they say, is always 20/20. The clues were there, and had my eyes been open, I would have recognized them.

I had been warned, too. A dear friend, an insightful woman...she knew. Somehow, someway, she knew. I didn't listen. I couldn't see what she saw, and I should have. After all, we share the same faith.

Yes, I said faith. That was the key. That *is* the key. Had I bothered to see the situation through the eyes of faith, I would have recognized the lie and maybe made a difference, maybe kept all this from happening. But I didn't. I suppose this video is as much a confession as it is an attempt to get the truth out to any who will listen.

Will you listen? I can't force you to believe me, but maybe, just maybe, my account will ring with enough truth you'll be able to recognize it. At any rate, it's the best I can do now.

That's why I have to do this and do what comes next. That's why this video...

Where to begin...

Chapter One

WHAP.

Priscilla Simms jerked in her chair and snapped her head in the direction of the sound. Something small and gray fluttered against the large window that formed one wall of her office. A bird-shaped smudge remained just to the right of the window's center.

Priscilla studied the powder residue the luckless bird left on the floor-to-ceiling pane. She had seen such things before. Occasionally, an inattentive bird would mistake glass for open space, smash into the window, and leave the fine powder that covered its feathers as evidence of its mistake. Most flew away unharmed; some were less fortunate.

Returning her attention to the computer monitor, Priscilla began to type.

Whap.

"Not again—"

Thud. Whap.

Another bird hit the window. Then another. She stood and looked over her cubicle wall. The window wall that ran the length of the open office bore the hit marks of a dozen birds.

Then she noticed the others. Birds flock in a panicked mass: pigeons, sparrows, and others, dipping and climbing and swooping and dropping as if each one had forgotten how to control their flight.

Then she heard it.

And then she felt it.

In the one and a half seconds that passed between the two moments, Priscilla Simms felt cored out by fear, and the empty space filled with scorching terror. Her heart clinched like a fist, and for a moment she believed it would never start again.

"What was that...?" Someone began but never finished. Priscilla didn't expend the mental effort to determine the speaker.

What began as a distant rumble of thunder over a mountain soon became a vibration in her feet—then a sharp jolt familiar to every Southern Californian. The rumble that first sounded like little more than a car stereo with an exaggerated baseline turned too loud, becoming a freight train roaring through her office cubicle.

A scream erupted from her lips. The frightened emanations of forty other people on the floor joined in a cacophony of panic. The rumbling announcement was familiar. The motion of the floor beneath her made her stagger backward, striking her chair and sending it crashing into the cubicle divider behind her. The thought of it barely registered when another jolt arrived and Priscilla stumbled, grasping madly for support from her desk. The flatscreen computer monitor danced across the surface as if magically brought to life. Papers slipped from the edges of the desk and cascaded to the floor. The large window that formed one wall of her workspace rattled.

Priscilla dropped to her hands and knees and scrambled into the kneehole of her desk, then covered her head with her hands. She managed a two-word prayer: "Dear Jesus." She repeated it several times.

The building swayed as if trying to bend over backward. She reminded herself it was what high-rise buildings did in situations like this. Swaying was better than breaking. Her head knew this; her heart harbored doubts. She thought of the six stories of building above her and the eight stories below. If the building collapsed, she would be sandwiched between them—she and all her co-workers.

The expansive windows rattled like the skin of a bass drum; plastic diffusers fell from the fluorescent lights above, crashing to the floor and shattering over office furniture. Priscilla pulled herself as far into the kneehole as possible, knowing that if the building collapsed, such an effort of self-preservation would be useless. No desk—not even the industrial metal one under which she cowered—could hold up hundreds of thousands of tons of steel and concrete.

The next jolt extracted another scream. The floor moved as if some giant had kicked it from beneath. Papers flowed from the desk and adjoining side table. File drawers sprung open as if a malevolent polter-geist had gone on a rampage. From somewhere in the office a large piece of furniture fell over and crashed to the carpeted floor. She heard the sound of glass breaking and first assumed the windows had given way but then rejected the thought. The windows would've been much louder. Besides, they were made of glass resistant to breakage. It was unlikely—

The window next to her desk exploded, and small cubes of glass rained like hail. The morning wind blew unhindered into her space and through the office, carrying the violent symphony of car alarms from the street nearly one hundred feet below.

The building flexed with the jerking of the ground, and Priscilla could feel the desk slide to the side—the side with a hole where once a window stood. The image of her falling eight floors, still wedged beneath the desk, flashed on her mind like a strobe light.

Finally the jolt passed, leaving the floor vibrating like a violin string.

But the third jolt was the worst. Priscilla felt the floor drop from beneath her, and she waited for the fall. It never came. The building still stood, quivering like a tower of Jell-O. Maybe *she* quivered.

She shifted in the small space, pressing her back to the side of the kneehole furthest from the missing window wall and dug her heels into the thin carpet. It took a moment for her to realize that she and the desk were still several feet from the broad opening.

Dust rose from the streets and buildings outside, riding manic air currents into the office and snatching up bits of office debris and scores of loose pieces of paper.

Another rumble rose, but this time the jarring movement had changed to an easy roll. Another, half the force of the last one, followed.

Then it stopped.

The building ceased its twisting, bending, and undulating.

Priscilla waited, afraid that her movement would invite the earth-quake to return.

She felt a new shaking, but this did not come from the ground. It came from her hands, which trembled as if stricken with palsy. Her lips quivered. Her stomach did gymnastics.

Seconds stuttered by as she waited. Nothing. Just the sound of car alarms, the feel of unwanted wind, and the sense that doomsday had just paid a visit.

Priscilla oozed from beneath the desk, crawling on the rounded shards of tempered glass. By design, such windows shattered into small pieces with rounded edges, but they were still sharp enough to cut two holes in her panty hose and leave painful red impressions on the heels of her hands.

She stood and swayed. Her heart had yet to settle and her body had not finished shaking. Brushing the bits of cubed glass from her hands and legs, Priscilla looked around her cubicle. The window next to the desk was gone, open from sill to head and from jamb to jamb. A tentative step forward allowed her a view of the street.

The dust in the air hung like a fog. Below, citizens raced from buildings and stood in the middle of the street. She could see that the façade of one of the older buildings, a historic office structure from the 1930s, had come loose and fallen. The concrete and brick facing had collapsed on several cars parked along Tenth Street. Several people moved with limps, and she saw others grasping their arms and heads.

"Get away from there, Priscilla. Have you lost your senses?"

Priscilla turned to see Leo Hart, face flushed, dust clinging to his thin white hair, standing just outside her cubicle. Two quick steps later, she had her arms around the man's neck. "Are you OK, Leo? I mean..."

"My heart is fine, kid. I'm just old, not decrepit. How about you?"

She gave the associate publisher another heartfelt squeeze. He'd lived sixty-two hard years and was the best journalist Priscilla had ever known. He had endured reportorial duty in Vietnam and lived through some of the most difficult reporting work a newspaperman could, and it had taken a toll on his heart and lungs.

"I'm fine, Leo. Actually, I'm scared out of my wits. I thought I was going to ride my desk to the ground floor."

"Yeah, but you didn't. That's the important thing to remember. Now we have work to do—"

"Leo...you're OK...Priscilla, are you hurt? Your window..."

Chris Conlin's extremities shook.

"Take a breath, Chris." Leo stepped to his boss's side. Chris was twenty years junior to Leo, but the wisdom of Debatto Media had given the less-experienced man the helm. Not that Conlin was a novice, just that on many levels he was the lesser of the two men.

"OK." He inhaled deeply. "We should do something."

"You got that right." Leo waited, then made eye contact with Priscilla. "OK, first things first. We need a head count of employees. Find out if there are injuries." He paused. "It may take some time before medical help can reach us."

"Christina Banner." Priscilla looked down the row of cubicles and into the open space of junior reporters.

"What about her?" Conlin still seemed dazed.

"She was a medic in the army. Saw lots of action in Afghanistan. You know that."

"Good idea," Leo said. "Let's hope she's all right."

"This is a big story, Leo. Real big. We need to get someone on it."

"People first, Chris, then the story. People first."

The sounds of moans and weeping rose and hung in the air.

The fear that had gripped Priscilla moments before melted under the heat of determination. There was work to be done. "I'll take this aisle."

She moved from cubicle to cubicle checking on each employee. Leo was right behind her. Conlin had disappeared.

Steve Toomey rapped his knuckles on the door so hard he thought for a moment he'd broken the skin. He waited one second and then opened the heavy slab and plunged into the room.

"Steve. What's the meaning of this?" Governor Patrick Merrell sprang to his feet. "You know better than to interrupt a meeting like this."

Steve looked at his boss and could see a tinge of red rise in his rugged and handsome face. At fifty-three, the man looked ten years younger. His shoulders bore the same square angle they did when he played football for UCLA. The three decades that had passed since those days had not bowed his head or taken the luster from his hazel eyes. He still could turn a woman's head.

"I'm sorry, Governor. I'm afraid this can't wait."

"Everything can wait, Steve. You're supposed to be meeting with the Democratic leadership on the budget." He turned to the two men seated on the sofa opposite his padded chair. "I apologize, gentlemen."

Steve gave the lieutenant governor and the state attorney general little attention. Instead, he marched to a large plasma television screen set in a maple entertainment center and pushed the power button. Before the picture flashed on the screen, cell phones hanging from the hips of the men on the sofa sounded in unison.

Steve turned up the volume, then faced his boss.

"...early reports indicated moderate damage and scores of injuries." The CNN newscaster struck an even but concerned tone, his voice steady, as if reporting on a downturn in the stock market. "As yet, no deaths have been reported. Of course, we don't know the status of those in the Windom Building in downtown San Diego..."

"San Diego? What happened?" The governor paled.

"Earthquake, sir. It happened ten or fifteen minutes ago. They don't have a Richter number yet, but some are guessing in the low sevens."

"The epicenter?"

"Don't know yet. We should have word from the Office of Emergency Services in the next few minutes."

"Steve..."

The chief of staff didn't need to hear the questions. "I'm trying to get word from someone on the ground. The news reports say it's her building, but we haven't confirmed that yet."

"Whose building?" Jon Banks was now on his feet. The attorney general looked fragile. Both men hung up their cell phones. Steve could guess what they had heard.

"The Windom Building. My daughter has a law office there."

Banks swore.

The lieutenant governor, Nicholas "Nick" Lodge, rose. "The news anchor didn't say what happened to the building."

"That's because we came in late," Steve said. "The building..." He stopped.

"Say it," Governor Merrell demanded. "Just say it."

6

"Apparently it fell in on itself, crushing a couple of the lower floors."

"First floor." Merrell answered the unasked question. He picked up his cell phone.

"Who are you calling?" Steve asked.

"My wife. She's in Orlando with the grandkids. Took them to Disney World. She...I don't want her to find out over the news media."

In the awkward moment, the two politicos joined Steve in front of the television, leaving Merrell an opportunity to speak to his wife without their eyes fixed upon him.

The CNN newscaster continued his monologue of earthquake facts, filling time as he waited for off-camera people to feed him new information. His fellow anchor, a woman who looked like she had stepped off a model's runway rather than through the door of a journalism school, helped. An expert, who had no more information than they, waxed on about the causes of earthquakes and what might be expected over the next few days.

"I'm...just a moment." The male anchor tilted his head to a side as if someone whispered in his ear. "I've just been told that we have a video feed from a local San Diego television station and they...yes...yes, they're at the Windom Building. I think we'll be showing that to you in just...we have it now?"

He disappeared from the screen, replaced by the image of a multi-story building that looked as if it should be on a bombed-out street in Iraq.

"Governor." Steve stepped to the side, allowing Merrell a clear view of the television.

"Oh, dear God." He crossed himself.

The first floor was gone, crushed beneath incalculable weight of concrete and steel.

Over the distance that separated Steve from the governor, he could hear the weeping coming from the phone's handset.

"Steve. Get me on a plane. I'm going to San Diego."

"The airport will probably be closed."

"Then get me close, and we'll helicopter the rest of the way. I don't care if we have to land on Interstate 5."

7

"I'm on it."

Merrell kept the phone to his ear. "I'm going to San Diego. I'll keep you posted." He listened. "No, not yet. If you fly back now, we'll lose contact. Stay put. I'll have someone charter a jet for you. It will take a little time." He paused and listened again. "I know. Waiting is the hardest work of all, but that's the way it is. Go back to the hotel and get your things ready. I'll call you when I can. Once the charter jet is ready, someone will call you. OK?" He hung up. Tears filled his eyes.

The image on the screen became more vivid, more detailed, as if it were morphing from 2-D to 3-D.

Merrell turned to Lodge. "I'm afraid your job just got a lot more difficult. If the worst...I mean, if..."

Lodge placed a hand on the governor's shoulder. "I'll handle things from here. I'll keep the government running until you're ready to strap on the harness again. For now, your only concern is your family." The lieutenant governor stepped to Merrell's desk and picked up the phone. "This is Nick Lodge. Get me OES." He looked at Merrell. "Get out of here. Go check on your daughter."

Chapter Two

PRISCILLA REACHED THE LANDING OF THE LAST SET OF STAIRS, HER legs reminding her that she was no longer as fit and limber as she was in college. She'd considered the elevators, but only for a second. She had no idea what the earthquake may have done to them and felt no desire to stretch her luck.

She and Leo had spoken to each of the forty people who worked on their portion of the ninth floor. Only a few had injuries, but none were serious: some cuts, some bruises, and two bumps on the head. How others on other floors fared she didn't know. That was the problem with natural disasters: too many people for one person to help.

At the bottom of the stairs was a door that led to the outside. Priscilla hesitated a moment, then pushed the panic bar that released the door. The dim light of the stairs gave way to the bright glow of the morning. She felt grateful that the earthquake had come during the day. Things would have been far worse had it happened at night. She didn't know why, but her building had not lost power. She assumed that such would not be the case for most of the city.

Priscilla had lived through several earthquakes before, but none with such intensity. In some cases, items fell from shelves and pictures slipped from their moorings on the walls, but never before had she experienced such widespread damage. She reminded herself that things could be worse. She'd seen video and studied pictures of cities hit by major earthquakes. Often rubble filled the streets and the death toll rose by the hour, but when she exited the emergency stairwell, she saw little of that. Some buildings, like her own, had lost windows; some displayed cracked plaster; and only one showed any real damage—the building she saw from the ninth floor. Chunks of its façade rested in the street.

People, employees of the various businesses and offices, stood in the road not willing to trust the safety of their buildings. A few wept, some stood in shock, and two men laughed nervously, apparently the only emotion they could release.

The car alarms had given up their effort to garner attention, replaced by the ululating sounds of sirens from emergency vehicles. Smoke began to rise a short distance away, but the blocks of mid-rise buildings blocked Priscilla's view.

She turned south and moved through the shadows of the tall buildings, bits of broken glass grinding beneath her feet. She felt as if she were in a war zone. San Diego had been lucky—this time.

After traveling two blocks, Priscilla stopped and stared in the first-floor window of a delicatessen she liked to frequent. Its front window lay in jagged shards on the street and on the tables that lined the inner wall of the restaurant. She pushed through the door and saw the damage the earthquake had left in its wake. A wire metal stand that held individual-sized bags of potato chips had walked away from the wall and tipped itself over. Ceiling tiles rested in pieces on the tables, chairs, and floor. Dust from the space above the tiles coated everything. She heard a sound of water spraying and saw a growing puddle ooze its way beneath the refrigerated counter and serving area and mix with the detritus on the floor.

"Mr. Chen? It's Priscilla. Mr. Chen? Are you all right?"

A string of hot Chinese words filled the air. Priscilla didn't speak Cantonese, but she recognized swearing when she heard it. The sound of spraying water ceased.

"Mr. Chen? It's me, Priscilla."

A head of thin white hair rose above the counter, and the unhappy face of Mr. Chen gazed back at her. Chen had owned the deli for as long as Priscilla could remember. He had once revealed that he'd inherited it from his father, who established the eatery when Chen was just a boy.

"Oh, hello, Ms. Simms." He gave a short bow. "I am fine, as is my wife. She is in the back restacking supplies."

"You're wet."

He looked sad and gazed at the water that covered him from neckline to somewhere below. The counter kept Priscilla from seeing the extent of the soaking. "The earthquake broke one of my water pipes. I am lucky that it broke above the cutoff valve or I would have to shut off the water at the meter."

"But you're not hurt, right?"

"I'm fine. My wife is fine, but scared."

"Everybody's scared, Mr. Chen. No shame in that."

"I may be out of business for a few days." He looked crestfallen, and Priscilla's heart went out to him.

"You'll be back on your feet in no time. You still serve the best pastrami in the city. No earthquake is going to change that."

"I hope you're right."

"I am. I'm always right."

The ground began to shake, and Chen's eyes widened. The floor rose and fell in even undulations. A thousand noises made by items in the deli assaulted Priscilla's ears. A few seconds later, it was gone.

"Aftershock," Chen said. "We can expect a lot of those."

"I know. Not that I want to hear it."

Priscilla wished him well and returned to the street, continuing south along the path she had begun two blocks ago, her eyes set on the rising column of smoke. As she moved past another street-level store, she caught a glimpse of her reflection and was surprised to see how disheveled she looked. She still wore her red hair to her shoulders, and the strong, distinctive features that once made her the darling of the television news business were still in place, albeit softened with wrinkles carved into a slightly paler skin.

There had been a time when her appearance mattered more than anything, a time when she worried about every new crease at the corners of her eyes. Ten years ago, when she sat behind the "big desk" and faced the cameras, reading news from a teleprompter and joking with the weatherman, such things were crucial. But she was not a stupid woman. She had gone into journalism not to be famous but to make a difference. She had earned her right to report the news, first by getting the best education she could and ultimately taking home a master's degree in

11

journalism. She had paid her dues as an on-camera reporter, giving the details of everything from the local dog show to four-alarm fires. She'd covered politics, crime, and everything else that came her way.

But no amount of education, experience, or fame could halt the progress of time. She, like everyone else, had aged, and the camera noticed. For a time it didn't seem to matter. No one said anything. Ratings didn't decline. Local television stations, unlike their national counterparts, had found something of value in having a woman of middle age announce the news. But the industry began to change. The twenty-four-hour-a-day national news programs began to populate the ranks of their anchors with women who dressed and made themselves up as fashion models—and what the networks did, Priscilla knew, would sooner or later make its way to the local stations.

She reached the breaking point when a colleague had taken an extended vacation and returned with a brand-new face. People told the woman how wonderful she looked, how the surgery had taken ten—no, fifteen—years off her appearance. That wouldn't have been so bad had the colleague not approached her, set the business card of the plastic surgeon on Priscilla's desk, and followed it up with, "It really wasn't that bad." She gave Priscilla a wink and left.

At one time Priscilla would have given such a hint serious consideration, but those days were gone. In the early years of her career, she was ruthless and ambitious, willing to roll over anyone who got in her way, but a series of events had changed her in the unseen places of her heart and soul.

Last year, she had left television news, leaving KGOT-TV behind and turning to print media, where content mattered more than appearance. When she first considered the change, she assumed that she might find a job at some newspaper; instead, she found a willing employer in the Debatto Media Group, specifically at *Today News*, a news outlet that published both a weekly magazine and a daily Internet edition. With offices around the globe, Priscilla had her choice of assignments. She chose to stay in San Diego and had yet to regret it.

As she moved along the sidewalks and across the streets, Priscilla paused and raised the digital video camera she carried. By using a video camera, she could shoot footage that would stream over the Internet or be snipped into individual "frames" for use in the magazine. She shot footage of the fallen façade, the broken windows of her office building, the stunned faces of citizens, and the dark column of smoke that drew her.

Other reporters from *Today News* were doing the same along different streets. That's what happened in a crisis—firefighters fought fires and conducted rescues, police officers controlled the streets, and reporters recorded it all.

Priscilla moved across Broadway and made her way to Eighth Street. As she rounded the corner, she heard more sirens and saw, one hundred feet in the distance, the red flashing lights of fire trucks and police cars. Priscilla quickened her pace, moving as fast as she could and still taping everything before her. In the old days, she had more than once guided a cameraman as they jogged at the scene of some breaking bit of news. She had no one to guide her here.

A dozen strides later, Priscilla realized that the emergency before her was taking place at the famous Windom Building, a landmark in downtown San Diego, one of the older and more beautiful structures in the city. She angled through the crowd reciting a mantra of, "Excuse me. Press. Excuse me, I'm with the press."

She managed to get close to the action and, for a moment, wished she hadn't. Priscilla knew the Windom Building to be ten stories tall—it was now one story shorter.

Priscilla removed her cell phone and looked at the small color display to check the signal. In a remarkable testimony to the resilience of technology, the cell phone system was still operating, and she punched in the number for her office. Of course, just because the cell phones were working didn't mean landlines were still intact.

She waited for the call to connect but instead heard the fast-busy signal that indicated overtaxed airwaves. Pressing the END button, she redialed. Again a busy signal. On the fourth try, Chris Conlin answered.

"Chris, it's Priscilla. I'm at the Windom Building on Eighth Street. It's collapsed in on itself."

"You mean the whole thing's fallen down?"

"No, I mean that the upper floors have crushed the lower floor. It looks like it may have sunk into the basement. The Windom Building does have underground parking, right?"

"Yeah, I've parked there myself a time or two. What about other buildings?"

"Aside from a few broken windows, this is the only real damage I've seen—except for the façade on our street."

"That's good. That's good." Priscilla could imagine him thinking and wished it had been Leo Hart who answered. "OK, learn everything you can. Shoot everything. Then get back here. Believe it or not, the Internet is still up, so we can post an article right away."

"Chris, you understood me when I said that it was the Windom Building, right?"

"Yep, I got it the first time. Listen, I can put Maria on and you can dictate the story to her—that way we'll get the story online even faster."

He wasn't getting it. "Chris, you're missing my point—"

"Priscilla, you're not the only reporter out there. I'm getting calls from a dozen people who left right after you did. I can't let you dominate the phone or my time."

"Shut up. Chris. Take a deep breath, but keep your mouth shut for a moment. I'm standing by the Windom Building, and the whole first floor is gone, probably smashed into the parking structure below. First floor, Chris. Does that mean anything to you?"

"Should it?"

"Of course it should. There was a law firm on the first floor: Godwin, Reed, and Merrell. *Merrell*, Chris."

"I understand, Priscilla. There was a law firm…oh. Oh my."

"'Oh my' is right. Merrell—as in *Governor* Merrell. His daughter's a partner in the firm. We did an article on her last year. She headed up the San Diego office of his reelection campaign. There are plenty of rumors that she was going to run for Congress in the next election."

"And you think she might have been in the building."

"There's no way for me to tell if she was actually in the building, Chris, but it is her office, and it is work hours. Do the math."

"You're going to need help with this, but I've already sent out most of the reporters."

"Send Leo."

"I need him here."

"No, you don't, Chris. Even if you do, this is more important. Leo has more experience than any five reporters combined. Besides, he has great connections with the fire and police departments. We may need his influence."

"Maybe you're right."

"No maybe about it, Chris. Just send him."

Priscilla flipped the phone shut, ending the call, and let her eyes drift to the scene. "No one could survive that."

Chapter Three

S OON PRISCILLA WAS ON THE PHONE AGAIN, DICTATING FACTS TO Maria, who took them down in the office. The dust that permeated the air three hours before had settled to the ground once again, coating anyone who stood outside. A crowd had gathered around the firefighters and police officers who worked the scene. The uniformed officers spent most of their time keeping the crowd and media back, allowing the firefighters to do their work. Yellow caution tape ran the perimeter of the scene. The crowd was smart enough not to press too close, and those who wanted to run the risk backpedaled with each aftershock. Although no one had officially said so, there was a general consensus that the building might fall again.

Firefighters had used every means possible to evacuate those trapped on the upper floors. Some who were on the top floors when the earthquake hit had to work their way to lower levels so that brave men on long ladders could rescue them. A ladder truck had stretched its 110-foot extension at a sixty-degree angle to one of the windows on the sixth floor. Debris kept the truck from getting any closer and the large ladder from reaching any higher.

One by one, firefighters helped residents onto and down the ladder.

"Hang on, Maria. Leo's coming back." Priscilla removed the phone from the side of her head. "Got anything?" Leo had been working the fire chiefs who were trying to bring order to the chaos.

"A few things." Leo looked wearied and stunned by the sight before him. "I spoke to Battalion Chief Gonzales. We belong to the same Rotary club. He wouldn't talk long, but he gave me a few tidbits.

"First," Leo continued, "he confirms that this is the only building in downtown that has suffered significant damage, or, as he put it, 'life-threatening damage.' He has no idea how many people are trapped below, but his best guess is that it's not many. The law firm took up half the floor space, and the other half was recently rented to a company that hadn't moved in yet."

"It's too many, if you're one of the people trapped." Priscilla held the cell phone between them so that Maria could take down Leo's comments.

"I won't argue with that. Chief Gonzales confirmed that Merrell's law firm was on the first floor. He couldn't say how many people from the firm were still in the building at the time of the earthquake. The other two principals of the firm are here watching the firemen do their work. Gonzales interviewed them, and they estimated that perhaps half the employees were still in the building. The other half were either in court or at meetings away. That would mean maybe ten people are trapped or crushed below." Leo paused, then added, "Both principals said Ms. Merrell would have been in the office."

"That's horrible. I can't imagine being trapped with the whole building on top of me."

"That's assuming you survived in the first place."

Priscilla returned the phone to her ear. "Did you get all that, Maria?"

Leo held up a finger. "There's more. Gonzales let it slip that the governor is on his way."

"Here? Forget that. Stupid question. Where else would he be going? When is he expected to arrive?"

Leo shook his head. "Gonzales didn't know, but he's expected fairly soon. You best keep your camera ready."

Priscilla looked at the readout of the video camera. "I should have enough memory to catch everything that happens, but I'll have to be more careful with the number of shots I take."

"It wouldn't be good to run out just as the governor arrives. Conlin would have your head, and probably mine, too."

"It wouldn't be your fault."

"Since when has that mattered?"

Priscilla nodded. "I see your point."

She looked at the Windom Building, once a glorious feat of architecture and engineering and the pride of 1940s San Diego. Now, almost seventy years later and fully refurbished, it had become a prestigious place to work. The midcentury engineering, however, had not planned on an earthquake seven decades into the future.

Making her way along the yellow caution ribbon, Priscilla studied the scene. The smoke she had seen and followed did not belong to the Windom Building but to a small Mexican restaurant nearby. First on the scene, firefighters had quickly suppressed the blaze. She couldn't know for sure, but Priscilla assumed a gas line had likely broken and ignited.

She returned her attention to the Windom Building. Two skip loaders took turns pulling close to the rubble-lined walk along the crushed floor, allowing rescuers to remove chunks of concrete, brick from the façade, and other debris and place it in the hefty machine's bucket. When the bucket filled, the tractor pulled away to be replaced by another. Men worked with hands, crowbars, and anything else they could find.

Priscilla returned to where Leo stood. "Do you think they'll find a way in?"

"Yes. They'll find a way in all right, but will they do it in time? There have been people who survived for days beneath crumbled buildings. Maybe someone got lucky."

"They're going to need more than luck."

Leo gave her a long look. "You're the religious one, kid. I'm sure the victims and the families would appreciate any prayers offered up on their behalf."

"Prayers have been going out since the earthquake hit."

A thumping in the distance caught Priscilla's attention. She turned toward the sound and raised a hand to shield her eyes from the sun's glare. The sound echoed off the tall buildings, making it difficult to track the thumping. A minute later, she saw a small, dark object in the sky.

"News copter?" Leo turned his gaze to match Priscilla's.

"Maybe. There have been several of those. This one sounds heavier."

A few moments later, the distant thump became a bone-vibrating, rhythmic thudding.

"Military," Leo said with authority. "I'd recognize that sound anywhere. Maybe the national guard is coming to help."

"Perhaps." Priscilla thought for a moment. "If you were the governor, how would you get here?"

"That would be a good way. Take a corporate jet to the closest open airport and have the Air National Guard bring me in the rest of the way."

"That's my thinking." She lowered her gaze. "Look at the cops. Something's up."

Priscilla watched several uniformed officers collect into a group. A moment later, three patrol cars drove off.

"He can't land on the street." Leo moved his head around, taking in the scene. "A couple of the taller buildings probably have landing pads on them."

A movement on the rubble heap drew Priscilla's attention to the rescue efforts. Very little debris had been removed, and to Priscilla it seemed that the fire department was taking its own sweet time. The logical side of her brain understood the need for caution; a hasty rescue could bring new danger to the site, and a careless act made for all the best reasons could kill the very people they longed to help. Her heart, however, told her that every minute that chugged by was a minute of life lost, of pain felt.

The hand-removal of debris had stopped, and the skip loaders rested in their places. A fireman knelt on chunks of sharp-edged concrete, removed his yellow helmet, and lowered his head into a dark hole created by the digging. A second later, he straightened and shook his head. He pointed at one of the skip loaders and said something to one of the other firemen. The second man faced the tractor's operator and drew his hand across his throat in a cutting fashion. He repeated the action with the other operator. The chugging metal beasts fell silent as their drivers cut the engines. The crowd took the hint and ceased talking. Only the thick pounding of the approaching helicopter continued to make noise. They could do nothing about that.

Again the firefighter bent and placed his head to the small opening.

"What's he doing?" Priscilla whispered the question.

Leo's voice was just as low. "I think he's listening for any sounds that might indicate someone is alive."

"That hole goes all the way to the building? It looks too far away."

"Rubble doesn't fill up all the available space. Maybe they think they're close enough to hear a cry for help." He paused. "Come with me."

"Where are we going?"

"I just caught Chief Gonzales's eye again. I'm going to squeeze him for more info."

Priscilla followed, pushing her way through the crowd to Gonzales's side.

The view from the helicopter gave Governor Merrell an unobstructed view of the Windom Building. It was a view he wished he had never seen and one he knew he would never forget. No nightmare had been more disturbing.

From the air, the Windom Building looked ready to topple forward, filling the street with its shattered bones. Near the front of the structure, firemen worked in slow motion. Merrell knew their pedestrian efforts were an illusion. They were working as fast as they should. Still, he wondered how fast they'd labor if each of them had a daughter under the crush of debris.

"We need to talk, Governor." The pounding of the rotors, the military grade microphone, and the whistling of wind around the HH-60 helicopter could not conceal Steve Toomey's intensity.

Merrell didn't respond. Fear had glued his gaze to the cockeyed building where his daughter worked and—*Please, dear God, no*—may have died.

"Governor?"

Merrell turned his head and looked into the eyes of his aide. They looked the same as they always did: firm, unflinching, cold.

"I know this is hard, Governor. I can't imagine what you're going through."

"You're right. You can't."

Steve pursed his lips.

"I'm sorry, Steve." Merrell's voice sounded foreign through the helmet headset. His stomach roiled with fear, and his mind busied itself erecting walls to keep out the truth. "I'm not at my best."

"No one in your condition would be." Steve leaned forward and placed his head near the governor's, as if ready to whisper a secret that the microphone he wore would not pick up. "There's bound to be media down there. You know how those folks are. They swarm over…" He started to say "death," but caught himself. "…tragedy."

"Maggots on rotting meat." Merrell intended the words to be harsh, but they lacked the heat he wanted. "I've had enough trouble with the media."

"I agree. That means they're going to want a statement from you."

Merrell tightened his jaw. He had lived on a steady diet of news reports since he first became interested in public office. Every time some airhead reporter stuck a microphone in the face of a person who had just lost someone he loved and asked, "How are you feeling at this moment?" he had wanted to scream obscenities. On several occasions, he had. Dealing with the media came with any political office, all the more so for the governor of the most populated state in the Union. Being the executive leader of 36 million people made him a person of interest to the media not only in his state but also in every other state.

"I can't talk to them, Steve. Not now. I can't do anything but think about my daughter."

"Yes, sir. I want you to let me handle it. I can be more blunt than you. I've arranged for police officers to be present the moment we touch down. There should be enough to keep the crowd and reporters away. I'll do all the talking."

"I want on the site."

"I'll get you as close as I can, sir, but there is still concern about the integrity of the structure."

"Get me on the site."

"Sir—"

"That's not a request."

It took a moment for Steve to reply. "Yes, sir."

The helicopter slowed, and its nose rose a few degrees as the pilot powered back. He hovered the craft for a moment, then eased it down

21

on the concrete helipad. Merrell stripped his helmet from his head and started through the open door. A hand took him by the arm.

"Just a moment, sir." Steve pointed up.

Merrell waited ten seconds as the engines began to wind down, but that was all he could abide. He pulled free and stepped to the roof of a building he estimated to be twenty or more stories tall. A man in a suit and two uniformed officers met him just beyond the swinging blades. The man in the suit extended his hand. "Governor Merrell, I'm Lieutenant William Arkin of the San Diego PD. I've been assigned to escort you to the site." He spoke loudly to overcome the noise of the military craft.

Merrell took his hand. He didn't ask the name of the other officers, and Arkin didn't offer. "Thank you for your help."

"This way, sir." Arkin started toward a small structure that sat near the center of the roof, well away from the landing pad. A single door and two wire-glass windows decorated one wall. One of the uniformed officers jogged ahead and opened the door. The police lieutenant led the way, and Merrell dogged his heels. Steve followed only a step behind.

Arkin punched the button for the elevator and the brass-clad doors parted, revealing a cab paneled in expensive Brazilian rosewood.

"This is the executive elevator," Arkin said. "We'll have you on the first floor in a few minutes."

"Tell me what you know." Merrell didn't think it was possible, but his anxiety grew with each floor the elevator passed.

"I'm afraid I don't know much, Governor. I'm sure you already have more details than I do. I've been on-site since dispatch received word of it. Firemen have been at it hard and heavy."

"Survivors?"

"Dozens, all from the upper floors."

"What about the first floor?"

Arkin hesitated.

"Shoot straight with me, Lieutenant; I'm too stressed to be diplomatic."

Arkin's spine straightened as if called to attention by a superior officer—a hallmark of a former military man. "We estimate at least half a dozen people trapped below."

"Any evidence that they're alive?" Merrell thought the question the most difficult he'd ever asked.

"No, sir. On the flip side, there's been no evidence that they're not alive."

"I see."

"You received my instructions?" Steve asked Arkin.

"Yes, sir. We've cordoned off an area away from the equipment and the crowds. I've assigned officers to keep the media away."

"I want to be close to the action, Lieutenant. You're not putting me off someplace."

"The situation remains dangerous—"

"Do you have children, Lieutenant?" Merrell kept his words firm but his tone quiet.

"Yes, sir. A son and a daughter."

"And if you were in my place, what would you do?"

Arkin didn't answer.

"I asked you a question, Arkin. I expect an answer." He watched the man squirm.

"I'd stand aside and let the experts do their work."

Merrell swore. "No, you wouldn't. If you could, you'd dig through the debris with your bare hands. Every father worthy of the name would do so. I don't care what it takes, I want my daughter out of there."

"Sir—" Steve began.

"Shut up, Steve. This isn't politics, gentlemen. Right now, I don't care about my image. I don't care about my office except for the authority it affords me over everyone in this elevator. My only child is trapped, and I want her out. I don't care what I have to do to make that happen. Am I clear?"

"Yes, sir. Crystal clear, sir."

"Mrs. Merrell will be arriving when she can. She's already airborne and headed back to Sacramento. Once she has the grandkids taken care of, she'll be on her way." His vision blurred. "I just hope to have some good news for her when she arrives."

The elevator reached the ground floor. Merrell moved from the cab before the doors had finished opening.

"So, how do we do this, Leo?"

"Talk to the governor?" He shook his head. "It's going to be tough, probably impossible."

Governor Merrell marched their direction surrounded by a phalanx of police officers. With him was a young man in a dark suit and an older man. Merrell wore a gray business suit, white shirt, and yellow print tie. The tie hung loose at the neck.

"I think we should leave him alone," she said. "We can take a few stills and some video but keep our distance."

"Conlin will scream. He'll say this is one of the biggest stories of the year."

"I know, but the man's daughter is under that building. I doubt he has any patience for the likes of us."

"I'm telling you he'll scream."

"Then let *him* come down here and approach the governor. I think the man should have as much room as he wants."

"They don't agree." Leo pointed to a pretty woman and a bulky cameraman. The woman held a microphone with a printed collar that identified the crew as employees of Priscilla's old station.

The governor and his entourage brushed past the reporting team and moved to where Chief Gonzales stood. The media team followed, but two police officers peeled from the group and stopped them. The woman appeared angry, and Priscilla watched as her partner pulled her away.

"Ah, television reporters are such an example of restraint," Leo said.

"Watch it, Leo. That was me fifteen years ago."

"Yeah, but you outgrew it."

"The man with Merrell. He looks familiar."

Leo agreed. "I've seen him a few times. He's the governor's top aide. A real behind-the-scenes kinda guy. Name is Toomey. Steve Toomey."

Priscilla raised her camera and pressed the RECORD button. She pushed the zoom and focused on Merrell's face. His skin looked ashen and eyes wet. "Poor guy."

A shadow eased over Priscilla.

The air turned cold.

Priscilla looked up.

Her knees went weak.

Chapter Four

D ENNIS DeGUERE WAS HELPING WITH TRIAGE, AND THE PRESSURE of it weighed upon him. The emergency room of San Diego Regional Hospital was always full. A sizable earthquake had taxed the waiting area beyond its design. When the ER lobby became standing room only and its aisles clogged with patients sitting or lying on the floor, something had to be done. New arrivals were moved to the main lobby, and a doctor, two interns, a nurse practitioner, and a registered nurse assessed the wounded, treating the ones they could. DeGuere was that doctor.

The hospital had held emergency drills in the past, but the real thing proved more challenging and irritating. Emergency medicine was not his specialty. Like all doctors, he had served in the ER as part of his training. He hated it then, and he hated it now.

The hard walls amplified the groans and complaints of the patients, each certain their injury deserved attention before any other. One man, convinced his wife deserved the front of the line, had seized DeGuere by the lapels of his smock and threatened to beat him into unconsciousness. A security guard separated them, forcing the man back to his seat with a warning: "You can wait here or you can wait in jail."

Neurology. DeGuere's field was neurology. Seldom did he have to deal with broken bones, contusions, sprained ankles, and hysteria. In the last three hours, he had seen more of such cases than he could count. Most he was able to send home after only a cursory exam. Others, including two men who complained of chest pain, he moved directly to the ER.

Glancing through the glass wall that separated the walkway and parking lot from the lobby, DeGuere saw what he hoped to see: the end of the influx of patients. He let his eyes trace the mass of people. He and the others had quizzed each one, looking for signs of life-threatening trauma. All that remained were those banged up from falling objects or bearing minor cuts from broken glass.

Things could have been so much worse.

He caught sight of a woman holding a child on her lap. The boy had hair that couldn't decide if it wanted to be blonde or brown. He held a bulky towel to the side of his head. DeGuere approached, dropped to one knee, then said, "Hi."

The boy looked at him and then pulled closer to his mother. His mom looked a couple of years shy of thirty. She also looked tired. "Tell the doctor hi, Danny."

"Hi."

If DeGuere had been another two feet away, he wouldn't have been able to hear him.

"You don't like doctors, do you, Danny?" He studied the boy's eyes. Danny shook his head slowly.

"Me either," DeGuere said. "They walk around like they're so smart, wearing white coats and using big words."

"But you're a doctor," Danny said.

"Huh?"

"Aren't you a doctor? You're wearing a white coat."

"Oh, I guess I forgot. In that case, I love doctors. They're so smart and help people feel better."

The boy looked at his mom and rolled his eyes.

"So, Danny, tell me. You married? Got any kids?"

"No. I'm only nine."

"Nine, eh? You're right. You should wait until you're eleven or twelve. Why are you here? Come for the food?"

He laughed. "No. I bumped my head."

"Actually, a book fell on his head."

"A book? What kind of book?"

"A big book. It fell off the shelf in our living room."

"And landed on your head? Let me take a look." He reached for the towel and pulled it away. There was no blood, and the towel felt cool.

Wrapped inside its folds, he could feel a plastic bag filled with ice and water. Much of the ice had melted.

The examination took only a few moments. The boy's pupils were responsive and equal. He showed no signs of dizziness or headache.

"Did he lose consciousness?" he asked the mother.

"No, but with it being his head and all, I got worried."

"Understandable." To Danny he said, "Let me look in your ears. I need to see if your brains leaked out."

Danny allowed it. DeGuere then felt the back of the boy's neck. "Do you feel sleepy, Danny."

"No. I just wanna to go home."

He continued the exam for another few moments. "OK. Pupils look good, motor skills seem unimpaired, communication is what I'd expect, ears are clear of cerebral spinal fluid, and the injury looks minor. I think you can go home. Keep an eye on him. If he suddenly becomes sleepy or you have trouble waking him, get him back in here. Otherwise he looks fine. The ice will help keep the swelling down."

"Thank you, Doctor." The woman stood.

"Is your husband at home?"

She shook her head. "He's in the military, overseas."

"Well, Danny, you're going to have a great story to tell your dad—"

A sharp beep emitted from the pager on DeGuere's belt. He glanced at the number on the display. The notification bore a code that he had long ago learned to hate.

He turned and jogged to the elevator foyer but avoided using the elevator, choosing instead to run up the stairs to the third floor. Forty-five steps later, he burst through the door. Before he could make the turn to third-floor west he knew something was wrong. Alarms on several medical devices cut the air. Beeps and squeals combined in a cacophony of ear-splitting noise.

"What the..."

He raced to the nurse's station. No one was there. He started down the corridor most familiar to him, a corridor that led to rooms where six patients lay one step from death, each locked in a coma that now defined their world. The first room held a patient DeGuere knew well. The man had been comatose for most of the year.

Inside, two nurses struggled to calm Allen Sloan. The forty-five-year-old man was doing his best to push them away, and for a man who had been in a level-1 coma, he was doing a good job.

DeGuere plunged into the fray. Seizing the frail man by the shoulders, he pushed back and down, forcing Sloan to the bed. "Mr. Sloan, I need you to relax."

Sloan gagged and reached for the intubation tube in his throat.

"I know. I know. I can't take it out until you relax. Do you understand?"

Sloan nodded then gagged again. A second later, he tried to snatch the tube.

With a nurse on each shoulder, Sloan finally gave in. It was no surprise. The man had been inactive for months. His muscles would tire quickly.

"Got him?" DeGuere asked the nurses.

"Got 'em," one said.

"Mr. Sloan, I'm going to take out the tube. On the count of three, I want you to exhale as hard as you can. Do you understand?"

He nodded.

This is unbelievable. DeGuere took the tube and counted down. As soon as he reached *one*, he pulled. The breathing tube slipped from Sloan's throat.

"He's here! He's here!" Sloan began to weep.

Priscilla's mind filled with a jumble of thoughts, all of them nonsense. She could not be seeing what she was seeing. Impossible. Unbelievable. She entertained the idea that the stress of the earthquake and her near fall through the shattered window of her office had led to a stroke, causing her mind to fabricate nonsensical images.

"What is that?" Leo's voice sounded thin.

Knowing that Leo saw the same thing should have made Priscilla feel better. It didn't. The crowd murmured. Several screamed. Priscilla lowered her gaze in time to see scores of people sprint into buildings or down the street. Others stood as if their feet had taken root in the asphalt.

Overhead, an object descended slowly like a child's balloon that had lost too much of its helium. Not an object—objects, Priscilla corrected herself. No—a single object. She couldn't decide. There was something about it that she couldn't define. It seemed a single mass like an inverted diamond, a coal-black faceted diamond the size of a ten-story building. It reflected none of the sunlight that reached its surface. One moment it appeared a single unit, and then the facets began to pull away from one another.

"Tell me you're shooting this."

"What?"

"Pictures, Priscilla. Take pictures."

"Um, right." She raised the camera, chastising herself for being so slow on the uptake. Gazing through the viewfinder, she noticed the object appeared different, as if its shape confused the camera's electronics. She forced her hand to steady and her stomach to cease its gymnastics and continued to shoot video.

"I don't believe what I'm seeing." Her words erupted louder than she intended.

"It's there. It's as real as anything." Leo's voice quavered.

"But what is it?"

"I have no idea."

The object continued its descent. Priscilla moved her eyes from the viewer back to the real thing. It mesmerized her. "I think we had better back up. It looks like it's going to land on our heads.

"It can't land here. It won't fit in the street."

"You're willing to bet our lives on that?"

"Maybe you're right." Leo took her arm, and they moved a few yards down the street. "I can't hear any sound from it. Can you?"

"No. How does it stay in the air? There are no wings, no rotors like a helicopter. It just hangs there."

"Maybe it's some secret aircraft. Maybe the governor pulled some strings with the military."

"Do you really believe that?"

Leo shook his head. "No. I just can't bring myself to say what I really think."

Priscilla said it for him. "It's a UFO. It's...I don't know what it is."

She forced her reporter's mind to the front, trying to analyze, memo-rize, scrutinize. Confusion threatened to dissolve her training into fear. Her knees felt weak, but she stood her ground—something most of the remaining crowd chose not to do.

At what Priscilla estimated to be about five hundred feet, the object stopped, hanging in place with no visible means of support, no engines, no anything. It rotated slowly, as if an invisible wire were connected to the diamond's point. A breeze blew along the street, stirring dust and loose papers, but had no affect on the obsidian object.

"I don't think this day can get any stranger, Leo."

"I wouldn't bet on it."

A motion near the collapsed building caught Priscilla's eye.

"Let go of me." Governor Merrell jerked his arm away from Toomey's grasp. Anger and fear battled for his mind.

"Governor, it's important that we get you to safety." Toomey spoke low but firm. He took the governor's arm again.

"Steve, we go way back, but if you don't let go I'm going to deck you."

Toomey released his grasp. "But, sir—"

"Forget it. I'm not running and hiding. If you want to take off, then go ahead."

"Sir, Mr. Toomey is right." The police lieutenant spoke without taking his eyes from the unbelievable object. "We don't know what that thing is. It would be wise to retreat to some protection."

"I'm staying here. This is as close as I can get to my daughter. I'm not leaving. Not even for...for...that thing. You and your men are dismissed."

"No, sir. You're my responsibility while you're here." Arkin swallowed hard. "I go where you go."

Merrell admired the man's courage and might have said so had he not returned his attention to the floating object.

"The thing is as big as a mid-rise building, yet it just hangs there." Merrell raised a hand to shield his eyes against the sun's glare.

"And if it falls, we're all dead," Toomey said.

"I told you, you could leave." Merrell turned his attention to the rescue site. The firemen had stopped working. Some gazed into the sky; others had backed away. He knew the courage it took to stand there. If his daughter weren't somewhere under the rubble, he would have taken Arkin and Toomey's advice and sought shelter.

The work had stopped. Merrell wanted to shout at the firefighters, tell them that their work wasn't done, that his daughter could still be alive, but he didn't. He couldn't blame them for the fear they felt.

"Why now?" he wondered aloud.

No sooner had he finished those two words than the object fragmented. Pieces detached from the whole and began to fall.

Merrell raised his hands as if such an action could protect him.

Priscilla ducked and covered her head. She felt something covering her, and it took a moment to realize that Leo had pulled her next to him and was doing his best to interpose his body between her and any falling debris.

She waited for the impact, for the sound of hard, unknown material crashing to the pavement and sidewalk, crushing parked cars and killing those who hadn't exercised enough common sense to run.

But there was no sound. No crashing. No screams from crushed bystanders.

She opened her eyes and saw a shadow on the ground, straight dark bands with alternating bands of light. Straightening, she gazed at the object overhead, except the object was gone. In its place, spiraling out from a central disk, were triangular slabs of black, each floating within feet of one another but never touching. A ring of rainbow marked out the circumference.

"It blew up," Leo said.

"Not in an explosion. There was no sound. It just flattened out." Priscilla raised her camera. "Amazing. Unbelievable. There must be fifty or sixty pieces up there."

She used the camera's zoom to see more detail of the impossible sight, but while she could focus on a single piece, she could see nothing

32

new. Each fragment was so black that she could see no edges and no reflection.

"Look." Leo pointed at the center of the floating jigsaw puzzle. The central disk, the only piece that had no straight edges, began to descend—ten feet, twenty feet, fifty feet—then stopped, still hovering five or six stories above the street. The other facets held their place but began to spin, slowly at first, then faster. Priscilla tried to hold the camera steady, but her hands shook.

"Now what?" Leo asked.

Priscilla didn't have to follow her friend's gaze. He stared at the same thing she did: the white hole that appeared in a blink at the center of the disk.

A sphere appeared. To Priscilla, it looked fifteen feet or so in diameter and made of swirling water. Rainbow colors flashed around the vessel as it slowly lowered until it touched the macadam surface of the street.

"It's so beautiful. What is it? How does it work? Is that really water or something else?"

"Priscilla, stop. I have no answers. I'm working on staying conscious."

Then the bubble burst and the fluid fell, but it never landed on the ground. It just ceased to exist.

A figure stood where the sphere of water had been.

"Leo?"

"Yeah?"

"I think I'm going to be ill."

Chapter Five

Easy, Mr. Sloan. Take it easy." Dennis DeGuere pressed his patient back on the bed. For a man who had been in a coma for the better part of a year, he displayed an amazing amount of strength. Judging by the terror DeGuere could see in the man's eyes, that strength came fueled by adrenaline.

"I saw him. He's coming."

"I need you to calm down, Mr. Sloan. Please lie back." He glanced at one of the nurses who had retrieved a vial and hypo. He shook his head. The last thing he wanted to do was sedate a man who had just come out of a coma. He wanted to talk the man down.

"Who are you? Why are you fighting with me?"

Sloan's blue eyes were wide and wild. His brown hair lay flat on his head, plastered there with oil and the pressure of a head set on a pillow. His sallow skin looked like parchment but reddened with exertion.

"I'm Dr. DeGuere. I'm your doctor. Now, if you'll relax for a minute, I will explain everything."

"He's here. Don't you understand? I'm telling you he's here."

"The only people here are doctors and nurses. You're in good hands, Mr. Sloan, but you must stop fighting me."

"I don't belong here. I belong...I belong...?"

"It will come to you, Mr. Sloan. Now please lie back or I will have to sedate you."

"I don't want any drugs."

"And I don't want to give you any. Just relax. Will you do that?"

DeGuere felt Sloan give in, not by choice but because his underused muscles fatigued from the struggle. DeGuere kept his hands on the man's shoulders for a few moments.

"Restraints?" a nurse asked.

"No," DeGuere said. To Sloan he added, "You don't need restraints, do you, Mr. Sloan?"

"No." The reply was sheepish, the consent of a man who understood he was outnumbered. "I don't understand." His gaze darted around the room.

"Confusion is normal, Mr. Sloan. You've been out for a long time."

"I feel weak." He touched his arms, then ran his hands over his chest and abdomen. He stopped and fingered an unseen tube. "What have you done to me?"

"That's a feeding tube. You've been out of it for some time."

"What do you mean, 'out of it'?"

"Your questions are good, Mr. Sloan, and I'll answer every one of them, but first I need to ask some questions of my own."

DeGuere pulled a small pen light from his pocket, leaned over Sloan and examined the man's eyes. "Are you in any pain?"

"No. I don't think so."

"That's good." He placed two fingers in Sloan's right hand. "Can you feel my fingers?"

"Yes."

"Good. Give them a squeeze."

Sloan did, and DeGuere watched the thin fingers wrapped around his own. The grip was good, better than expected. He moved to the foot of the bed and lifted the white sheets from over Sloan's feet. He pinched the great toe on Sloan's right foot.

"Ouch! What are you doing?"

Without a word, DeGuere did the same on the left foot. Sloan pulled his leg back.

"You some kind of sadist?"

"Sometimes I have to be. Tell me, Mr. Sloan, how do you feel?"

"With my hands."

"Humor is a good sign. I mean—"

"I know what you mean. I feel...funny. Odd. Out of place. Confused."

"Physically?"

"My back is sore, but not as sore as my toes."

To the duty nurse DeGuere said, "Let's get a BP, then draw some blood for a panel." He moved to the side of the bed. "Do you know what day this is?"

"I think it's Thursday, but I've got a feeling I'm wrong."

"What makes you say that?"

"You said I had been out for some time. That, and I have a feeding tube. I don't think you put a tube in a man's stomach for the fun of it."

DeGuere had to smile. A deep coma patient suddenly regaining consciousness wasn't unheard of, but it happened far less often than urban myths said. "Your mind seems to be working well."

"Why shouldn't it? Have I been in some kind of accident?" He raised his hands to his head as if searching for injuries. He noticed the IV lines connected to the shunt in his arm. Then he looked at his hands. "I've lost weight." He grabbed his stomach. "I used to have a potbelly. It's gone."

"You've lost about forty pounds."

DeGuere watched as Sloan examined his arms. "Stroke? No, not a stroke. My speech is clear and my hands work fine. Doctor, what's happened?"

"One-forty-five over ninety, pulse eighty-five," the nurse said.

DeGuere nodded. "A little high, but considering the effort you just spent, Mr. Sloan, I'd say it's pretty good." He paused, then asked, "What is the last thing you remember?"

"I don't know."

"Give it a try."

Sloan's brow furrowed. "I remember leaving the studio. I needed… I needed, what? Wood. Basswood. That was Thursday."

"Basswood?"

"Yeah. Great stuff. Carves easily."

His memory is more intact than I would expect. "You carve basswood?"

"I work in other woods. I'm an amateur furniture artist. I make furniture for the fun of it. I've been trying my hand at some carving." He stopped and looked at his hands. "Gone."

"What's gone, Mr. Sloan?"

He clinched his fists. "Calluses. They're gone. That means...Doctor, what happened to me?"

"So you make furniture for a living?" DeGuere knew he didn't.

"No, not for a living. I told you, it's a hobby. I'm a communication exec. I'm high enough up the ladder that I can take the occasional afternoon off. Some businessmen golf, I make furniture."

DeGuere pursed his lips. "First, the important thing to remember is that you're awake, and so far your mind seems undamaged. That's remarkable, considering everything."

"What's everything?"

"You've been in a coma for nearly eleven months, Mr. Sloan. There are many kinds of coma. Yours is—was—the kind that people normally think of: unresponsive to verbal stimulus or pain."

"I've been here for a year?"

"Almost."

Sloan looked lost. DeGuere stood by quietly to give his patient time to process the information. "I can't believe it."

"I don't blame you. It's hard to take in. Nonetheless, it's true."

"But I don't remember being sick or in an accident."

"You were in an auto accident and suffered several major injuries, including head trauma and a perforated liver. You were bleeding out when the paramedics brought you into the ER. I can't tell you exactly why you slipped into a coma, but the most likely cause was your response to anesthesia. The surgical team put you under and you never came out. That's when they called me in. I'm a neurologist. Other doctors treated your injuries. My job was to keep you alive and try to bring you back. I'm afraid I wasn't very successful."

"A whole year gone." Tears filled his eyes.

"Listen to me, Mr. Sloan. Many coma patients never come out. You may have lost a year, but you didn't lose a decade." DeGuere decided not to tell him that many patients slip away again.

"What now?"

"I'm going to give you some time to let all this sink in, and then I need to run some tests—CAT scan and a few other things. For now, just rest."

"I've been resting for eleven months."

37

"If things look good, I'll see about getting you off the tubes."

"Thanks, doc. I'm sorry…" Sloan stopped and tilted his head to the side. "My family. I have a family. A wife and a…a son. We need to tell them."

DeGuere's stomach constricted. "I'm sorry, Mr. Sloan. They were in the car with you when you had your accident."

The being—that was the only term Priscilla could think to call it—stood in the middle of the street. He turned his head from side to side, looking first at what remained of the crowd, then at Priscilla and Leo, and then at the debris-strewn street in front of the Windom Building.

"He's got to be eight feet tall," Leo whispered. "I've never seen anyone that tall."

Priscilla started forward, camera still pointed at the visitor.

"Where are you going?" Leo asked.

"Don't talk to me, Leo. I might change my mind."

"Maybe you should."

Priscilla ignored him and moved slowly toward the being. He wore what looked to Priscilla like an off-white linen jumpsuit. She saw no buttons or zippers. It seemed to be a single piece of material formed into a garment that gave off a hint of color in the sun.

She stopped ten feet from the stranger. Leo had been right; the man—did he have gender?—stood eight feet tall or more. His face impressed her as masculine with a strong jaw, square cheekbones, and deep, dark, jade eyes that rested an inch above a tiny nose. She couldn't see pupils. His mouth was thin but obvious, not like the pictures she had seen of little gray aliens so popular with the UFO culture.

The being turned and studied her with such intensity she felt she might be sucked into those dark eyes. His gaze shifted from her face to the camera. In a slow, fluid motion, he extended his right hand. It took a moment for Priscilla to interpret the action. She held out the camera and he took it. The hand had five narrow fingers. It didn't register at first, but she realized the fingers had one more joint per digit than her own. She saw no fingernails.

Every muscle tightened as their hands met. Fear made her twitch, and for a moment she questioned her own sanity for daring to approach.

The being took the camera and examined it. He turned it so the lens pointed at Priscilla. She watched as he looked at the tiny monitor, then did the unexpected. He smiled. The grin looked unnatural, as if his thin lips were unaccustomed to expression.

Priscilla returned the smile and almost laughed as the alien moved the camera around, his eyes fixed on the monitor. Then she heard what she could only think of as a chuckle. It was a lyrical sound, like a dozen birds singing the same few notes.

He returned the camera and then raised a hand to touch her red hair. Priscilla couldn't decide if she were being brave standing there or if she were just too frightened to move. The long fingers fondled her hair, and he tilted his head as if seeing hair for the first time. Maybe he was. Priscilla saw no hair on the alien's head or arms.

He laid a hand on her head, and electricity cascaded through every muscle, every bone. It was exhilarating, as if he had quick-charged her mind and body. She had never felt so good.

Lowering his hand, he turned to the area where the governor and others stood. With long strides he moved forward, but not toward the others. Instead, his long legs carried him to the heavily damaged Windom Building. Priscilla had to run to keep up with him.

"Priscilla!"

She ignored Leo's call and focused on keeping pace with the alien. He moved with such ease, such grace, she wondered if his feet ever really touched the ground. A gasp of air surprised her. She had been holding her breath.

As the being approached, firemen and cops backed away. Priscilla saw that several officers had hands firmly placed on their sidearms. Two had drawn their weapons from leather holsters but had not raised the muzzles.

Keep things cool, boys.

The silent advice clashed with her own emotions—she felt anything but cool. The shock of what she had seen and what she had just done divided her into two persons: one who wanted nothing more than to flee down the street, the other dedicated to learning everything she could about the…thing…person…creature…alien.

They had covered less than ten yards, but Priscilla sucked air like a runner at the end of a marathon. Her heart fluttered like the wings of a hummingbird.

The being slowed at the rubble-covered sidewalk and stared at the half-crushed building. A policeman approached, and the being gazed at him. The cop backed away without a word. Priscilla stepped to his side.

"Did you…I mean, did your ship…cause this?" *Nothing like an incoherent reporter. I don't even know if he speaks English. Why would he?*

The being shifted his gaze from the building to Priscilla.

"Do you understand me?" she asked.

He raised his left arm and pulled back the sleeve. For a moment, Priscilla thought the man from the spaceship was checking his watch, but she saw no dial or digital display. Wrapped around his long forearm was a dark blue, almost black plastic device. Priscilla stretched her back and neck, standing on tiptoe to see. The plastic—if that's what it was— ran six inches up from his wrist. One moment it appeared nothing more than a smooth, blank surface, but a blink later Priscilla saw it come to life. Lights and characters danced on the surface and—to her amazement—just above it.

"Four. One breathes."

His voice was soft and smooth but made Priscilla think three people were speaking in unison.

"Four? Four people? One is still alive?"

"Weak. Cessation is near."

"Cessation—death? The person is about to die?"

"Let go of me!"

The heated words made Priscilla jump. She turned in time to see Governor Merrell freeing himself from the man Leo identified as Steve Toomey. Toomey had had both hands secured around the governor's left arm, and Merrell had to yank hard three times before he freed himself.

"Governor, please."

Merrell ignored him and marched up to Priscilla and the man from who-knows-where.

"Are you responsible for this? Did you cause all this destruction? Did you kill my daughter?"

The being tilted his head to the side as Merrell approached.

"I want to know," Merrell demanded.

The being didn't respond. Instead, he returned his attention to the device on his arm, studied it for a moment, and then lifted his hand toward the governor. Merrell stopped in his tracks. Several officers shouted, "Hold it!" and pointed their weapons at the stranger. He gave no indication of being intimidated.

Merrell stopped mid-step, then took a step back as if he expected lightning to flow from the creature's fingertips.

"Priscilla, get out of there." Leo's words rode currents of fear.

"*Wait*. Everyone just wait." Priscilla raised her hands and tried to sound like she felt more confident than she did. "He says someone is still alive down there."

Merrell's mouth opened. "How can he know that?"

"I don't know. I'm only telling you what he said. Let's just all take a breath—"

"One is yours." The being's harmonic voice filled the area. Priscilla had to turn to see that he was speaking to Merrell. He looked back at the armband. "Offspring."

Merrell eased forward. "How do you know this?" To Priscilla he said, "How does he know this?"

"Don't ask me. I'm just repeating what I heard." She paused, then added, "I think he just read your DNA."

"You can't know that," Merrell snapped.

"You're right, Governor. I know nothing, but that thing on his arm seems to be some kind of...what? Scanner?"

"Offspring breathes," the stranger said.

"She's alive? My daughter is alive?"

Priscilla could see Merrell's legs weaken.

Lowering his hand, the being turned to face the fragmented structures hovering overhead. A second later, they began to move, creeping along the sky until they were centered over the Windom Building.

Priscilla could detect no sound, no vibration, and no indication that what was above her was anything more than an illusion. They moved as quietly as a cloud.

When the black facets stopped, the being moved easily over the remains of the fallen façade and approached an area cleared of debris by one of the bulldozers. A few small fragments of concrete remained, which he swept away with his foot—a foot clad with a form-fitting shoe that looked more like a sock than any footwear she had ever seen.

With no hesitation, he centered himself in the clearing and tapped the thing on his arm. A moment later, he dissolved as if made of powder.

"What...?" Priscilla had no words to finish the sentence.

"What did I just see?" Leo had stepped to her side.

Priscilla shook her head. "I have no idea. One moment he's there, the next, he's..."

Before she could finish the thought, a swirl of water rose from the concrete like an upside-down waterfall, the top of it reaching ten feet above the walk. Leo took a step back tugging Priscilla with him. She resisted his efforts. She wanted to see—to see everything.

The circular water curtain dropped away, leaving no sign that it had ever been there. The being stood where he had been the moment before. In his arms rested the battered form of an unmoving woman. Her opened eyes didn't blink.

"Martha!" Merrell charged forward, stumbling over loose bits of debris. His toe caught a large chunk of concrete, and he came close to falling. Toomey, who lagged behind by half a step, caught Merrell's elbow and kept the governor from crashing to the ground. Merrell showed no sign of noticing the help. He finished the short distance. "Let me have her."

The being refused. Instead, he brushed past Merrell and moved to the center of the street.

"Is she alive? You said she was alive." Merrell stayed within inches of the visitor.

When he reached the center of the road, the being bent as if hinged in his middle and laid the motionless body on the warm asphalt.

Merrell dropped to his knees and caressed the side of his daughter's face.

Tears brimmed Priscilla's eyes as she fought to maintain a reportorial detachment.

"Martha, oh baby. Martha." Merrell wept. He laid his face near her mouth. "She's not breathing." He looked up. "Someone help me." He pointed at Chief Gonzales. "You! Get over here!"

Gonzales looked at the creature, then back at the lifeless form on the street. He lowered his head and started forward. As he did, he motioned for the nearest paramedics to join him. They hesitated. He barked an order, and they started forward.

"She's dead." Merrell looked up at the being. "You told her that one was still alive." He turned his attention to his stricken daughter. "Too late. Too late."

The paramedics knelt beside Martha Merrell and began what must have been a well-practiced routine. They listened for a heartbeat. One, a man who looked more like a boy to Priscilla, shook his head. "CPR. I need an airway."

The second paramedic looked at his victim. Priscilla looked, too, despite the strong urge to turn away. The right side of the woman's skull was caved in. Blood covered her face and matted her hair. One eyelid hung half closed; the other looked frozen open.

Years of reporting had made Priscilla an expert in body language. She had seen people tense when they lied, had seen jaws tighten when anger took over someone she interviewed who didn't want the intrusion. Now she saw a trained paramedic look at his partner with an expression that said, "CPR will be a waste of energy," but he kept his thoughts to himself. He opened a med case and removed a plastic device that looked like the letter J and handed it to his partner, who gently pulled Martha's head back and opened her slack jaw. With a practiced movement, he inserted the plastic device down the woman's throat, then gave it a slight twist. As he did, the older paramedic handed the Ambu bag across the body. He repositioned himself, and with his right hand ran his fingers along her sternum until he reached a point just above the abdomen. He placed the heel of his left hand at a point just an inch or two higher, then set his

43

right hand over his left, leaned forward, and sharply pressed down the area between her breasts. "One, two, three…"

It struck Priscilla just how desperate an act CPR was.

Before the paramedic could finish his fourth compression, he left the ground. The being held the chunky man, kicking and flailing his arms, in two hands. Then he turned and set the man down behind him. Turning to the other paramedic, he extended a long arm, but the younger man recoiled faster than Priscilla thought possible, just escaping the long, thin fingers.

"Leave them alone!" Merrell's face had gone from pale white to crimson.

The alien paid no attention to the grieving Merrell. He crouched, folding in a way that the knees of his long legs reached the middle of his head. Priscilla thought of an insect.

He touched Martha's hand, then her head, as if studying her injuries. Gently, he pulled the sleeve of her pantsuit coat up until the bottom of the sleeve was near her elbow. Priscilla saw bruises and bumps that she hoped weren't from the jagged ends of broken bones seeking escape from their suit of flesh.

She keyed the small video camera.

In fluid moves, he removed the device from his arm, attached it to Martha's left arm, and tapped it in a manner that made Priscilla think he was typing on an unseen keyboard.

"What are you doing?" Merrell asked.

The being didn't answer. He raised his hands to his head. The position reminded her of Edvard Munch's painting, *The Scream*, except the alien looked at peace.

The black device changed from black to crystalline blue.

Merrell started forward again but stopped when the being shot out a hand and finger. "No."

Merrell froze.

A mist grew around Martha, rising in gossamer waves like steam from a hot cup of tea, but instead of rising into the air and disappearing, the mist thickened and hung just above her body. Mist became fog; fog became fluid; fluid became plasticlike.

Uncertain she could trust her eyes, Priscilla kept them fixed on the morphing mass as it settled around Martha, cocooning her. It took less than a minute, but time felt elongated.

"What are you doing?" Merrell's question lacked the lightning-bolt snap Priscilla was certain he intended.

"I think he's helping her." Priscilla's words sounded foreign in her own ears.

"How do you know?"

"I don't. I just think it's true."

Toomey moved from behind the governor. "Maybe we should move you to safety."

"Forget it, Steve. I'm not going anywhere."

Martha's body jerked.

Toomey swore. Merrell raised a hand and bit his knuckle.

The body jerked again, then shuddered. Spasm followed spasm. Shudder led to tremor. Then Priscilla saw it. Martha raised a hand and pushed against the envelopment. Then her other hand. She kicked at it with her feet.

She tried to sit up, but the thick material around her prevented it. It was as if a living person were suffocating in a plastic bag. *How can a dead person suffocate—*

"It can't be." She looked at Leo. His ashen face and wide eyes said it all. "I'm not seeing what I'm seeing."

"Don't ask me."

"Martha?" Merrell's words were soft.

The being looked up and motioned for Merrell to approach. He did, crossing the distance in four long strides. Kneeling by his seizing daughter, he asked, "What do I do? She's in pain."

"Wait," the visitor said.

"But—"

"Wait."

Priscilla moved to get a better angle.

The cocoon thinned. Then, like the water curtain and the sphere before it, it seemed to turn to fluid and fell, again leaving no sign that it had ever been there.

"Dad? Dad!"

45

Merrell took her in his arms and began to weep. "Martha... Martha..."

"What happened? I was—" She looked over her father's shoulder, and Priscilla expected her to scream. She didn't.

The governor followed his daughter's eyes. "It's all right. It's all right. He made you well. He's a friend."

"But..."

"I'll explain later. Are you in pain? Can you stand?"

Martha nodded. "My head. Everything is unclear. I was... the earthquake!"

"Yes, you were trapped." Merrell kept an arm around her. "Our friend... he... I don't know what he did, but he saved your life."

"The others? There were others with me. Judy, Emilliano, Jim..."

The being shook his head. "Gone the way of all flesh. Too much time passed." Then, as if an afterthought, "I regret their death."

Merrell held Martha, tears of joy coursing down his face.

Extending his arm, the being laid his long fingers on Martha. "Death is an illusion. Death matters not." He began to move away.

"Wait." Merrell faced him but kept one arm around his daughter. "I don't know what to say. I... thank you, Mr..." He stammered. "Do you have a name?"

The being tilted his head again, his jade eyes seeming to see through Merrell. "Call me Aster."

"Aster," Merrell repeated.

"It is from one of your languages."

Merrell nodded as if he understood, but Priscilla doubted he did. She didn't.

"Thank you, Aster. I owe you a great deal."

Aster did his version of a smile, tapped the armband, and stood still as a stone while the water sphere Priscilla had seen minutes before surrounded him.

He and the sphere disappeared.

Overhead, the fragmented ship drew together, then slowly rose until it disappeared from sight.

The sound of a cell phone chiming filled the air. Those who remained looked at Toomey, who snapped the phone from his belt. He held the

46

cell phone to his ear. Nodding, he said something and then held it out to Merrell. "It's Mrs. Merrell."

"I'll take it," Martha said. "Mom?"

Priscilla's cell phone chirped to life. The caller ID indicated Chris Conlin was on the other end. She answered.

"Why haven't you been answering your phone? I've called several times."

"It never rang here, Chris." It occurred to her that no cell phones rang since the thing overhead had appeared. *Come to think of it, all the radio traffic from fire and police had gone quiet, too.* In the midst of destruction and death, everything had gone silent—peacefully silent. "I think something interfered with communications."

"Well, what's happening? Have you got enough footage?"

"Oh, I've got footage, Chris. Boy, do I have footage."

Chapter Six

Tom Clyn was on a bridge spanning Interstate 8 when the earthquake struck. Seated in the driver's seat of his moving 1985 Toyota sedan had altered his perception of the event. His car felt light and the road slippery, as if he had hit a patch of ice. Ice in San Diego wasn't likely. As he struggled to remain in his lane, he caught sight of rising dust and the erratic actions of the other cars in the northbound lanes of the 805 freeway.

That's when he knew.

Although he had driven over this bridge more times than he could count, he had never given thought to how high above the Mission Valley floor he was. He thought about it now.

Where some men might have prayed, Clyn cursed. Images of his old car plummeting a hundred, two hundred, three hundred feet—whatever the actual distance—and being buried in concrete and rebar sent his stomach plummeting and his heart stuttering.

He let off the gas but didn't touch the brakes. He wanted off the bridge. It took all the restraint he could muster to keep from pressing the accelerator to the floor. Doing so might send the Toyota out of control. At the moment, he was still on course, although he used more of his lane than normal.

He felt it before the sound of crunching metal reached his ears. The back of his car jerked to the right, and what little traction he had gave way. The car spun across two lanes before slamming into the concrete barrier rail.

When he came to rest, his car faced the wrong way. He gazed through his windshield at oncoming traffic. A short distance away, light posts swayed. He forced himself to look out the driver's side window, over the rail, and down the long distance to the coursing cars on I-8. Some swerved. Some came to an abrupt stop.

Clyn turned his head and saw a black, late-model BMW with a crunched right front fender stopped and turned sideways in the lane.

Tires pressed to a sudden stop squealed in protest. The roar of an eighteen-wheeler thundered along the bridge as it came to a stop three feet from the Beemer. Drivers did their best to avoid collision. Most were successful.

The bridge shuddered.

The bridge swayed.

Clyn shook and stared at his white knuckles.

"Seconds," he muttered. "Earthquakes only last seconds." But high on a bridge, unable to move, surrounded by cars and panicked drivers, seconds oozed by at an impossibly slow pace.

He closed his eyes and waited for the fall to begin.

The rumble of an angry earth and the vibration of the bridge ceased so quickly, Clyn thought he had gone deaf. Opening his eyes, his vision fell on the small ornament hanging from his rearview mirror. The little flying saucer swayed like a pendulum. He placed a shaky finger to its side to stop the swinging.

He had survived. The bridge still stood and he was not buried in concrete rubble. He chuckled. Nothing about the situation was funny, but he couldn't help himself.

His left side hurt from where he impacted the door when the car hit the barrier. Other than that, he felt whole.

"Aftershocks." Clyn's heart ratcheted up again. *An aftershock can be nearly as powerful as the initial earthquake. And if the bridge has been damaged—*

He pressed the gas pedal, but the car didn't move. Red lights on the dashboard told him the engine had died. He turned the ignition key, but nothing happened. *You're not thinking. Think. Of course. The car is still in drive.* He slipped the gearshift lever into PARK and tried again. The engine churned but refused to start.

"Come on, come on."

He tried again. Nothing.

"Great. Just great." He slammed his palms on the steering wheel.

He reached for the door release and then realized he couldn't open the door against the barrier. Crawling across the seats, he exited through the passenger door. Several other drivers stood by their vehicles.

"I'm sorry, pal." A young man in expensive clothes walked toward him. "The car just lost traction. Next thing I knew, we were banging bumpers. You OK?"

"Yeah, no thanks to you."

Clyn guessed they were about the same age, twenty-eight. They had the same build, thin. There the similarities ended. Clyn's brown hair hung to his shoulders; Mr. Beemer's looked like the product of a fifty-dollar haircut. Clyn wore dirty jeans and a black T-shirt with the image of a green alien on the front and the words THE TRUTH IS IN HERE. The Beemer's owner had *successful entrepreneur* written all over him: casual brown pants, sport coat, and collarless shirt.

"It was an accident. There's been an earthquake."

"Ya think?"

"Look, I'm trying to do the right thing here. We should exchange info and insurance."

"Normally, I'd agree, but I'm getting off this bridge."

"Why...?"

The bridge began to shake.

"Oh."

"Yeah, oh. Stay as long as you like. My car won't start, so I'm hoofing it out of here. If you're smart, you'll do the same..."

A movement caught Clyn's eye. He blinked, then blinked again. Several hundred feet overhead and moving at pedestrian speed south along the same line Clyn and others had been driving was a giant inverted black diamond. Beemer-guy followed Clyn's gaze and said something Clyn's mind didn't bother processing.

"Wow."

"What is that?" Beemer asked.

"It's a UFO, man. A real, right-in-your-face UFO." Something in his chest began to scrabble about like a rodent scratching and chewing through a cardboard box. It took a moment for him to realize the rodent was his heart.

"I thought...I mean, aren't...you know..."

50

"You thought all UFOs were saucer shaped?" Clyn frowned. "Don't be stupid. They come in all kinds of shapes and sizes. Just like cars. Of course, I've never seen anything like this. Never read about it, either."

"I...I don't think anyone has seen anything like this before."

"My camera! I'm an idiot." Clyn sprinted to his car, yanked open the passenger door, popped the glove compartment, and removed a small, rectangular digital camera. He took several shots, then set it to video and recorded several seconds.

A thought slammed forward. "Hey, buddy." Beemer-man shifted his gaze from the thing overhead to Clyn. "Go stand by your car."

"Why?"

"Just do it, man. I'm gonna make you famous. That, and I need to establish perspective."

A few steps later, Beemer stood next to his damaged luxury car. Clyn took more photos and shot more video. He wished for a better camera and a larger memory card. Within seconds, the card was full.

The black diamond passed overhead and continued along its course for another mile or so.

"It looks like it's headed for downtown."

"What's your name, man?"

"Ian Robinson."

"Ian. Figures. You look like an Ian."

"I'll take that as a compliment. You really know about these things?"

"Yup. I'm an expert among experts. Listen, Ian. I think you're right. I think that thing is headed downtown. My car won't start. Is yours still running?"

"Nope. After I hit you, I spun into another car. Oil and radiator fluid are bleeding out of every pore."

Clyn swore. He stepped away from Ian and raised his voice. "Listen, everyone. My car is toast and I need to follow that thing. I need a ride. How about it? Anyone?"

No one stepped forward. Someone shouted, "Forget it, freak."

"Come on, folks; this is big. This is history."

"So's your car."

All my life I wait for this and I'm stuck on a bridge over Mission Valley with a boatload of idiots.

He returned to his car and tried to pop the hood, but the collision with the concrete guardrail had bent the frame and body enough to jam the hood shut.

"You're going to need a body shop to open that hood."

"Thanks for trying to cheer me up." Clyn kicked the car door. He did it again and again, the sound of it echoing along the bridge.

"Keep doing that and no one will give you a ride." Ian put a hand on Clyn's shoulder. "Look. I think you're right. We should get off the bridge. Both our cars will need to be towed."

"I can't afford a tow truck."

"I can. I'll pay. I know a great body shop. Until then, I think we follow your advice about getting off the bridge. Who knows what kind of damage the earthquake did?" Ian took stock of their position. "Let's head south. Any help will be coming from that direction. We can wait over on solid ground, and you can tell me about what we just saw."

Clyn kicked the car one more time. "Might as well. Can't do anything more here."

Priscilla had to sit for a few minutes to catch her breath. The walk back and slow plodding up the stairs to the ninth floor had left her more than winded. She had a few more decades before she'd consider herself old, but she felt twice her age. An earthquake, a hike through downtown streets, the arrival of some kind of alien, and an unbelievable rescue and resuscitation were additional weights that encumbered.

It was resuscitation, wasn't it? I mean, it couldn't be anything else. Martha just looked dead. Because if she were truly dead, then she had just witnessed . . . no, that couldn't be.

Leo sat next to her. A spring breeze wafted through the opening where once her window had been.

"I can't work here," Leo said, his breath now steady. Aware of Leo's history of heart problems, Priscilla had made the climb up the stairs slowly, stopping at every floor to catch her breath, but, more importantly, to let Leo catch his. "That gaping hole makes me nervous. Let's use my office."

"I told you I'd have your office one day." She stood.

"Yeah, well, you're just visiting—although if I have to climb those stairs one more time, you may have it permanently."

"You told me you were OK. You *are* OK, right?"

"A little angina." He pulled a small brown bottle from his pant pocket, removed a small pill, and placed it under his tongue.

"Nitro?"

"Yup. I'll be ready to go dancing in a minute." Leo closed his eyes.

"Let's go to your office instead. My legs can't stand any dancing. Besides, I can't dance."

"I've heard redheads have no rhythm."

"That's because we have everything else. You sure you're all right?" Priscilla studied Leo's face.

"Fine. Want a piggyback ride?"

"I think I can make it. Lead the way, Leo."

Priscilla followed as they worked their way over the paper-strewn carpet. Books, pencils, paperweights, soda cans, coffee cups, and other office items littered the floor, detritus of the quake that could have been worse but was bad enough.

Before they crossed the threshold of Leo's office, a glass-enclosed structure near the center of the cubicle forest, Chris Conlin appeared, jaw tight and face red.

"It took you long enough."

"We decided to take in a movie and then a pizza."

"I'm under a great deal of stress, Leo. I don't need your smart mouth now."

"Chris, we got back as fast as we could, then had to march up nine flights of stairs." Priscilla's patience thinned. "You try doing that in a pair of pumps."

"OK, OK. My phone is going off like crazy. Between the other reporters and the higher-ups at Debatto Media, my mind is about to melt. To make things worse, I'm getting calls from nutballs about a flying saucer. Like we need that now."

The phone in Conlin's office, which shared a glass wall with Leo's, began to ring. He ignored it. "Gimme." He held out his hand and motioned for the camera. "I want to see the shots and video."

"You better sit down when you do." Leo plopped into his chair. Priscilla took one of the two seats positioned at the front of the desk.

"Whatever. You two get to work on the copy. We'll need material for photo captions, text for the online version. Also, we need to get material for the hard-copy edition. Think above the fold. Maybe six inches. No, ten inches."

"Do you think ten column inches will do it?" Priscilla asked.

"Sure. Best I can tell, the city is still standing and there's been minimal damage. Be sure to play up the governor angle. Leo, you write that piece. Priscilla, you take the broad picture."

"I think you'd better view the digital material before you settle on details." Leo picked up and repositioned a toppled coffee mug that bore the inscription *Los Angeles Times*—a memento of higher and happier days.

"Just do as I say. I don't need any more problems." Conlin exited with the same grim expression he wore when he entered.

"Think I should share my nitro with him?"

Priscilla chuckled without feeling the humor. "They couldn't pay me enough to have his job. Lead reporter is fine with me. Administration takes a different set of skills—skills I don't have."

"Skills he doesn't have." Leo rested his elbows on his desk and rubbed his eyes. "I think I just lived five years this morning."

"What did we see, Leo?"

"What do you mean? You were there. You took the pictures and video. You even talked to him. That's more than I could do."

"It all happened less than half an hour ago, and already I'm doubting my own eyes and experience."

"Why? Just because some kind of alien pulls his spaceship into San Diego and parks it over your head, appears in a big ball of water, rescues the governor's daughter from an impossible situation, and resuscitates her with some kinda science magic, then sails off again? What's not to believe?"

"I don't know whether to feel blessed or cursed. I mean, it was amazing. More than amazing. Clearly, he's not human. That means that he's...he's...what? From another planet? How can that be? How did he get here? How is it that he arrives right after an earthquake? Where did he learn English? Why—"

Leo leaned back and raised his hands as if surrendering to a gunman. "Ease up, kid. I don't have answers. Like you, I have nothing but questions."

He closed his eyes and Priscilla could see his eyes dart beneath thin lids like someone in REM sleep. "We are witnesses to the greatest event in human history. When this gets out, the world will go nuts."

"As if the world weren't nutty enough."

He opened his eyes and straightened in his chair. "And you, my dear Priscilla, are going to be in the heart of it."

"Why me? You saw as much as I did."

"True, but I didn't talk to Mr. What's-his-name. I didn't shoot the footage."

"Aster. He said his name was Aster. There was a television crew there. I'm sure they got better footage."

Leo guffawed. "You were too preoccupied to notice, but those guys left when Aster set down in the middle of the street. That thing he came from—that black diamond thing—terrified them. To be honest, it put the fear in me, too. I came close to scampering away myself."

"But you didn't. That's what makes you a great reporter."

"I stayed because you stayed. Didn't you hear me calling you?"

"I think so. I may have been a little overfocused."

"Overfocused? Is that what they call it these days?" He shook his head. "You are one piece of work, Priscilla Simms."

"That's what I keep telling people. Why does the name Aster sound familiar?"

"It does sound familiar." He turned his chair to the low-rise bookcase behind him and removed a large, well-worn volume.

"A dictionary. You know they have those on computers now."

Leo looked to the side of his desk. Priscilla saw the object of his gaze: a toppled monitor and keyboard. "At times, the old way is best."

He rifled through the pages. "Here we go. The first definition refers to a plant with daisylike flowers."

"I don't think that's it."

"Me, either. Second definition mentions star-shaped structures in a cell, sometimes called a cytaster. That's a new one on me."

"He said that his name came from one of our languages."

"OK, let's check the etymology." He ran a finger along the page. "Ah, this is interesting. Aster comes to us from the Greek through Latin. It means 'star.' Appropriate for a being from space." He turned the old dictionary so Priscilla could read the entry. "We get our word *asterisk* from it. You'd think an old newspaperman like me would know that."

"You can't know everything, Leo."

"Conlin does. If you don't believe me, just ask him."

Something else in the entry caught her attention, but before she could speak Conlin stumbled into the office.

"What's the matter, Chris? You look like you've seen a ghost."

"I don't know for sure what I just saw. You could have warned me."

"What, and miss this?"

"Give the man a break, Leo. Can't you see he's had a shock?"

Conlin settled in the other empty chair. "This is big, people. This is huge. It's the story of the century...no, it's the story of all history, and we have it. This is the greatest thing to ever happen to mankind."

"I hope you're right," Leo said. "We just learned that his name means star. Aster means star."

"I know. We get the word *asteroid* from it. That, and *asterisk*."

Leo frowned.

"I hate to be the party pooper, guys, but we also get the word *disaster* from it."

Chapter Seven

POLICE CARS ARRIVED BEFORE FIRE TRUCKS, AND THOSE, CLYN thought, took their sweet time about it. Splashes of red and blue lights played in the air as emergency personnel did their best to make sense of the pileup on the bridge.

"How long do you think before they clear things up?" Clyn asked. He and Ian stood at the threshold of the bridge.

"Can't know for sure, but I don't think it will be real long. I didn't see anyone with serious injuries. If someone had been killed, the road would be closed for hours while investigators try to find someone to blame."

Clyn looked to the sky again, an action he had done so many times over the last half hour that his neck and back ached. Redirecting his gaze to the more mundane scene of Mission Valley, he watched streams of cars move along I-8, only slightly slowed by the sight of emergency vehicles on the bridge over their heads. On the hills that framed the valley stood homes that, best Clyn could tell, had successfully rode the rolling ground that shook the region. A really big quake, like the one that nearly destroyed Irvine a few years ago, would have brought the expensive homes to the ground. Earthquake insurance was so expensive in Southern California that he doubted more than half the owners carried it on the houses they called home.

"They may close the bridge anyway. Someone's going to have to inspect it to make sure it's safe for traffic." Clyn shoved his hands in his pockets, removed them, then shoved them in again.

"I don't think so. The quake wasn't that bad."

Clyn snorted. "That a fact? It felt bad enough to me. You got a seismograph in your back pocket?"

"Hardly. Look around you. All the mid-rise buildings appear in good shape. I don't see any broken windows. I imagine some structures lost a window or two and probably have cracks in the plaster. I only saw one fire, and the fire department made quick work of that. The city was lucky."

Clyn looked around for the first time. He hadn't thought about damage other than that done to his car. "Yeah, maybe."

"No maybe about it. We had more trouble because we had the misfortune of being on a bridge when the quake struck. It swayed and cars lost traction. That's why my BMW and your car mixed it up."

"Sounds like you got all the answers, man."

"Not all. I'm just good at analyzing things. It's what I do. I'm a business consultant. I travel the country telling executives how to do a better job."

"Judging by your car, it pays pretty good."

Ian nodded. "I'm not hurting any."

Clyn removed his hands from his pocket and straightened as a police officer approached.

"Any of those cars yours?"

Clyn started to speak, but his words hung in his throat.

Ian showed no reluctance. "Yes, sir. Mine is the black Beemer convertible midpoint on the bridge. My friend's is the..." He looked at Clyn.

He cleared his throat. "The '85 Toyota against the guardrail."

The cop eyed Ian. "Either one drivable?"

"No, officer. Mine lost coolant and oil. I think something pierced the oil pan."

"What about you?" The officer locked eyes with Clyn.

"Nah. I tried to start it but nothing happens. It's dead, Jim."

"My name is not Jim."

"I know. It's a Star Trek thing—never mind." Clyn broke eye contact.

"I've called for a tow, officer. The truck should be here soon."

"Don't count on it. Tow truck companies have more than they can handle."

A loud air horn sounded a short distance away. A large tilt-bed, flatbed transportation truck worked its way along the shoulder and past stopped cars.

"There he is, now." Ian waved at the driver. A few moments later, the operator stopped the truck and got out.

"Hello, Mr. Robinson. Are you all right?"

The man stood two inches shorter than Clyn, wore a beige mechanic's coverall, and was the cleanest tow truck driver he had ever seen. His Hispanic face wore a look of concern.

"I'm just fine, Tito. How's the family?"

"The earthquake scared the kids, but everyone is fine. A couple of pictures fell from the wall. Nothing important."

"Good. What about your shop?"

"Came through fine. A few tools got scattered, but nothing big. I made the mechanics check on their families. Everyone is good."

"Well, I'm glad you could come. My car is in the middle of the bridge. I also want you to help my new friend. His is the classic Toyota against the concrete rail."

"No problem, Mr. Robinson. I'll put yours on the bed and tow Mr…"

"Clyn," Clyn answered.

"…and tow Mr. Clyn's."

"Thanks, Tito. You're the best. Put everything on my bill. I'm afraid I contributed to Mr. Clyn's problem."

"I understand." Tito looked to the officer. "Am I cleared to drive out there?"

"Yes, but we could use some help clearing the bridge."

Tito nodded. "You help me get Mr. Robinson and Mr. Clyn's cars, and I'll have two other trucks here before I'm gone. Will that do?"

"That'd be great. Are you under contract with the city?"

"No, but I'll do it anyway."

Tito jogged back to his truck.

Clyn looked at Ian. "You have your own tow truck driver? Sweet."

"He's not *my* tow truck driver, but I do a fair amount of business with him. I collect cars. It's a small collection right now. Tito is the best restoration man in San Diego."

The officer said, "So when he says he'll send a couple of trucks, you believe him? He's not just working me so he can retrieve your car ahead of others?"

"He's an honest man, Officer. He'll do what he says."

The officer started to leave, then stopped. "Let me ask you guys something. We got lots of reports of something…how do I put this."

"A big black diamond in the air?" Clyn said.

"Yeah. You saw it?"

"Oh yeah. We saw it."

"In fact—" Ian began.

"You missed something special, Officer. I don't think I'll ever forget it." Clyn put his hands back in his pockets. "You might ask around. Maybe someone took pictures."

"I'll do that."

Once the officer moved from earshot, Ian said, "I take it you don't want people knowing about the camera in your pocket."

"None of their business. I don't want anyone taking this from me. I've waited too long."

"Too long for what?"

"To see one. I've read every book about these things. Now I have pictures."

"And you're hoping to make a few bucks off them."

"Something wrong with that?"

Ian grinned. "No problem at all. In fact, I admire the sentiment. Seizing opportunity is what it's all about. Knowing what to do with opportunity is another matter."

"Knowing how to get home is what I'm wondering about."

Ian pulled his cell phone out and dialed a number. Clyn wished his phone had extra minutes on it, but he always used them up in the first week. *One of these days…one of these days.*

Ian turned and looked up the road. "Got it." He folded the phone and clipped it to his belt. "If you feel up to a little hike, I can get us out of here."

"A hike?"

"I called a limo service. The driver is about a mile up the road. He can't get closer until they open the bridge, but he can pull a U and get out of this mess. All we have to do is walk a mile."

"A limo? You hired a limo?" This bad day was getting better.

"Don't think stretch limo, Tom. It's just a Lincoln Town Car, but it will do."

"Why are you doing this?" Clyn studied Ian. "I gave you a pretty bad time."

"From your perspective, I deserved it. Not that I could have done much about it. Still, I feel a little responsible. I was on the phone when the quake hit. Had I had both hands on the wheel...well, who knows? It might have made no difference at all. I'm not the only one who lost control of his car."

Clyn didn't know what to make of Ian Robinson, but he did know that a ride in a nice car was far better than standing along the roadside.

"Lead, man. I'm right behind you."

"You spoke to it? You really held a conversation with the thing from outer space?" Conlin leaned forward in Leo's guest chair, bridging a few more inches that separated him from Priscilla.

"I think it's a he." She leaned back, trying to add back the inches between them.

"How can you know that?"

"Because that thing on his arm reminds me of a remote control, and we all know how you guys love those things."

"Funny. Very funny. Hilarious. Answer the question."

At least Leo smiled.

"I can't, Chris. He just struck me as male."

"We don't know they have males and females." Chris raised a hand to his mouth and nibbled on his fingernails. "Maybe they have three or four genders."

"There's a nightmare," Leo said.

"He touched you, Priscilla. I saw it on the video. What was that like?"

"It was interesting. I felt a sensation. I can't describe it. It might have just been adrenaline pumping through my body."

"Are you writing this down, Leo? I want an article on this. Our own reporter makes the first contact with an alien race."

"Hold on, Chris." Priscilla raised a finger. "We don't know that. Maybe he just had lunch with the mayor. I just happened to be on scene."

"I can't abide false modesty, Priscilla. You walked right up to this giant alien and spoke to him. You let him touch you. You've done what no one else has done, and I plan to let the world know. The video should be edited in a few minutes and streaming over the Internet. Our web people are setting up the online articles. They need input from you on captions. And how about that article? We need that right away, Leo."

"Chris—"

"I've already been on the phone with the suits at Debatto Media. They're thrilled. I have to coordinate things with their other media outlets."

"Chris—"

"There are going to be bonus checks around here soon, guys. Big, honkin' bonus checks."

"Chris, please."

"Our competitors are going to want to talk to you. I need a few minutes to think about how to handle that. Now—"

Leo spoke up. "Chris. Take a breath. Priscilla is trying to say something."

Priscilla inhaled. "I'm not comfortable with all this. I don't mind doing the reporting, writing the articles, but I don't want to be the focus. I was just one of many people there."

"How many did what you did?"

"I don't know."

"Yes, you do. It was remarkable. I'm sorry you don't like the spotlight, because you're smack-dab in the middle of it." He stood and hitched up his pants. "Roll those sleeves up, people. We got reporting to do."

He left silence behind.

"Finally," Leo said. "You OK?"

"Yeah, I guess. But the story isn't about me, it's about what happened."

"True."

"The focus should be on Aster, not me."

"True."

"Reporters shouldn't become part of their story."

"Truer still."

She paused. "You agree with him, don't you?"

"I'm afraid so, but don't tell him. It'll ruin my reputation."

"Leo, how can you agree that I should subject myself to interviews and share my video and stills?"

"Because you *are* part of the story, and the video and stills are not yours. They belong to the company."

"I'm not going to win this, am I?" She slumped in the chair and rubbed her temples.

"No, ma'am. The game is already over. Come on. We have words to put on the page."

Priscilla didn't move. The image of the tall being slammed to the forefront of her mind, and for a moment she felt ill. The electric current of fear snaked through her limbs and chest. Then she thought of his touch, of the peace, of the exhilaration, and the cold fear warmed like an embrace. How evil could a creature be that brings such joy with his touch? Should she be frightened of someone who saved a life like Martha's?

I'm a lucky woman.

Something inside her disagreed.

Chapter Eight

C LYN EXITED THE BACKSEAT OF THE LINCOLN AND WAITED FOR IAN and the driver to pull away. He watched them all the way down the street and waited for them to make a turn onto the street that would lead them out of La Mesa and back to Interstate 8. They drove at a speed fitting the residential neighborhood. Once the car was out of sight, Clyn walked in the opposite direction and south two blocks, past small stucco homes that sold in an inflated real estate market for hundreds of thousands more than they were worth. In less dreamy moments, he acknowledged that he'd never own one—not until his mother died, something she seemed to be resisting.

The walk took less than ten minutes, and Clyn began to second-guess his decision to tell Ian where he lived. He had lied, but he should have lied bigger. Two streets wasn't enough separation.

Eye-slamming pink paint made his house stand out on the street, as did the lawn with its patchwork of dead grass. Early spring warmth had kick-started jacaranda and ornamental plum trees. Spring came earlier every year and gave way to summer weeks before it should.

The house had been built in the post-WWII boom and had held up well against the years, mostly because of the weekend sacrifices of his father. Clyn had helped from his childhood years on. Since his father had died, he hadn't picked up a hammer or paintbrush.

Most houses in San Diego were slab-on-grade construction: wood framework affixed to a slab of concrete. Houses in this part of La Mesa stood a couple of feet above the ground. He had given it no thought until that moment, but the house still stood. In fact, the neighborhood seemed untouched.

Clyn breezed through the door.

"Tommy? Is that you?"

"Yes, Mom. It's me."

"You're late. I've been worried half to death."

What would get you to worry all the way? "Sorry. I was in an accident in Mission Valley."

"Accident?" A woman with artificially dark hair, lines in her face plowed by life, and a slight bend in her posture emerged from the kitchen. Goldie Clyn was seventy-two and had a mind that grew more childlike everyday. "Are you OK, baby? I mean, are you hurt? What happened? Where's the car?"

"Mom, Mom, relax. I'm fine. I'm a little sore and probably will be sorer tomorrow, but I'm fine. Nothing a few aspirin can't handle." He kissed her on top of the head. "And I've told you not to call me baby. It creeps me out."

"But the car..."

"The guy who hit me has money. He was driving a high-end BMW and lost control during the earthquake. We were crossing the bridge over I-8. He paid to have my car towed and then brought me home."

"He sounds like a nice man."

"I wouldn't know. What about you? You OK? The house OK?"

"The picture of your father fell, and the refrigerator danced halfway across the kitchen floor, but that's all. You're going to have to put the fridge back."

"Maybe later."

"It will only take a minute."

"I got something to do."

"Like what?"

"Mom, let it go. You wouldn't understand."

Her frown nearly touched her shoulders. She placed her hands on her hips. "You listen to me, Thomas Albert Clyn. I've been rearranging dishes and picking up I don't know how many knickknacks. And where were you? I could have had a heart attack and been lying on the floor unable to get up. All I can say is, if you ever want to eat another meal in this house—"

"All right. For the love...all right. I'll do it."

"Now?"

65

"Yes, Mom. Right now. Before I do anything else. Despite my busted-up side. Before I go to the bathroom…before I draw another breath, I will move the refrigerator back in place."

"That's my boy."

"If we had a better fridge maybe these things wouldn't happen."

"There was an earthquake, son."

"I know there was an earthquake. I almost drove off a bridge."

"You were in an accident?"

Clyn pinched the bridge of his nose. "Yes, Mom. I told you just a minute ago. I…" He sighed and walked into the kitchen. "Mom, the thing has barely moved."

"It walked away from the wall. We're lucky it's not in the back-yard."

"It's barely moved six inches."

"Are you going to put it back or not?"

Clyn gave up. The quickest way out of the endless loop of bickering was silence. He put his shoulder to the avocado green appliance and pushed. It made his side ache, but he didn't complain. That would only start the sniping and questions again. Questions he already answered. Thirty seconds later, he had the fridge back in its place. He started to walk away.

"Where are you going?"

"My room. I've got a couple of things to do."

"You're not going to tell your mother how work went?"

"Mom, there's been an earthquake. How my day at Circuit City went doesn't matter."

"You're a smart boy. You could get a better job. You know all that computer stuff. I've read that some people make a lot of money in computers. You could be one of them."

"I'll give it some thought. Maybe I can invent something before dinner." He moved down the hall hoping his mother wouldn't follow. He was lucky.

The room was less than one hundred fifty square feet and dominated by a singlewide bed he had slept in since he was ten. The solid blue comforter lay neatly spread over the mattress. Once again, his mother had entered his domain and made the bed. Clyn had told her to stay out a thousand times—at least twice a day—yet she persisted in the daily invasion.

Removing the small camera from his pocket, he set it on his desk—a smooth, hollow core door pressed into service as a work surface. Gracing its top were two laptop computers, each with an auxiliary monitor. Four monitors. He powered up each computer and entered the password when prompted. As the computers booted, he searched through a black, two-drawer filing cabinet he used to store cables and other odds and ends.

"Where is it?"

He pushed aside plastic tangles of phone cords, power cords, and speaker wire. Beneath an unopened package of cable organizers, he saw the target of his search: a USB wire.

He sat in a worn secretary's chair, hooked the camera to one of the laptops, and waited for the computer to recognize the connection. The computer's wallpaper image was a black background with large gold letters that read: CLYN PRODUCTIONS—DOCUMENTARIES THAT MAKE A DIFFERENCE.

"Someday."

The word had been his mantra for the last year. Twelve months ago, he saw a documentary on UFOs and felt it was his calling in life to contribute to the genre. He owned every DVD produced on the subject and subscribed to the few magazines dedicated to the topic. He also received online newsletters and belonged to an Internet chat group infatuated with flying saucers.

It took only a few moments for the photos to transfer from the digital camera to the computer. Clyn spent the next few minutes separating photos of the craft he had seen flying overhead from those of a beer party he had attended the week before.

"This will rock the world." He clicked on the video files and watched, wide-eyed, as the black diamond cruised noiselessly through the sky. He felt pleased with the result. An amateur would have been carried away by the moment, but not him—not Thomas Clyn. He had remembered to keep the camera steady, to zoom in and out, and to find other objects to help establish perspective. A single object in the sky with nothing but blue as background always brought suspicion. In a digital world, anyone could fake anything. *Jurassic Park* and almost every movie that followed proved that. He had thought long and hard about this, preparing for the day when he could shoot photos and video of a real UFO.

His only complaint was the camera. He spent much of every paycheck buying computers and software necessary to enter the field of documentaries, but he still had to work with a cheap camera, a low-end digital device that could take a few seconds of video as well as still photos.

Still, the quality proved better than expected.

There it was in all its glory, gliding across his primary monitor just as it had flown over his head. The small mic picked up garbled expressions of shock and disbelief. All the better—more evidence that the video was real.

He wondered if others had taken photos. If not, he might be able to sell his footage to the news outlets and earn enough money for a professional camera.

Next to the makeshift desk, resting on a battered microwave cart, was a small television. He turned it on and switched to the local news station. The talking heads yammered about the quake and filled transition time between field reporters.

"OK," said the male anchor. Clyn had seen his face almost daily over the last few years. He was a fixture in San Diego broadcasting. "Here's what we have so far. The earthquake that struck our city happened at 10:22 local time and centered three miles off the coast. Seismologists have given a preliminary intensity of 6.2 on the Richter scale. Damage has been minimal throughout the county with the exception of the Windom Building downtown. It's hard to believe that anything could eclipse an earthquake, but that's what has happened."

"That's right, Mitch." A beautiful blonde coanchor chimed in. "For those just joining us, a dramatic rescue was conducted at the site of the fallen Windom Building downtown. We're sad to report that as many as three people perished when the building collapsed in its basement. One survivor is in San Diego Regional Hospital, being attended to by physicians."

"And what a survivor. Martha Merrell, a partner in a law firm, is Governor Merrell's daughter. Helping in the rescue was...I don't know how to say this...an alien."

Clyn bolted to his feet, sending the chair rolling back several feet. "No way!"

He reached for, grabbed, and fumbled with the remote control, but managed to activate the digital video recorder.

Mitch the anchorman continued. "This is no April Fool's joke. I've reported many things in my day, but this...well, look at the video, and you decide."

The screen filled with the image of a collapsed building. Firemen worked cautiously in the rubble, and some kind of tractor was pushing chunks of concrete around. Standing in the street, a young woman held a microphone near her lips. Her expression showed considered concern. "I'm at the scene of the fallen Windom Building, and as you can see, little more has been done since my last report. Rescuers are moving carefully, fearful the building might further collapse.

"As we reported earlier, Governor Merrell's daughter is one of those trapped beneath the rubble. He arrived on scene a few moments ago. He maintains a prayerful watch, as any parent would. I spoke to his aide..." She looked at her notepad. "...Mr. Steve Toomey, who informs me that Emily Merrell, the governor's wife, is traveling back from Orlando, Florida. He didn't know when she would arrive or even if she would come to the site."

A slow-moving shadow crawled across the reporter's face. "The fate of Martha Merrell is in the hands of..." She looked up. "Oh...oh, my." She cursed and pointed.

The camera shifted from her to something in the sky—the same something Clyn had seen cruising over his head: a huge, black, diamond-shaped craft.

"I don't believe it. I've been scooped." Clyn looked for something to kick but found nothing that wouldn't do more damage to him than he to it.

He started to sit down, then realized just in time that his chair had gone missing. Pulling it close, he sat and rested his elbows on his knees and his head in his hands.

The image on the screen began to bounce and sway, and Clyn could hear swearing. *Amateur.* The station had not bothered to censure the cameraman's curses. *Not even the FCC suits can complain about this.*

There was more cursing, this time in a woman's voice. He heard a thump. The camera swung around in time to see the backside of the reporter as she fled.

Again, the cameraman turned his lens up just in time to capture the ship as it broke into fragments. Clyn was sure the pieces would fall, but they remained aloft and unperturbed by gravity or the law of physics as Clyn knew them.

He leaned closer, unwilling to believe his eyes. A sphere—a sphere of water—began a slow descent.

"Whoa."

When the sphere touched the surface of the street, it disappeared as if it had never been there. What did remain was the tall, odd figure of something he knew was not human. "Un…be…liev…able."

The creature looked at the scene, then at the cameraman. A second later, the video showed only the pavement.

"You ran?" Clyn cried. "You coward! You spineless, worthless, piece—"

The anchorwoman's face reappeared on the television. "As you can see, we experienced some technical difficulties." Mitch cleared his throat and the newswoman—Cybil something, Clyn thought—fought off a frown. "Fortunately, we have video from another source. What you are about to see was shot by Priscilla Simms of *Today News,* here in San Diego."

Clyn spent the next few minutes trying to remember how to breathe.

"*Newsweek* is on line three."

Priscilla acknowledged the message, switched off the intercom, and stared at the blinking lights on the silver and black phone. "*Newsweek* on three; CNN on two; NBC on one. I can't get my material written if I'm the subject of every other journalist's material."

Leo sat on the sofa at the back of his office. Only Conlin's office was larger. It was also home to a better line of furniture than Leo's. Leo didn't care.

Priscilla sat at his desk, trying to get the copy written that Conlin demanded as well as field questions from other news agencies—something else he insisted she do. "Just be sure you mention Debatto Media and *Today News*," he urged.

Priscilla felt glad that she had Leo's quiet strength to anchor her—that, and she appreciated the use of his office. Her work area was off-limits because of the broken window. Besides, Leo's office had a door and her cubicle didn't. Being interviewed required quiet.

"I bet when you got up this morning, you didn't think you'd get your fifteen minutes of fame today."

"I lost my hunger for fame a long time ago, Leo. I'm happy to have meaningful work, a few friends, and the occasional grilled-cheese-on-rye sandwich."

"Stop. I didn't eat breakfast, and we haven't had time for lunch."

"Want me to go get you something? I promise not to complain about the stairs."

Leo pointed at the phone. "You have more important things to do. Don't keep those guys waiting."

Priscilla looked at the flashing lights and groaned. She reached for the handpiece but stopped when Conlin burst into the room.

"How's it going?"

"Peachy."

"Great. Great. Fabulous. A couple of things. The building engineer has cleared the elevators. He says they're safe."

"My legs thank you," Priscilla said.

"Also, a man named Tim Wacher will be calling. Squeeze him in. He's the publicist for the execs at Debatto. He's going to handle your publicity."

"What publicity?"

"You know what publicity. You're the hot item for now. Only nuclear war can push you and that Aster character off the front pages."

"I don't want publicity."

Conlin laughed. "You say that like what you want matters."

71

"I could quit."

"Do you think that'll stop the press? It wouldn't stop anyone here, including you."

"Arggggh."

"Well said, but work on your vocabulary. I'll let you get back to the phone work. You're doing a super job. Your video has gone national, but of course we knew it would."

Conlin started to leave.

Priscilla stopped him. "Hang on, Chris. Pick a number between one and three."

"There's only one number between one and three: two."

"You know what I mean."

He grinned. "I'm sticking with two."

She looked at the phone. "CNN it is." She took a deep breath and picked up the handset.

A rumble ran through the building again, and the floor swayed beneath her chair. It lasted less than three seconds, but Priscilla held her breath for a full minute.

"Aftershock," Conlin said.

"You think?" She punched the blinking button on the phone. "Shaky Priscilla Simms here."

Allen Sloan sat in his bed and studied his reflection in the handheld mirror given him by Dr. DeGuere. The face that looked back looked familiar, yet that of a stranger. He touched his hollow cheeks, tallow skin that hung on his cheekbones like drapes. Stubble covered his jaw. He hadn't been shaved for at least two days, but a missing beard proved someone had been putting a razor to his face. *Nurses don't get enough credit.*

His hair had grayed a touch, and his eyes seemed two shades paler than he recalled. He raised his other hand and studied it: thin, with bruises from months of IV needles. His fingernails were too long and needed trimming. He leaned his head back and closed his eyes.

Shards of thought rattled in his brain like broken glass tiles. He had a thousand questions for Dr. DeGuere and the nursing staff, but patients needed them elsewhere. He had come awake after the quake. All he knew was that it had been sudden, sharp, and not as bad as it could have been. He supposed that was good.

Much of his muscle mass had gone missing. And something else was absent: emotion. While he felt a sense of joy at being released from a yearlong nap, he felt no euphoria. After all, he had no memory of being unconscious. *Not entirely true. The images. They're there from time to time.*

Images he couldn't see clearly but could sense scratching at the fabric of his memory. Their presence made him uncomfortable, but he couldn't tell why. The vague emotion chilled him, as if he were the house in a haunted house movie.

Thinking exhausted him. Sleep beckoned him. *I've slept enough for five years, but I'm still drowsy.*

He pushed the specters back in the basement of his mind and tried to focus on the family he lost. DeGuere had delivered the news softly but with clinical detachment: "I'm sorry, Mr. Sloan. They were in the car with you when you had your accident."

That was it. "I'm sorry. You're wife and son are dead. Other than that, how do you feel?"

He corrected himself. DeGuere showed the proper concern. Shouldn't such news move a man to tears? Shouldn't a husband grieve the loss of a wife and weep over the death of a son?

Yes. Yes, he should. Then why am I so...so unmoved?

No answer came. No tears flowed. No retched tearing of the stomach. Just detachment. He had shown more emotion in a theater during a romantic comedy.

The accident or the coma had left him stripped of emotion. He tried to feel bad about that but couldn't. Something wasn't right. Something in his head. His thoughts were like rowboats in a thick fog.

So sleepy. So tired.

But he didn't want to sleep. What if he closed his eyes only to sleep for another year? A twenty-first-century Rip Van Winkle.

"I've got to stay awake."

He set the mirror aside and saw the remote for the television mounted to his hospital room wall. The television awoke at the press of a button.

The grainy image disappointed him. "State of the art hospital and they can't fix the reception on something as simple as a television."

He flipped through the stations until he found a clear image of a news program. *Maybe I can get some details on the quake everyone is talking about.*

The news anchors faded away as a video began of something in the sky floating overhead. A sphere of water. A tall, odd looking alien—

Allen Sloan's screams filled the room and hallway.

Not every emotion was gone.

Chapter Nine

PATRICK MERRELL WAS A POWERFUL MAN. His bank account never dropped below the hundreds of millions of dollars—each dollar earned through one of several corporations he owned and through stocks and bonds. As governor, and to avoid conflict of interest, he had to place the stocks in a trust. He enjoyed playing the market, taking risk on some ventures, but kept most of his portfolio in stable, slow-growing markets. Most of his income came through Merrell Homes, a company that built hundreds of thousands of homes in the Southwest and all of California. The business continued to operate under the direction of a hand-selected president. Someday, if his political aspirations faltered, he'd return to the world of stick-built, slab-on-grade clone homes.

Being governor—a very rich governor—garnered special favors everywhere, including the busy emergency room of San Diego Regional Hospital.

Martha Merrell, thirty-eight, rested in a wheeled bed in a corner of the ER. Every bay, areas marked off by cheery drapes, held some injured person needing attention. There were no cries of pain or mournful moans. Advisors told Merrell that injuries from the earthquake were light. Still, gashes needed stitching, sprains needed wrapping, and head bumps needed examining.

Doctors and nurses slipped in and out of the bay. The head of emergency services, Dr. Caleb Rosen, had taken Martha's case, poking, prodding, questioning, listening, examining. He shook his head, then called for tests. Two hours passed and now he returned, slipping past the curtain. He brought with him another man, thin and distinguished. Merrell saw gray lightly painting the hair by the man's ears.

"Governor Merrell, Ms. Merrell, this is Dr. Dennis DeGuere. He's our top neurologist. I've asked him to consult."

"Doctor," Merrell said, standing from the fiberglass chair that had been his perch for the last two hours. They shook hands.

"It's an honor, Governor," DeGuere said. His hand felt warm and firm. Merrell had trouble trusting a man with a weak handshake.

The doctor turned his attention to Martha. "And you must be the reason behind the buzz in the hospital."

She smiled, and the sight of it warmed Merrell. Events had left him bone weary, and anything that looked like good news he welcomed.

"My father is the famous one. I'm just a lawyer."

"Your father? Did he do something special?"

She forced a laugh. "Um, he's governor of the state."

"That a fact? And just how long has he been governor, and can he fix that parking ticket I got the other day?"

Merrell caught DeGuere's glance, but his eyes immediately returned to Martha. Something lay behind the humor and questions.

"Are you kidding? Your ticket, your problem. Besides..." Martha trailed off.

"Besides what?" DeGuere prompted.

"Besides, I think you're testing my memory and mental acuity. And to answer your question, he's in the second year of his second term. He won the last election by garnering 63 percent of the vote."

"You're right, I was testing you. The fact that you used the phrase 'mental acuity' is impressive. Dr. Franklin here doesn't even know what *acuity* means."

"His name is Dr. Rosen. Dr. Caleb Rosen. He examined me two hours and..." She stole a look at a clock on the wall. "...twelve minutes ago. He had nurses do a blood draw, I've been x-rayed, run through a CAT scanner, and poked all over. So, as you can see, my short-term memory is working just fine."

"All of that good news."

Merrell took a step back as DeGuere approached the bed. He had her squeeze his fingers, wiggle her toes, and touch her nose with the tip of her finger. He peered in her eyes and ears. Much of what the new doctor did, Rosen had done two hours before.

DeGuere looked puzzled.

"What do you remember of the earthquake?"

"I remember being terrified beyond words. Several of us..." Her sentence faded. "Several of us were working when I heard a rumbling. It sounded like a big truck racing down the street, and then it hit. Before I could speak...it hit. The building shook. I heard glass breaking. Several people screamed. Maybe I did the screaming. Then the floor—well, the floor disappeared beneath my feet."

She took a deep, ragged breath. Merrell stepped to his daughter and took her hand. "The noise...the noise was deafening. I felt myself falling. I remember hitting bottom, but I don't remember anything more. I think something hit my head and everything went dark. When I woke up, I was outside looking at the sky—at something large and dark in the sky. And...I remember...him. I remember seeing him and thinking I was dreaming." She sighed. "Then they brought me here, but I don't know why. I feel great."

Merrell exchanged glances with DeGuere. The doctor acted like everything he heard was routine.

"You say you saw him. Who did you see?"

"I can't describe it. He didn't look human to me. Dad tells me it was an alien and that he saved my life."

"An alien?"

"Look, Doctor. I know it sounds outlandish, but it is what I experienced."

"It's been on the news," Rosen said. "It's got all the patients in the waiting room worked up. Some have left and gone home. They think the end of the world has come."

"I've been a little too busy to watch television." DeGuere's words revealed no criticism. "Ms. Merrell, here's the thing. I've been told that you sustained a serious head injury, that you were dead when paramedics looked at you, and now you're well. I've reviewed the X-rays and CAT scan. Your brain looks fine. Your neurological responses are normal."

"And you can't explain it."

"My job isn't to explain but to discover and cure."

77

Merrell couldn't remain silent. "She's not crazy, Doc, and neither am I. I saw the whole thing. She was dead, but he—it—made her well."

"A miracle? You're saying it's a miracle?"

"I don't know about miracles, Doc," Merrell said. "I only know that my daughter was dead and broken, but here she is in your bed, healthy and happy. You can watch the video footage if you don't believe us."

"Belief isn't the issue. Facts are. And the facts are that I can find nothing wrong with your daughter."

"So I'm free to go?" Martha asked.

"That will be up to Dr. Rosen, but I can't find a reason to keep you."

"Dr. Rosen?" Martha looked eager.

"I think we should free up the bed for a sick person. I'll start the paperwork."

Merrell stopped him. "Are you certain, Doctor? I mean...I don't want us to make a mistake."

"Let him go, Dad," Martha said. "I'm fine. Let's get out of here."

Conflict raged in Merrell. No matter how old the child, she remained a child in the eyes of her parents. "Do you know what your mother will do to me if I let you check out and then something goes wrong?"

"You're the governor. Call up the National Guard."

"They wouldn't stand a chance." He turned to the doctors. "Thank you. Any reason she can't fly?"

"I see no reason," DeGuere said, "but the last word rests with Dr. Rosen."

"I don't anticipate any problems," Rosen said, "but if there's any change, get to a doctor."

"I can't go to Sacramento with you, Dad. The firm needs me. Especially now."

"I need you more," Merrell said. "I can't go back without you. Your mother should be in California soon. I chartered a plane for her. She and the kids will be back from Florida and everyone is going to want to see with their own eyes that you're fine."

A buzzing noise rose from DeGuere's direction. He grabbed his pager and looked at the display. "I need to take this."

Cohen said, "We'll let you two duke it out. A nurse will come by in a minute with everything you need to sign out."

DeGuere and Rosen left.

"He seemed to know what he was doing."

Martha swung her legs over the edge of the bed. "Who? DeGuere?"

"Yes."

"He seemed capable enough. Great bedside manner. Of course, he thinks we're nuts."

"He won't when he sees the footage." He noticed Martha staring at him. "What?"

"I have to dress."

"So dress...oh, of course. Sorry. Your mind might be in good shape, but mine is pretty mushy."

"That's all right, Dad. Now leave."

"I'll go tell Steve to get things rolling. We'll need to find a way past the media. I can't face them now." He started to leave.

"Dad?"

"Yeah?"

"It really happened, didn't it? I'm not dreaming all this."

He pursed his lips. "It happened, and every second is branded on my mind."

DeGuere moved with purpose, his steps just shy of a jog. He wove through the busy corridor to the bank of elevators near the center of the hospital. Twenty people waited for the next elevator car. DeGuere brushed past them and into the stairwell, beginning a four-story climb to the neurology wing.

A man with a disciplined exercise regimen, DeGuere felt only slightly winded as he emerged into the lobby. He could see the nurses moving in and out of one of the rooms—the room with the enigmatic Allen Sloan. Ten steps later, he pushed his way into the room.

Chaos. Sloan kicked and fought against the large male nurse that pinned him to the bed. Two female nurses struggled to place straps around Sloan's emaciated ankle. It wasn't much of a battle. Sloan had been immobile for a year. His muscles no longer held the necessary strength to wage a physical battle against a skinny teenager, let alone the two-hundred-twenty-pounder pressing him to the mattress.

"Him! Him!"

DeGuere pushed his way to the head of the bed. "Mr. Sloan. Mr. Sloan!"

"Him! Him!"

DeGuere placed a hand around his patient's chin. "Mr. Sloan. Look at me. I said look at me."

"*Him!*" Sloan's eyes were fixed on something in the room, or something in his mind.

DeGuere followed Sloan's gaze and saw the television. A news program played, showing a heavily damaged building, rubble, fire and police cars, and—

He blinked several times. What was he seeing? Could it be—

"*Him! Him!* He's here!"

"Turn that off," DeGuere ordered. One of the nurses stretched to the wall-mounted television and switched off the power.

"*Him!* Him! Him." Sloan began to calm.

Again, DeGuere took Sloan by the jaw and directed his face closer. "Mr. Sloan. It's Dr. DeGuere. Everything is fine now. Do you hear me?"

A nurse stepped forward with a hypodermic.

"What are you doing?" DeGuere snapped.

"Sedating him. I just assumed—"

"I didn't call for sedation."

"With all due respect, Doctor, you weren't here when he went ballistic."

"I'll decide on the kind and type of sedation. Is that clear?"

Her face hardened like stone.

"Do you understand?"

She sighed for show. "Yes, Doctor."

Sloan had stopped struggling. "Ease up on him, Chuck, but stand by."

"Sure thing, Doc." The big, male nurse released Sloan's shoulders.

Sloan lay still for a moment, then raised his hands to his face.

He began to weep.

"Get his vitals."

The nurse felt for a pulse, then placed a BP cuff around Sloan's arm.

"Mr. Sloan. Do you know who I am?"

He nodded.

"Who am I?"

"DeGuere. Dr. DeGuere."

"That's right. Everything is fine. I need you to take a few deep breaths."

The nurse removed the blood pressure cuff. "Pulse one-twenty. BP one seventy-five over one hundred. Not good."

"Fear," DeGuere said. *More like abject terror.* "Give him a moment, then run the vitals again."

Sloan stopped sobbing and rubbed his eyes. He took several deep breaths.

"How are you feeling?"

Sloan nodded. "Better. I don't know what happened."

"You were watching television. Did something upset you?"

"I don't remember...yes. I was watching the news."

"That gets me every time, too. What do you remember?"

"Not much. Nothing." He took a few more breaths.

DeGuere turned to the others in the room. "All right, folks, let's stop breathing all of Mr. Sloan's air. Great job, everyone." He made eye contact with the eager nurse and nodded. "I mean it. Great job. Chuck, stay with me, please."

"Will do." Chuck began another pass with the sphygmomanometer. "One forty-five over ninety-five; pulse one hundred."

"Good. It looks like you're settling back in, Mr. Sloan. You gave us quite a scare."

"I'm sorry. I don't know what came over me. My mind is still a little weird."

"That's to be expected. Can you tell me any more about what set this off?"

"No. I barely remember it. It's like I slipped into a trance." His eyes began to flood again. "Am I going to be like this from now on?"

"I don't know. I doubt it. My guess is that your brain is still trying to process things it has ignored for a year. Give yourself time. Maybe the tests will tell us something."

"I'm sorry to be so emotional. That's not like me."

"No need to apologize, Mr. Sloan. Is there, Chuck?"

"Not to me. I cry at old *Lassie* reruns." He started the cuff again.

"At least you're showing other emotions besides terror. Regret and sadness are never fun, but they come with the human package. We'll get it figured out." DeGuere looked at Chuck.

Chuck smiled. "Almost back to normal now."

"I'm sleepy."

Chuck chortled. "I guess so. You put up quite a fight. Wore me out."

"Sorry."

"Don't be. I need the exercise, but next time I think I'll just go to the gym."

That brought a forced smile from Sloan.

"I'd rather not give you a sedative, Mr. Sloan. We're doing a few tests this afternoon and want your brain at normal."

"I don't want a sedative."

"Afraid you might not wake up?" DeGuere watched Sloan's eyes, looking for telltale signs of seizure or other neurological disorders. He saw none.

"Yeah. That's pretty much it."

"Well, you can't stay awake forever. I suggest you rest for awhile."

"I've been resting for a year, Doc. I want to get up and walk outside."

"Soon, Mr. Sloan. Very soon." DeGuere hoped he wasn't lying.

Chapter Ten

PRISCILLA WANTED TO CALL IT A DAY. Her mind said she should eat, but her stomach wanted nothing to do with food. She longed for a bath with the water temperature just shy of scalding. And candles— soft, flickering candles. Perhaps a book with no socially redeeming value. Anything to exorcise the stress, fear, and confusion that were exercising squatter's rights in her mind.

Instead, she scanned the computer monitor: *Larry King Live, Anderson Cooper 360, NPR, The Today Show,* even *Dr. Phil.* The list included thirty other shows, each one pleading for her time.

"It's impossible."

"You can only do what you can do," Leo said. A laptop sat across his legs. He hadn't left the office sofa for the last two hours.

"I don't think Chris and Debatto Media would agree. They want me to do all of them. I don't know why they're centering on me. Chief Gonzales was there. Firemen were there. *You* were there."

"I'll take whatever you can't, kid, but they want you because you were the closest, and it was your video."

"Why did that television reporter have to bail?" She rubbed her eyes.

"Same reason I wanted to. The question is why anyone hung around."

The phone rang. Priscilla grabbed it. "Leo Hart's office, this is Priscilla."

"Ms. Simms," a voice said. "It's an honor."

"Thank you. You are...?"

"Dave Debatto. I should have introduced myself."

It took two tries for Priscilla to say, "Mr. Debatto. I didn't expect a call from you."

Leo straightened and set the laptop on the sofa next to him. "Uh-oh."

"I should have called earlier. First things first: I know you have had an unbelievable day. Are you all right?"

"Yes, sir, I'm fine. A little tired." The image of the dapper forty-two-year-old CEO of Debatto Media floated to the top of her mind.

"Don't you mean 'a little exhausted'?"

Priscilla chuckled politely and stared at the phone set as if it would produce a three-dimensional picture of her boss's boss. "Maybe a little exhausted."

"I believe that's an oxymoron. I'm toast, and I didn't live through an earthquake or chat with an alien. You're a hero in my book."

"That's a generous thing to say, Mr. Debatto—"

"Just Dave. Mr. Debatto makes me feel my real age. I prefer to believe I'm much younger. May I call you Priscilla?"

You sign my checks. You can call me whatever you wish. "Please do. Listen, Leo Hart is with me and he was the lead reporter on the scene. May I put this on speaker phone?"

"Who else is with you?"

Odd. "Just the two of us."

"Are you in an office with a door?"

"Yes. Leo's office has a door."

"Close it and put me on speaker."

Priscilla motioned for Leo to close the door. She punched the SPEAKER button. "Can you hear us OK?"

"I hear you fine. Hello, Leo."

"Mr. Debatto."

"Same rules for you, Leo, as for Priscilla—call me Dave. Now on to business. Your video has gone out to..." Priscilla heard papers shuffling. "...about two thousand outlets worldwide, and more are going out every minute. It's been a big day for Debatto Media and *Today News*. More importantly, it's a monumental day for the world. Nothing will ever be the same."

"I can't argue that," Priscilla said.

"Conlin has been keeping me posted on the calls coming in down there, and of course I've read the Internet material you and Leo posted. I'm not exaggerating when I say you need to clear a place on your mantle for a Pulitzer and every other journalism prize out there."

"That's kind, Mr...Dave. I haven't thought past the next hour."

"I imagine you're overwhelmed. That's why I'm sending someone to help."

"Someone to help?"

"You need an assistant. This thing isn't going to go away overnight. Life isn't going to be the same in general, and it's certainly not going to be the same for you anytime soon."

Or ever.

"That's very kind, but I'm not sure it's necessary."

Leo raised an eyebrow.

"Hey, Leo. I take it Priscilla is pretty independent."

Leo laughed. "You don't know the half of it."

"Priscilla, I know what I'm doing here. I bet you have a list of people wanting to interview you. Am I right?"

Priscilla didn't want to admit it. "Yes."

"It's a long list, isn't it?"

She said it was.

There was a pause. "Look, I have no doubts about your abilities or judgment, but what you have is just a fraction of what you can expect. It's only just begun. I promise you, you will thank me."

"Yes, sir." She clinched her teeth.

"He should be there soon. I sent him by private plane. San Diego International is still closed while they examine buildings and runways for damage, so he will set down at..." Paper shuffled. "...at Montgomery Field. Is that far from you?"

"No. Maybe twenty to thirty minutes. Traffic will be heavy. A lot of people are headed home after the quake."

"But that should be traffic out of the city," Leo added. "Coming into downtown should be a little easier. Word is, all the roads are open. We did have a backup on a bridge over Mission Valley, but that's been cleared."

"Good."

"Dave, exactly what is your man going to help me with? Is he a journalist?"

"Not in the sense you're thinking. He's a facilitator—a consultant. His job is to juggle the media requests and to help you prepare for on-air interviews."

"Sir, I spent a great many years in front of a camera. I know my way around a studio."

She heard him sigh. "Interviewing is not the same as being interviewed. I'm aware of your résumé, Priscilla. I'm also aware that you will not only be representing your experiences but Debatto Media."

"I see."

His tone softened. "Listen, every day I trust scores of writers and photographers, not to mention dozens of executives and hundreds of other employees. Trust is part of every business. We've trusted you for years now and have never been disappointed. It's time for you to trust me."

"I understand. I meant no disrespect."

"I'm not offended. I...hang on a sec..."

Priscilla waited as seconds dripped by.

"Sorry," Debatto said. "He's just called in. He's on the ground and headed your way."

"Already?" Leo said.

"I sent him as soon as I saw the video."

"So," Priscilla said, "this has been in progress for some time."

"Only if you consider three or four hours 'some time.'"

"I'm sorry, sir. This day seems a month long."

"No need to apologize. Priscilla, listen to what Wacher says. Heed his advice. He's the best communications consultant on the planet. I know. I pay him to be."

"Wacher." Priscilla tried the name.

"Tim Wacher. You'll like him. Not that that matters." Someone in the room with Debatto spoke but Priscilla couldn't make out the words. "I have to move on to the next thing. Thanks for your great work. Oh, you and Leo—in fact everyone in the San Diego office—can expect a little surprise in their paycheck."

Before Priscilla could speak, Debatto had hung up. She punched the SPEAKER button again, silencing the dial tone.

"When did I lose control of my life, Leo?"

"I'm not so sure we ever had control. If I did, I'd be younger, richer, and a whole lot better looking."

The door to the office swung open, and Chris poured in.

"Sorry, boss," Leo said. "I didn't hear you knock."

"I didn't knock."

Priscilla caught Leo's intent even if Chris didn't.

"I just got an e-mail from Mr. Debatto. He's sending some kind of—"

"Communications expert," Priscilla said.

"How do you know? He sent you an e-mail, too?"

"He was just on the phone."

"He—what? He called you?"

"Sure, Chris. Why not?"

"No reason. Did he mention me?"

Dave Debatto swiveled his high-backed suede office chair away from his glass-and-metal desk and directed his eyes over the San Francisco skyline. Evening approached, fading a brilliant day to muted colors. Soon headlights and taillights would streak the lanes of Market Street and human night crawlers would fill the void left by the daytime San Franciscans. The city had a split personality that changed each time the sun rose and set.

"She didn't sound all that thrilled." Debatto didn't need to see the woman speaking. He had gazed upon her smooth skin, red lips, and cold eyes for five years. He had memorized every variation in her dark hair, every curve in her body.

"She's had a tough day, Erin. She could have won the lottery and not had enough enthusiasm to shout, 'Yippee.' We're lucky she has held together at all."

"You said you trust her." Erin Boyle stepped next to Debatto's chair and laid a hand on his shoulder. He kissed it, then returned his gaze to the bustle of the city.

"They're talking about it down there. In every car, every office, every coffee shop—everywhere. Those that haven't seen the footage yet, soon will."

"And every second of it bearing the Debatto Media logo and *Today News* tag. Giving it away was brilliant."

"That remains to be seen." He stood and walked to the window. The street twenty stories below grew more congested with each moment. "What a day. Earthquakes and aliens. Sounds like a bad science-fiction movie."

"Do you think it will change things?" Erin stepped close. Their shoulders touched.

"Yes. I think everything has just changed. Everyone will be affected, from the pope to the president. I don't know if it will be good or bad, but the change has begun. I plan to be riding the crest."

Tom Clyn replayed the video. He didn't keep count, but he had watched the news footage thirty times or more. He had watched the grainy video he had taken with his low-end camera almost as many times. He made still copies of certain scenes, running them through photo software, adjusting color, contrast, hues, and everything else he could think of to coax detail from the digital images. One image drew his attention more than any other: the tall alien touching the red-haired reporter.

"Why you?" he said to her image on the monitor. "What makes you so special?"

He set his HP printer to photo quality, slipped an 8½ by 11 inch sheet of glossy photo paper into the tray, and printed the image.

"Priscilla Simms. First contact," he muttered. "This can't be a coincidence."

"Who are you talking to, Tom?" The voice pressed through the door.

"Mom! Leave me alone. And stop hanging around my door."

"What do you want for dinner?"

"I don't know. I don't care. Anything."

"That's not very helpful."

"I'm trying to work, Mom. Go away."

He returned his attention to the photo. "For an older woman, you're still a babe."

He set the photo down and redirected his Web browser to the *Today News* Web site. He searched for new information and then clicked on his intended destination: the bio of Priscilla Simms.

Chapter Eleven

S TEVE TOOMEY CONSIDERED HIMSELF A FORWARD-THINKING MAN. If he were a comic book superhero, his superpower would be planning and execution. He prided himself on his ability to absorb and retain information faster than any man he knew. His constant focus on strategy and contingency plans proved valuable once again, as he replaced the battery in his Blackberry. A lesser man wouldn't have brought a back-up battery.

If he were a superhero, then his kryptonite was impatience. Waiting for the governor in the hospital set his teeth on edge. The greatest event in history had occurred and very little was being done about it. The governor of California had spoken to a nonhuman creature—actually carried on a conversation. This made him unique in history. Well, and there was that reporter woman, but like all reporters she would fade into the background. Merrell needed pushing.

"We're going to have to do something about the press," he said into the phone. On the other end, Nick Lodge grunted. The lieutenant governor had been overwhelmed with phone calls from media and state representatives wondering about the well-being of Martha Merrell and the events on the downtown San Diego street.

"He must address this whole alien thing." Lodge made a sound that Toomey took as a forced laugh. "I can't believe I'm using the word *alien* in any context other than immigration. Unbelievable. Sacramento is buzzing like a beehive with a bear at its door. You were there. What was it like? I mean, you were within feet of the thing...er, him. Sheesh, I don't even know which pronoun to use."

"I haven't taken time to think about it. I've focused on the governor. I just received word that his daughter is fine. The doctors are going to release her any minute."

"That's great. I assume someone has told Mrs. Merrell."

"The governor called her, and Martha spoke with her."

"I imagine she's very relieved."

"Yeah. We all are. Listen, it's important that she not be bothered. She's due to touch down soon. We need to make certain the press doesn't mob her. She's not all that good with the press."

"That's for sure."

"Or the good of the governor. I hate to put this on you, but could you make certain that a limo is there to pick her up and take her straight to the mansion? Security should be increased, too."

"I've been thinking the same thing. I also think the grandkids should go with her."

"Good idea."

"Have they heard from Teresa and Bill?"

Toomey nodded as if Lodge could see him. "They've exchanged phone calls. Both are flying in from Idaho. They weren't supposed to pick the kids up for another couple of days."

"I'll make sure they get picked up and taken to the mansion."

"I want to set up a press conference. I want it held in Sacramento. We'll have more control there, and I can use the time to pull together a statement and coach the governor on the approach he should take."

"I wouldn't phrase it that way to him. You know his ego."

"I'll be more diplomatic. His ego is part of his strength." *It's also part of his weakness.* "We'll do the press conference in the media room. That way we can limit the number of reporters."

Lodge said he'd make certain the room was ready, then stated, "I'm getting a ton of e-mail alerts from the national news networks. The reporter seems to be the darling of the talking heads. She's going to be the featured guest on Larry King and a dozen others."

"That attention should go to the governor. It was his daughter the sky-guy saved."

"Sky-guy. I like that. But you've been around long enough to know that what should be is seldom what is."

91

"I'll have the press office send out a press release from the governor's office."

"I assume you've cleared that with Governor Merrell."

"I have my end taken care of." He hung up but placed another call ten seconds later.

Tim Wacher looked younger than Priscilla expected. He stood six-two or six-three and carried enough weight for two men. His head bore a thick crop of dark hair pulled back tight and lacquered with something shiny and apparently strong. Not a hair was out of place. His eyes were set deep and his jaw straight and sharp. When he spoke, his words gushed in *basso profundo* tones that seemed to make the furniture vibrate. He wore casual clothes: Docker pants, a white collarless shirt, and a black sport coat. On his feet were an expensive-looking pair of Nikes. A laptop bag hung from his right shoulder.

"Ms. Simms," he boomed as he entered Leo's office. "I'm Tim Wacher. My friends call me Wacky...Wacky Wacher."

"I hope that's just a play on your name." Priscilla stood and shook his hand. "This is Leo Hart, the associate publisher for *Today News*..." She paused as Chris worked his way into the room. He looked like a child afraid of missing something the adults were doing. "And this is Chris Conlin. He calls the shots around here."

Hands were shaken, but Wacher wasted no additional time getting to business. "I understand Dave gave you a call. Is that right?"

"Dave?" Chris asked.

"Dave Debatto," Wacher replied.

"Oh...of course...Dave."

Priscilla acknowledged the phone call.

"Good, then you know why I'm here."

"Not fully," Priscilla said. "All I know is that you're supposed to help me with the interviews..."

"And you think that as a reporter, you've got the interview thing down. Am I right?"

"I think I can handle myself in front of the camera. I did on-camera reporting for—"

"For a local station—KGOT. You did the work for over ten years. Things have changed Ms. Simms...may I call you Priscilla?"

"Well—"

"Thanks, and call me whatever you like. Look, it's crowded in here. Not much air. Can we meet someplace larger and better ventilated? Guys my size like well-ventilated places."

"My office has plenty of air." Priscilla tried to look innocent.

"Great. Is it larger than this place?"

"As large as all outdoors."

Conlin sighed melodramatically. "I'm afraid she's trying to be funny."

"Ah," the big man said. "I take it the cubicle with the broken widows is yours? I saw it on the way in."

"Sorry," Priscilla said. "I'm a little weary, and all of this is like being run over by a freight train."

"That's why I'm here: to pull you from the tracks and put you on the train."

"Come on," Chris said. "We'll set up in the conference room. Plenty of elbow room there. Leo, I think you can continue—"

"He's coming with us." Wacher started for the door. "He was there. I need him." He stopped and looked at Conlin. "Were you at the site?"

"No. I was manning the office here..."

"OK. Feel free to skip the meeting if you want. There's nothing for you to do there."

"She's my reporter, and my publication put the news out. I prefer to stay in the loop."

Wacher shrugged. "Suit yourself. Now, where is this conference room?"

"I'll show you," Leo said.

"Oh, and I'll need whatever list you've compiled on interview requests, raw video footage, edited footage, any stills, whatever you have. I'll also need a wireless connection. I assume this place has wireless."

"Of course," Conlin snapped. "We're state-of-the-art here."

"Good. I need the network password so I can log on."

"I'll have tech—"

"I don't need help from IT. The digital key will be enough." To Leo, Wacher said, "Lead on, McDuff."

"Lay on," Priscilla said.

"What?" Wacher looked confused.

"Shakespeare wrote, 'Lay on, McDuff.' Not 'Lead on.' It's from *Macbeth*."

Wacher blinked several times then smiled. "I think I'm going to like you."

The conference room was familiar territory to Priscilla. Senior staff met there daily, discussing stories and making assignments. The room, located near the center of the cubicle forest, was partitioned from the larger room by floor-to-ceiling glass panels.

Wacher took a seat at the head of the table as if he had sat there a hundred times before. Conlin narrowed his eyes but said nothing. He took the seat at the other end.

Four seats remained on each side. Priscilla sat one chair away from Wacher and set the list of interview requests in front of her. Leo settled in the chair opposite her. Wacher set his laptop on the table. "Key, please."

Conlin recited the password.

"List." Wacher pointed at the paper in front of Priscilla then wiggled his fingers in a hand-it-over motion. She slid it over, feeling proud she could do so without snide response.

He studied it, comparing it to whatever he saw on the laptop monitor. He grunted. Typed on the keyboard. Grunted again. "You're going to be one busy woman." He slid the paper back to her.

"OK, here's what were going to do. I'm going to print out your first twenty interviews. The first one begins sooner than you might think, so we don't have much time. First things first: no local interviews. We need to maximize your exposure and thereby increase the exposure of Debatto Media."

"What's wrong with local news interviews?" Priscilla asked. "I've given a good hunk of my life to local news."

"Physics. You can't be in two places at once. Every minute you spend talking to the local yokels is a minute off the global stage. Wolf Blitzer on CNN is set to do a report on the late edition of his program. You'll follow that with Larry King. It's too late to fly you to New York, so I've set up a feed from your old haunt at KGOT-TV. Next—"

"Hang on a sec." Priscilla raised a hand. "Don't I get a say in any of this?"

He smiled. "Well, of course not. No offense, but you'd make a hash of it."

"I beg you're pardon?"

"Listen, Priscilla, if we had more time I'd be kinder, but we don't. You've experienced what no human has. You stand unique in humankind."

"There were others present. Leo was there—"

"And I have plans for Leo, but you were the one who spoke to the alien and took the pictures. I know the governor was there, but we don't have immediate access to him. You work for Debatto Media. You're our asset."

Before Priscilla could speak, someone knocked on the door. "Must be the video you requested."

Wacher raised an eyebrow. "That was quick."

"We're not amateurs, Mr. Wacher. We've been through a significant earthquake and managed to cover the greatest news story ever." Conlin's mood had soured and Priscilla couldn't blame him. Wacher was a human steamroller, and no one appreciated being squashed into the pavement.

"Of course. You're to be commended—"

Priscilla expected one of the video/photo techs to be standing at the door, DVD in hand. Her attention had been fixed on Wacher, his computer, and the list, so she didn't notice two men walk past the glass partition and approach the door. Both wore suits, and both were tall; one was white, and the other looked Samoan.

"We're looking for Priscilla Simms and Leo Hart."

"Who are you?" Conlin demanded.

In what struck Priscilla as a choreographed move, each removed a leather billfoldlike case and opened it. "Federal agents, Department of Homeland Security."

Priscilla groaned. "Oh, this just gets better and better."

Chapter Twelve

Ms. Simms, I assure you this is routine." The Samoan pasted a smile on his face that looked rehearsed and insincere. "I'm sure you can understand our need to ask a few question."

"Routine for you, maybe, but it's not routine for me."

"Guys, listen." Wacher tried on the same pasted smile and had no more success than the fed. "We're right in the middle of something here, and we're way behind. I'm trying to do a month's work in ninety minutes."

"I'm so very sorry, sir," the other agent said. "We'll just put the security of the country on hold while you go about your business."

"Great. I knew you'd understand. Now, if you don't mind..." He nodded at the door.

They didn't move.

"I think he was being sarcastic," Leo said.

Wacher shrugged.

The Samoan made another attempt to look friendly. "Ms. Simms, I need you to come with us so we can ask you some questions."

Conlin sprang to his feet. "Oh no, you don't. She's not going anywhere. She's done nothing wrong."

"Who are you?" the Samoan asked.

"Conlin. Chris Conlin, and I run things around here. Who do you think you are?"

"I'm Agent David Tiumalu, and this is my partner Agent Robert Jay. Now, I'm going to ask you to take a step back."

"No way. You have no right to barge in here and spirit away one of my reporters. No, sir. Not on my watch. Do you have a warrant?"

"I don't need a warrant, but I can get one if you like. Right now, we just want to talk to Ms. Simms, but I can get a warrant to search the premises if you like."

"You can't have her. You'll have to arrest her."

"Whoa, Chris. I appreciate you looking out for me, but don't volunteer me for jail." She addressed Tiumalu: "Can't you ask your questions right here? I'm really stuck between a rock and a hard place. I'm supposed to be interviewed on several news shows, the first of which starts in..." She looked at Wacher.

"One hour, twenty-two minutes." Wacher didn't look at his watch, but Priscilla had no doubt the man knew the schedule to the minute.

"One hour and twenty-two minutes."

Conlin's red face darkened another shade. "What business is this of Homeland Security? You have no right to barge in here and interfere with our work."

Agent Jay closed his eyes then opened them again. "Think about it."

"Think about what?" Conlin looked around the room. "What?"

Leo cleared his throat. "An alien, presumably from someplace other than Earth paid a visit."

"I know that. We've been dealing with that all day...Oh." His outburst of laughter surprised Priscilla.

"What's so funny?" Tiumalu asked.

"You. You think this is an invasion? You think maybe Aster is some kind of space terrorist?" He laughed again. "I'm surprised Immigration isn't here. I doubt the being has a passport—that makes him an illegal alien, doesn't it?"

Only Conlin laughed.

Priscilla stood. "I left my purse in Leo's office." She moved to the door.

"We'd appreciate you coming along with us, too, Mr. Hart."

He stood. "I figured you'd get around to me sooner or later."

"That's it!" Conlin reached for the phone on the conference table. "I'm calling our lawyers."

Before leaving the room, Priscilla stole a glance at Wacher. He was punching numbers on the keypad of his cell phone.

The office for Homeland Security was in a familiar part of downtown—common knowledge to any experienced reporter. What wasn't common knowledge to the public or to Priscilla was the plain, concrete, tilt-up building in Kearny Mesa, a good fifteen- or twenty-minute drive from the downtown offices.

"This doesn't look right." Priscilla and Leo sat in the backseat of a large Ford sedan.

"You're right." Leo leaned forward to address the two agents in the front seat. "What's the deal, guys? Your office is downtown, not in Kearny Mesa."

Tiumalu sat in the passenger seat. "*One* of our offices is downtown. We live in a post-9/11 world. Putting all of one's assets into a single location is unwise."

"I don't see any signage indicating a government office."

"You're not going to, either."

Jay pulled the car around back. A large metal door typical of industrial buildings opened, and he pulled the car in. The door rattled closed behind them.

Agent Jay killed the engine and, before it could completely die, exited the vehicle. Tiumalu moved with the same speed and purpose.

Priscilla waited until Tiumalu had opened the door and asked her to exit. She didn't want to but couldn't think of anything else she could do that wouldn't make things worse.

She slipped from the backseat. Leo worked his way out the other door as Jay held it open.

"This way, please," Tiumalu said.

At least he's polite.

He led them to a gunmetal gray door. A keypad hung on the wall near the doorknob. Tiumalu punched a long number sequence into the keypad and then pressed his right thumb on a small glass panel just below the numbers. The panel glowed red, then green. Priscilla heard the lock disengage.

Tiumalu pulled the door open and motioned for the others to enter. Priscilla felt like shrinking. *The door of no return.* She told herself she was being silly. It wasn't convincing.

She didn't walk very far. The door led to a small room just large enough to hold five or six people. It reminded her of an elevator cab. Her eyes traced the space of details. A small video camera was overhead.

"I suppose this leads to your secret underground lair," Priscilla said.

"It's a capture room," Leo said.

"A what?"

"When I was a young man, I worked for a bank. That was before I found my true calling. I worked in the credit card division. That was in San Francisco. We made our own cards. You needed clearance to get into that part of the building. If you had the clearance, you had to pass through two doors. One you could open, but the second opened only if a security guard permitted it. If you didn't belong, a flip of a switch kept you from leaving until the police arrived." He looked around. "I imagine this is a little more sophisticated."

"It's a little claustrophobic," Priscilla said.

Jay approached another keypad, entered a code, then looked at a small camera mounted next to the door.

The door unlocked and they stepped from the small room into a vast open area, marked off by a maze of cubicles much like Priscilla saw every day at work. To her right was a row of rooms, the only ones with partitions that spanned floor to ceiling. Each room had a large window facing the hall.

"If you'll follow me." Tiumalu moved down the corridor, cubicles to his left and enclosed, windowed rooms to his right. Leo followed him, Priscilla followed Leo, and Agent Jay brought up the rear.

"Dead reporter walking."

"What was that, Ms. Simms?" Jay asked.

"Nothing, just my nerves talking."

Priscilla glanced in the first room and nearly came to a stop. Through the observation window, she saw the woman television reporter that had been at the scene with them and then fled when Aster arrived. She sat at a cheap metal table. A man and woman whom Priscilla assumed were agents sat opposite her. It looked to Priscilla like the reporter had been crying.

In the next room sat another familiar figure: the cameraman she had seen with the reporter. A pattern was shaping. In the third room sat Chief Gonzales. A pair of men in suits grilled him.

Priscilla exchanged glances with Leo. Words weren't needed. The feds were gathering as many people from the site as possible.

"You got the governor here, too?" Leo asked.

"That's none of your business," Agent Jay said.

Tiumalu took a more courteous tone. "If we did, we couldn't tell you—but we don't."

"I imagine he's a little more difficult to cart off." Priscilla felt proud her voice didn't betray the apprehension that roiled within her.

"You haven't been carted off, Ms. Simms. We just have a few questions."

"You could have asked questions back at our building," Priscilla said.

"Then they wouldn't have home-field advantage." If Leo was nervous, he wasn't showing it. He remained as Priscilla had always known him: unflappable.

They reached the end of the corridor. "You're in this room, Mr. Hart. Ms. Simms, you're in here." Tiumalu opened a door.

"You're splitting us up?" Priscilla didn't like the idea.

"Routine. That's all." The agent motioned for Priscilla to enter. She took a deep breath and crossed the threshold.

The room was Spartan and identical to the others she had seen: a simple metal table and two metal chairs. Priscilla took a seat. Tiumalu did the same on the other side of the table. "Can I get you anything? Soda? Coffee? Water?"

Priscilla smiled. "I once saw a movie where the interviewee was given lots to drink, then deprived the use of the bathroom."

"No such intent here, Ms. Simms. Just trying to be polite." He turned and pointed at a small video camera in the corner. "I need to inform you that this meeting is being video recorded. What you say will be preserved for the record."

"Am I under arrest?"

"No."

"It sounds like you're reading me my rights."

"I'm not, but I am obligated to inform you that we are recording this interview."

"Interview. That's a nice, soft term. Since I'm not under arrest, then I'm free to answer or not answer as I see fit. Correct?"

"This will go a lot faster and easier if you would just cooperate."

"Easier on whom? Me? You've pulled me from my office, forced me to cancel major interviews, and kept me from doing my job. My cooperation only makes *your* job easier, not mine. So please don't pretend you're doing me favors."

"Ms. Simms—"

"If you want this to go easier and faster, then drop the I'm-a-big-bad-federal-agent attitude."

Tiumalu sighed. "Look, lady. It's been a long day. Let's just get down to business."

"Long day? You've had a long day?" Priscilla snickered. "I almost fell out of a ninth-floor window, and I've walked the streets after the earthquake and saw what no one would believe." She frowned. "There are moments when I don't believe it myself."

"Ms. Simms, I have informed you that this conversation is being recorded. I need you to acknowledge that for the record."

She frowned again. "I understand that you're recording this."

He began to speak in what seemed to Priscilla like a conversation with the open air. "This is Agent David Tiumalu, conducting an interview with Ms. Priscilla Simms of *Today News*. Ms. Simms is here of her own free will—"

"Hah!"

"—of her own free will." He recited a case number, gave the time, and said they were in room 6.

"Ms. Simms, you work for *Today News*. Is that correct?"

"Didn't you just say that?"

"Is that correct?"

"Yes, I work for *Today News*, a division of Debatto Media."

"And what is your position?"

"I'm one of the senior reporters."

"Earlier today you were at the location of the Windom Building, downtown. Correct?"

"Yes."

"And while there, you took video footage of the damaged building?"

"I did."

"And you further took video footage of individuals present?"

"Yes." *This is getting old.*

"That footage has been uploaded to the Internet via the *Today News* Web site. Is that correct?"

"You know it is."

"What I know isn't important at the moment. What *you* know is."

He's laying a foundation. The question is: what is he building?

He pressed on. "Was that video in any way edited?"

"Of course."

"Of course?"

"You look surprised, Agent."

"I didn't expect you to admit it."

Priscilla tipped her head to one side. "I don't think we're talking about the same thing here, Agent. You're aware that almost all video is edited to some degree. Raw footage is seldom posted or aired."

"Explain."

"Excuse me?" She leaned back in the chair.

It was his turn to frown. "Could you *please* explain?"

Priscilla struggled to pull her emotions in. During her early years, she had built a reputation for being tough, opinionated, aggressive, and often rude. It was part of her nature. Much of that had changed over a decade ago when she became a Christian. Still, the old patterns often rose to the top, especially when she felt stressed.

"One of the first things we do with video is remove unwanted material. Not stuff that is important but shots that bring nothing to the table."

"Who gets to decide what gets cut and what remains?"

"I think you're reading too much into this. What's being removed are things like blurred shots. Sometimes a reporter moves from one action shot to another. The image may blur when the reporter moves the camera. Since it adds nothing to the report, it gets cut."

"But you can edit video to show just what you want?"

"And since what I want to show is the truth, that's what we broadcast."

Tiumalu nodded as if he understood. "Did you add anything to the video?"

"Add?"

"Did you or any of your fellow workers or anyone you know create footage of events that did not happen."

"You're accusing me of fabricating a story?"

"I'm just asking questions."

"No, you're not. You're insulting me and my profession."

"I have said nothing insulting. Please answer the question."

"The answer is: no. I did not fabricate anything in that video, nor did anyone I know. We don't do that."

"It wouldn't be the first time a news agency—"

"The video I took is an accurate account of what happened."

"A spaceship appeared over the city? An alien being beamed down—"

"He didn't beam down. That's a science-fiction contrivance. He floated down in a waterlike sphere."

"Oh, well. That's better."

"It's on the video. Now you're just trying to goad me."

"You said, 'he.'"

"What?

"You referred to the alien as a he. How do you know he's male?"

"I don't. His action. His voice—weird as it was—his mannerisms made me associate him with males. I use the pronoun as a convenience."

"Do you watch television, Ms. Simms?"

That came as a surprise. "Of course."

"Then you know that almost anything can be done with digital media. Photos can no longer be trusted. Neither can video. A good technician can make a very believable image that's almost impossible to refute."

"We did not do that."

"You must admit that it all is too much to believe."

"Of course it is. That changes nothing."

"I couldn't help but notice that your video seems to be the one everyone wants."

"I don't own the video. Debatto Media does. Why would I fabricate such a thing?"

"Fame. Money. How's your career? Things good at *Today News*?"

"You're wasting my time, Agent. You know I didn't make that video up. I'm no special-effects expert. Besides, you have the television reporter a few doors down; you have her cameraman; you even have Chief Gonzales in one of your little cells."

"They're not cells. This is an interview room."

"Lovely as it is, it's an uncomfortable place. It's been designed to be uncomfortable. I'll tell you what. Don't take my word for it. Scores of people saw the events I taped, including the governor. Why don't you drag him down here and put him in this seat? Listen to his story. Ask him about his daughter."

"My focus is on you."

She stood. "We're done."

"No, we're not."

"Unless I'm under arrest, I'm leaving."

The door to the room opened. Agent Robert Jay poked his head in. "Got a sec?"

"What?"

The door opened wider and a man in an expensive dark suit and maroon tie pushed his way in. He was tall with silver hair. His face looked as if it had been chiseled from marble.

"Who are you?"

"I'm counsel to Debatto Media, and, by extension, Ms. Simms's attorney."

Tiumalu snapped at Jay. "How did he get in here?"

"The director called. He wants us to cut Hart and Simms loose."

"Someone got to him?" Tiumalu swore.

The attorney smiled. "Mr. Debatto has many friends."

Chapter Thirteen

PRISCILLA MADE IT HOME JUST BEFORE ELEVEN. If she counted the time she spent getting ready for the day, then she had been working for nearly eighteen hours. In those hours she had endured an earthquake; narrowly escaped the one-hundred-foot fall to unyielding concrete; walked the streets of downtown reporting on the effects of the shake; watched a nearly indescribable spaceship fragment overhead; observed a watery sphere float to the ground, disappear in a wink, leaving no trace of its existence and leaving behind a being that no one could mistake for anything human. She had then watched as that very same visitor made an impossible rescue and resuscitate someone who looked as dead as a corpse.

Such events were enough excitement to fill several years of life, but they had only been the beginning. When her alarm clock sounded this morning, she was just a reporter for a respectable print and online publication, invisible and hidden behind a byline, but now millions had seen her face on the video that circled the world over the Internet and television screens as she did one interview after another.

And in between? In between, two federal agents had escorted her from her office to a little-known building and quizzed—no, interrogated—her as if she had been the cause of everything.

Enough was enough. Priscilla had locked the door to her apartment, examined her living space for damage, and uttered a prayer of thankfulness that nothing had been broken. The only signs of the earthquake were crooked paintings on the wall and a fallen stack of books and magazines she had been meaning to put away. Her Bible had been resting on top of the stack, but now it lay half-buried beneath the glossy paper of magazines and thick tomes of novels. She picked up the Bible and set it on the coffee table. She left the rest of the stack on the floor.

An amber light on her phone winked at her in unvarying rhythm. She dialed the number that would access her message center and entered the code.

"You have thirty-eight new messages and no saved messages. To listen to your new messages—"

Priscilla hung up.

Locking the entrance door had not been enough. Priscilla longed for more separation from the world. She entered her bedroom and locked that door, ran a tub full of hot water in her bath, stripped and crawled in, but not before locking the bathroom door.

Three locks. Paranoia reigns.

She eased herself deeper into the jetted tub; the hot water enveloped her in a womblike embrace. Tight muscles tightened more, then slowly released their hold.

It was a good place to think, to reason, to relive the day and discover new perspective. She wanted none of that. She longed for a few moments of oblivion.

The phone rang. She didn't care. It rang again. Priscilla turned on the jets, and streams of water and bubbles caressed and massaged her body. They also helped drown out the ringing of the phone.

Thoughts boiled in the cauldron of her mind, and she struggled to turn down the emotional heat: images of the UFO, of Aster, of the half-crushed head of Martha Merrell, of the emotionally crushed governor—and of the healing.

Had she really seen it? Would she wake up soon to discover that her subconscious had played a horrible trick on her? She wished it would be so. She prayed that it would be so.

The phone began to ring again.

"I can't believe this." Taking a deep breath, she slipped beneath the churning water allowing it to cover her head. When she needed air, only her face broke the surface. The gentle pounding of the jets drove out the sound of the phone.

Bliss to be alone. Joy to be unable to hear the invasive ringing. Ecstasy to be surrounded by warm, soft water.

Slowly, she opened her eyes and stared at the ceiling: flat, white, glistening with dampness.

She sighed, blowing out a silent stream of air through puckered lips. Tension began to dissolve.

Turning her head, she gazed over the rim of the wide tub—then screamed.

Ian Robinson was a night owl. He did his finest work after most people went to bed. He felt his best when he slept only four and a half hours. Why he needed less sleep than others remained a mystery to him, a mystery he gave very little attention to.

As the clock in his Point Loma home inched its way toward midnight, Ian jogged on his treadmill. He had been at it for thirty minutes and had another half hour to go. In front of the treadmill stood a chrome-and-anodized stand that held four small flatscreen monitors. Three were tuned to various news channels, one monitored the Internet. In his right hand, Ian held a white, sweat-drenched towel; in his left, a remote control. Every time one of the news stations went to commercial break, he changed the channel. Now, FOX News, CNN, and MSNBC played, but he had also consumed information from Bloomberg, Headline News, and others.

Someone once accused him of being an info-junkie. He didn't deny it, but he did offer a spin: "I'm an info-connoisseur." Information was his diet. He took in more information in a day than most did in a month, and he had a mind that could retain it. A near-perfect memory had been his greatest skill since childhood. Eidetic memory, the school psychologist called it. He didn't care what term the medical profession used, he knew that it was a skill very few others had. While other students spent hours studying, Ian would glance over his classroom notes, do a quick read of the book material, then ace every test.

He graduated high school at the top of his class, earned a free ride scholarship to Stanford, and graduated a year early. He did MBA work at Harvard, and close to fifty of the Forbes Top 100 companies tried to recruit him. He chose to work for a leading communications company but left during his first year. When asked why he was leaving, he responded simply by saying, "Genius wilts in the presence of medi-ocrity."

It was an arrogant thing to say, but he was an arrogant man. He began a consulting business that earned him a mid-six-figures income that deftly turned into millions through real estate and the stock market.

While the money was good, it wasn't what drove him. He had enough wealth to last a family of five three lifetimes. Achievement is what mattered. Mastery of some business. Beating the other guy. That was the real thrill.

The monitors replayed the image of the UFO. The craft matched the one he had seen while dealing with the waste-of-flesh named Tom Clyns. As repulsive as the long-haired moron was, he did know things that Ian didn't. That made him useful—and useful people could be used.

Ian's mind drifted from the images before him and began crafting a script all his own.

He punched a button and took his job to the next level.

The scream caught in Priscilla's throat. She thrashed in the tub, sending small tsunamis over the bath's rim. Pushing herself up, she tried to cover herself with her hands, then reached for the towel, which was just out of reach. She'd have to stand to reach it, and there would be no modesty in that.

"What are you doing here? Get out!"

Aster tilted his head and squeezed out another pathetic attempt at a smile.

"How did you get in? Never mind. Get out. Get out now! I'll scream."

Aster looked puzzled as Priscilla took another swipe at the towel. He pointed at it. "That is what you want?"

"Just leave. That's what I want. Can't you see I'm...bathing?"

The oddly angled grin disappeared as Aster looked at Priscilla in the tub and then at the towel on the rack mounted just out of reach. He moved to the towel, pulled it from its holder, then handed it to her.

She grabbed it and pulled it into the tub to cover her naked body. Aster seemed even more puzzled. His small mouth turned down. He looked around the room. Priscilla saw his gaze fix on a white terrycloth robe hanging from a hook near the other end of the tub.

Priscilla struggled to her feet, wrapping the wet towel around her.

Aster removed the robe from the hook and held it in his long fingers. He turned to her. Priscilla knew it wasn't possible, but he seemed a foot taller than she remembered. His head missed the ceiling by an inch.

"Apparently you don't know the meaning of privacy."

"Privacy?"

"It's a noun. It means free from attention of others."

He nodded. "You are frightened because you are unclothed?"

"I'm not frightened." She held the towel in front of her and reached for the robe with the other. "OK, maybe I *am* frightened. I didn't expect company in my bathroom."

"Not frightened?" He seemed lost in thought. "*Embarrassed*. Is that the right word? It is also a noun?"

"No, it's an adjective—what am I doing? I'm giving an English lesson to an alien in my bathroom while I'm in the nude."

"Nakedness is wrong? It is natural. Are you not born naked?"

"Yes, but that's not the point."

"The point is what?"

She carefully stepped from the tub. Water ran from her body as she turned her back on him and slipped into her robe. When she turned, she felt the heat of her embarrassment radiate from her face. "A person doesn't enter a private room like a bathroom when someone else is in there."

"Are you ill? Your color has changed."

"Forget my color. What are you doing in my bathroom, and how did you get in here?" She looked at the door and saw the knob was still locked. She remembered his first arrival. "Forget the last part. Why are you in my bathroom?"

"Bathroom," he said. "Called such because of the bathtub." He looked around, studying the pedestal sink and the mirror above. He seemed amused by his reflection. He turned the faucet on, then off. "Efficient." Again his eyes traced the small room until they fell on the toilet. He moved to it and pushed the flush lever. The swirling water seemed to amuse him. "What…biological waste? You come here to bathe and to—"

"Aster, what are you doing here?" She backed up to the door, slipped a hand behind her, and unlocked it.

"I have been monitoring your electromagnetic transmissions. The people of your world hold you in high regard. They let you speak about me."

"I'm a reporter—nothing more, Aster. It's my job to tell others what I see." She opened the door slowly.

"That is good. It is your help that I need."

"My help."

"Are we going to another room?"

Priscilla sighed. "Sure. Why not?"

"I frighten you?"

"Well…yeah, you do."

"I mean you no harm—only good."

"You barged into my bathroom while I was in the tub. That's more than a little disconcerting."

"Because you are without clothes."

"Back to this." She raised a hand to her head. "Yes."

"I have told you, naked is good. Naked is normal. Even one of your myths says that male and female were created in nakedness and that it was good."

"It's not a myth, and…how can you know that and not know what a toilet is?"

"There is much for me to learn. I want you to teach me. I need to communicate. That is what you do, correct? You communicate?"

"Yes, but there are others better trained than me—more important than me—who could do a better job."

"Better? Persons are not better than other persons. All are the same."

"Great people have been teaching that for centuries, but it never seems to catch on."

The door was fully open, but Priscilla stood her ground. Where could she go? The creature appeared in a locked room; she doubted she could outrun him.

"This is a strange world to me. The beings are confusing."

You think we're confusing?

"I can understand how you'd feel that way. The feeling is mutual."

"Will you help me? I must speak to many, but I do not wish to offend."

"Such as popping into an occupied bathroom unannounced."

"Yes. Like that."

"I don't know, Aster. I may not be the right person. I don't know what to think of all this."

"Perhaps you will discover what to think."

"Exactly what do you want me to do?"

"Guide me in the ways of humanity."

"Oh, is that all?"

"Yes, that is all."

Priscilla laughed. Some of it came from her still-raging embarrassment, some from her confusion, and some from the ridiculousness of the situation. She imagined what another interview with Larry King would be like. "Priscilla, you say the alien named Aster appeared to you in your home?"

"Yes."

"What were you doing?"

"Sitting in the tub, naked as a jaybird."

She laughed some more, then stopped when she heard the sound of wind chimes.

Aster was laughing.

Chapter Fourteen

MARTHA MERRELL SAT AT THE DINING ROOM TABLE AND POKED HER eggs with a fork. She had been up since dawn and still hadn't worked up an appetite.

Around the table sat her mother and father. Patrick Merrell wore a crisp white shirt, a powder blue tie, and dark gray suit pants. His suit coat hung on a rack nearby. Emily had dressed casually in brown slacks, a tan, long-sleeved blouse, and walking shoes. Her hair was pulled back with every strand in the right place. Her makeup could barely be noticed. She had become an expert in being understated.

"Something wrong with your eggs, sweetheart?" Emily asked.

Merrell bit off the corner of a piece of rye toast and studied Martha. They had arrived home in Sacramento a little before eight the previous evening after successfully avoiding the press and returning on the same business jet that had carried him to the horrific scene in San Diego. He wanted to provide a comfortable and safe place for her. Events had traumatized her enough without the press hounding her. Even now, he knew members of the media were squatting outside the wrought-iron gate and brick wall that marked off the governor's property. Capital security, a function of the California Highway Patrol since the late 1990s, kept them at bay.

"No, the food is fine," Martha said. "I'm just not hungry."

"I suppose that's understandable. Did you sleep?"

Martha shrugged. "I'm not sure. I don't remember."

Merrell joined the conversation. "Are you not feeling well? Should we take you to a hospital?"

"No, no. Please don't. I've had all I want of hospitals. I'm just... I don't know what."

"Depressed?" Merrell suggested. "It would be normal if you were. Posttraumatic stress can be very disruptive."

"I guess. I feel—blank."

"Blank?" Emily's face clouded. "I don't understand, sweetheart." Merrell recognized the tone in his wife's voice. Both of their daughters were in their late thirties, but she still spoke to them as if they were ten. Mothers, he decided, never stop being mothers.

"I feel empty, blank like a blackboard that has been erased. I know it doesn't make sense, but it's how I feel."

Emily rose and walked around the table, pulled a chair near her daughter and laid a hand on her shoulder. "I'm sure it will pass, dear. Give it time. The shock must have been horrible. I mean..."

"You can say it, Mom. I lost several friends and nearly lost my own life. Here I sit, looking at eggs and bacon, and co-workers are lying in the morgue."

"But that's not your fault," Emily said. "There's nothing you could have done."

"I know, Mom. I'm not suffering from survivor's guilt. I don't feel guilty. I don't feel overcome with remorse. I just don't feel at all."

"I'm staying home today." Emily shifted in her seat, an air of concern that Merrell could almost see surrounded her like an aura. Emily had an office in the capitol building where she worked on charitable efforts on behalf of her husband.

"Dad, was I really dead?"

Merrell set the toast down. "The paramedics said you were."

"But you would know, wouldn't you? I mean, can't you tell?"

He didn't want to have this conversation. They had discussed things best they could last night, but with the grandkids present they had to avoid some issues. The conversation became freer after Merrell's other daughter, Teresa, left with the children. She needed a police escort to avoid press and paparazzi.

"Dad, I have to know."

Merrell cleared his throat and looked deep into the eyes of his daughter, a daughter he thought he had lost. Her eyes looked blank. She had been through unspeakable events.

"I can't say that I would know, but...yes, to me you looked dead. I was certain I had lost you." His eyes began to burn.

"Then how is it that I'm alive now?"

"People have been resuscitated before," Emily offered.

"Not like this, Mother." Martha set her fork down. "I remember so little. We were on the first floor when everything began to shake. It felt like a train running through the hall. Then the floor fell beneath us. Desks...chairs...everything fell around me."

"You don't have to do this now," Emily said.

"Yes, I do, Mother. I have to try and remember. I have to know what happened to me."

"It's OK, sweetheart." Merrell thought his words sounded dumb. "Go ahead."

"That's just it, Dad. I can't go ahead. That's all I remember: the quake, falling, something hitting me on the head, then nothing—almost nothing."

"What do you mean, 'almost'?" Merrell pushed his plate away but waved off the butler when he came to retrieve the plate. The butler disappeared from the room.

"I don't know. I've been thinking about it all night. There's something in the back of my mind, but it's too faint to see—a mental tickle. I can't bring it forward."

"Maybe it's an artifact of the trauma."

Martha nodded. "Maybe...but..."

"But what?" Emily held her coffee cup in her hand as if drawing strength from it.

"I feel like I should remember something, but there's nothing. No heaven. No hell. No nothing. Shouldn't I remember some of that? A tunnel of light or something?"

"I don't know, Martha. I really don't." He paused to fight back the pressing tears. "I do know you're here alive and well. For that I am thankful."

"I'm here, I'm alive, but I'm not well. And who do you thank, Dad? God? He let the whole thing happen. The alien? He's the one who brought me back from the dead."

"We do owe him a great deal," Merrell said.

Emily said, "Amen."

Martha gave her a strained look.

"You know what I mean."

"I want to meet him, Dad. I want to meet Aster."

"Everyone does. I'm surprised the president hasn't called."

"Is he in South America?" Emily asked.

"Due back today. I may get a call yet."

"I'm serious, Dad."

"I know you are, but there's nothing I can do. He didn't leave a calling card."

"But if he contacts you again, you'll let me know?"

Merrell viewed this as an easy promise to keep. What were the odds of his ever seeing Aster again? "Yes, I will." He stood. "I want you to get as much rest as possible today."

"I'm not a child, Dad."

"Oh, I forgot. I was supposed to stop loving you and worrying over you on your twenty-first birthday." He smiled, stepped over to her, and kissed her on the head—then remembered how her head looked less than twenty-four hours ago.

"I want to check in with the principals of my firm. I also want to call the families of..."

"I understand. You know where the home office is. Make use of it. If you need anything from me, I'm just a phone call away."

"Thanks, Dad."

"Excuse me, Governor."

Merrell turned to see the butler. "Yes?"

"The car is here, sir."

"Thank you. Please tell them I'll be there in a moment."

"Very good, sir." The butler slipped from the room.

Merrell moved to his wife and gave her a peck on the cheek. "I'll be home by dinner." He started to walk from the room but then stopped, turned, and faced his daughter. "Martha, sometimes we don't know the why, and the best we can do is focus on the what. In this case, you were brought back to us. I don't know how, but I know it's true, and that's enough for me." He paused. "I've always loved you, but I didn't realize how much until I saw you lying on the asphalt." This time he did nothing to stop the tear that crept down his cheek.

🔱

"Shut up, girl. He didn't!"

"Oh yes, he did." Priscilla and Elizabeth "Lizzy" Svoboda made their way across the macadam of the Starbucks and into the store. Lizzy stood taller than most women, just over six feet. As long as Priscilla had known her, she had remained in the zone between thin and "solid." Her light brown hair fell only to her jaw and curved in a gentle fashion that reminded Priscilla of a sixties style. Her blue eyes sparkled, and her sharp features were perfectly proportioned for her size. She had turned her share of heads.

"Right there, while you were *bathing*?" Lizzy whispered the last word.

"Scared me out of my skin. I would have crawled down the drain if I could have managed it."

"I guess so. I'm surprised you didn't scream your lungs out."

"I recall hearing someone scream."

Music playing a dozen decibels too loud poured from overhead speakers and mingled with the white noise of a dozen conversations, a roaring blender, and a steam-spewing coffeemaker.

"I want to hear everything. Spare no details."

"I don't have much time. I'm due at the office." Priscilla approached the counter as the person in front of her finished giving his order and putting his change in a worn leather wallet.

"So talk fast."

"Good morning. Can I help you?" The employee looked fresh from high school. Although she and Lizzy met at this Starbucks every Wednesday, she didn't recognize the worker. That wasn't unusual; the company moved employees from store to store. There were often new faces.

"Venti, half-caf hazelnut, please."

"Name."

"Priscilla."

Lizzy leaned forward. "Venti chai tea." She pulled open her purse and reached for her wallet.

"No, you don't. It's my week to pay." Priscilla set her purse on the counter and opened it.

"Nope. I'm paying. You're providing the entertainment." To the clerk, she said, "Her money is no good here." Before Priscilla could extricate her wallet, Lizzy tossed a twenty on the counter. "It pays to be fast."

"I was just thinking that it pays to be slow."

"Hey, aren't you...yes, you are. You're that reporter chick." The clerk's eyes widened. "I saw you on television last night. You spoke to that alien dude."

"Sorry, I'm not her," Lizzy said with a grin.

"Not you. Her." He pointed a finger in Priscilla's face.

"Easy with that thing." Priscilla took a step back. "You could poke an eye out."

"You're her." His voice rose. Priscilla noticed others looking her direction.

"Um, look..." She gazed at his nametag. "...Ronny. I'm just here for some coffee."

"Man, this is so cool. Can I have your autograph?" He started looking for a pad of paper. No one had asked Priscilla for an autograph since she left television news. Not finding a blank pad of paper nearby, he seized a cup and handed a pen and the cup to Priscilla. She took it and signed it the best she could.

"Are you really her?" The question came from a mother with two small children sitting at one of the tables.

"I'm just a woman looking for a decent cup of coffee."

"What was he like?"

"Was he as tall as he looked on television?"

"Is he coming back?"

The questions began to come in waves. Priscilla looked at Lizzy, who turned to the young man behind the counter. "That order will be to go, please."

They managed to escape to Lizzy's car, a late model Chevy Silverado extended-cab pickup. It still struck Priscilla as odd that her gregarious friend cruised around town in a hefty truck. She knew the reason. Lizzy owned a small furniture shop specializing in custom and art furniture. She often used the truck for deliveries.

Once in the vehicle, Lizzy locked the doors. "Doesn't look like anyone followed us."

"This is nuts."

"You're famous, kiddo."

"Fame isn't all that great if it interferes with my morning latte."

"OK, now dish the details." Lizzy wiggled in her seat like a person settling into a theater chair and waiting for the movie to start.

"Not much to tell, really."

"Nonsense. I've lived longer than you, and not once has an alien paid me a visit while I was bathing, or doing anything else, for that matter."

"Well, it's not all it's cracked up to be. I'd rather it didn't happen."

"So you didn't interview him?"

"I'm afraid I didn't have my camera or recorder on me."

Lizzy filled the cab with her laugh. "No, I suppose you didn't. So one minute you're alone, then the next you're entertaining extraterrestrials."

"Nothing entertaining about it." Priscilla took a sip of her coffee, then told the whole story.

Lizzy listened intently, occasionally asking for clarification. When Priscilla finished, Lizzy looked concerned. She bit her lip. "So, what are you going to do?"

"What do you mean, do?"

"He asked for your help. Are you going to give it to him?" Her tone had weight to it.

"I told him I'd have to think about it. He gave me a strange look, like, 'What's there to think about?'"

"And he said that nudity was a good thing?"

Priscilla shook her head. "Not really. He just seemed puzzled that it bothered me. At least he didn't offer to disrobe."

"That could have been awkward. Imagine what the church gossips would make of that."

"I don't want to." Using the "objects-may-be-closer-than-they-appear" side mirror, Priscilla looked back at the Starbucks behind them. Several people stood outside. One pointed in their direction.

"What was it he said at Windom Building? Something about death."

"He said death is an illusion, that death doesn't matter."

"Hmm."

"Hmm, what?"

Lizzy gazed into the distance. "Just thinking. Those seem like odd things to say."

"Every culture has its own philosophy. I imagine that's true for people on other planets. Now there's a sentence I never expected to utter."

"If he's..."

"If what?" Priscilla prompted.

"If he's from another planet."

The comment stunned Priscilla. "Of course he is. Where else could he be from?"

"Has he claimed to be from another planet?"

"Not to me. What are you thinking?"

"I'm thinking I'm nervous about this whole thing. My mind is disquieted."

The statement didn't surprise Priscilla. Lizzy attended the same church and taught the women's Bible study, and she was good at it. She should be. Both her college and graduate degrees were in biblical studies. Once she had told the class that she hoped to teach Bible at the college level but had difficulty finding a position. Teaching theology was still an uphill climb for women.

"I haven't had any time to think about the theological implications."

"Yeah. You had a full day yesterday."

"To say the least...are you OK, Lizzy?"

"Huh?"

"I asked if you were OK."

"I'm fine." She sipped her chai tea. "Why?"

"I've known you for years, woman. Your body is here, but your mind is elsewhere."

"I think you should avoid this Aster creature."

120

"He's a person, Lizzy, not a creature. He thinks, speaks, acts with purpose, and shows a high level of intelligence."

"Are those reasons to trust him?"

"He did bring the governor's daughter back to life."

Lizzy nodded. "Maybe."

"What do you mean, 'maybe'? I saw the whole thing. And even if she just appeared to be dead, he was able to heal her crushed skull. That was no magic trick."

"Priscilla, doesn't it bother you that you're speaking of a resurrection?"

"Not really. But as I said, I've been a little preoccupied. I'm working on just a few hours of sleep. Every time the wind would blow in the night, I'd wake up and say, 'Aster, is that you?' Makes sleeping a little tough."

"I imagine. But something's not right, Priscilla."

"Look, Lizzy, the world has just experienced a historical event—maybe the greatest in history. Of course we're all going to be a little uncertain."

Lizzy's normally upbeat expression turned sour. "Priscilla, the greatest event in history is the resurrection of Christ. Everything else is secondary."

"OK. I know. I didn't say it well. My point is, it's not every day we learn that we're not alone in the universe."

"The Bible has taught that from the beginning."

"What? That there's life on other planets? I don't recall reading that."

A sigh flowed from Lizzy's lips. "The Bible is filled with accounts of nonhuman intelligences."

"Like angels?"

"Yes, like angels. But *angels* is a catchall term. We use it too broadly. The word means 'messenger.' But angels are called other things: seraphim, cherubim, angels, principalities, and the like. At the tomb of Christ—after the resurrection—several angels are described. Six, if memory serves."

"OK."

"My point is this: the Bible has always taught the existence of nonhuman intelligent life. Granted, there's no mention of life on other planets, but that's not the point."

"What are you getting at, Lizzy?"

"I'm worried for you, Priscilla. In less than twenty-four hours, you've gone from reporter to chief contactee. Why you? Why not some diplomat or political leader?"

"Maybe he watches the news and doesn't want to have anything to do with the way we humans do government. After all, we haven't had very many fine hours."

"No." Lizzy moved her head from side to side slowly. "Something isn't right."

"We don't know that. To my knowledge, I've had more contact with Aster than anyone else, and the sum total of that can be measured in minutes."

Lizzy said nothing, and Priscilla hoped she hadn't offended her friend. She took a different tactic. "I'll admit that I'm uncomfortable around Aster. Truth is, I wouldn't shed a tear if I never saw him again, but there's a part of me—maybe it's the reporter part—that needs to see this through."

"So you're going to be his mouthpiece?"

"He didn't ask me to speak for him, just to guide him in the ways of humanity."

"Oh," Lizzy said. "If that's all he wants. How do you plan to do that?"

"I have no plans. Still, this is the biggest story I'll ever cover."

"You have visions of the Pulitzer dancing in your head." Lizzy lifted her tea.

"Not really. OK, maybe a little."

"Be careful, Priscilla. Be very careful. Use your brains, but let the Holy Spirit guide you. Promise me that."

"I promise. Thanks for the coffee and the advice."

"Get going. You have to find a place to put your Pulitzer."

"I think I'll put it right by the stuffed bear I won at the carnival."

Chapter Fifteen

WHEN PRISCILLA WALKED INTO HER NINTH-FLOOR OFFICE, SHE noticed two things. First, the broken window by her cubicle space had been repaired sometime during the night or in the wee hours of the morning. Workmen had replaced the furniture, and someone had reset her computer, printer, and other desktop items. A lone cube of tempered glass resting on the floor by her chair glistened in the fluorescent light. Stepping into the space brought conflicting emotions. At first, she felt at home; a second later, the terror of the previous day returned. She did her best not to look out the window.

Second, Priscilla noticed the frenetic pace of the reporters and assistants. The sound of fingers pounding computer keyboards rose from the other cubicles.

Several televisions hung from the ceiling and near the exterior wall, the volume set low. Priscilla always thought the monitors were ill-placed. Glare from the afternoon sun made viewing difficult. Each television was set to a different news station. News anchors sat behind desks and gazed into the single eye of a camera.

"Priscilla! Get in here!"

The command came just as she put her purse in the lower drawer of her desk. She looked over the padded partition and saw Chris Conlin making sharp, come-here-right-now motions. He looked like a father who had just witnessed his child carving initials in the neighbor's fence.

"Coming."

"Today, Priscilla!"

Priscilla wondered how long she could take getting to the conference room. Maybe she should powder her nose, go out for breakfast, or watch a movie. "Keep your pants on, Chris."

When she entered the conference room, Chris stood with his arms crossed, doing his best to look intimidating. It was something he did when frustrated. Priscilla found it humorous. Also in the room were Leo and Tim Wacher. Both were seated.

"Gentlemen," Priscilla said, casting a questioning glance at Leo. He responded with a raised eyebrow.

"Glad you could make it this morning." Chris's tone was cold.

"I'm on time, Chris. In fact, I'm ten minutes early." She checked her watch again: 8:50.

"On a normal day, yes, but this isn't a normal day. Sit."

"I beg your pardon?" She faced Conlin. "I'm not a dog. You might want to rephrase that."

"Just take a seat, Priscilla. We can deal with your ego later."

"My ego? What about your—"

Leo cleared his throat loud enough to be heard outside the room. "Chris, what say you close the door?"

Conlin did as Leo suggested. When he turned his back, Leo motioned to one of the chairs. Priscilla took it. Before Conlin could sit, Leo said, "There have been some events that pertain to Aster."

"I figured something was up. I know I have more interviews today, but I still have several hours before the first one."

"This isn't about interviews," Wacher said. "By the way, you did a stellar job, but I have a few more pointers for the next few, some background information, and I need to give you a list of some new media events—"

"Can we stay on track here?" Red tinged Conlin's face.

"Sure," Wacher said. "Sorry." His grin belied his apology. Priscilla doubted Wacher felt sorry. He didn't seem the type.

"So, anyone going to fill me in?" Priscilla wished she had brought her latte with her.

"While you were sleeping, things have been happening all over the world." Conlin stabbed the tabletop with an index finger.

"Things? Could you be more specific?"

"Aster," Leo said. He sat scrunched in his chair and looked five years older than yesterday.

"You'd know this if you answered your phone or checked it for messages."

"Do you know how many messages I had when I got home last night...*late* last night? It would have taken an hour to get through them all."

"What about your cell phone?"

"It died on the way home. I used it a lot yesterday, as you know."

"Enough!" Leo's tone startled Priscilla. Normally unflappable, Leo seldom raised his voice. "Chris, get off her back. She's here now, so let's get down to business."

"I'm running this meeting."

"And running it badly," Wacher said. "You're wasting my time. Get to it, man."

"You're not part of this staff," Chris snapped.

"Mr. Debatto might disagree."

Leo swore, sat up, and leaned over the conference table. Priscilla noticed he rubbed his left arm and his skin looked ashen.

"Here's the skinny," he said. "Aster has been making appearances around the world. Rome, London, Athens, even Reykjavík."

"Iceland? He appeared in Iceland?"

Leo nodded and pursed his lips. He looked ill. "The guy gets around."

"He never stays long," Conlin said. "Sometimes he appears to a large group, sometimes to just a couple of people. Some reports are dubious, but many come from reliable sources."

"Such as?"

"The BBC, for one." Conlin seemed more settled, but enough agitation remained to irritate Priscilla. "It looks like he's made about ten stops, eleven counting yesterday in front of the Windom Building."

Twelve. Priscilla decided to keep last night's incident to herself. Headlines that read, ALIEN VISITS BATHING REPORTER didn't sit well.

"Where did he appear in Rome? The Vatican?" Priscilla asked.

"Nope," Conlin said. "He appeared near the Colosseum. Caused quite a traffic problem. We have video of his ship hovering over the ancient stadium. It looks incredible."

"And then what did he do?"

Leo answered. "He spoke to the few brave enough to approach him. This time he had a message: 'Behold, a new day dawns. Humankind is about to take its next evolutionary step.'"

"Evolutionary step? He actually said that?"

"Pretty much. He spoke in Italian. A reporter for CNN assigned to Rome translated it."

Wacher said, "I've got to admit I was impressed before, but now— I mean, he speaks English, Italian, and, get this, Icelandic. In Reykjavík, he spoke in Icelandic. Do you know how difficult a language that is?"

"There has to be more message than that." Priscilla's mind swirled.

Conlin shook his head. "That's pretty much it. Each visit was short, and each happened outside. I'm certain that has to do with the way he moves from his ship to the ground. He probably can't appear anywhere except outdoors. Makes sense."

If you only knew. "What about time?"

"What do you mean?" Wacher asked.

"You said his appearance caused a problem with traffic in Rome."

"Yup. And in London. All the big cities. Rush-hour traffic is bad enough without extraterrestrials plopping down in the intersection."

"So he appeared about the same time in each place?"

"I guess," Conlin said. "Give or take."

Priscilla thought for a moment. "He's moving from east to west."

Leo straightened. "I think you're right."

"What about in the U.S.? Has he made more appearances here? If he's traveling east to west, he's following the sun."

"That's the time when most people will be out—people traveling to work, taking kids to school." Wacher raised a hand to his chin. "He's going for maximum exposure. I of all people should have noticed that." He laughed. "It's a media tour."

"How's that?" Leo asked.

"Simple. Pretend he's not an alien, but an entertainer. He wants to be seen by as many as possible. Television and news media will flock to wherever he is. He even appears early enough that the event will be carried on morning, afternoon, and evening news. This guy is great. I wonder if he's looking for a job."

Priscilla ignored Wacher's comments. "London, Rome, Reykjavík...all capital cities."

"I know where you're going," Leo said, "but he didn't always appear in capital cities. He appeared in Russia but not Moscow. He also avoided Berlin and Paris. I can't figure out why."

"It's noon in DC," Priscilla said. "That's well after morning rush hour. Did he appear there?"

Conlin said, "Not that we know of. He did appear in Asheville, North Carolina—go figure. In the Midwest, he set down in Omaha. He also paid a visit to Colorado Springs, Colorado—not Denver, mind you—Colorado Springs."

"Maybe he's trying to keep us from anticipating his next location." Leo reached into his coat pocket and removed a bottle Priscilla recognized. A second later, he popped the nitro pill in his mouth.

"Are you OK, Leo? You look pale."

"I'm fine. A little angina. Don't worry about me."

"You sure?"

"He said he was fine, Priscilla. Give the man a break." Conlin tapped the table again. "As you can imagine, the world is going nuts. Two streets down, a group of people have taken over the rooftop of Western Bank. They're up there with signs and gazing at the sky. I want you to get over there and get some footage and do a few interviews."

"I'll go with you," Leo said as he stood.

"No, Leo. I think you should take it easy today."

"Nonsense. I'm fine. As long as we don't jog over there, I'll be great."

Priscilla looked to Conlin. He frowned, then said, "Priscilla's probably right. You look a little peaked."

"I always look peaked. It comes with age."

"It comes with a heart condition," Priscilla said.

"Thank you, Dr. Simms, but I know what I'm capable of—you don't. I'm going. You coming or not?"

She stood. "You're taking this 'cranky old geezer' thing too far. If you die on me, I'll never speak to you again."

"Deal. Just as long as I get a byline."

Wacher cleared his throat. "Don't do anything that will make you late for your interviews."

"Yeah," Conlin added. "What he said."

"If things go long, I'll tell our visitor from another planet that I have an appointment."

"Was that sarcasm?" Wacher said. "That really sounded like sarcasm."

Priscilla forced a smile and left.

Western Bank towered forty stories above the downtown streets. The building was a new addition to the San Diego skyline built just five years before. A glass and concrete structure, it was really two towers blended together by the magic of engineers and architects. It reminded Priscilla of two fingers pointing to the sky.

A crowd had gathered at the base of the structure, and police were busy trying to keep streets clear so traffic could flow. Priscilla and Leo had to show their press passes a half-dozen times to get into the building and ride the elevator to the top.

The elevator doors opened to a glass lobby. From there, they moved to the patio area. Before they left the lobby they could see a mob of one hundred or more people milling about.

The roof was more than a flat area to keep rain away. The architects had designed a parklike area to the west, affording a stunning view of the bay and the blue, arch-supported San Diego Coronado Bay Bridge.

The center section of the roof was partitioned off by a ten-foot-high, tile-covered wall that screened the large equipment necessary to heat and cool such a large building.

A breeze, pregnant with the salty smell of the nearby ocean, wafted over the Plexiglas barrier that circumscribed the large patio.

"Looks like a party," Leo said.

Priscilla agreed. People mingled and joked. Someone had brought a boom box that played New Age music. Priscilla was surprised to see the mix of ages. She had expected a host of twentysomethings. Instead, people well past forty made up the bulk of the group. Some carried signs reading BEAM ME UP and TAKE ME HOME. One young lady had penned LET'S DO LUNCH.

"Unbelievable." Priscilla raised her small camera and shot several seconds of footage.

"See what you've started."

Priscilla was glad to hear the humor in Leo's voice. The nitro must have done its work.

"Sure, blame me. All I did was shoot a few photos and video."

"Yeah, right, that's all you did. Talking to him. Letting him touch you. Standing up for him when the governor looked ready to take his head off."

"I'm just a simple-minded reporter. Why don't you ask the questions, and I'll work the camera. I know how you old guys are with technology."

"Nuts to the old guy talk. I've fixed your computer more than once."

"I just wanted you to feel needed."

"Hey, that's her!" The voice came from her left and belonged to a rotund woman of fifty years. She had a yellow stripe of dyed hair running over her left ear—someone who couldn't let go of the punk rock days. "It's her. That reporter woman."

Leo leaned close. "Think they'll put that on the Pulitzer—That Reporter Woman?"

"With my luck."

"Don't point the camera at her. It will only encourage her."

The crowd pressed forward. Questions came in a wave.

"What was it like?"

"Was he really that tall?"

"Is he coming here?"

Priscilla backed up, moving slowly toward the lobby. The one hundred looked like five hundred. "Um...Leo..."

"Follow my lead. Keep your camera up. Let's go."

"To the elevators?"

"Of course not. Let's go." He took her by the arm and moved toward the crowd.

Priscilla raised the camera and pressed the RECORD button. "I hope you know what you're doing." She whispered the words.

"Ma'am. Ma'am." Leo walked to Yellow Streak woman. "I'm Leo Hart with *Today News.* We're taping right now. I wonder if I could ask you and your friends a few questions. Let's begin with you."

The force of his words and actions stopped the crowd. The woman stroked her hair, trying to put in place wayward strands blown by the wind. "We're on the air now?"

"Soon. We're taping, and then it will go around the world. Can you tell me why you're here?"

"Um, well, yeah. I mean, this is a big deal. Now we know for sure that we're not alone in the universe. Of course, I've known that all along. After all, I've talked with them many times."

"Spoken with whom?"

The crowd fell silent as the woman spoke. Everyone wanted to be on the news.

"The aliens. They started abducting me when I was a child. They told me I'd be one of their messengers, but no one believed me. They believe me now."

I doubt it. Priscilla kept the camera steady.

"What do you hope to achieve here?"

"I want them to come and get me. It's time."

"Time for what?"

"You know. The world is going to change. It *has* changed. We're moving onto the next evolutionary plane."

"They planted us here, you know," an elderly man with a bald head said.

"Planted us?"

"Life didn't originate here. Even scientists acknowledge that life is too complex to have evolved here. It must have evolved elsewhere and been planted here by space travelers."

"That's right, man. Now they're coming back to check on us." The speaker was one of the few in his twenties.

Leo kept control. "So you want Aster to come back to San Diego?"

130

Several in the crowd said yes. A couple cheered. Then someone began chanting, "Aster, Aster, Aster." Dozens joined him. Priscilla panned the camera to take in the crowd.

Leo returned his attention to the woman, and Priscilla redirected the camera. "Did the aliens who abducted you look like Aster?"

"No, they looked different. But that doesn't matter."

A movement to her left caught Priscilla's attention. Holding the camera still, she stole a glance. A television crew had made it to the rooftop. Priscilla recognized the reporter and cameraman who covered the Windom Building collapse. The ones that ran when Aster appeared.

Priscilla noticed something else. A shadow crept across the rooftop— a shadow cast from a cloudless sky.

"Look!" Someone in the crowd pointed to the sky. "He's here! He's here!"

The shadow darkened.

Chapter Sixteen

FEW THINGS LEFT TOM CLYN WITHOUT WORDS, BUT SEEING IAN Robinson standing at his door was one such thing. The doorbell had chimed at 9:10, just as Clyn exited the kitchen with a large bowl of Cheerios.

"Who's that?" his mother asked.

"How should I know?"

"Well, answer it. I'm fixing eggs for breakfast."

"Mom, I already have a bowl of cereal. I don't want eggs."

"You're a growing boy. You need your protein."

"Mom, I'm an adult, not a growing boy." He closed his eyes and tried to control the volume of his voice.

The doorbell chimed again.

"Answer the bell, Mr. Adult."

When he swung open the door, the sight of Ian almost made him drop the sloshing bowl. "What...what are you doing here?"

Ian wore a pair of white, pleated, twill slacks, a black dress shirt, and a blue-and-white-patterned silk tie. His shoes looked expensive. Clyn wore a pair of beige baggy shorts, frayed at the legs, and a sky blue T-shirt with the phrase STOP THE COVER-UP emblazoned over the chest. He wore no shoes.

"Hello, Tom," Ian said with a smile.

"But...I mean, hi."

"I imagine you're wondering how I found you, especially after you had me drop you off in front of a house several blocks away."

"Well...yeah."

"No magic, really. Your car's registration is in the glove compartment."

"Oh."

Ian laughed. "I understand, Tom. I'm a cautious man myself."

"What are you doing—" Goldie Clyn's voice rumbled out of the kitchen.

"It's just a guy I know, Mom. Don't worry about it." He rolled his eyes. "Mothers."

"I've got one myself. Lives in Florida."

"Bet she's nothing like mine."

Ian shrugged. "Look, I'm sorry to just drop in, but I was up and about early and took a few minutes to go by the body shop. I'm afraid it's going to take longer than expected to fix your car."

"It wasn't munched that badly."

Ian seemed embarrassed. "I think it was on its last legs, if you know what I mean. It's pretty run down."

"Maybe, but it's the only car I got. If you're trying to get out of repairing it—"

Ian raised a hand. "If I were trying to get out of it, I wouldn't be standing here, Tom. I brought you these." He held up a pair of keys. On the ring hung a medallion with a Lexus logo.

"What's this? I mean...this is a joke, right?"

"Come and see."

Ian turned and stepped off the porch and moved down the walk. Clyn stood as if his feet had been glued to the floor. Two seconds later he had set the bowl on the kitchen counter and raced out the door before his mother could form a question.

It sat in the driveway like a diamond: a silver Lexus SC Luxury Coupe. At the curb sat the same limo that had delivered him to his neighborhood. Ian must have driven the car with the limo following. Why? He sensed something was up.

"She's a pretty nice car, isn't she?" Ian looked like a proud father. "I'm offering it as a loner until we can get you better wheels."

"This is your car?"

"One of them. I collect cars like some women collect shoes. It's an addiction. I picked this up three or four months ago but haven't driven it all that much. Odometer reads twenty-five hundred miles."

"I can't pay for a rental like this."

"No pay. It's just sitting in one of my garages. This way I know its being put to good use."

Clyn walked around the sporty car. "This thing has to run fifty grand."

"I spent over seventy for it. Bluetooth connectivity, 288 horsepower delivered by a 4.3-liter V-8. Six-speed sequential-shift automatic tranny. As they say, it'll pick 'em up and put 'em down."

"Are you being straight with me, man? I mean, you're really going to loan me this car?"

"Actually, I do have a different goal in mind." Ian slipped his hands in his pockets.

Clyn studied him. "I knew this was too good to be true."

"Rein in your paranoia, friend. What I really want to do is give you the car."

"Why would a guy I just met yesterday want to give me a seventy-five-thousand-dollar car?"

Ian stared at him and Clyn felt like the man's eyes were boring holes in his head. "You have something I want."

"That's a laugh. You're obviously rich, and I'm a minimum-wage grunt who lives with his mother."

"You're more than that, Tom. You are a man with information, and information is as good as money if you know how to use it."

"Really. And what info do I have that you can't get someplace else for a lot less outlay?"

"We both saw something yesterday, something incredible."

"The UFO."

"Exactly. I've been watching the news, and it's piqued my interest. I want to know more. In fact, I want to know as much as possible."

"Why come to me?"

Ian smiled. "Don't freak out, but I did a little research on you. The T-shirt you wore yesterday—the one that read THE TRUTH IS IN HERE—the one with the green alien face on it."

"Yeah, that's a fave. I had it made special. Been thinking about marketing it over the Net."

Ian nodded. "I like an entrepreneurial spirit." He paused like he was searching for just the right words. "Look, I want to learn everything

I can about what we saw and anything else that might be related. Now, I can track down someone with a high profile in the UFO community—yes, I did a little research last night—but I find that the best info comes from people behind the scenes. You've posted to several UFO blog sites, and I like what I read. I assume no one takes you seriously."

"That's an understatement. I've tried to get invitations to the radio shows that cover the paranormal, but no one returns my calls. They will, though."

"Why is that?"

"Look, man, I know I don't look like much, but I got plans. I got dreams. I know more about UFOs than anybody except those who fly them—if you know what I mean."

"I know. What's your dream?"

"I want to make a documentary, one that tells the whole truth."

"Do you know the whole truth?"

"Of course, man. I spend my life studying this stuff. If they taught this in college, I'd have a PhD."

"Will you help me?" Ian asked. "Help me, and you get to keep the car."

Clyn looked at the car, then back at Ian. What could be better? A sweet set of wheels as free as the sun, and all he has to do is talk about his favorite subject.

"It's a deal, man!" He held out his hand and Ian shook it.

"Before I give you the keys, there's one more thing."

"Uh-oh, here it comes. I knew there had to be a catch."

Ian gave him a slap on the shoulder. "Nothing like that, Tom. To legally transfer ownership, money needs to be exchanged."

"How much money?" He felt the car slipping from his grasp.

Ian tossed the keys to him. "Got a buck?"

The VC-25A aircraft crossed the Mexican-U.S. border at thirty-seven thousand feet, clipping through the thin air at a leisurely three hundred fifty knots, propelled by four General Electric engines pumping fifty-six thousand pounds of thrust. The modified Boeing 747-200B, one of two in the presidential fleet, was the most high-tech flying office in the world, and President Dwight Mohler loved it. Nothing said *president* more than a city-block-long, six-story-high, blue and white aircraft dubbed *Air Force One* the moment he stepped aboard.

The craft was capable of flying halfway around the world without refueling, and there were days when he wanted it to do just that. The last year, the third of his first four in office, had been especially grueling. Gas prices had crossed the five-dollar mark, and the country was still firmly attached to the oil umbilical. Any one of several countries could put the nation into a serious hurt just by saying, "No more oil for you."

The trip to South America had been part of his effort to make nice with oil-exporting countries. Venezuela and the U.S. were still on the outs, and visiting a country that made no secret of their hatred of the U.S. was unwise—probably disastrous. Sill, Mohler had been able to make vague comments that people in the know would understand as conciliatory.

It galled him to have to make such gestures. Several times he had confessed to his wife, Jana, that invading such countries would be easier. She reminded him that voters elected him to bring peace, not more strife.

"They're weary of needless death," she said.

"They're weary of rising oil prices. It's not just the oil used for gas, but used for everything else. When the price for a barrel of oil goes up, everything goes up."

He had campaigned on the need for real alternative energy—not just political posturing, not just the simple tossing of terms like "alternate fuel," "fuel-cell technology," "biodiesel," and other high-minded talk.

The people believed him and said so with their votes—and each year the gas prices rose. People in the Northwest and Upper Plains states suffered bitterly in the winter when the poor could no longer buy furnace oil or propane.

Congress had turned against him, each member finding some novel way to cover his or her fanny. The best way to divert voter barbs was to deflect them to the White House.

"We've elected a president who doesn't understand or refuses to understand the very nature of the problem," the Republican majority leader had said recently.

Truth was, he knew better than anyone on the Hill. Understanding wasn't the problem; big businesses so entangled with one another that separation was impossible—that was the problem. Auto manufacturers thrived on oil dependency. Tiremakers depended on carmakers. Oil companies needed automakers. Consumers needed parts for cars. Whole industries lived and died by auto sales.

To introduce a truly unique technology could put tens of thousands out of work and upset a global economy in the process. Russia teetered on economic ruin every year. Oil was one of the few things the rest of the world wanted.

Mohler thought of these things as he made his way from the presidential cabin, through the plane, and into the conference room. He took in each detail. The way things were going, he'd be flying commercial airliners in a little over a year.

As he stepped through the doorway to the room, two people stood. "Mr. President," they said in near unison.

"Take your seats, folks." He moved to the head of the table and found a briefing folder waiting for him.

"Did you get some rest, Mr. President?" Dian Schub sat to Mohler's right. Fifty-one, with keen hazel eyes, the former congresswoman was the country's first female chief of staff, a job she took seriously. Mohler thanked her for asking.

"I did. I'm afraid some of the food didn't agree with me, but I'm up and moving."

"Do you want to see the doctor?"

"No. I've lived long enough to know indigestion when I have it. I feel pretty good now." He pulled the file close. "This is it?"

"It's what we have so far." Ben Gerson opened his copy of the file. The deputy director of Homeland Security was a chunky man that looked like he hadn't exercised since graduating high school. He once joked he was allergic to physical effort beyond the lifting of a glass. Mohler knew the man's body might be out of shape, but his mind was as keen as any he had known. "This came straight from the director. It's up-to-the-minute."

"It figures that I'd be away when this happened. Do you think the news media will blame me?" He smiled at his rhetorical question.

Mohler read the file. He had already been briefed, but the file contained photos enhanced by Pentagon experts. What he saw amazed him. "I don't see a lot of notes on the photos."

"I spoke with the head of the optics division, and he said they did their best to enhance detail but failed. It's his opinion that there is *no* detail to enhance, and then he said something odd. He said it was like the spacecraft wasn't really there."

"What kind of nonsense is that? I'm looking at photos of the thing, and I understand that there have been hundreds of eyewitnesses."

"He can't explain it. He's working on video and photos taken by observers overseas." He paused. "There's something else."

"Let's have it, Ben."

"NORAD didn't track it."

"Come on, Ben. NORAD tracks everything. They're monitoring us right now. They know every plane in the air and every piece of space junk above the atmosphere."

Ben shrugged. "I understand that, Mr. President, but they told the director that they didn't get a single blip on their radar."

Dian added more. "It's not just NORAD, Mr. President; our people have interviewed air traffic control in San Diego, LA, Phoenix, and a half dozen other places. All say the same thing: nothing appeared on their radar."

"Are you saying this craft is so stealthy that we can't detect it at all, even when it hovers over one of our cities?"

Gerson nodded. "It's terrifying. Allied countries that were visited last night report the same thing."

"And it moves silently?"

"That's what the witnesses say," Dian replied.

"Let's see the video."

A wide, flatscreen television opposite the president came to life. The wall-mounted unit flickered as Dian executed a command on her

laptop. A moment later, the image of a dark craft, impossibly large, impossibly slow, moved across the screen.

"Unbelievable," Mohler whispered. "How does it stay up? I don't see any engine exhaust."

"No one knows, sir," Gerson said.

"And no one can pick this thing up on radar? What about satellite photos?"

"We've checked with the Pentagon and our allies. Nothing. China called the State Department and asked the same question. They denied we had such capabilities."

Mohler frowned. "An unnecessary precaution. They know we have more spy satellites than any two countries combined, and they're catching up quick."

The phone on the conference table sounded. Dian snapped it up. "Just a second." She pressed her hand over the receiver. "It's Clayton. He wants to speak to you, Mr. President." Clayton Cook led Homeland Security.

"Put him on speaker."

Dian did.

"What's up, Clay?"

"May I ask who's with you, Mr. President?" The voice filled the room.

"Just Dian and Ben. The door's closed. We were just talking about the...what do we call it?"

"Visitation?" Dian offered.

"That'll do for now." Mohler set his elbows on the table.

"That's why I'm calling. The thing is back." Clayton sounded stressed.

"I've already heard about the round-the-world appearances."

"No, Mr. President. I'm sorry. I haven't been clear. Right now, as we speak, it's back."

"Where?"

"San Diego again."

The phone chimed again. Dian glanced at the caller ID and recognized the code name. "It's Chairman JCS."

"Hang on, Clay. Joint Chiefs is calling." Mohler nodded to Dian who switched lines.

"General. I assume you're calling about San Diego."

"Yes, Mr. President. We just received word. I already have two F-18s from Miramar Air Station in the air. I'm planning a fly-by."

General Gordon Lewis, U.S. Army, was quick to act but never without thought. Mohler knew him to be a proactive man, never reactive. "I'm being told radar is no good with this thing and that we haven't been able to use satellite."

"I've ordered a sat recon. We got lucky and have one passing overhead."

"Great. The F-18s will be taking photos?"

"Video, sir. I'll make sure you see it ASAP."

"Very good, Gordy." He turned to Dian. "Let's crank up the sit room. I want a full briefing as soon as we get back."

"I'll see to it."

"Conference in Clay."

Dian punched buttons on the phone. The president took the lead. "Clay, we're teleconferencing with General Lewis. You say the spaceship is in San Diego. I assume you have men on the scene."

"They're on the way, Mr. President. I also have a man headed up in a sheriff's helicopter. Police were already on scene to monitor a gathering of...UFO fans."

"*Fans*, that's a good word for them," Mohler said. "Be advised that Gordy has called for a military fly-by. Make sure your man in the helicopter knows a couple of jets are headed his way."

"Yes, sir."

"We'll meet in the sit room as soon as I can get there."

"Hang on a second, sir." General Lewis said something that didn't make it from Washington to *Air Force One*. "I've just been handed photos from the satellite..." He trailed off. "I can see the bank building and the people on it, but the UFO doesn't show at all. I...stand by."

Mohler looked at Dian and Gerson and raised an eyebrow.

"The F-18s report visual contact, but nothing shows on their on board radar."

"That's consistent with other reports," Mohler said. "How is that possible?"

"I don't know, Mr. President, but I sure want to. That kind of stealth could change warfare."

"Suggestions, General?"

"We need to put the military on full alert. This thing appears where it wants, and we can't see it coming. That makes me nervous."

"Me too," Clayton said. "All federal agencies need to be brought to bear on this problem."

"How do we know it's a problem?" Dian asked. "Why assume that the visitor means us harm?"

"For all I know," the general said, "they've come to watch a Padre game, but until we know that for sure we need to assume the worst. I'd rather explain why I overreacted than didn't react at all."

"Move cautiously, gentlemen, and keep me informed. I want a full report the moment I cross the threshold of the White House."

Mohler motioned for Dian to hang up.

"I expected many things when I decided to run for president. I prepared myself for economic problems, assassination attempts, and war. But this...I never prepared for this."

Chapter Seventeen

PRISCILLA STOOD HER GROUND DESPITE THE DESIRE TO FLEE. She held the camera steady, then became aware of her ragged breathing, knowing that every exhalation was being recorded by the camera's microphone.

It didn't matter. If anything, it made for better news.

"Priscilla, get out of there." Leo's voice cut through the excited, frightened chatter of the rooftop crowd.

She didn't move. Aster's ship hovered overhead and a moment ago disgorged the same kind of bubble she had seen in front of the Windom Building—the same bubble that bridged the distance from ship to street and brought Aster to the earth.

"Priscilla, move!"

"In a sec. It's moving slowly. I don't think I'm in any danger."

Priscilla lowered the camera angle to take in the crowd. All had backed away, each gazing skyward and seeing what they never imagined they would. A cry to her right grabbed her attention. Priscilla turned the lens in the direction of the sound. Scores of people were fighting to escape through the glass lobby and to the elevators. Several ran for the emergency stairwell exit. The cry had come from a woman who lay on the warm concrete of the patio. Her head was bloody, and Priscilla could see scrapes on the woman's knees and elbows. Around her lay several other people—people who had tripped over her.

"Run. Run!" The voice came from a young man.

Panic spread. Previous "believers," eager to catch sight of the man from another world, had become a frightened mob. Only a handful remained in serene calm.

Leo raced to the fallen woman's side and knelt by her. Over the years, Priscilla had watched him cultivate the detached reporter persona, an image he relished but could never pull off. More than once, he had stopped his duty to help the subject of his report. It was one reason, Priscilla assumed, that he was in second position at *Today News* and not first. Here he was again, shedding his reportorial mantle and revealing a very human heart. Priscilla loved him for it.

She kept the camera on him for a moment. The shadow over her head darkened. He looked at her. His eyes widened. "Priscilla—"

She looked up. The liquid bubble had increased its rate of descent and was only ten feet above where she stood.

Priscilla began a sprint—a sprint that lasted two steps.

The bubble dropped.

Everything around her disappeared.

Allen Sloan tested the floor with another step like a man testing the ice over a frozen lake. He shifted his weight carefully onto the foot. A year of unbroken recumbent living had left little muscle mass to operate the tricky task of standing and walking. Children learned the art of motoring on two feet through trial and error, wiring their brains with each step, each stagger, and each fall.

Allen didn't mind learning the steps, but he desperately wanted to avoid the falling part of the ritual.

"I'm amazed. You're doing so well, Mr. Sloan." The nurse was young, blonde, and attractive. She didn't look old enough to be an RN. Walking with them was a nurse practitioner from the physical therapy department. Unlike the young nurse, this woman was well into her fifties, round and stout, with a thin mouth nestled in wrinkles. She radiated a I-will-tolerate-no-resistance countenance, but Allen saw a deep well of compassion in her eyes. If she were tough with a patient, he figured, she was so because she cared.

"I feel like a toddler."

"You've been inactive for a long time," the older woman said. "All the massages and treatments we give coma victims can't replace real physical effort. It's amazing you can stand and take a few steps."

"Let's go into the hall." Allen directed his aluminum walker toward the door.

"Not so fast, Mr. Sloan," the older woman said. "Standing and taking a few steps is all we're asking for today."

"I want to go a little farther. Just into the hall."

"That may be a little too far," the blonde said. Allen saw her exchange glances with the NP.

"I can do this. Just into the hall, one door down and back. I promise that's as far as I'll go." He pushed the walker forward, taking one small step after another. He didn't want to give them time to object.

"You know if you fall and break an arm, it will go badly for me." The senior nurse stayed closed to his side.

"Go badly for *you*?" Allen smiled. It helped cover the grimace.

Stepping into the hall made him feel like he had crossed the finish line in a marathon. His heart was pounding, his ankles hurt, and his arms felt taxed. A dozen small steps later, he stood before the door to the next hospital room. Inside, a woman lay with a thin, white sheet pulled up to her neck. The bed was angled so she could see the television. The odor of hospital food wafted into the hallway.

Allen began the arduous task of turning around on Jell-O legs.

"Excellent, Mr. Sloan," Blondie said.

"You can see the bubble coming down. It's been descending slowly so far. As you can see, the ship continues to hover above..."

Allen's heart began to pump ice.

"Uh-oh," the young nurse said. "It's time for us to go back to your room." Her face stiffened into an expression of concern and fear.

Allen turned the walker and started in the room.

"No, Mr. Sloan," the NP said. "We don't want a repeat of yesterday."

"I'm fine. I have to see this."

"Maybe once we're back in your room."

"The doc had you disconnect the television. I'm all right. Really."

The blonde took his arm.

"Let go. If you don't want another scene, then you'll let go."

The older woman nodded.

"Trust me on this," Allen said. "I promise to be a good boy."

144

The squeaky plastic wheels of the walker protested as if they were in agreement with the nurses. Allen pushed on.

"Hi," he said to the woman in the bed. "I'm your next-door neighbor."

She raised a finger. "Hi. Have you been watching this?" She nodded at the television.

"My television is...broken. May I watch with you for a moment?"

"As long as you don't sit on the bed. Truth is, I could use a little company. My family doesn't come by much."

"I'm sorry to hear that." Without removing his eyes from the television, he said to the nurses, "Ladies, I could use a chair."

On the screen was the image of a huge, black ship. The reporter and cameraman were in a helicopter, circling a tall, downtown building.

"As you can see, a portion—maybe half—of the rooftop crowd are doing their best to flee the area. Some have fallen. Others are taking the arrival of the spacecraft calmly."

Allen plopped into a wide chair pulled behind him by one of the nurses. His legs shook from the strain of walking from his room to his neighbor's. A movement at the door pulled his eyes away from the television screen. Several other nurses, including two males, stood nearby. They stared at him.

"Really. I'm fine. I promise not to start screaming." He focused on the image and shook his head.

"I've never seen anything like it," the patient said. "Never in my life."

Allen nodded.

"I have."

Chapter Eighteen

PRISCILLA HEARD LEO SCREAM HER NAME, AND SHE CHASTISED herself for not taking his advice. A second later, the bubble that had been descending as slow as a feather dropped like a stone.

She covered her head, bent low, and tried to scamper from beneath the sphere.

She failed.

It touched the back of her hands, then her spine, and then swallowed her like a wave over a careless surfer. She raised her head and looked for Leo. He was on his feet charging her direction...

...then disappeared.

Priscilla fell to the ground, hands still cupped behind her head.

She shivered.

She whimpered.

She waited for the crushing to begin.

It never came. The outside sounds of the newscopter, of people shouting, of traffic on the street below disappeared.

She took a deep breath and felt relieved that nothing hindered the expanding of her lungs.

Maybe it had stopped just above her. Maybe Aster sensed she was below and stopped in time. Maybe...

Priscilla opened her eyes and looked up. She saw sky. Not the sky she had seen a moment before—not the azure of another San Diego day—but a sky of jade green.

She pushed herself into a sitting position and discovered that she sat not on the concrete of the rooftop patio, but on grass—dark, blue-green blades in tight tufts that reminded her of carpet.

"How...? Where...?" She struggled to her feet. *I must be dead. Can this be heaven?*

The surroundings were lovely enough to be heaven. In the distance, green-tinged mountains rose, giving the horizon a gentle sawtooth look.

Priscilla struggled to her feet and swayed like a young tree in a stiff breeze. Dizziness churned in her head, and for a moment she thought she'd faint.

Bending, she placed her hands on her knees and took several deep breaths. The air smelled like... *like what? Pomegranate?* The air also had a taste, but not like fruit. More like freshly mowed grass.

With each deep inhalation, her heart slowed a few beats. At first, it had scrabbled in her chest like a squirrel trapped in a cage, and she had been certain it would claw its way out.

She straightened and took another look around. Her mind refused to believe the images before her eyes: a green sky, green ground, green mountains, carpetlike grass—if it was grass at all. No sun hung in the sky. No moon. No stars. Nothing flew in the air. No breeze blew.

Priscilla turned, taking in as much as her mind would allow. She saw no buildings, roads, or signs.

She was alone. She had never been or felt so alone.

"Think, Priscilla. Think." She spoke to herself in low tones. The words sounded slightly distorted, altered in a way she couldn't describe. "I was on the roof patio. Aster's ship arrived. The bubble descended. It fell on me. How did I get here? It doesn't make sense."

Should she move? Should she walk from this spot? Or would traveling make things worse?

The desire to crumple back to the ground overwhelmed her. Only her tenacity, cultivated by a lifelong commitment to stubbornness, kept her on her feet.

"Hello!" She shouted, but the word seemed to hang in the thick air. She tried again. "Can anyone hear me?"

"I can."

Priscilla jumped and spun around to face the voice behind her.

Aster looked as he did the day before: tall and angular, but his chiseled features were softer.

"Aster!"

"Priscilla!" He pushed out a smile. This one looked closer to normal than what she had seen at the Windom Building and in her bathroom.

"Where am I?" She wasn't sure if she were glad to see him or not.

"Where you were before."

"What? I was on the rooftop of the Western Bank building. This isn't it."

"It isn't?"

"No. Of course not. There were people and...and...everything you find on the top of a high-rise building."

"It is all still there."

"But where are we?"

"At the place you described."

She frowned. "That makes no sense." She waved her arm toward the horizon. "This is not San Diego."

"It is the San Diego you do not see."

"Aster, please tell me what is going on. I'm scared out of my wits."

He tilted his head to the side as if processing the sentence. "Be not afraid. This has happened to you to bless you."

"Bless me?"

"And bless the world."

She rubbed her temples. "We have got to work on your communication skills."

"It is why I need you. As I explained before."

"In my bathroom. While I bathed."

He nodded. "This time, I waited until you were not in your bathtub."

"I can't tell you how much I appreciate that, but I'd appreciate a straight answer, Aster. Where are we?"

"What do you remember last?"

"That bubble thing of yours. That thing that transports you to and from your ship."

"Yes. We are there."

"But where is everyone else? Are we...no...are we on another planet? That can't be...distance too great...not enough time...maybe..."

148

"No, not another planet. Same planet. Same place. Different space."

"What does that mean—different space?"

"It does not matter now."

She raised an eyebrow. "What you're really saying is I'm not smart enough to understand."

"Not experienced enough."

Priscilla stared at the tall creature. Nothing about him seemed evil. He spoke plainly but with no emotion, yet she sensed that there was more to Aster than she could see.

"Aster, why am I here?"

"To see. To help. To believe."

"To see what?"

"To see why I have come and what I have to give. To know why I need your help."

"We went through this, Aster."

He stepped forward and reached his long, thin arm in her direction. The sleeve of his garment retracted with the reach, and she saw the smooth, plasticlike device on his arm.

"You are blessed, Priscilla Simms of Earth. You shall take a message of glad tidings to a needy world."

"Glad tidings?" *Odd expression.*

"I bring good news to humankind. The world needs what I have to offer."

"Aster, I'm just a reporter. You should be talking to heads of state, not me."

"I shall, but I speak to you first. I need you to help me."

"But I'm just a reporter."

Aster pressed his lips together. "Are you not a seeker of truth? Do you not write the truth so others will know it?"

"Well, yes, to a degree." Priscilla took another deep breath and wished that breathing came easier. "But I don't cover politics... I mean... Look, I'm just one reporter among hundreds that work for my firm. There are reporters who speak to the nation every night."

He lowered his head, then raised it a moment later. "See." He raised the arm with the plastic cuff and touched its surface.

"See what—?"

149

The green sky turned blue; the distant mountains flattened; the turf beneath her feet became dirt. Around her milled thousands of people. By skin tone, dress, and the few words she could make out, she knew she was in India or a neighboring country.

"Do you know this place?"

"No. Maybe India."

"Bangladesh. What do you see?"

"People. Lots of people."

"This country is one of the most populated in the world. Two thousand eight hundred humans live on every square mile. It is subject to flooding in the coastal areas. Thirty years ago, one half of one million people died after a hurricane."

"Cyclone," Priscilla corrected without thinking. Aster looked puzzled. "Sorry. A hurricane is called a cyclone in this part of the world."

"I do not see how that is relevant."

Priscilla shook her head. "It's not. How come no one is reacting to you?"

"They do not see us. We see them."

"So we're not really in Bangladesh."

"We are. Look. See."

Priscilla gazed at the bustling crowd. They stood in the narrow confines of makeshift buildings. It took a few moments for her mind to register the sight. The "buildings" looked thrown together from miscellaneous materials, mostly mismatched lumber, plywood, and cardboard. The structure reminded her of a pigeonhole cabinet used for sorting memos and letters. Slots, wider than tall, were stacked one upon another. Each compartment was no more than four feet tall and, she guessed, eight feet long. Inside each, she could see old, soiled, tattered cloth.

"Are those? No, it couldn't be." She studied the compartments again. "They're sleeping quarters."

"They are homes," Aster corrected. "You see people in the only houses they will know."

"Those slots...those compartments are their homes? Men and women?"

"And children. Families."

"That's horrible." Priscilla felt ill.

"Tens of thousands live like this here and elsewhere in the country. The storms—the cyclones—come every year, and thousands die."

"Why don't they move to a safer place?"

"They are too poor and too unwanted. Their culture keeps them here. They starve. They endure disease needlessly."

"Why show me this?"

"I can make this good."

"Make it good? You mean, make it right?"

"Yes, make it right."

"You can stop poverty?"

"Yes." He stared at her. "You do not believe me."

"It's not that—OK, it is that. Poverty has always been a human struggle. How can you change that? How can anyone change it?"

"There is more you should see."

The cramped, filthy street disappeared, and Priscilla stood again in the green-hued landscape. She started to speak when the terrain disappeared, replaced by another startling scene.

Priscilla stood at the foot of a mountain, but not a mountain of stone and dirt. Towering scores of feet above her was the largest mound of garbage she had ever seen. The odor made her gag.

"Look. See."

"I am looking, and I've seen enough."

"Look, Priscilla Simms. Look and see."

She forced her eyes open. The mountain of trash buzzed with flies, and the smell of the place turned her stomach. Uneaten food, bits of raw meat, dead animals, animal feces, paper trash, aluminum cans, and items she didn't want to recognize festooned the mound. Smoke rose from fires on and in the man-made mountain.

More toxic to her mind than the decay were the women and children who walked barefoot over the surface of the massive pile, digging through the loose material that appeared to have been recently deposited. A woman who looked forty but whom Priscilla guessed was really in her early twenties clutched aluminum cans and scraps of metal to her chest. Near her, two barefoot girls, neither older than eight, followed their mother's example. They were just a few of the hundreds that worked the gigantic garbage heap, many of them carrying soiled burlap bags.

"Smokey Mountain." Priscilla whispered. One of the little girls picked up something and put it in her mouth. Again, Priscilla closed her eyes.

"You have been here?" Aster's eyes remained fixed on the soul-freezing sight.

"No. I read about it. We're near Manila in the Philippines."

"True."

"Wait a minute. Didn't the Philippine government dismantle this place? They did. I remember. It was sometime around 1995."

"They did as you say. The people moved to this site. A different place, the same problem. Three hundred thousand in slums in this area. Twenty thousand live near places like this. I can make this good."

"I don't see how."

"You will."

The mountain of trash and the mass of poverty dissolved like a billion fireflies, replaced by the green land. This time, Priscilla didn't relax. She suspected Aster had more on his mind.

A moment later the ground disappeared, and churning ocean replaced it. Priscilla gasped and reached for Aster's arm. She looked down and saw no ground, just the blue of ocean. Priscilla stood firm on the surface of the water. A wave ran over her feet, but she not could feel the cold or the wet of it.

"You are safe with me," Aster said.

"You have *got* to start giving me a little warning." She raised her eyes from the frothy water beneath her feet to the shore thirty feet away. A small wood home with a galvanized sheet-metal roof, rested at the water's edge. A woman sat on a stool, working what looked like fruit in her hand, seemingly oblivious to the incoming tide that lapped at her feet and ran over the wood porch where she sat. Young children played at the side of the shanty.

"Now where are we?"

"Your maps call this place Funafuti, Tuvalu, Polynesia."

Priscilla took in the scene. While the woman and children certainly were poor, they did not seem as impoverished as those on the edge of a gigantic mound of garbage.

The children began a game of chase. "This beats the last two places."

"You think this place is better than the last?"

"Of course. The woman and children look well-fed and happy. Granted, they'd be considered poor in many parts of the world. Their home is little more than a shack, but they don't appear in distress."

Another wave passed without touching either.

"In some years, the ocean will make their home unlivable. The ocean is rising."

"Wait, are you talking about global warming?"

"I speak of rising oceans. Climate change is one factor. It is the major issue."

"Our scientists are still arguing about the reality of global warming."

He looked sad. "Arguing is what humans do best. I have monitored your planet's discussion. Most of your scientists agree that climate change is underway; most agree global warming is the reason; most know that human-produced gases are the major cause. Denying it does not keep the ocean from rising."

"It's a hot topic. I don't know what to think."

"I am telling you what to think. The ocean will force this family and many others to relocate. Fifteen to twenty million around your Beijing will be affected. Two times that around your Shanghai. Sixty or seventy million in Calcutta and Bangladesh will be driven from their homes. It can be repaired."

"What can? The ocean?"

"The climate, Priscilla Simms. The atmosphere."

She started to speak when the scene evaporated replaced with the green terrain.

"Is that it?"

"There are many more things, but I will show only one more."

This time the setting shimmered but didn't change. Priscilla heard something behind her.

She turned.

She screamed.

Her heart sputtered to a stop. Fear forced the air from her lungs. She backpedaled then ducked behind Aster. Her knees went hollow, and her hands shook.

"You are safe," Aster said.

"What is that? Make it go away!"

It buzzed.

"It must remain for now."

The creature raised its wings, fluttered them, then brought them to rest on its dark red body. Priscilla peered around Aster's thin frame and tried to ignore what her eyes showed her: an insect the size of a pickup truck. It moved but seemed unaware of their existence.

"Do you know what this is?" Aster asked.

"It's a monster; that's what it is. It's the biggest bug I've ever seen."

"What kind of bug?"

Priscilla straightened but kept Aster between her and the freak of nature. "I don't know. It looks like...it looks like a gigantic mosquito."

Against her desire, she moved her gaze along the body of the insect. Its head was small compared to its body. Black eyes returned her gaze. It stood on long, spindle-like legs. From the head protruded a four-foot-long proboscis.

"You are correct. The small animal is the deadliest creature on your planet."

"You call that small. Man, I don't want to visit your planet."

Aster's laugh chimed. At least, Priscilla considered it a laugh. "This is not from my homeplace. This is from your land. I've made it larger to help you remember."

"Trust me, I'm not going to forget this. Is it real?"

"What is reality?"

"Don't go philosophical on me, Aster. I'm on the verge of a nervous breakdown. Is it real or not?"

"It is, but it is not here. It cannot harm you. You may touch it if you wish."

"That is not going to happen."

Aster moved to the creature and walked around it as he spoke. "Many diseases are spread by your insects. Mosquitoes are the most dangerous. Your doctors treat malaria, dengue fever, yellow fever, and many more. During every one of your years, three hundred million people are infected with malaria—nearly two million of them will die. Treatment is becoming more difficult. The parasite carried by the mosquito is now resistant to your drugs. The coming climate change helps the mosquito and endangers the human. New diseases will come, too."

"And you can fix that?"

"Yes, I can. I can fix that, the poverty, the climate, and more. Thirty thousand people die every day due to malnutrition. Malnutrition is the most curable of diseases. It responds well to food."

"Now you sound sarcastic."

"You number your centuries. True?"

"Yes. We're in the twenty-first century."

"Tell me, Priscilla Simms. How much has the world improved from the century before?"

"We have a great deal more technology."

"And your poor, hungry, displaced, imprisoned, and enslaved are fewer?"

"I don't know. Maybe."

"They are not."

"The problems are too great for us. There are too many of them."

He shook his head. "That is not the problem. Very few care. I care. I can make a difference."

"How?"

"The telling of that is too long for now. Trust me. Help me tell the others."

"Why me?"

"Because you have not shown fear around me. Because people read your words and listen to your news reports. Because I trust you."

"I don't know what to say."

He raised his arm and tapped the arm piece. The mosquito dissolved into dust that left no remains. Turning, Aster took Priscilla's hands and turned them palm up. The same electricity she felt when he touched her yesterday fired through her. For a moment, glitter sparkled in her eyes.

"Lives rest in these hands. The world needs what I have to offer. The world needs you." He smiled.

Priscilla started to speak, but before a word could pass from her lips the green field and mountains were gone and Priscilla stood on the hard concrete of the rooftop patio, her hands turned skyward.

Chapter Nineteen

Y OU DIDN'T SAY YES, DID YOU?" Lizzy Svoboda directed her truck off the 163 freeway and onto Clairmont Mesa Boulevard. Streetlamps shed puddles of light on the asphalt.

"Traffic's not bad," Priscilla said. She leaned against the door and fought to keep her eyes open.

"It's almost eight thirty; it should be a little lighter. You didn't answer my question." Lizzy had met Priscilla at home and persuaded her to go out for a late dinner since Priscilla hadn't eaten since breakfast.

"I didn't?"

"No. And you still haven't. I'm developing an emotional complex."

"Then my job here is finished." Priscilla glanced at Lizzy and saw the frown etched on her face. "Are you sure you want to eat here this late at night?"

"This isn't dining; it's therapy. My best friend has lost her mind, and I'm trying to save her from herself."

"And you think lasagna at Filippi's is going to do that."

Lizzy nodded. "Lasagna fixes everything. It's biblical."

"Hah. The Bible doesn't mention lasagna."

"Sure it does. The Hebrews called it manna."

Despite the length of the day and the emotional weight piled on her shoulders over the last two days, Priscilla laughed. "I know you have a couple of degrees in Bible, but I'm pretty sure you're wrong about that."

"Maybe. It depends how you translate the word." She turned right on Kearny Villa Road.

"You mean you don't care about accuracy."

"Exactly. Now answer my question or you'll get stuck with the bill."

"No, I didn't say yes."

"Good—wait, 'No, I didn't say yes.' Are you trying to confuse me?" Priscilla rubbed her eyes. "I'm much too tired to be clever. You asked if I told Aster yes to his request for help. My answer is: No, I didn't."

Lizzy sighed loudly for effect. "Good. Great. So you told him no."

"I didn't say that."

"Oh, brother." Lizzy made a right onto Kearny Villa Way and into a small parking lot, pulling in front of the Mediterranean-styled restaurant.

"I didn't agree to anything. I didn't reject anything." She paused. "Frankly, I was trying to keep my senses. It's not every day I get bounced around the world in a gigantic water bubble. Of course, it's not really a water bubble, it's a...a...I don't know what it is."

"It's scary is what it is." Lizzy parked and switched off the truck. "Come on. I'm famished."

"You're always famished. Wait until I get my hat."

"A girl has got to eat."

They walked into the restaurant. The noise of patrons mixed with the aroma of cheese and tomato sauce being fashioned into Italian meals that Priscilla was sure she'd be eating for the next two days.

A young woman with dark hair and large eyes greeted them. Lizzy asked for a table away from the other patrons. "We have some business to discuss. I promise to reward the server for the extra steps."

A few moments later, they were being led to the back of the restaurant, away from other diners, and the hostess walked away with a five-dollar bill in her hand.

"I don't think she recognized me." Priscilla slipped into one of four wood seats around a table with a red-and-white-checkered tablecloth.

"No one will as long as you wear that getup. I've known you for years and you look like a stranger to me." Lizzy took a seat opposite Priscilla. "We don't want another Starbucks episode. After today, you won't be able to walk down the street."

The ball cap Priscilla wore belonged to Lizzy. A yellow lightning bolt adorned the front of the cap. Lizzy was unashamedly a Charger fan.

Priscilla also wore jeans and an extra large T-shirt with Lizzy's business printed on the back: Furnishings by Liz.

"Admit it, Liz. You're not protecting my identity; you're advertising your shop."

"Never crossed my mind. Could you turn a little to your right? The other customers can't see the back of the shirt."

"Very funny. If I weren't so tired, I'd laugh."

"The food will perk you up."

This time, Priscilla did laugh. "No it won't; it'll put me in a food coma."

A waitress came by and they ordered a plate of lasagna to split and cheese bread. Both ordered diet sodas, something Priscilla thought amusing considering the carbs they were about to consume.

Once alone again, Lizzy said, "I'm serious, Priscilla. You need to stay away from this guy."

"It's not like I'm stalking Aster, Liz. He pretty much finds me."

"That alone ought to chill you to the bone."

It did, but Priscilla didn't mention it. "I've never felt threatened in his presence."

Lizzy's frown almost reached the table. "Priscilla, he abducted you."

"And returned me safe and sound to the same spot. Leo says I wasn't gone more than one or two minutes. It sure seemed a lot longer than that."

"As I said before, something is wrong with this whole thing."

Priscilla looked at her friend. Lizzy was a unique person—a character—full of quirks, a quick wit, and many opinions. Still, she had never known Lizzy to be rude or condescending. On many occasions, she had seen her take time to help others in the church and in the community, at times spending more money than she should.

"I come back to the question of yesterday: Why you?"

"I think he trusts me."

"I think he knows you can be a benefit to him."

"Lizzy, if you could have seen what I saw—the poverty, the pain, the real and potential loss—you'd see what he is trying to do."

"Then why not let him do it? Why does he need you? Wouldn't it make more sense for him to be meeting with heads of state?"

159

"Maybe his kind doesn't think that way. I don't, Lizzy."

"I don't have a peace about this, Priscilla. Something is wrong, spiritually wrong. Surely you feel that."

"Feelings can be misleading."

"No, don't start that. You—" Lizzy stopped as the waitress approached and set the glasses of soda on the table. After she left Lizzy continued. "Can you honestly tell me you have a peace in his presence?"

Priscilla stalled by taking a drink of diet soda.

"Come on, Priscilla. I know you better than your mother does."

"No, I can't say I feel anything but confusion and some fear—OK, a lot of fear. But...but there's something about him that's—convincing."

"Priscilla—"

"What's eating you? This is twice you've gone off on me about this."

"And I'll do it again, Priscilla. You're my best friend. You're my sister in Christ. We look out for each other. That's part of our faith."

"How do you know Aster isn't part of God's plan? For all we know, he might be a messenger from God."

Lizzy leaned back. "Do you believe that?"

"Maybe. He did show me the poor and downtrodden and said he could fix the problems of disease and poverty. Probably more."

"And you believe him?"

"I don't know what to believe. I didn't ask for this. I'm just a simpleminded reporter. Life was just the way I like it."

Lizzy leaned forward and touched Priscilla's arm. "Who knows whether you are come to this place for such a time as this?"

"That sounds familiar."

"It's a personal paraphrase from the Book of Esther. You remember the story of Esther?"

"Yes. You taught it to our Bible study class last year."

"Two years ago. Time moves fast. What do you remember?"

"Esther was a Jewess who became queen of Persia by marrying Ahas...Ahes..."

"Ahasuerus, also known as Xerxes. Go on."

"God used her to save the Jews in Persia against the pogrom planned by one of the king's advisors. Haman, right?"

160

"Exactly. Her cousin, a righteous man name Mordecai, encouraged her to speak to the king even though it might mean the end of her life. He told her that everything that had happened to her might have been preparation for this one event."

"I'm not Esther."

"I'm not saying you are, but I am saying that you may have been thrust into the middle of this for a reason."

"What reason? Thrust by whom?"

Lizzy straightened. "Only you can say."

"You didn't answer my question," Priscilla said. "How do you know Aster isn't part of God's plan?"

"You've told me everything you've seen him do and heard him say, right?"

"Yes."

"I don't recall you saying that he has ever mentioned God. Has he?"

Priscilla didn't answer. Judging from Lizzy's expression, she knew she didn't need to.

Martha stood at the tall french window in the west wall of the guest-room where she was staying. This was not her room. She had moved from home before her father entered politics. She had stayed here many times during his first term, so the room felt comfortable—normally.

Tonight it felt more like a tomb. She had been sequestered since yesterday's events, avoiding contact with anyone other than her parents. She had called her law partners, but little information was exchanged. She learned that the bodies of the unlucky employees... *unlucky* didn't seem the right word. She searched for another term but came up empty.

It didn't matter. The gruesome point came easy: the battered and broken bodies had finally been recovered and sent to the medical exam-iner's office. Autopsies would be performed but only because the law required it. Should a lawsuit for wrongful death come, then such infor-mation would be needed.

It was the right thing to do.

It made sense.

It would all be legal and correct.

Then why did it feel so wrong? More to the point, why couldn't she feel anything at all? Sadness had filled her like a black fog, but it lacked the proper intensity. The dead were her employees and, to a degree, her friends, but no matter how often she stoked the coals of regret and remorse she felt no worse. It seemed to her that any true emotion, any true feelings, had been cored out of her.

A knock on the door captured her attention. Martha stepped to the paneled oak slab but didn't bother asking who had knocked. She recognized the rhythmic tapping of her mother's knuckles. It was a sound she associated with growing up. Her mother was prone to check up on her. She did so when Martha was six and would do so if Martha were sixty and her mother ninety. A woman never outgrew motherhood.

She opened the door. "Hi, Mom. I thought you went to sleep hours ago."

"I went to bed. There's a difference. You OK?"

"Yes. Come in."

"My motherly instincts say different."

"Dad asleep?" She moved to the bed and sat. Her mother joined her.

"Yes. You know him. He's snoring before his head touches the pillow."

Martha faked a laugh and hoped her mother bought it. She didn't.

"Still feeling down?"

"Yeah, I guess so."

"You've been thinking about your poor employees. I know it's hard, but you can't dwell on it. It's not your fault."

"I'm not dwelling, Mother. I think of them, but I'm not dwelling. In fact, I can't seem to dwell on anything."

"What do you mean?"

Martha shrugged. "I don't think I can explain."

"Try."

"I don't feel the same. I don't...feel at all. I think about the people who died in my building, but I don't feel the grief I should."

"You've had quite a shock, sweetheart. It'll come. Just give yourself time."

"It's more than that. I slept last night. It was restless sleep, but I slept. I took two naps today."

"As you should. Rest is the best medicine for you. It gives you time to adjust to everything that has happened."

"No, you don't understand, Mother. I sleep, but I don't dream."

"You don't remember your dreams. That's the way dreams are."

"Mother, stop it. You're not listening to me. You're reinterpreting everything to make it sound better. I'm not a child and I'm not in shock."

"OK. I'm just trying to help." Emily lowered her head.

Martha took her hand and gave it a gentle squeeze. "Mom, I'm not trying to be aloof or cruel. I'm just struggling to understand what has happened to me." She looked at a painting hanging on the wall opposite them, a French impressionist piece that Martha couldn't recognize. The dim light in the room washed out the muted colors of the art piece.

She continued. "When I say I haven't dreamed, I mean exactly that. You know me, I've always had bizarre dreams—not always frightening, but usually odd. I didn't dream last night. I didn't dream during my naps. I don't feel the emotions I normally do. I touch things, like your hand, and it feels artificial. And..."

"And what, sweetheart?"

"And when I look in the mirror, I don't see me."

Her mother looked puzzled. "I'm afraid I don't understand."

"I know. Lawyers make their living with words and I can't pull together a simple, coherent sentence about what I'm experiencing. Let me try again. When I look at my reflection, I don't recognize myself. It's like I'm looking at someone else, someone who doesn't belong in my mirror."

"I...I don't know what to say."

"I know. I don't expect any words of wisdom."

"But the doctors said you were fine. That the...um..."

"The head wound. I think of it as the 'damage.'"

"That the head wound was gone and everything else about you checked out. This must be from the shock of what you experienced."

"Maybe, but I doubt it."

"I wish you hadn't watched that video footage. You didn't need to see that."

Martha stood. "That's another thing, Mother. I watched that video of the Aster creature and of me on the ground. I saw that half my head was caved in. No one could survive that. I didn't. Yet here I am." She touched the side of her head.

"Let's not talk about that." Tears brimmed in her mother's eyes.

"Ignoring it won't make it go away, Mom."

"Give it time, sweetheart. Your life will be back to normal soon."

"I don't think so, Mom."

"But why, dear? People have lived through tragedies before, some worse than this."

"It's not the earthquake, it's not the fallen building, or the fact that I was trapped. It's not even the fact that I was...I was dead."

"What then?"

Martha approached the bed and knelt. "Mom, I don't feel anymore. I don't sense fear, or longing, or hope, or love. I can't feel anything. I should be a bigger basket case than I am. I'm...numb. Emotionally paralyzed. I'm empty inside like a drained soda can. What was me is somehow gone."

"We should see the doctor tomorrow. He'll know what to do."

Martha rose and stepped to the dark window. "This is beyond doctors. I think maybe I need a preacher or a priest or a rabbi."

"Your father could ask the Senate chaplain to come by. I'm sure he'd be happy to do so."

"Do you want to hear what I really think my problem is, Mother?"

"Of course."

"I don't think I'm alive. Mother, I think I'm still dead."

Chapter Twenty

WACHER CALLED EARLY THE NEXT MORNING. He had been working through the night and was happy to say that he had arranged for a television interview to be simultaneously cast at noon that day. Priscilla didn't share his joy.

"Look," Wacher had said. "I did all this to make it easier on you. This way your old television station will serve like a pool reporter. One taping, and everyone in the world will get the same material."

"With Debatto Media sniped at the bottom of the video."

Wacher sounded hurt. "Well, of course. You make it sound evil. It's not. It's business."

Priscilla, still in pajamas, sat staring at the blue letters of her alarm clock as 6:28 became 6:29. "Sometimes I can't distinguish between the two."

"You're not a morning person, are you?"

"I'm sorry. After yesterday, I'm a little edgy. I didn't sleep well. I need a couple of days off. Make that a couple of months."

"I imagine you do."

"But I'm not going to get them, am I?"

Wacher laughed. "No. Priscilla, you may not know it—although I don't see how you couldn't—but you're the most important person on the planet."

"Nonsense." She slipped from bed and stretched her back.

"I'm serious."

"So am I. Nonsense. Worse than nonsense."

"Name one person who has spoken to a nonhuman."

"Mary the mother of Jesus spoke to an angel."

His sigh came over the phone clearly. "I mean a real person."

"Mary wasn't real? I know a few million people who would disagree with you."

"Priscilla, you have spoken to a being from another planet, not once, but twice. No one can make that claim."

"I didn't ask for the privilege."

"No one said you did. I just think you're keeping yourself from seeing the magnitude of your part in all this."

Priscilla walked into the bathroom and, cradling the remote phone between her ear and shoulder, squeezed toothpaste on the bristles of her electric toothbrush.

"Tim, I need you to get to the point. I'm about to brush my teeth, and if you're still on the phone you'll hear some repulsive noises."

"Be at KGOT at eight. They'll set you up in-studio and arrange for the network feeds."

"Who's doing the interview?" She turned the cold-water knob, then let her eyes drift to the mirror. She looked pale and the flesh beneath her eyes was puffy and dark. She wanted to climb back in bed.

"Tedi Stewart."

"The new anchor on *This Day*?"

"She's the one. She's the hottest TV property going. Since joining the show, the ratings have doubled."

"She's not property, Tim. She's a person."

"We'll see if you agree after the interview."

"Swell. You think she'll use this to increase her currency with the network and her viewers?"

"Wouldn't you?"

"At one time, Tim. At one time."

"Well, use it to increase your currency for the company that writes your checks. You're not only the darling of the world, but also of Debatto Media."

"I'm all atwitter."

Another sigh. The man was losing patience. "I don't get you, Priscilla. There are people that would kill to experience what you have. You are the conduit of communication with a new species—at least new to humanity."

"I'm sorry to be a pain, Tim. I don't feel well. I'm weary beyond description. To be honest, I can't believe any of this, yet I'm living through it."

"I understand."

"No you don't. If I don't understand, then neither do you."

"You know what I mean."

Her reflection seemed to grow thin and frail. Her red hair hung flat against her face. She ran her free hand through it. "When should I be there again?"

"Eight. I'm sending a limo."

"A limo? Why? I've got my car."

"I don't think you should be driving around alone. This way you can focus on what you're going to say. Go straight to makeup. They'll make you even more lovely."

"Tell them they're going to need a trowel and a spray painter."

Several familiar faces greeted her, people from her days as anchor of the evening news. Most looked older and worn. A year or two after Priscilla left the camera lens behind, KGOT had been sold to a high-powered media firm in New York. Their take-no-prisoners approach to the news drove many employees away. Those who stayed endured a new level of stress. Priscilla considered it a blessing that she left when she did.

"Sit right here, Ms. Simms. I imagine you know the drill." The makeup tech was a twentysomething male with delicate features who spoke with a hint of nasal resonance. His brown hair displayed blond highlights and was spiked with enough gel that Priscilla feared he would put out someone's eye.

"Thanks. Sorry I'm late."

"Doesn't matter to me. I get paid no matter what." He pulled a small cart to the barber-style chair and opened a container of foundation. He studied her. "Actually, a few extra minutes would have been useful."

"Thanks. And the sarcasm is intended."

"Don't mind me. I don't know any better than to speak my mind."

Priscilla closed her eyes while the artist made her camera-ready. She hoped her closed lids would signal her desire to avoid conversation. She was disappointed.

"So tell me what's it like hanging out with that alien. He's amazing looking, isn't he? I'd just love to meet him."

"I don't hang out with him. I just happened to be in the right place at the right time."

"Oh, you're just being modest. You can't fool me."

"Look, I need to get my head in the game. You're a professional in this business. You know what it's like."

"Have it your way."

Ten minutes later the floor director met Priscilla. "I'm Bob Henry. I understand you used to work here." He led her to the studio news desk.

"That was before you guys moved to the new studio complex. We weren't in East County then."

"Before my time. Have a seat, please." On the desk rested a lapel microphone. "Please remove your coat."

Priscilla wiggled out of the dark gray coat that was part of the pant-suit she wore. He draped a wire over her shoulder and down her back. Priscilla placed the ear monitor in her left ear and slipped back into her coat. The motions brought back a cascade of memories, and for a moment she missed her previous life as a television journalist. He attached the microphone to her lapel.

"I know this is all old hat to you, but let me run through things. Tedi Stewart will be conducting the interview from New York." He pointed to a small flatscreen monitor mounted to the camera. "You'll be able to see her on that monitor. We'll only be using the one camera for this. As you know, you'll hear her through the ear monitor. If the director needs to speak to you, you will hear him the same way. Can you give me a count?"

"Ten, nine, eight, seven..."

"That's good, Ms. Simms." The voice came through her ear monitor and sounded young.

Bob backed away. Priscilla noticed that he wore an earpiece like hers. The space around the cameras seemed dark, and the lights that lit the news platform seemed too bright.

Bob held up a hand. "We go live in five, four, three..." He faded to silence but continued the countdown with his fingers. When he reached "one," he wagged his finger and pointed.

The monitor came to life, and Priscilla could see Tedi Stewart sitting in a set that looked like a designer living room. Tedi was a dark-skinned beauty with a keen mind and a dazzling smile. Priscilla had wondered where the name Tedi had come from. She assumed that it related to Tedi's East Indian background, but rumor had it that the name was a concoction designed to make her seem more exotic.

"The world is abuzz with news about the alien called Aster. Well, he did it again, appearing suddenly in San Diego to the amazement of onlookers. We are fortunate to have with us this morning Priscilla Simms, the only person to have repeated contact with Aster. Welcome, Ms. Simms."

"Thank you, and call me Priscilla, please."

"I should say right up front that Priscilla is with us this morning through the kind arrangements of Debatto Media and *Today News*. Priscilla, there are reports that the alien has taken a liking to you, that he has appeared to you twice."

Priscilla almost corrected her and said, "Three times." She decided to keep the bathroom encounter secret a little longer. It wouldn't help and would only draw unwanted questions. "I spoke to him at the Windom Building after the earthquake and on the rooftop patio of the Western Bank building, which is also downtown."

"Isn't it true that you were taken into his...well, what do you call that waterlike bubble?"

"I don't know what to call it. It looks very much like a sphere of water. Best I can tell, it allows Aster to travel from his ship to the ground."

"So it's like a smaller ship."

No, it's nothing like that. "That's one way to look at it. It is, however, more."

"More. Explain."

Priscilla looked into the camera as if she were really looking at Tedi. "It's inaccurate to say I was taken into the bubble. It sorta fell on me. One moment, I was on the patio roof, the next I was inside the thing. At least, I think I was."

"You *think* you were?"

"There's no way to fully describe this. I think I was in the bubble, but it seemed to me I was somewhere else."

"Where?"

"I don't know. No place I have ever been."

"A place where humans have been?" Tedi leaned forward and looked deeply interested.

"I wouldn't know. I saw only Aster there."

"Can you tell us what else you saw?"

"Yes, but it's going to take some time."

Tedi nodded. "Then let's wait until after this message."

Priscilla waited until she could see Tedi relax. On the monitor, she saw someone step forward and touch up the woman's makeup. Priscilla thought Tedi would make small talk. Instead, she studied her notes and spoke to someone off-camera. Priscilla assumed it was the director in New York.

Back in one minute. Priscilla nodded.

Tedi shifted in her seat, cleared her throat twice, then looked into the camera. "We're back with our earthshaking interview with Priscilla Simms. Priscilla, you were about to tell us what you experienced. We're going to run some of the video from the last two days. Feel free to comment on it."

Video replaced Tedi's image.

Priscilla told the story, holding very little back. It took a solid six minutes to recount the events—an eternity in morning television news.

"So Aster says he can cure malaria, poverty, and the effects of global warming."

"That's what he said."

"Why you? Forgive me, but what makes you special?"

"Tedi, I don't have a clue."

"But he wants something from you. What?"

Priscilla thought the question odd. "He wants me to help him interact with us—with humans."

"That's amazing. Are you going to do it?"

Priscilla didn't respond at first.

"Priscilla? You still with us?"

"Yes."

"Yes, you're with us, or yes, you plan to help Aster?"

Images of the poor living on trash heaps and scouring through the toss-offs of others just to survive, of the displaced poor, of...everything she saw yesterday.

"Yes."

The studio felt suddenly cold.

Tom Clyn felt nervous. His life had changed over the last few weeks. A happenstance accident in Mission Valley had turned into a gold mine. Ian Robinson had officially hired him to compile all the information he could about Aster, his spaceship, and his actions. The money was good, and Ian promised much more to come if he continued to provide good information.

He did.

At first, Clyn couldn't believe his windfall. At last he was doing what he was meant to do: research UFOs and make documentaries about them. Life grew sweet.

Clyn analyzed every report, every photo, every frame of film, and every second of digital recording. He questioned experts—discreetly, as Ian had demanded—and compiled more information than he thought possible.

He worked late into the night, often sleeping in his office chair. Ian had made certain that he had the best in equipment, computers, and software. For weeks he felt like a kid who just learned that every day from now on was going to be Christmas.

That feeling faded.

A gentle knock on his door pulled him from the blanket of his thoughts.

"What?"

"It's your mother." The closed door muffled her voice.

"Of course it's you, Mom. Who else would insist on bugging me while I work?"

"Don't be mean, son. You have a guest. Mr. Robinson is here to see you."

Clyn sprung from his chair, sprinted to the door, and unlocked it. "Why didn't you say so, Mom? Come in, Ian."

"I'll just leave you two to your work. May I fix a glass of milk for anyone?"

Clyn rolled his eyes and Ian smiled. "No thank you, Mrs. Clyn. That's very kind, but I'm fine for now."

"I don't want anything, Mom." He shut the door the moment Ian crossed the threshold. "I have got to get a place of my own. She's driving me nuts."

"Is that your way of asking for more money?"

"No...I only meant...no, I'm more than happy."

Ian laughed. "I'm sorry to hear that, because I have good news—news that will make you wallet swell with pride.

"Really? Here, take my chair."

"No. You're the one who had better sit down."

Clyn did. "What's up?"

"When we first met, I told you that I am a business consultant. I've done some work with Debatto Media. I'm going to be doing more—actually, *we're* going to be doing more. Because of Priscilla Simms, Debatto leads the world's media in Aster-related content. Aster has been very open with them. It looks like that's going to continue."

"OK..."

"They want me to help them control the flow of information."

"You mean they want to keep it for themselves."

Clyn watched Ian eye him, and he didn't like it.

"I assume you mean that in a good way."

"Yes, yes, of course."

"Debatto Media wants to develop product they can sell. Information is a hot commodity, and they have the best source in Priscilla Simms and in you."

"Me?"

He nodded. "That's what I said. Your knowledge and connection have proved invaluable. It's time to move you up the ladder. The documentary you're working on is now fully funded. You have a blank check for equipment and crew."

"Wow. You're kidding."

"I never kid about business. Here's the deal. I am your only contact on all matters related to Aster. You talk to no one but me. Got it?"

"I've been sharing info with other key researchers. They've sent me a boatload of information. I kinda owe them."

Ian shook his head. "You owe them nothing. Me you owe, not them. Got it?"

"But they'll wonder what happened. It will ruin my cred in the UFO community."

"Your cred will be sky-high once the video is released."

"But—"

"It has to be this way. I have another researcher in the wings. I'd rather stay with you, but if you feel that you can't do the work..."

"I didn't say that." Clyn fell silent. Had he kept all the information to himself, he could use it to leverage a compromise, but he had shared everything with Ian. "I'm, um, happy to help."

"Glad to hear it." Ian said the words in a way that made them sound like a threat.

"You should know something." Clyn spun in the chair and brought up a document.

"What's that?"

"It's a list of inconsistencies. I've been studying Aster's ship, and something doesn't fit. I've looked at reflections, studied the video and digital stills of the ship, the shadow it casts, and more. I've also spoken with radar operators from various airports and get the same story: the ship never appears on radar."

"So it's stealthy. It's a great angle for your documentary."

Clyn nodded slowly. "Of course, of course, but it ain't right, man. I mean, UFOs often appear and disappear from radar, but those are always distant. Aster's buggy sat right over downtown, and I can't find a single radar return. Then, when I use photo software to study images, things don't add up."

"Like what?"

"Like reflections, angles that shouldn't be there, the way the ship fragments but stays aloft. A dozen things, man. I'm just getting into that part of it, but we should probably tell someone about this."

"Like whom?" The words were cold.

"I don't know. The execs at Debatto, maybe."

"I told you that I am and will remain your only contact."

Clyn raised his hands as if surrendering to a gunman. "OK, man. Chill. I'm just trying to be a good little researcher."

"So what's your point?"

"I don't think Aster is what we think he is. I have reason to believe that he may have lied to us."

Thick and heavy silence hung between them. "You come to that conclusion based on that little bit of information? Seems like a mighty big leap to me."

"I can't prove it to you, Ian. Not yet. But when I put two and two together, I'm not getting four. You know what I mean? The more I study this, the less things jive."

"Who else have you told about this?"

"Not a soul. Too early. I'm still gathering info. Right now, you're the only one I've mentioned this to."

"That's good," Ian said. He placed a hand on Clyn's shoulder and squeezed hard. Clyn writhed under the powerful hand. "Listen to me, Tom. Debatto Media has spent a fortune staying ahead of the curve on this. They have broadcast hours of video touting the truth that Aster is from another planet. It would be a bad thing for their credibility if it turns out they're wrong."

"And bad for their checkbook." Clyn had to force the words through clinched teeth.

"You understand that that would be bad for me, too, right? And what's bad for me is horrible for you. Clear?"

The hand tightened.

"Yes. All right. Let go."

Ian did. "You talk to me and no one else. Got it?"

"Yeah, I got it." He rubbed the bruised muscle. "Man, that was so unnecessary. Just what kind of consultant are you?"

174

"The kind that makes sure his clients aren't bothered by crusaders and do-gooders. A lot of people hate big business. My job is to make sure people don't act on their morals."

"You do the dirty work?"

He smiled. "It pays the bills." His eyes narrowed. "Do we have an understanding?"

Clyn nodded and rubbed his shoulder some more.

PART II

18 Months Later

Chapter Twenty-one

Last Will and Testament of Priscilla Cloe Simms
Digital video recording from somewhere in Minnesota

MY NAME IS PRISCILLA SIMMS. Yes, *that* Priscilla Simms. This is my last will and testament. Being of sound mind and weary body, I make this recording of my own volition and under no compulsion. Before I pass my earthly belongings on, I wish to make a statement, to give an account of what has led me to this place and what will likely lead to my death."

I stifled a laugh. I felt no joy and no happiness. I had no reason to laugh, yet laughter tried to percolate out. With a touch, I stopped the recording, closed my eyes, and leaned forward until my head touched the ping-pong table upon which the camera rested. Tears burned my eyes, but I fought them back. It was important that I appeared sane and stable, although I ceased feeling either months ago.

Raising my head, I leaned back in the folding metal chair, activated the camera, and tried not to squint against its bright light.

"I'm recording this from a secret location...scratch that. By the time you see this, I'll be in another location—or dead. Probably dead. Since I can't edit this video, I'm afraid you're going to have to endure raw footage. Sorry. I wish I could do better, but things aren't ideal for me. Not anymore."

I looked into the lens and continued. "I doubt I'll be here much longer. I have to keep moving—keep hiding—but I suppose it's only a matter of time. From reporter to rebel in eighteen months seems too much to believe. Half the time I think I'm dreaming, but when I open my eyes the nightmare continues.

"As you can probably tell, I'm not in a studio. No one will have me anymore. I'm not sure I care. Career no longer seems important. Instead, I'm twenty-three hundred feet underground in what used to be the Soudan Mine—an iron mine. Miners pulled iron ore here from the 1880s to 1962. A few years ago, scientists converted it to the Soudan Underground Laboratory. They used it to search for dark matter in the universe. That was when humans did their own science. Instead of taking as truth everything that comes from the mouth of Aster." I tried not to spit out his name.

"I know you—whoever you are—don't need me to tell you all that has happened since Aster's arrival, but you do need me to tell you what few others will: the truth."

I ran a hand through my hair, now cut short, partly for convenience—I don't get a regular shower these days—and for disguise.

"You know some of the story—the parts he wants you to know, the parts we all believed, the parts I helped broadcast to the world. There's more—much more. All the goodness you see..." I trailed off. "Things aren't what they seem, and I'm not what the authorities say I am. I wish I could prove that to you—to the world—but I harbor no illusions about that. Still, I must try. This is bigger than me or my opinion. This is larger than any one person. This goes beyond this life. It extends into eternity."

I rose and moved across the makeshift rec room where once scientists took time off from trying to understand a universe of dark matter. I didn't bother turning off the video camera. My new constant companion, apathy, rose to fill my heart. Caring was becoming difficult. When a person faces the impossible, it is difficult to remain positive.

This underground laboratory, twenty-seven levels below the surface of the earth, held the best in technology. Pipes and electrical conduits designed for one thing: detecting the missing ingredient of the universe. Sensors, shielded from ambient radiation on the surface and cooled to near absolute zero, waited for the impact of what researchers called WIMPs—weakly interactive massive particles. I only know this because they were some of the first scientists to abandon their work, and I dutifully reported it.

Across the room, just ten steps, stood a refrigerator that looked as if it had been manufactured two decades before. I opened the fridge and removed a Dr. Pepper. It wasn't diet; it wasn't caffeine free. Such concerns were too trivial to occupy any portion of my mind these days. When you're certain you're going to die any moment, sugar content seems such a small thing.

I returned to the metal chair, lowered myself in front of the camera, popped open the soda, and took a swallow.

"I should have known better, really. Hindsight, as they say, is always 20/20. The clues were there, and had my eyes been open I would have recognized them.

"I had been warned, too. A dear friend, an insightful woman..." The tears rose again, and this time I let them flow. What did it matter? "She knew. Somehow, someway, she knew. I didn't listen. I couldn't see what she saw, and I should have. After all, we share the same faith."

I set the soda down on the ping-pong table, then thought that I should find a coaster so as not to leave a moisture ring. Odd how such thoughts occur.

"Yes, I said *faith*. That was the key. That *is* the key. Had I bothered to see the situation through the eyes of faith, I would have recognized the lie and maybe made a difference, maybe kept all this from happening. But I didn't. I suppose this video is as much a confession as it is an attempt to get the truth out to any who will listen."

I looked straight into the small lens. "Will you listen? I can't force you to believe me, but maybe, just maybe, my account will ring with enough truth you'll be able to recognize it. At any rate, it's the best I can do now.

"That's why I have to do this and do what comes next. That's why this video..."

I reached for the soda can, took a sip, then returned it to its previous resting place.

"Where to begin? I suppose I should pick up from where the truth stopped and the lies began." I thought for a moment. "The medical examiner's report would be a good place to start..."

"Priscilla? Where are you?"

"I'm almost home, Leo," I said into my cell phone. "What's up?"

"Can we meet somewhere?"

I directed my silver Mazda off the freeway and up Friar's Road. I would be in my condo in ten minutes. A glass of milk, a piece of whole grain bread, then bed. That sounded great.

"Leo, I'm whipped. These have been the most difficult few days of my life. I'm really looking forward to writing THE END on this day."

"I wouldn't ask if it wasn't important."

That was true. Leo made few extra demands on my time. As one of my bosses, he never hesitated to insist on excellence, but he never interfered with my free time.

"OK, but it's going to cost you a piece of chocolate pie. How does Busters sound?"

"Too many people."

"Leo, it's almost eight o'clock. How busy can it be?"

"Something smaller. How about Bean There. We've had coffee there before. I can't buy chocolate pie there, but I know they have some decadent pastries. And there won't be as many people."

"That's twenty minutes from here."

"I'm still at the office. It'll take me that long to get to College Avenue."

"Fine, Leo, but this better be important. You don't want to get between a weary woman and sleep."

"Sleep is overrated." The connection went dead.

I turned on a side street, pulled a U-turn, then headed back to the freeway. *This had better be good, Leo.*

Bean There, despite its trendy name, was a small, plain coffee shop that specialized in coffee grown in Hawaii. I don't know why, they just do. I arrived before Leo, and he had been correct: only two other people were in the strip-mall joint. An elderly bearded man sat at a small table that looked like a castoff from Starbucks. Before him rested a shiny new computer. He wore a set of headphones and nodded to the beat of music only he could hear. In the center of the seating area sat a college-aged man with a thick textbook in front of him. He marked passages with a yellow highlighter.

Mounted to a wall behind the counter and near the ceiling, a flatscreen television set turned to MSNBC showed video of Aster's ship hovering over the Western Bank high-rise.

"May I help you?" The woman behind the counter seemed this side of twenty, had close-trimmed locks dyed deep black with orange highlights. Her lower lip bore two piercings filled with silver rings.

"Thanks, I'm waiting for someone."

"Can I get something started for you?"

"What do you have that gives the greatest degree of guilt?"

"I know just what you need. It's not on the menu, but I've never had one come back."

"I'll take it. Just make it decaf. I need my sleep."

"OK. You look familiar."

"Do you watch the news?"

She shook her head. "I only get so many brain cells; I don't want to use them up on that stuff."

"Good for you."

"Priscilla."

I turned and saw Leo enter. In his hand he carried a manila folder. He looked wearier than I felt. I remembered him gobbling his nitro pills earlier that day. "Hey, Leo. You OK?"

"Fine. Just fine."

I looked back at the young woman. "This guy is paying."

"Fine by me."

Leo ordered decaf coffee black and in a real cup. I shrugged at the woman. Some people learn coffee shops exist to serve the different.

He insisted we take a seat as far from the others as possible.

I spoke in hushed tones, just loud enough to be heard over the steamer squealing behind the counter. "OK, what's so important that I had to turn around and leave my warm, comfy bed waiting at home?"

"No one goes to bed this early. It's not even eight thirty."

"After what I've been through, I may go to bed early for the rest of my life. Besides, I didn't say I was going straight to sleep. I was going to watch a movie and forget about the world."

He looked drawn and worried. "I don't know what to do with this. I wanted you to see it." He set the folder on the table between us. I reached for it. "Not yet."

The server brought Leo's large coffee in a ceramic mug with the name of the shop emblazoned on it. In her other hand she carried a clear plastic cup that looked large enough for two to share. The contents looked dark and chocolaty. "Let me know what you think," she said to me.

"I can't drink all that, and it looks so rich." I took a sip. Heaven.

"You want me to take it back?"

"Not if you value your life. I can't figure out why you made it so small."

She laughed. "I get a lot of that."

"Do I want to know what's in it?"

"It's legal unless you're on a diet."

I thanked her profusely and took another sip of what might be the best drink I've ever had. Leo was going to have to work hard to keep my attention.

He opened the folder, and my drink soured. "This is a medical examiner's report. How did you get a copy of an ME file?"

"Keep your voice down." He glanced at the student who hadn't lifted his head since I entered.

"Fine. Answer the question."

He shrugged. "I know a guy who knows a guy who knows a guy."

"Uh-oh. In other words, you're not going to tell me."

"I'm not going to tell you."

"So much for trust between friends." He seemed to catch the humor in my voice.

"It's because we're friends that I won't tell you."

"You're a pal." I pulled the file close and looked at the contents. "There are three reports. Are you going to tell me what all this means, or do I need to read everything?"

He leaned closer, pushing his coffee aside. He had yet to drink any of it. "These are the reports of the three employees of the law firm that died in the Windom Building collapse."

"That was fast." I looked at the names: Judy Stone, Jim Cass, and Emilliano Neri.

"They were the only deaths from the earthquake, and since the law firm Godwin, Reed, and Merrell are influential in the city, the ME made the autopsies a priority."

"Not to mention that one of the partners is the governor's daughter."

"Not to mention."

"So what am I looking for?"

"TOD."

"What's so special about time of death? We know to the second when the earthquake took place. We know what time Aster saved Martha Merrell, and at the time he said the others were dead."

"I know what he said. My contact knows what he said, and that's why he contacted me. It doesn't add up."

"What doesn't?"

He looked exasperated. "Let's see if I can lay this out. The fire department rescue teams were able to recover the bodies about three hours after the quake. Of course, they found three corpses, as expected. Each body was removed and transported to the medical examiner's facility. By routine, they used the typical methods to determine a precise time of death. They did a liver temp and whatever else the people down there do."

"And?"

"And...two died within minutes of the earthquake. One, Jim Cass, lived longer."

"How much longer."

"Close to three hours."

"That's horrible. I can't begin to imagine what it's like to be trapped for so long. I wonder if he was conscious...wait, three hours? That can't be."

"Exactly what I said." Leo shifted in his chair. He said nothing more. He waited for the truth to dawn on me.

"Leo, that means that..."

"Jim Cass."

"...that Jim Cass died shortly before the fire department extracted him. If they could have gotten to him sooner..."

"They might have been able to save him." Leo finished the sentence for me. "But they didn't save him, and one reason is the fire department boys didn't rush. Why should they? Rushing increased their own risk, and they had been told that everyone else was already dead."

"Leo, it goes beyond that. This would also mean that Aster left a living person behind to rescue Martha Merrell."

"Who was already dead. Remember the paramedics pronounced her dead, then Aster did his magic trick and all of a sudden she was alive."

"No, I don't buy it. Why would he do that? What does he achieve?"

"How about the gratitude of the governor?"

"OK, Leo, this is nuts. You're assuming Aster knew that one of the trapped people was the daughter of a government leader. How could he know that?"

"I don't know, Priscilla. How does he know English?"

"Maybe he monitored all those *I Love Lucy* episodes that get beamed into space. I think there is an error somewhere."

"Something's wrong, that much is certain."

I forgot about the unforgettable drink. "Are you telling me that Aster purposely misled us and the world?"

"I don't know that. What I do know is that things don't add up. Aster lied or is mistaken. Either way, I'm suspicious."

"Maybe the ME is wrong. You said they sped up the autopsy. Haste makes a ripe field for error. It plagues our profession. Maybe their equipment was faulty."

"Maybe, and maybe it is exactly as it appears."

"So, when does the news come out?"

"I don't know that it will. What we're looking at wasn't meant for our eyes. We have to be careful with this."

"I should say so. I'm betting the ME goofed up."

Leo lowered his head. "Why are you defending Aster so much? Do you really think he can end poverty, reverse global warming, and end diseases like malaria?"

"Only time will tell. I do know—and so do you, because you were there—that he brought a woman back to life. Maybe this Jim Cass was too far gone, too damaged for Aster to help."

Leo's face hardened. "You're much too good a reporter to have such shoddy thinking. Martha Merrell's head was caved in. Read the report—Jim Cass's injuries were minor by comparison. He died from shock and from the slow buildup of fluid in the lungs. I'm no doctor, but as bad as that sounds it seems a whole lot better than having half your head crushed."

I had no words. Leo had always been a proactive person, steady in all situations. He had seen more in his life than most, and I had always valued his opinion.

He softened his tone. "Priscilla, all I'm saying is, be careful. I felt as thrilled as anyone that someone from another planet paid a visit to this tired, old planet. To be part of the team that reported it has been the highlight of my career. It's the kind of thing a man my age hopes for, to end a long career on top." He bit his lip and rubbed his chest. "I may be all wet, but something isn't right."

The words made me think of Lizzy's comments. She too had said that something wasn't right. What was wrong with these people? True, I felt leery at first, but Aster promised so much good and so far had asked nothing in return.

I broke eye contact with Leo as my brain chugged along trying to make sense of what I had just learned. The old man with the computer stared at me. The moment our eyes met, he diverted his gaze back to the laptop's screen. His face held no expression.

"Priscilla, I'm sorry if I upset you...but as...your friend...Oh, no."

Leo's reached for his coat pocket, then his head dropped forward.

"Leo?"

"Oh, no, no..."

He dropped to the floor.

"*Leo!*"

I knelt by him. "Leo? Leo? Stay with me, Leo." I rifled through his pocket looking for the small bottle of nitro he carried. He had been reaching for it when he collapsed.

Found it.

"Call 911. Now! Someone call 911!"

The student came and knelt beside me, and the server rushed to my side. The old man with the computer closed the lid and walked from the shop.

"I said, call 911. Now! Do it now!"

The server disappeared.

"Help's on the way, Leo. Just stay calm..."

His eyes were open and stared at the ceiling.

He didn't blink.

Chapter Twenty-two

MINUTES IN THE HOSPITAL PASSED LIKE DAYS. It took an unending twelve minutes for the ambulance to arrive, and each minute passed at a glacial speed. The paramedic team was composed of one middle-aged man who was balding on top and a much younger man who looked too young to shave. Flashing emergency lights pushed through the storefront windows and splashed on the coffeehouse walls. The two emergency personnel strode through the door at a leisurely pace as if they'd come for coffee instead of administering life-saving procedures. I've been at enough emergency scenes to know that calm was required and that paramedics did no good by arriving in a panic. I felt panicked enough for all of us.

Dizziness filled my head. The student and I had been doing CPR on Leo—he did the chest compressions, and I did the mouth-to-mouth. Sweat dripped from the student's face and plopped on Leo's white shirt.

"One...two...three...four...five..." The kid sounded winded. Compressing a man's chest for nearly a quarter of an hour was hard work. I blew air into Leo's lungs.

The paramedics set their kits down and took over, leaving me to watch and pray. And answer questions.

"When did this happen? How long has he been unconscious? Does he have a history of heart problems? How old is he? Is he taking medications? What was he doing before he collapsed?"

I answered them all.

They hooked up a heart monitor. Flatline.

They broke out defibrillator paddles and sent currents coursing through Leo's body. He jerked with each shock. So did I.

After the third jarring electrical assault, Leo's heart began to play music. Not the kind that comes from a radio; the kind that means a dead heart has come back to life. The beep-beep-beep song sounded better than any sound I have ever heard.

My joy wasn't shared. The paramedics studied the readout and frowned. I wanted to ask what concerned them, but I couldn't bring myself to form the words of the question.

Fifteen minutes later, the ambulance pulled from the parking lot with Leo in the back. I followed behind, steering my car down the lane and doing my best to keep up with the ambulance as it stretched the meaning of the posted speed limit. There was no siren, but the emergency lights spun like beacons.

I lost them at a stoplight and fought the urge to pound the steering wheel and swear. Instead, I substituted prayer for the foul language.

Before leaving, the paramedics had told me they would take Leo to San Diego Regional Hospital. I knew exactly where that was.

I arrived five minutes after the ambulance and told the ER admitting nurse who I was and why I was there. She studied me for a moment, and I knew she recognized my name and appearance. I waited for the questions about Aster to begin, but she proved herself a professional and kept her queries in check. Apparently, I looked frazzled enough to dampen her curiosity.

"I'm sorry, but I can't allow you back in the ER area. You are welcome to have a seat in the lobby. I'll let the doctors know you're here."

"Thank you."

The lobby held fewer people than I expected. The few times I had been in an ER lobby, there had been too many people and too few seats. It must have been a slow night because only three other patients waited for attention. Of course, that could change any moment.

Ten minutes became an hour; an hour became two. At eleven forty-five, a dark-skinned, thin man in a white coat entered the lobby. From his features and skin tone, I took him to be Pakistani. He glanced around the lobby, saw me, and motioned for me to join him in the hall.

I did, and he led me a few steps down the hallway and into a small consulting room. My heart hit my chest like a wrecking ball.

The room was about half the size of a small bedroom and contained a desk, a wall-mounted lightbox for viewing X-rays, and a telephone. I didn't need to be a detective to know that the space was seldom used. He motioned for me to sit in one of the plastic chairs. I did, and he sat behind the desk. I searched his eyes for any clues as to what he was about to say. All I saw were the indications of a man who'd been working too long, too hard, and on too little sleep.

"I'm Dr. Salim Shaikh." He rubbed his face. "The nurse told me that you were with Mr. Hart when he collapsed. Is that true?"

I said it was. "Is he..." I couldn't finish the question.

He sighed before he spoke, which didn't make me feel any better. "He's alive, Ms. Simms, but he's had a serious cardiac event. He's not out of the woods yet. We've been able to get him stable, and he's breathing on his own. Of course, I'm admitting him to the hospital for further treatment and observation. He's being transferred to the cardiac wing right now."

"What are his odds, Doctor?"

"I'm not a gambler, Ms. Simms. I don't know anything about odds. I can tell you he's in grave condition. You should know he may not make it through the night."

The cork that held my last few ounces of hope gave way, allowing my optimism to drain. I took a deep breath, partly to stall the realization that my friend and mentor lay dying, and partly to keep from fainting.

"He'll be in the coronary care unit tonight, and probably for several days."

"I...I see."

His face softened. "I have learned that no matter how dark the circumstances, there is still room for hope."

"Thank you. Will I be able to see him?"

"You're not family?"

I shook my head. "I'm the closest thing to family that he has in San Diego. I think he has a younger brother on the East Coast and a daughter in Florida. I'm not sure of the cities. He didn't talk much about his family."

"We'll need to contact them as soon as possible. Any help you can provide will be useful."

"I'll see what I can do."

He stood. "I'll make sure the people in CCU know about you and will grant visiting rights." He moved to the door. "I know this is hard news to take. Feel free to use this room to gather your thoughts. I wish we had time to visit. I have many questions about your alien friend."

"Everyone does."

"I imagine they do."

He left.

I spent close to an hour in the little office, doing my best to track Leo's family. Thankfully, Leo still had some old-school ways about him. I called one of the late-shift reporters at *Today News*, and he found an address book in Leo's desk. A "Richard Hart" was listed under the Hs. His address showed he lived in Rhode Island. That jogged my memory enough to know that I had the right man.

The search for Leo's daughter took longer. I couldn't remember her name—if I ever knew it. I felt guilty. All these years of working together and I knew so little about the man I admired. We were work friends. Seldom had we interacted in a social setting. Meeting at a coffee shop was the closest thing to hanging out we ever did.

Leo kept a paper calendar, too. The reporter rifled through it and found a birthday reminder for Tempest Howard. "Tempest" rang bells. It's a hard name to overlook. The address book listed her home in Miami.

Both lived on the East Coast, three hours farther along in the day. I checked my watch: a quarter to one in the morning—and a quarter to four on the East Coast. What was the ethical thing to do? Call and wake them or wait until a decent hour? I decided to leave that up to the medical professionals. I wrote down the information on paper from a small notepad that I carry in my purse. I used two pages: one for the hospital, and one for me.

Then I exited the office, handed the numbers to the ER nurse, and made my way to the third floor.

The wee hours made the hospital an eerie place, the kind of place Stephen King writes about. Nurses, doctors, and janitorial staff moved through empty corridors. To reach the CCU, I had to move down a long corridor of rooms. The doors were open. Inside each room, one or two patients lay asleep. In a few rooms, patients watched television, perhaps unable to sleep in a strange surrounding.

A large gray door sealed off the end of the hall. A sign identified it as the coronary care unit. I found an intercom to the side of the door and a white button. I pressed it and identified myself.

"I'm sorry, Ms. Simms. The nurses are still working with Mr. Hart. You'll need to come back during the posted visiting hours."

"I can't see him now?"

"No. I'm sorry. Hospital rules prohibit it."

I thanked the disembodied voice and wondered what to do next. I supposed I should go home, but that didn't appeal to me. There was the matter of Leo's car. I would have to get that from the coffee shop tomorrow and…and…

It landed on me. All of it. The fears, the despair, the uncertainty, the weariness, the confusion—it all dropped on me like sacks of concrete.

I leaned forward and rested my head against the wall, fighting back an eruption of tears.

"I think you'll be more comfortable in there."

I turned to see a thin, pale man in a hospital gown leaning heavily on an aluminum walker. He looked drawn and his brown hair stuck up at odd angles, no doubt a bad case of bed-head. His eyes were blue and exuded kindness and intelligence. Thirty pounds heavier, and he'd be attractive—assuming he wore more than the hospital gown. Pale green wasn't his color. I guessed him to be on the young side of fifty—maybe mid-forties.

"Pardon me?"

"There's a small lobby for CCU. I think you'll be more comfortable in there. It will be more private."

I followed his gaze. A closed door bore a sign indicating a waiting area.

"Thank you."

193

He approached, pushing his walker in front of him. "If you don't mind, I need to sit for a few minutes, too. I'm afraid I've gone one too many laps."

"Should I call a nurse for you?"

"No, I'd rather you didn't. I'm not supposed to be out." He smiled as he moved into the lobby. I followed, in case he fell.

"You're not supposed to be out?"

He lowered himself into one of the ten or so padded chairs and seemed relieved the moment he was off his feet. "I'm supposed to be sleeping. Can't sleep and when you've been in bed as long as I have—getting up and moving around is a compulsion. Please, have a seat."

"I should be going."

"Really? It looked to me like you could use the company of a sympathetic person."

"The last few hours have been rough."

He nodded. "Husband have a heart attack?"

"No. I'm not married."

"Father, then?"

"Friend." I settled into the chair, my purse situated on my lap.

"And they won't let you in? They seem touchy about their rules around here. Not a free spirit among them."

"It sounds like you've been here for awhile."

"Almost a year."

"I'm sorry to hear that." I couldn't imagine a year in a hospital.

"No need. I've only been awake for the last two days. The rest of it is lost to me. Coma, or so they tell me."

"But you're awake now? That's amazing."

"I'll bet your reporter instincts are already working on an angle for a story."

"As a matter of fact…how do you know I'm a reporter?"

"You are Priscilla Simms aren't you?"

Uh-oh. "Look, I'm not really in the mood to answer questions—"

He raised his hand to cut me off. "Please. I'm not here to bother you. I was walking by, if you can call this walking, and I heard you give your name."

"Oh. Of course. I'm sorry to have snapped."

194

"Don't apologize. I didn't need to hear your name. I would have recognized you anyway."

"From the television."

"Well, there is that, but...how do I say this? I've been seeing you a lot lately."

"Over the last two days—"

"No, over the last year."

"But you said you were in a coma."

He nodded, then stared at me for a long time. "I knew you'd be here tonight."

"How?"

He pressed his lips together as if fending off a frown. "I don't know, Ms. Simms. I just knew. I also knew about the thing called Aster. I knew before he arrived. Before your reports and broadcasts."

He looked harmless, intelligent, even insightful, but I knew he was a nut case.

"I see. Well, I really need to be going." I stood.

"Please sit down, Ms. Simms. I'm no threat to you, and I haven't lost my mind. I couldn't attack you if I wanted to, and I don't. I just want to talk for a moment. Please, sit."

I did, but it went against my better judgment. "Look, a very good friend of mine is just beyond those doors. A doctor told me he didn't expect him to make it through the night, so I'm in no mood for questions or requests for favors."

"You think I want Aster to heal me?"

"Why not? If you saw the broadcasts, then you saw what he can do."

"May I call you, Priscilla?"

I started to say no. "Yes."

"Thank you. I'm Allen Sloan. Call me Allen." He shifted as if the chair hurt his back. "I'm in good physical condition. I'm just weak because my muscles have atrophied over the months. My strength is returning. Soon I hope to leave this place, although I don't know where I'll go or what I'll do."

"Why not just go home?"

"I'm not sure I have a home. A car accident landed me in here. It also...it also killed my family. I was an only child, and my parents died over a decade ago. The same is true for my wife. I haven't had opportunity to check, but I imagine my house went into foreclosure and the bank seized it. Some other family is probably living there."

"That's horrible."

"I won't argue that, but I don't tell that story to make you feel sorry for me. I don't want you to think that I want a healing from Aster."

"I couldn't arrange it if you did. If I could, I'd have him here fixing up Leo."

"The man in CCU?"

"Leo Hart. One of my bosses, and a friend."

"I'm sorry. Losing a friend is hard."

The comment angered me. "He's not dead yet."

"No, of course not. I'm still tripping over my words. Forgive me."

"I should be the one to apologize. The last few days have been tough, and now this."

He took a deep breath. "Priscilla, Aster isn't what he seems to be. You should stay as far from him as possible."

I thought of the folder Leo brought, the file now hidden under the seat of my car. I felt that Leo had been wrong, that he had overreacted and drawn conclusions based on too little evidence. Now I had this guy in front of me.

"I have no reason to believe that Aster intends anyone harm. In fact, from all I've seen, he will bring great good to the planet."

"Not everything is as it appears."

"How do you know this?"

He hesitated. "While in my coma, I saw things. Much of it is gone now, and what remains is fragmentary. I seem to lose more of it with every passing hour."

"And you saw Aster."

"I saw Aster, his arrival, the earthquake—and I saw him for what he really is."

"Which is what?"

"Nothing of this world."

I laughed. "Excuse me, Allen, but that much is already known."

"It's not from any other planet, either."

"And this you know because you dreamed it?"

"I know it sounds crazy."

"That's because it *is* crazy."

The door to the lobby swung open and a thirtysomething woman in a nurse's uniform appeared. A short, dark, male nurse stood next to her.

"Mr. Sloan, what are you doing down here? You're supposed to be sleeping."

He grinned. "I must have been sleepwalking. Yeah, that's it. Sleep-walking."

"I doubt that," the woman said. She gave me a hard look.

"Don't do that," Allen said. "She has nothing to do with this. I was feeling the need for a little rest. She helped me out. She has someone in CCU."

"I'll get a wheelchair," the male nurse said.

"No need. I can walk back." Allen struggled to his feet, then looked at me. "Four-twenty-two," he said.

"I don't understand."

"I know."

He let the nurse guide him from the room.

Chapter Twenty-three

I FELL SILENT, STARING INTO THE UNBLINKING CAMERA LENS. Then something, perhaps the silence, brought me around. "I'm sorry," I said to the camera. "I'm afraid I drifted into my memories."

I cleared my throat. "If you followed my story in the media, then you know this next part. Leo died." The words seemed harsh and caustic. There's no good way to say your friend died.

Pushing aside the emotion, I continued. "I sat in the lobby for an hour or so, then decided to go home and freshen up, maybe get an hour or two of sleep. Before leaving, I rang the CCU nurse's station again and asked for a nurse to come to the door. I gave her my card. I had written my cell phone and home number on the back.

"I had just dozed off in bed when my phone rang. My alarm clock read five thirty. The ringing of the phone at that hour could only mean something bad, and I knew what that something bad was. I was right. The nurse apologized for the hour and then gave me the word as if she were announcing a sport's score.

"Although I had been warned that he might not make it through the night, the news hit me like a speeding car. I began to weep, and, to the nurse's credit, she didn't hang up. After I regained some composure, I asked the time of death. I assumed that Leo expired a few minutes before the phone call. I heard the sound of fingers hammering a computer keyboard.

"'The doctor lists the time of death as 4:22.'

"For a moment, I couldn't breathe. Four twenty-two was the number Allen Sloan told me to remember. How could he know?

"He couldn't know. It had to be a coincidence, a lucky guess, or, at most, intuition. Still, the conversation we had in the lobby came to the forefront of my mind.

"I hung up and failed to stop another wave of weeping.

"I used the bathroom and then went to the kitchen to make coffee. It was my usual routine, and I needed a few moments of the usual. I also needed time to prepare myself to make the call. The hospital would take care of notifying the family. It fell to me to notify my boss, Chris Conlin. At six, I telephoned him at home. I also told him I would be late coming into the office. I needed some time alone. For once, Chris seemed to understand."

I took a long draw from the soda.

"I also called Lizzy. She arrived within half an hour. We spent the next hour crying. I wept for Leo; Lizzy wept for me. When the water-works died down, I told her the whole story. She took in every word.

"I can't tell you everything that happened in the weeks that followed. I don't have enough digital memory on this camera, nor do I have the time. Things are telescoping now. I've been able to hide in this mine, safe from Aster and his pals. That's right, his pals. I learned that he did not travel alone." I paused long enough to sigh. "I'm getting ahead of myself. Lately, my thoughts resemble scrambled eggs and are almost as difficult to put back together.

"The two weeks that followed Leo's death were a whirlwind. I did more television interviews and was questioned by every three-letter government agency: FBI, CIA, DIA, DOD—you get the idea.

"They treated me well—too well. After my experience with the Homeland Security agents, I expected to be pushed around, at least emotionally. Instead, they gave me the royal treatment. I found out why later.

"During those weeks I also attended Leo's funeral. My pastor led the service, then took me aside to quiz me about Aster. He seemed nervous.

"Aster didn't appear again for nearly three weeks. To this day, I don't know why. I have a thing about dumb questions, especially those asked by people in my profession. You know the kind I mean. A home burns down and the family barely escapes and someone asks if the fire frightened the children. Well, I got those kinds of questions by the truckload. 'Where is Aster? When will he return? Why has he been out of sight for so long?' Someplace along the line, people began to think of me as Aster's personal assistant and press manager.

"Someone got my address, and soon I had to wade through a line of photographers and reporters just to get to the front door. Debatto Media moved me into an upscale hotel. I did most of my work there. Chris let it be known that he didn't appreciate having to drive to meet me. I told him to take it up with Mr. Debatto.

"Three weeks with no Aster, and the country slipped into anxiety. After all, he promised to fix some of our biggest problems. But while the world mourned the missing alien, I started to relax. I wanted to see an end to malaria, poverty, and global warming as much as the next woman, but being with Aster always took an emotional, intellectual, and even physical toll. I spent some of my time trying to push Leo's death, the medical examiner's report—which I still didn't understand—and everything else to the back of my mind.

"The effort was wasted.

"Three weeks, two days, and four hours after his last appearance, Aster returned."

The phone on my desk rang. I sat on a patio chair at a wrought-iron table on the balcony of my hotel. My fingers clicked the keys as I tried to write yet another story on the world's response to its first out-of-this-world visitor. I had just finished my professional blog entry that Chris wanted. The number of its visitors ran in the tens of millions each day, setting new records for that type of media. Some foreign countries began to reprint my articles and Web postings in their own publications, keeping the Debatto creative rights attorneys busy. I didn't care. Readers were readers.

I lifted my cell phone to my ear. "Simms."

"Priscilla. Have you seen it?"

"That depends on what 'it' is, Chris. Can you be a tad more specific?"

"Aster's ship. It's over the city."

"Where?"

"The phones are ringing off the hook. The city has gone nuts."

I asked again, "Where, Chris?"

"I'm looking out the window and the streets are filling with people. Apparently word is getting out."

"It's not getting to me, Chris. Focus. Where is Aster's ship?" I stood, scanned the skies, and saw nothing.

"I can't believe you can't see it. I'm looking right at the thing."

For a moment, screaming into the phone seemed like a good idea. I missed Leo. Without him, Chris ran uncontrolled. More than once, he had to beg some key employee not to quit. "From the north? The south? Help me out here, Chris."

"It looks like it's headed your direction—"

If he said anything else, I didn't hear it. A shadow fell over the balcony. Overhead, the diamond-shaped craft of Aster's appeared, eclipsing the sun and leaving me in the shadow.

The air filled with electricity. I could feel the hair on the back of my neck stand. The ship made no noise. I estimated that it hovered not more than twenty feet above the hotel roof. As with the first time, the craft's facets fragmented and spread across the sky.

"Priscilla...Priscilla..." Chris's voice seemed distant—as it should. I was holding the cell phone by my hip. The water sphere I had seen twice before descended slowly from the craft.

Even from eight stories up in the twenty-five-story hotel, I could hear the confused noise of people in the streets below. Cars came to a stop. People poured out of buildings like ants out of an anthill. I returned my gaze to the glistening orb. I had a feeling where it would stop.

The undulating bubble stopped its descent at my balcony, hovering nearly one hundred feet above the concrete, asphalt, and accumulating humans below. There was no getting used to a sight like this.

Instinct said I should run back into the room, but remembering the way Aster appeared in my bathroom made the thought absurd. Besides, despite the warnings of friends and one wacky patient in San Diego Regional Hospital, Aster had never been anything but polite and fascinating. I reminded myself that three weeks ago I had publicly agreed to help him.

Seconds dripped by, and I wondered if Aster were waiting for an invitation. I moved to the railing. Wind sent invisible fingers through my hair. The deck vibrated to a tone or force I couldn't detect.

A slit appeared in the bubble from top to bottom. It reminded me of a cat's eye. The slit widened into an opening several feet across. Aster, dressed in the same beige garment, appearing as he always had, stood gazing at me.

"Hello," I said. "Long time no talk."

He gave the slightest of bows, then tipped his head at my words. "It has been a short time."

"Three weeks, but I'm not complaining."

"It is time."

Somehow I knew he would say something like that. "Um, do you want to come in?"

He stepped to the very edge of the opening and gazed down. The height didn't seem to bother him, but then why should it? He flew around the universe.

"A crowd gathers. It would be best if you joined me." His English had improved. He held out his hand.

That made it my turn to look down. The sphere hovered ten or more feet from the edge of the balcony. "I can't jump that far."

"There is no need to jump." The bubble moved a few feet closer, but not enough to make me comfortable. I looked inside the sphere. Last time I stood in the device, I saw an entire terrain. This time the interior looked like the exterior—water as walls; water as floor.

As I began to object about the still-too-wide gap from balcony to sphere, the globe began to change. A protrusion grew from the bottom and formed a two-foot-wide bridge. Not a solid bridge—a bridge of fluid.

"Come," he said.

"What? Across that? It won't hold me."

"Trust me, Priscilla. I mean you no harm. The span is more than it appears."

My mind flashed to a sermon I heard about Peter walking on the water. Everything went well for him until he doubted. Except with Peter, he sank in a stormy sea—I would plummet to the ground below. For a moment I wondered if falling to my death would be ruled a murder or a suicide. Aster wasn't forcing me to cross, but he was compelling me.

He stood with his hand out.

"I hope no one is taping this," I said aloud, more to myself than to Aster. I climbed over the iron rail, turned my back to Aster and his bubble, and gazed into my hotel room. I wanted nothing more than to climb back over the rail, enter the room, and close and lock the sliding-glass door.

Of course, I didn't. I clinched the rail until my knuckles blanched. I looked back over my shoulder. Aster hadn't moved. He stood as if a statue with his arm stretched my direction.

I released one hand and turned halfway around. I stretched my arm, hoping my reach would meet his. It didn't.

"Come, Priscilla. We must meet."

"Yeah, right. Why couldn't you come to the front door?"

He didn't answer.

I leaned back a little and felt the iron railing lean with me. Every organ inside me threatened to let go of whatever held them in place and drop to my feet.

The wind picked up.

Slowly, I set my right foot on the undulating bridge while simultaneously questioning my sanity.

The phone rang. It took every bit of willpower I had not to climb back over the rail and answer it. I let the phone ring.

I pressed further into my first step until my foot rested on the clear surface. I could see through the bridge to the ground below. I felt ill.

A cool sensation worked up through my shoe. It felt like ice, a sensation that made my fear soar. Spectator pumps were never designed for such insanity.

"Priscilla, please trust me."

I put even more weight on the surface. It held. One deep breath later, I stepped onto the bridge and started for Aster. I made the distance in four short strides and turned in time to see the bridge rejoin the sphere.

"Thank God. Thank You, God." I looked up. Aster looked different, sterner. I had yet to see his expression change other than the few times he tried laughing. I have no idea what he might look like when angry, but this could be it. "I'm sorry I took so long. It's my first time walking on water."

The catlike pupil of the ship closed, but the light in the sphere remained unchanged. Unlike the scenery I had seen before, this time I was enclosed by water—or what my mind persisted in thinking of as water. The only thing flat was the surface I stood upon.

"Our journey begins."

"Where are we going?"

"I wish to speak to your president."

"I know he wants to meet with you. I've had enough visits from government officials over the last few weeks to know that. I'll need to set up a meeting, though I have no idea how to do that. Agents from the Department of Defense gave me a number to call—"

"Such is not necessary."

"Aster, one doesn't just walk up to the front door of the White House and knock. There are procedures to follow, clearances to obtain—"

The bubble dissolved, and for a half second I knew I would fall.

I didn't.

Instead of plummeting to my death on the sidewalk a hundred feet below, I was standing on blue carpet. I snapped my head up and looked around. I had never been in this room, but I recognized it. I also recognized the man behind the wide wood desk.

"Hello, Mr. President," I said.

"What the—?"

Doors to the Oval Office sprung open. Several men and women charged in with handguns drawn.

"Aster, don't move," I said.

He moved. He took a step toward the president. Two of the agents shouted for him to stop. Aster took another step. One agent, a man the size of a football player, threw his body at Aster while two other agents seized the president and drew him from his chair. Another agent superimposed his body between us and the leader of the free world.

The big agent plowed into Aster like a truck hitting a building but with less luck. Aster didn't budge, and the agent fell to the carpet floor in pain. He held his shoulder, and judging by the loud pop I heard when his body collided with Aster's, the man had broken his shoulder.

Every open door slammed shut. Aster had pressed a long finger against his wrist device.

Two other agents stepped within arm's reach and held their handguns as close to Aster's face as possible. It proved a stretch even for the tallest of the agents.

"Please put down your weapons," Aster said. "I wish no one harm. Your president has requested to see me."

"Let go of me." President Mohler struggled with his own agents.

"Mr. President..." I began. "I'm sorry for the interruption. I didn't expect to arrive like this. Aster has his own way about things."

"He needs to learn a little about how we do things here," one of the agents next to Aster said.

"Stand down, Bill." The president straightened his tie and began tucking his shirt back into his pants. "If Mr. Aster wanted me dead, I assume I'd already have breathed my last. Is that true, sir?" He looked at Aster.

"It is. I mean you no harm."

Mohler looked around. "Bill, I said stand down."

"But, sir."

"No buts. We've been hoping to meet. Now that we are, I prefer our guest not get the wrong impression about us."

The agents lowered their weapons and took two steps back, but no more.

"Won't you have a seat, Mr. Aster, Ms. Simms?"

"I do not sit." I could detect no emotion in Aster's voice.

"I do." He walked to the center of the room where two sofas and two heavily padded chairs waited. "You still sit now and again, don't you, Ms. Simms?"

"I do, Mr. President. I think I could use a few minutes off my feet. It's been an unusual day."

"So it seems."

The president took one of the chairs, and I sat at one end of one of the sofas.

The president looked at Aster as if he entertained aliens every day. "I've been hoping to meet you. What shall we talk about?"

"It is time to save your planet."

Chapter Twenty-four

WHAT YOU SUGGEST, MR. ASTER, IS GOOD IN PRINCIPLE BUT NOT easy to implement. There are other factors to consider. Besides, your claim that our planet's climate is changing is still unproven."

"I have followed the literature your scientists have shared. Most have seen the problem clearly."

Mohler smiled his best politician's smile. "There are those who disagree."

"Only those who find the facts inconvenient."

The president looked at his uninvited guest. "Aster, what you suggest is wonderful, and I wish it could all be true, but you need to understand the ramifications of making wholesale changes to the oil and auto industry. Tens of thousands of jobs are at stake. Perhaps we could handle that with time, but there is the matter of international relations. For example—and of course there's no reason for you to know this, you being a visitor and all—but the importing of foreign oil helps support some of our allies. Take Russia, for instance. They're already financially challenged since the breakup of the Soviet Union. Oil exportation is one of the country's greatest sources of income. If the United States ceases importing oil tomorrow, several countries would be in distress. And when a country is in distress it gets—cranky. I'm sure you understand."

"There is no foreign oil. Planetary resources belong to planetary inhabitants," Aster said, "but yes, I do understand. The technology I offer will lower harmful emissions while you still use oil. I will also give to you several other technologies to allow your people the same mobility without the destructive consequences."

The president nodded as if extremely grateful. "Look, I don't know how things are done where you come from—by the way, where do you come from?"

"The place is unknown to you or your science."

"Well, here on this planet we are closely tied to financial movement. It is what keeps our people employed and enjoying a high quality of life."

"Many of your people do not enjoy a high quality of life. Many are poor; many more cannot seek medical treatment when needed."

"Yes, it's true, we still have many problems."

"Problems that could have been solved long ago. I know that commerce drives all countries. I will show you how to institute the needed technology and still allow your businesses to thrive."

"That's very kind of you."

Aster folded up again, just as I had seen him do over Martha's body. Again, he laid his large hands on the side of his head as if he had a migraine. At first I thought it was a sign of acquiesce or frustration.

I was wrong.

"Mr. President. You have been very kind to receive me in your place of power. I now owe you a courtesy. My courtesy is this. I have come to you first because you are the leader of the land of Priscilla Simms. Since you show no interest in what I propose, I shall now go to other countries and allow them to have what I offer you."

The president stiffened. "I've been under the impression that you were going to offer this to them as well."

"That is true. But I offer it to you first. There is some power in being first, is that not true."

"Yes, yes, I suppose it is. I need to confer with my advisors."

Aster stood erect again and seemed to me to be a foot taller. "I will be back tomorrow."

I don't know how many moments had passed in silence. The video camera's lens stared at me and I stared at it. Time chugged by, and I had very little of it to waste. My eyes burned with weariness. Lack of sleep left me worn and too weary to think. I inhaled deeply and let the air out in a slow exhalation. Then I continued.

"At this point, the details no longer matter. The president capitulated. Over the next few days, Aster, with me in attendance, appeared to the heads of state for all the major countries. In each meeting, he promised or delivered something of great value to the people of that nation. In France, he provided plans to improve the recycling of nuclear material from their power reactors. They were already leaders in that field, but Aster gave them technology that would make nuclear waste material usable for things I couldn't begin to understand. To the Russians he gave information that would allow them to better grow and harvest wheat and other crops. To all oil-producing nations, he gave technology to treat oil and gas products so they produced much less pollution. He educated Chinese engineers in ways to power their coal plants while eliminating carbon emissions and the need for carbon sequestration. On and on it went.

"For the most part, I felt useless. At times, Aster would ask about a human custom, the proper way to address a dignitary—advice he routinely ignored—or asked my thoughts on the response of the leaders.

"I fielded questions like, 'Why do the Iranians hate Americans so? The French and the British seem uncomfortable with each other. Why?' I did my best to answer his questions, but I always felt he already knew the answers and that his queries were to give me a sense of involvement.

"I did more than answer the occasional question and formally introduce Aster to presidents and prime ministers; I also set up the meeting between Aster and the heads of the world's pharmaceutical firms. It wasn't easy. Competition in that field is intense, with billions of dollars at stake. Many of the CEOs didn't want to be in the same room as their competitors.

"But Aster insisted. In one case, the CEO of a European drug firm refused to attend. When we arrived at the designated meeting area in Cairo, Aster saw that the man was missing. Then the bubble appeared and Aster was gone. Five minutes later, he was back with the chief exec…still in his robe."

I smiled at the memory despite my lack of joy. Aster was nothing if not insistent.

I continued. "At that meeting, Aster gave—from memory—a brief lecture on malaria, AIDS, and several other global diseases. As in almost every case, someone challenged him. These guys didn't get wealthy and powerful by being timid.

"He said, 'I will give to each of you the cures and preventative chemical structures to eradicate these diseases and more, but you must promise to make these available to the world at large and at a price that can be easily paid by even the poor.'

"An American CEO said, 'That's not how we do business, Mr. Aster. What if we refuse? I don't believe you can force us to comply. We have a duty to our stockholders, and that fiduciary relationship is paramount—'

"Aster looked at me for a second, then said, 'I will give it to the world for free. There are those more noble-minded than you, and they will make these cures available.'

"The exec called Aster's bluff. Aster seemed to sigh and waited for the others to respond. None did. That's when the bubble began to appear. Someone called out, 'Wait!' Aster did, and the deal was done.

"After each trip, I was delivered to my hotel room. I began staying in the suite to stay out of sight of my fellow journalists and the overzealous Aster followers—a group that grew exponentially every day. Having Aster's ship appear overhead every day and the bubble deliver me to my balcony—I became pretty good at crossing the water bridge—undid my secret location. I continued to live in the suite because it was easier to provide security. Debatto Media had hired an executive security firm to guard my door, my floor, and the lobby. It cost them an arm and leg, but I paid for it in other ways—mostly isolation.

"I did have one visitor not on the list of the security firm's approved personnel. He brought his own approval."

After a few weeks in the hotel room, I came to appreciate small, local television stations. The networks were almost completely filled with video, audio, eyewitness accounts, and more, all dealing with Aster, but the local, independent stations, lacking some connections provided by their national counterparts, continued their around-the-clock provision of classic television. Andy of Mayberry was on the set, sitting on the front porch, playing a simple folk song on his guitar and chatting with Barney Fife and Opie. The simple lifestyle appealed to me. I would have given last year's salary for a few days on that front porch, a few minutes of simple folk songs, the amusing antics of Barney, and the gentle wisdom of Andy. But life intervened. Andy Griffith had grown into an elderly man, Don Knotts was dead, and Ron Howard had become a talented Hollywood director.

Still, I could allow myself a few moments of mental displacement and pretend that the country still held a few real Mayberry-like towns. Maybe the time had come to leave the big city behind. Not that my longings mattered. Aster could—and would—find me in Mayberry or any other place on the planet.

The phone rang, something that happened only on occasion. To call me, a person had to be on the approved list.

"Yes."

"Ms. Simms, you have a visitor."

"Who?"

"I shouldn't say on the phone."

Odd. "OK, give me a sec."

I hung up and instinctively glanced around the suite. It looked presentable enough.

My guest turned out to be three. When I opened the door, Governor Merrell, a woman I knew to be his wife, and Martha Merrell were waiting for me.

"Governor, I . . . please come in." I stepped to the side. The threesome entered, and we took seats in the living room. "I'm afraid I don't have much to offer you. I have a few sodas."

"No, thank you, Ms. Simms," Merrell said. "We won't take much of your time."

"Are you sure? I can call room service."

He looked at his wife and daughter. Each declined. The governor cleared his throat. "This is my wife, Emily. You already know Martha.

And of course, I had the pleasure of your acquaintance from...that day."

I studied my guests. Merrell looked concerned, Emily appeared worn, and Martha looked crushed.

"Yes, I remember."

"Ms. Simms—"

"Please call me Priscilla."

Merrell nodded. "Priscilla, no one but my closest advisors know we are here. We would appreciate your keeping this in the strictest confidence."

"Of course," I said.

"I know...we know how busy you have been. Your face appears on television more than the president's. That's saying a lot."

"I'm just a passenger most of the time. Frankly, I don't know why Aster carts me around the way he does."

"Priscilla, we're here about Martha."

I directed my gaze to the woman. Her eyes were fixed on me, but I saw no hope, no life in them. "I hope nothing is wrong."

"Everything is wrong," Emily said. Merrell put a hand on her knee. Tears added a sheen to her eyes.

"Are you ill?" I asked Martha.

"No. I'm dead."

I blinked a few times. "I'm sorry. I don't understand."

"I'm dead."

Merrell slipped an arm around his daughter's shoulders. "Martha has been upset since the incident, and her emotional state is declining."

He said it as if she weren't sitting on the sofa next to him.

"I'm sorry to hear that, but I still don't understand about the dead part."

"You were there," Martha said. "I've seen your video footage. You know that I was as dead as a rock. A chunk of concrete or a steel beam or something caved in my skull."

"True, but you look healed and normal to me." I kept my voice low and soothing. It occurred to me that Aster may have healed her body but not her mind.

212

"I don't dream, Priscilla. What emotions I had have dissolved. I don't feel anything anymore. I used to adore my parents, but I don't feel that anymore. I...I can't describe it. I don't feel the same as I did before the accident."

"Maybe you're still working through the trauma."

"Don't psychoanalyze me." The words were hard and direct, but she didn't snap at me. In fact, her words came across as hollow. I know that makes no sense, but that's how I perceived them. "My parents have retained the best psychiatrists in the state to look at me. They haven't been of any help."

"I'm sorry, but I don't know what to say. I don't see how I can help."

"I want to see Aster." Martha used her best lawyer tone.

Merrell spoke before I could respond. "Martha is right. The specialists—and there have been several of them, not just the psychiatrist—are at a loss. They insist nothing is wrong. We think that Aster might be able to help. We want you to contact him."

I slumped back in my chair. "I don't know how. It doesn't work that way."

"You're the only human he takes with him when he goes bouncing around the globe," Martha said.

"To my knowledge that is true, but I don't contact him. He comes for me. I never know when or where he's going. He just appears where I am then whisks me off."

"But he listens to you, right?" Emily said.

"I wouldn't phrase it that way. I advise him on interacting with humans, but much of it he ignores."

"Are you refusing to help us?" Martha asked.

"That's enough, Martha," Merrell said as if speaking to a ten-year-old.

"That's all right, Governor. I can sense the stress you are under. Being a public figure can't make it any easier." I tried to pull my thoughts together, and then I turned to Martha. "I don't pretend to know how you feel, but I don't see how you can believe you're dead."

Martha shook her head from side to side so many times I thought she was in the beginnings of a seizure. She stopped abruptly. "I can't explain it. I don't feel alive. I'm not depressed. I'm—empty. It's as if my soul is gone but my body remains. Please talk to Aster."

"I will," I promised. "I can't speak for him, but I will certainly tell him about all of this. That's the best I can do."

Merrell stood. Emily and Martha joined him. Emily gave me a hug, Merrell shook my hand, and Martha just stared at me with eyes that seemed emptier than when she arrived.

"Again, if you follow the news—and who doesn't these days—you know what follows. Aster didn't show until five days after my meeting with the governor and his family. But three days after my meeting with the Merrell family, Martha threw herself off a freeway overpass. She had timed it so that an eighteen-wheeler ended her existence and forever changed the life of the driver.

"Emily Merrell had to be institutionalized. Governor Merrell, gutted by the loss of his daughter and the crumbled mind of his wife, resigned and went into seclusion.

"Of course, even before Martha took the fatal plunge, she was already dead. She said so herself."

Chapter Twenty-five

I RETRIEVED A DIET SODA FROM THE REFRIGERATOR IN THE UNDER-
ground lab's rec room. I also found a Snickers bar. I'm not prone to
eating sweets, but I needed the carbs to keep me going. I took a bite
of the candy bar and washed it down with the soda, giving only a
moment's thought to the irony of chasing a mouthful of candy with a
gulp of diet soda. What did it matter? Stranger things went on in the
world—much stranger.

Setting the candy bar and soda on the ping-pong table, I started taping
again.

"The meetings with heads of state continued. Aster met with medical
researchers. There were more who wanted more of Aster's time than
Aster was willing to give. Two U.S. senators even had the temerity to
lead one of their committees to subpoena Aster. I explained the situation to him. He chimed his unusual laugh. That ended the discussion.
Public outcry kept the small group of lawmakers from declaring Aster
in contempt of Congress.

"There are a thousand stories to tell, but I'm trying to confine myself
to just the highlights—or maybe I should say lowlights.

"Two weeks after the governor's visit, I received from Aster two
assignments. First, he would allow himself to be interviewed by representatives from various academic disciplines. The second: he wanted to
'meet the people.' After a few questions, I learned that he had a large
meeting in mind with hundreds of thousands in attendance. I had
no idea how to arrange such things, so I turned to someone who did
know: I called Tim Wacher. I figured, with his connections, he could
make it happen."

I paused and rubbed my hands over my face. Tired. So very tired.

"Forgive me," I said to the camera, "I'm getting things out of order. Before the meeting with the people came the meeting with the leaders—the UN leaders. I told him I didn't know how to arrange that. I should have known that he did. A bubble trip later, Aster and I stood in the Secretary General's office in the UN building in New York. The poor Brazilian man had been so startled that for a moment I thought he'd keel over. Ten minutes later, the date had been set."

On the day of the meeting we arrived just outside the main building, and security escorted us into the lobby. Dr. Paulo Amado, the UN Secretary General, escorted us through the doors and into the massive assembly room.

I said *we* walked into the room. I mean more than just Aster, Dr. Amado, and me. When I had stepped into the bubble a few minutes before, I expected no other travelers, but two others stood waiting for me. Both looked similar to Aster and wore the same linenlike garb. While similar, they did appear different in some ways. Both were shorter than Aster by a good six inches, and their features were sharper and more pronounced. They showed no emotion at seeing me, yet I felt uneasy in their presence. They stared at me too long, following each step I made. I had the impression they were leering.

Until that moment, Aster had always appeared alone, and I had come to think of him as a solitary being. Seeing the others brought me to my senses. Aster's ship was huge. Surely it was home to more than one alien.

Why the other two were there, I couldn't guess. Aster didn't introduce them and they didn't introduce themselves. I said, "Hello," and received only a nod in return. Before I could ask Aster who the other two were, the bubble dissolved and we had made the three-thousand-mile journey to New York and stood at the entrance to the United Nations.

When we crossed the threshold of the assembly room, the delegates and guests stood and applauded. Aster did nothing to acknowledge the welcome; he just followed Amado down the aisle to the platform. I was the caboose of the line. When we reached the platform area, a man in a suit motioned for me to sit in the front row. He looked at the unexpected alien additions and froze. There were no free seats.

I whispered, "Don't worry. They never sit anyway."

Aster followed Amado up the steps and stood to the side as he was introduced.

I had a sense of déjà vu. I had never been in this building before, but the scene seemed familiar. It finally hit me. My father loved old science-fiction movies, the stuff from the fifties and sixties. I don't know how many black-and-white sci-fi flicks I watched, but it was clear they still resided in my memory. In several of those, as well as more contemporary movies, an alien visitor speaks to the UN. I was living through a cliché.

Through his thick Brazilian accent, Amado introduced Aster, the being who "single-handedly was changing the world." More applause. The others—that's how I began to think of the two new beings—bent at the waist in a bow as Aster took his place behind the lectern.

The place buzzed, both from the presence of Aster and the addition of the others.

"Your presence today honors me." He bowed to the crowd. Still more applause.

For some reason, I found myself holding my breath. Aster held the bow for several seconds then straightened to his eight-foot height. No matter how many times I'd seen him—and I'd seen him more than any human—he impressed me.

He continued. "I have been among your people for many months now and observed you for years before that. I have been aided by Priscilla Simms, who has been a friend and advisor."

He looked my direction and paused. I stood and gave a polite bow and wave to the audience. As I did so, I noticed the cameras at the back of the room. I wondered if all this was being broadcast live. Turning to Aster, I nodded then sat. The others stared at me again. Their gaze unsettled me.

"In our time together, I have made myself aware of your history. The United States president Ronald Reagan stood in this room and spoke of a force that could unify your world. He suggested that a threat from the outside, like a force of aliens, might force warring countries to get along." He paused and for a half second I thought he might have just threatened the world.

"President Reagan's idea is interesting but unnecessary. Countries can achieve peace by choice and without the threat of mutual destruction."

That brought applause.

He raised a hand. "Peace is the right of every evolved species. Your evolution has led you from primordial seas to land and from land to trees. Then, when your ancestors left the trees and became social monkeys, society began. By working together, they survived and evolution continued its course. Today, those social monkeys have become intelligent creators."

Again, applause. I didn't join the ovation. My stomach burned and my spine chilled.

"We have come to remind you that your future is your choice. I have given to your world new technology that will alleviate the global warming that is leading to climate change. Your world is sick with such poisoning. In the next few years, if you as leaders utilize the technology I freely give, then you shall see improvement around the globe.

Over the months, I had noticed Aster's speech had become more fluid and natural, less stiff. I should have expected that a being as intelligent as Aster would continue to learn. For some reason, that made me even more uncomfortable. I know the power of words. I have spent my life using them, and I recognized the sway Aster had over the gathering. I was as quick to see what effect they were having on me.

"I have bestowed upon your race a way to eradicate some of the worse diseases, like malaria and AIDS. I am capable of helping with many other threats to human life, such as cancer. It is my hope to give to you biological knowledge to double your life span."

He paused to let the audience respond, which it did with gasps and then a wave of clapping.

"Poverty is curable. Genetic disorders can be managed and treated. What I have given, I have given without cost or obligation. But one problem remains. The human race has ceased to evolve. You are bound by fear. You mark off territories to keep others out and label them immigrants even though they share the same planet. You create businesses that must destroy other businesses to succeed. Your executives love investors over consumers and themselves over investors. You create situations that create crime, then punish those who are the natural outcome of your own creation."

I noticed that no one applauded.

"Your science has become competitive instead of cooperative. You elect leaders who show the greatest skill at lying or who have the most money, not based on their ability to further humankind's growth.

"And worse, you still allow artificial and contrived belief systems to flourish, blinding young minds and deceiving the thoughts of the elderly.

"Call these systems what you will: Christianity, Buddhism, Hinduism, Islam, and all the variations. This makes no sense to my kind, those of us who have traveled the road of evolution longer and farther." He shook his head. "I have observed your sports and notice that when a swimmer competes, he does not first tie a weight to his feet; when a runner enters a race, she does not first chain her feet together. Such actions would be foolish, yet the human race has shackled its mind and creative spirit with myths and stories that have long outlived their usefulness in the evolutionary process."

He spoke softly, but his words struck me the way a dart hits a dartboard. I pushed my emotions to the side, deciding that I would think on these things later. Some thoughts, however, refused to be pushed. I told myself what he said couldn't be true. Could it? For a moment, I wondered what Aster would do if I walked away.

I should've walked away.

I didn't.

"I have come as your friend. I speak to you as your brother. My people long to call you neighbor, but your infighting fueled by religion and greed hold us at arm's length.

"We have much to learn from one another. My people can enrich your world in ways too lengthy to mention here and beyond your imagination. In return, we get friends and the great satisfaction of helping yet another race further its path of evolution." He folded his hands and set them on the lectern, which looked dainty and tiny in front of him.

"I have been asked by my leaders to encourage you to strip away old habits that hamper your progress, to free yourself from old ways of thinking and to embrace the light of the future. We can help you do this.

"It is not our desire to control your thoughts. We would not do so even if we could. Your history is rich with the accounts of well-meaning humans like Buddha and Jesus. Honor their memory and their contribution to evolution, but do not fail to realize that ancient stories do not open the door to the future."

Aster lowered his head as if sad. "I have spoken to my leaders and told them of all that I have given so far and have received their blessing and praise. I have more to give. Much more. If you will allow me, I will give knowledge that will increase food production tenfold. I will show you how to harvest your oil and coal and use it in a manner that will not harm the planet for your children. I will also give technology that will make oil and coal obsolete before those resources become too scarce to use.

"To my right is Tanra. In our world, he is the leading medical scientist. We have very little illness, and our lifespan is over two hundred of your years. He can teach you methods of extending every life on the planet by one hundred years or more. He can show you how to heal the children in your hospital so they can lead normal and very long lives. No child needs to die of leukemia or any other disease. He can do all that and more, and still show you how your doctors today can continue to have meaningful and satisfying careers. They will still be needed.

"To my left is Geel. In our world he is what you would call an engineer or maybe an architect. He has volunteered to work with your world's engineers to guarantee every human a worthwhile home and to create buildings that are almost alive.

"This and much more is yours."

By now the crowd was on its feet, but only for a moment. Aster motioned for them to sit.

"Please. Your response is humbling, but there is something you should know. My leaders fear that your adherence to old ways of thinking might lead you to be irresponsible with this new technology. I am not allowed to give any more than I have already until we know that your intentions are set only on the betterment of humankind as a whole. By giving you these things, we know that we become at least partially responsible for your actions with them. When your scientists like Einstein and Oppenheimer gave you nuclear power, you killed others with it. Even today, you teeter on oblivion.

"When your scientists gave you an understanding of biology, you made weapons out of it. This must stop. If not, we will leave, never to return. We can make transportation almost instant, communication faultless, space travel ordinary, and do it all through existing and new businesses. No one suffers; no one loses. But you must change."

I glanced around the room. Every eye was fixed on Aster. It seemed I was the only one who didn't want to look at him. Still, when I thought of all he offered...when I recalled all I had seen...

"Are you ready to evolve to the next level of existence, to a place free of disease and where every human has value? Are you ready for a world with long life and no mental illness? If so, then we will help you. If not, we will leave. The choice is yours.

"Give up your battles. Give up your myths. Embrace your evolutionary future."

Aster stepped back from the podium.

The crowd rose as one. I couldn't see every seat, but I suspected I was the only person still seated. My knees were too weak to stand. I wondered where the ladies' room was—I needed to vomit.

I glanced up to the podium. Aster bowed to the audience several times. The other called Geel stared at me, and for a moment I felt as if he were reading my thoughts—and worse, my soul.

Chapter Twenty-six

HAD A MILLION QUESTIONS FOR ASTER. My mind was as frenetic as a beehive. As soon as we left the assembly building, I planned to press Aster about his comments.

We exited up the same aisle we entered and in the same order. Once in the lobby I tried to position myself next to Aster. Geel stepped between us, and the air around me took on an arctic quality.

Just as I started to call Aster's name, Dr. Amado stopped the procession, turned, and asked him, "There are several people who've asked permission to speak with you. I wonder if you could spare a few moments to answer their questions."

Aster studied the man, then said, "People? What kind of people?"

"They are scientists, philosophers, and theologians from around the world. I know this was not part of our original arrangement, but we would consider it an honor to be able to spend a few more moments with you."

Aster glanced my way. I shrugged. I expected him to look at his newly arrived cohorts, but he didn't. Instead, he said to Amado, "It would be my honor."

Amado led us from the lobby and down a hall, all the time surrounded by security. At the end of the long corridor, we passed through a door and found what looked like a briefing room. Tables were arranged in a horseshoe fashion with a chair in the center. Amado motioned for Aster to take the chair, but as usual he refused to sit. Instead, he stood behind the chair, his hands folded near his abdomen. I also noticed a man with a broadcast-quality video camera standing at the back of the room. Another stood at the front, making it a two-camera shoot.

When we first entered, the other chairs were empty, but they were immediately filled by thirty eager questioners. They were a mix of men and women, each dressed nicely for the event. Amado introduced each one, then made some opening remarks. Present was an astrophysicist, a medical researcher, a geneticist, an American politician, a representative from the British Crown, the delegate from China who also held a PhD in history, and a theologian from Harvard. I can't remember the names of the specialties of the others. I was still reeling from the speech.

During the talk, several questions struck me—not so much the questions themselves, but Aster's answers. One set came from the astronomers. Several wanted to know what star system Aster hailed from. A fair question, I thought, but Aster refused to be specific.

"My home world is many light-years from anything you know."

"Can you tell what area of the sky we should study to find your world?" This question came from the astrophysicist.

Aster answered, "Yes, but I won't."

When asked why, he simply said, "Your technology is insufficient to detect my origin. It would be a waste of time."

That didn't satisfy the scientists in the room. Several similar questions were asked, but Aster sidestepped them all. The biologist wanted to know everything from reproduction to Aster's offer to cure major diseases.

"It would be inappropriate to answer in detail."

"Why?" As I recall, the man was a biochemist at MIT.

"The introduction of technology into a society without proper control can create more problems than it solves. It has happened in your own history. One race steals control of land from indigenous inhabitants and the evolutionary pace becomes disrupted. Those who control the technology control the people. If my people give our technology too quickly, your economic systems will crumble and the world will have larger problems. I came that your people might have life and have it in abundance."

His words rang a familiar note with me. It also caught the attention of the Princeton theologian. "Excuse me. Those words are very much like those spoken by Jesus: 'I came that they may have life, and have it abundantly.' Are you quoting Jesus?"

"No, of course not. The old traditions should be set aside."

The theologian pressed the issue. "Christians have been following Christ for two thousand years."

Aster shook his head. "You are mistaken. Christians have been following Jesus's teachings for two thousand years. I am certain you can discern the difference. I am familiar with the teachings of Jesus. Many of His words were good and true. His intent has been useful to your development."

The word *Jesus* seemed unnatural coming from Aster's mouth. I can't tell you why. It just did.

The theologian had to speak quickly to keep other participants from redirecting the discussion down another path. "You say some of his words were good and true. Are you saying that some were *not* good and true?"

"All beings are subject to error," Aster said smoothly. "It is why we need each other. Self-correction is not always enough. We need friends to help us see what we are blind to. Jesus taught of love and commitment to one another. Those are good and noble thoughts. You should learn from them, but his...I need a word...spiritual, yes, spiritual teaching was—imaginative."

"An interesting choice of words. Are you saying that Jesus's teaching about heaven and hell, about God being spirit, about—"

"Well-meant myths told to meet the needs of his day. There is no hell. There is another level of existence beyond the physical. After biological death, the conscious continues. Our scientists have been able to look into that dimension."

"You've seen heaven?"

"Heaven is not what your religious leaders teach. Consciousness continues on another existence level."

"And the resurrection?"

Aster's odd laugh echoed in the room. "We live a very long time by your standards. I myself am one hundred fifty years old by your calendar and am still considered in my middle years. The day will come, however, when my flesh will no longer contain life. My consciousness will move on, but my body will decay. It is the way of all life."

"You're saying that Jesus could not have risen bodily from the dead?"

"Your myth is that his body remained in a tomb for three days, true?"

The theologian said yes.

"Decomposition, cellular breakdown, and loss of energy from every cell would make such resuscitation impossible. If you must believe in a resurrection, then believe that his consciousness ascended to the next level."

The theologian laughed. "I've been teaching that for years."

The man might have thought the revelation humorous, but it sickened me.

Other questions were asked. Scores of them—maybe hundreds. I don't know. I could no longer concentrate and couldn't retain what I was hearing.

I rose from my seat and slipped from the room. I don't know if Aster or his pals saw me and I didn't care. I needed fresh air, different air.

I had walked into that room as a Christian and walked out a doubter.

Once home again, once left to myself and away from the unblinking eye of the camera and the soul-stripping gaze of the aliens, I wept.

I wept for the loss of my faith.

Chapter Twenty-seven

A SOFT, METALLIC POP WOKE ME FROM MY STUPOR. The soda can in my hand bore the bends and dents of my abuse. I raised my eyes to the patient video camera waiting for me to continue.

"I'd be lying if I said it didn't depress me. To think that everything I had come to believe was a lie. My commitment and my faith crumbled like dry bread. It wasn't just me. Some pastors led their churches to close their doors, sell their property, and give the proceeds to 'more worthy' nonprofit organizations. In some parts of the world, others responded negatively, even violently. Feeling cheated and deceived, they burned churches to the ground and killed clergy. Members who had given money over the years now wanted those tithes and offerings back and leveled thousands of lawsuits against churches. Parachurch organizations folded within months.

"There were those, of course, who tried to argue against what Aster had taught. Conservative theologians, priests, and pastors railed against the heresy, but their numbers were too few and their support too little.

"It was no surprise to me that atheist groups and some scientists, humanists, and others who had battled the church for so long found a new and willing market. Aster spoke softly in sentences that were sometimes awkward, but all that did was lend credibility to the man from outer space. Always consistent, always sincere, he became the poster child for unbelief. Humanity had learned to argue with itself, but we seemed unwilling to argue with someone from a distant planet.

"I became a Christian a good number of years ago. Prior to that, the church had never been my home. Brought up by loving parents, they were nonetheless skeptics, and that skepticism rubbed off on me. Only

226

after an unusual set of circumstances and the testimony of a pastor named Adam Bridger did I see the truth and power of the gospel. Not once in my fifteen-year journey as a Christian did I doubt. Not once did I waver. Bible study, worship, and prayer had become as much a part of me as eating and sleeping. Church was a refuge, a place to recharge my spiritual batteries, to connect with other believers, and most of all to connect with God.

"Aster killed that, murdering my belief and my hope. I try to comfort myself by saying that it was all for the best, that the truth was always better than myth. I put away my Bible, and my morning routine of prayer ended. There was no sense in praying to a God who did not exist, no wisdom in trusting a savior who was just a man.

"Oddly, there seemed to be great joy about Aster's announcement. Hearing that we were moving along the evolutionary path and that that road led to better and more positive things—to longer life, better technology, the end of life-endangering disease—blanketed the country and much of the world in euphoria. But it was not all joy and celebration in the streets. Within a few weeks, word began to circulate in the media that the number of suicides had increased dramatically, as had admissions to mental institutions.

"As for me, my depression deepened. I made several more journeys with Aster, and each time—in an effort to keep the mortar of my already-crumbling faith from eroding any more than it had—I tried to press him for more information, tried to challenge him about his opinions of Jesus, but he always sidestepped them. It became clear he had no patience for spiritual matters, no tolerance for faith. So I argued with him in my mind, laid out reason upon reason, point upon point, as to why he was in error, but I couldn't get my mind to cooperate. Over the years, I had read the Bible, but it had become clear to me that I had failed to study it. It had become for me the book of solace, a text of wisdom, a history book, a source of strength when I felt weak. What I had not let it become was the knowledge of my heart and soul, the book of evidence, the proof of the truth of God. I felt miserably stupid, a new sensation for me. Until then I felt I was smart and resourceful. Now I felt ill-equipped to deal with the challenges that lay before me.

"Lizzy made countless attempts to reach me. She called my cell phone. She left messages on my answering service. She called the hotel repeatedly, but I rebuffed my friend's every effort. I couldn't face her. I couldn't tell her that I had been shaken to the core and that the faith I had held so dear and for so long was dwindling to a cold, lifeless ember.

"Three weeks after the UN speech, my cell phone rang. Caller ID told me it was Lizzy. I didn't answer. It sounded a short and shrill phrase from Beethoven's Ninth, and I tried to drive the sound of it from my ears. It stopped. Ten minutes later, I dialed for my messages, of which there were several, but I focused on the one from Lizzy.

"She got right to the point. 'Priscilla, it's Lizzy, but I suspect you already know that. You've been avoiding me. It's time we got together, and I'm not asking. I'm stating it as a fact. So, here's what's going to happen, girl. I will be in the hotel on your floor at 3:10 this afternoon. I know you have security to keep riffraff like me away, but I'm coming anyway and we're going to talk. So if you hear a scuffle outside your door, you can decide whether to let me in or let them haul me off in handcuffs. It's your call, Priscilla. I'm your best friend, and you know I love you, and you also know we need to talk. I know there is a chance that you'll be cruising around the globe with Aster, but I'm coming anyway. I'll just have to take the chance. It's the only way I'll get to see you.'

"She wasn't kidding."

I heard voices just outside the door. Two men were arguing with a female. I stepped to the door of my hotel room and peered out the peephole. What I saw was what I expected. True to her word, Lizzy had arrived at precisely ten minutes after three and engaged the two security guards situated in the hall. I knew there were other security agents assigned to my protection in various places of the hotel; they would descend upon Lizzy in a matter of moments. I had a decision to make.

I listened for a moment, then turned my back on the door with the intent of walking to the window, gazing at the skyline, and forcing from my mind the mental image of the confrontation a few feet behind me.

"Ow!"

"Miss, you can't be on this floor."

The first voice belonged to Lizzy, the second to one of the two security guards I'd exchanged pleasantries with on numerous occasions. He was tall, he was broad, and I had never seen him smile. Their voices came through the door clear enough for me to hear every syllable.

"Back off, thug." Lizzy sounded hot. "Priscilla knows I'm coming; just tell her that I'm here."

"I'm sorry ma'am, but you're not on the approved list."

"I should be."

Those three words were like arrows in my back; the pain of them ran through my mind and my heart. Lizzy had been my closest friend, my confidant, the one with whom I went to church and sang praise songs and hymns. She was my Bible study teacher. She was my coffee-drinking buddy. In all the years that I had known her, she had always been there for me, and now I stood with my back to the door, trying to forget that I ever knew her.

I couldn't do it.

I returned to the door, turned the knob, and swung it open. The bruiser of a security guard, the one with no sense of humor, held Lizzy's wrists. The other guard was on his radio, calling in reinforcements or maybe the police.

"Lizzy! It's great to see you." I wouldn't have admitted it at the time, but the sight of her gave me more joy than I imagined possible. "What...what is going on here?"

"I'm sorry, Ms. Simms, she's not on the approved visitor's list." He seemed stunned to see me at the door.

"I suggest you let go of her right now." I tried to sound angry. "This is my good friend Lizzy Svoboda, and I won't have her manhandled."

"I'm sorry, Ms. Simms, but I'm just doing my job and following my orders."

"I know that, and I appreciate it, but I would also appreciate it if you'd listen to me—let go of my friend."

He exchanged glances with his partner and then did as I asked. I thanked him and invited Lizzy in, closing the door behind us. I led her from the door, through a small corridor, and into the living-room section of the expansive suite. I then offered her a seat at the round oak table situated near the sliding glass doors that led to the balcony.

I began with a simple question: "Have you lost your senses, Lizzy?"

"One of us has." The phrase was hot and sharp, and it cut deep into my emotions. "You've been avoiding me. If we were husband and wife, I would've expected divorce papers by now."

"Oh, stop acting like a jilted bride. Everything has changed; the world has changed; *I've* changed. I can't think of anything that hasn't changed." For some reason I felt like crying, and when I feel that way I become combative.

"I can think of a few things that haven't changed, but it's clear that our friendship has."

I shook my head and turned my gaze from her to the view outside the window. She looked hurt and fragile, like a china doll, and the sight of her caused me even more pain. "Now you're just being dramatic. Our friendship is the same as it's always been."

Lizzy began to laugh, and it made me angry.

"I don't see what's so funny. Care to enlighten me?"

"We're having our first fight." She spoke the next words softly. "I never thought it could happen."

That was one straw too many. The dam I had been using to hold back the mounting waters of frustration, fear, uncertainty, and loneliness gave way. It began with a tear, then two, and then sobs came. I wept as quietly as I could, fearful that the guards at the door would think Lizzy had done something to me and come bursting into the suite.

Lizzy said nothing. She offered no hollow words, no useless phrases, no meaningless encouragement. She just let me cry for a while. I shuddered and shook; I sobbed and moaned. The release of months of pent-up emotions in me made me feel lighter and cleaner. When the waterworks ceased, I looked up and saw the serene face of my longtime friend. Her smile said our friendship was still intact.

"Oh, Lizzy, I owe you such a big apology. I owe you a hundred apologies and a thousand explanations. I never meant to cut you out."

"Then why did you, Priscilla?"

I hadn't expected her to be so blunt. I shrugged and stood, retrieved a box of tissues from the coffee table, and returned to my seat. I blew my nose—loudly. "I don't know...actually, I do know. I was afraid."

"Afraid of what?"

"Afraid of your disapproval. Afraid I would have to explain my involvement in something I don't want to be involved in. Afraid I would have to admit my fear."

She leaned forward and placed a hand on my arm. "You never have to be afraid of me, Priscilla. There are, however, many other things to fear."

"I take it you're still not a big Aster fan."

"That's putting it mildly. But first tell me how you're doing."

"Just look at me. I'm doing great. I'm one of the most famous people in the world. I can't walk down the street without being recognized. My face has been on every television station and in every newspaper and magazine. Debatto Media has been paying me an obscene salary, far more than I could get anywhere else. I have everything I want: fine food, fine lodging, and all the loneliness a girl could ask for." I blew my nose again. "I'm living every girl's dream."

"Maybe it's just me, but I'm detecting a wee bit of sarcasm here."

"And here I thought I was being so sincere."

"That's one of the things I love about you, Priscilla: your sincerity. Did you know that *sincerity* comes from the Latin meaning 'without wax'?"

"What?"

My confusion gave Lizzy a reason to grin. "And you call yourself a journalist. *Sincere* comes from a compound Latin word meaning 'without wax.' In the days of Rome, sculpting was a big business. Everyone wanted a statue of some god or another in their home. But like anything that is hand-manufactured, imperfections would some-times appear in the marble. Sometimes the sculptor just made a mistake, other times the material was faulty. Less scrupulous sculptors would mix marble powder with wax and fill cracks with it. The more noble sculptors would hang a sign over their shop that read *sine cere*—without wax."

I blinked several times before responding. "Only you would know an obscure piece of trivia like that."

"Endearing, ain't it? And aren't you glad I appreciate your waxlessness?"

That made me laugh, which I'm sure was her point. Her tone turned serious. "Back to the question. Dish it. I'm not leaving until you open up."

I knew there was no joking or cajoling my way out of an answer. "I'm lousy. I'm lost, adrift, and more confused than I can explain. A year and a half ago, I thought the worst thing that happened to me was the earthquake. For several very long moments there, I thought I would fall through the broken window to the street below, riding my desk all the way. The other night I caught myself wishing I had." I shook my head and fought back more tears.

"At what point did it all turn bad for you?" Her words were soft and fluid, devoid of any condemnation or superiority.

"I've never been comfortable with any of this. Oh, at first I was impressed with Aster; and being one of the first humans to meet an alien from another planet, well, that's every reporter's dream." I paused, allowing my mind to skip back through the months to that first day, the first moment the world learned we were not alone. "To this day, Lizzy, I can feel his touch and the electricity it sent through me. I was fearful and thrilled all at the same time. Then to be chosen to help him deliver his message, to see inside his transportation bubble, see the world as no human has seen it—that was an honor that could not be ignored."

"Your feelings have changed?"

I broke eye contact and nodded. "Yes, I think so."

"You *think* so?"

"What do you want me to say?" I snapped.

"Just the truth. You *think* your feelings have changed, or you *know* they have changed?"

"They've changed."

"I bet I can tell you when they changed, but I'd rather hear from you." She leaned back in her chair.

"You want something from room service? They treat me quite well here."

She pressed her lips together. "Will they bring me a straight answer?"

I sighed. "Everything changed after the UN speech and especially after the group interview."

This time Lizzy looked off into the distance. "I saw the news reports. Very disturbing. Why did things change for you then?"

"You know why."

"You're right, Priscilla, I do know why, but I want *you* to know why."

"I'm not stupid, Lizzy. Everything he said about faith, everything he said about Jesus, struck me like hammer blows. I'd been so full of faith and love for the Lord, and Aster came along and crushed it all."

"You blame Aster for your loss of faith? That's pretty narrow thinking."

"Is it? Who do you suggest I blame?" I leaned back in my chair, not to be comfortable, but to put more distance between us. I didn't like where she was going.

"I blame you."

"Well, isn't this great. Just what I need—more guilt. I'm not the one who called Jesus a myth. Aster did that. He's the one that's convinced the world that Jesus was just a man, albeit a well-intentioned one. I don't see how you can blame me"

"Tell me, have you ever received those spam e-mails from Nigeria? The ones that say they need help from someone in the United States to cash a monstrous check and whoever helps them will receive a payback in the tens of thousands of dollars?"

That came out of nowhere. "I think everyone with e-mail has received that at some time. What does that have to do with our conversation?"

"If I told you that I received one of those letters and that I responded to it and paid all the fees they asked me to, whose fault would you say it is that I got took?"

I didn't answer.

"I see the cat has your tongue. Let me answer for you. You'd blame me, and you'd be right. I can understand someone who is confused being taken in by such a fraud. I can understand someone greedy beyond control being taken advantage of, but I can't understand anyone with a minimal amount of common sense believing such a cockamamy pitch."

"You're saying I'm the one responsible for what Aster says?"

"Not at all. I'm saying you're responsible for *believing* what Aster says."

The balloon of my indignation popped. I knew exactly what she was getting at, and no matter how much I wanted to argue against it, her logic was spot-on. "I don't want to say any more. My faith has been stripped away from me."

"Priscilla, for being one of the smartest women I know, you sure are a goof. No one can strip away your faith. It's yours to keep, and it's yours to give away. Everything that Aster has said is a lie. You know that in your heart. You know that in your mind. And you know that in your soul. Do you know why you feel so bad?"

"I've given you a few ideas."

"It's called conviction, Priscilla. Every believer has the Holy Spirit living in her. When one of the faithful begins to wander, the Holy Spirit convicts them of their sin. The Holy Spirit serves like an alarm. He warns us of trouble; He warns us when we face lies and subterfuge on spiritual issues. Priscilla, what you're feeling is not confusion; it's a lack of peace. When we walk in faith, we have a sense of peace. Sometimes we get too used to it, so much so that we don't even notice it. But when that peace goes missing, there's no ignoring it. Inner turmoil replaces the peace we once had, and we feel like, well, like you're feeling now."

"So you're saying the Holy Spirit has left me." That didn't make me feel any better.

"Nonsense. The Holy Spirit doesn't leave believers, but believers can stop listening to Him. Personally, you know in your heart of hearts that Christ is just as real and as true as He has ever been. Simply because a man, or something appearing like a man, says that everything we believe in is nonsense doesn't make it so. Let me say it again: Aster is a liar."

"But he's been so convincing, so believable. He promised a cure for malaria, and all the early tests show that it's highly effective. Countries without the strict FDA testing requirement are already using it in the field with remarkable results. Some experts are predicting a complete eradication of the disease.

"And the information he gave to agricultural scientists has been tested and is yielding the results he promised. He warned us about global warming and climate change and gave us the means to prove the problem really exists and quiet the skeptics. I can go on for an hour with examples, Lizzy. Everything else he has said has been true."

She leaned forward again. "I didn't say he was a *lousy* liar. In fact, he's one of the best there's ever been. But the quality of the lie doesn't make it true—a lie remains a lie." She frowned. "Have you ever owned a dog?"

"What's that got to do with anything?"

"I'm trying to make a point here. Have you ever owned a dog?"

"Not recently, no. We had one when I was a child. A cocker spaniel."

"Did you or your parents ever have to give the dog a pill?"

"Well, sure. She scratched her leg on the fence and it became infected. The veterinarian gave us a bottle of antibiotics and we had to medicate her twice a day. I was only eight or nine years old, but I remember that the dog hated the pills."

"I'm guessing you tried different ways to get the dog to take the pill." She kept her eyes fixed on me as if analyzing every response, reading every thought.

"I remember Dad hiding the pill in a small piece of hotdog. That worked well."

"Let me teach you how to tell a lie and have people believe it."

I raised an eyebrow. "Doesn't that pretty much come naturally to everyone?"

"Not the big lies. The bigger the lie, the more difficult it is to believe. The best way to tell a lie is to start with the truth. Tell one truth, make another truthful statement, offer another factual opinion, then slip in the lie. It's similar to what your dad did with your dog. The dog doesn't want the pill; she wants the hotdog. Every time you gave her the treat in the past she enjoyed it, so she wouldn't be suspicious when you offered her one with a pill inside."

"You're telling me that Aster has been hiding a lie in all the goodness he's done."

"That is exactly what I'm telling you. If you do enough good for people, they will forgive you for doing wrong. If you tell enough truth, people will trust you when you lie. What Aster said and showed you about climate change, global diseases, our ability to overcome global poverty, and all the rest of it is true. Everything he said about Jesus is false."

"Lizzy, I try to come up with all the arguments against what he said, but I keep coming up blank."

"There's so much for you to learn, but you know enough. Your faith isn't gone; it's just sequestered. It's time you free it. God has not changed, but you have. The good news is there is always a way home."

Something began to stir within me, something I had not felt for a very long time. The tears began to flow again.

"Priscilla, I can't let you go through this alone. I'm here for you. I will always be here for you."

I started to say something when a movement outside the balcony caught my attention.

Aster's bubble was descending.

"Uh-oh."

Lizzy directed her attention out the sliding glass door and over the balcony railing at the descending aqua-bubble. "I take it you weren't expecting him."

"Not this early. It appears I may be cutting our visit short." I rose from the chair. "I'll walk you to the door and let the guards know that I'm leaving."

Lizzy pushed her chair back and stood. I rounded the table, gave her a hug, and started toward the door. I walked halfway down the corridor when I heard the sound of the sliding-glass door opening. Turning, I saw that Lizzy had not followed me but had moved to the balcony and opened the door. "Lizzy?"

She didn't respond. I moved quickly down the hall toward Lizzy, who had already stepped onto the balcony. Aster's bubble hovered as it always had, several feet away from the balcony edge. By the time I stepped from the suite, the cat-eye-like aperture opened and Aster stood looking back.

Lizzy showed no fear. She stood there staring into the opening and into Aster's eyes. The water bridge had already begun to extend from bubble to balcony, but halfway across it stopped.

"Lizzy? What are you doing?"

She didn't answer; her eyes seemed glued to the alien. Then something I didn't expect happened: the water bridge that I had crossed so many times before retracted as if Aster were afraid that Lizzy would make use of it. The bubble's opening closed and the sphere shot skyward.

"Do you mind telling me what just happened, Lizzy?"

"I should go," she said abruptly. "He was here to take you to Mojave, wasn't he?"

"Yes. Tonight's the big rally, the meet-the-people event."

"Then we don't have much time. "

That puzzled me. "Much time for what?"

"Do you trust me, Priscilla?"

"You know that I do." The question hurt me, but after avoiding her for so long, I could understand her doubts.

"Then here's the deal: I need you to trust me now more than ever. I want you to come with me."

"Where?"

"Do you remember our last conversation, the last time we talked before you went into isolation?"

I remembered it well. "Yes. I was upset at Leo's death, and I called you. As I recall, I told you everything."

She stepped back into the suite and I followed. "You told me about a file that Leo had given you. Do you still have it?"

"Of course. Why?"

"Bring it. You also told me about a man named Allen Sloan, right?"

"Yes."

"I've been doing a lot of research. I'll fill you in."

"What about Aster? I'm supposed to go with him to the Mojave Desert for this rally."

"It's time you stopped worrying about Aster; it's time you started worrying about yourself. You'll get there. I'll drive you if I have to. It's only a few hours, and I was planning on being there anyway."

"You were?"

"It's best that we go now."

Two minutes later, we walked out the door of the suite.

Chapter Twenty-eight

THE LAST TIME I SAW ALLEN SLOAN HE WAS HUNCHED OVER A walker, dressed in a greenish hospital gown, and looking so thin and frail I feared he would break in half if something bumped him. The man I was looking at now looked nothing like that. He wore a dark blue, pinstripe suit, a white shirt, and a bright gold tie. Over the intervening months, he had gained at least thirty much-needed pounds. His face was full, and his head supported a full shock of dark brown hair.

The environment was different, too. When we first met, it was in the CCU waiting lobby of San Diego Regional Hospital. This time I was seated in the conversation area of a well-appointed office in a mid-rise building of Kearney Mesa. Lizzy had driven, and as we pulled into the parking lot I read the sign identifying the building: DigiTV. I recognized the name, and I should have—I'd been using their service for years. DigiTV is the nation's third largest satellite television provider. Over the last five years, it had made great inroads as one of the toughest businesses on the planet. When we first entered the building, I expected to find Allen Sloan in the technical department or perhaps marketing. I didn't expect to see the word PRESIDENT emblazoned on his office door.

"It's been a long time, Ms. Simms." He sat in an overstuffed, brown leather chair, his feet on a matching ottoman.

"Well over a year," I said. "Honestly, I never imagined we'd meet again."

He smiled and nodded at Lizzy. "I suppose we have your friend to thank for that. And by the way, from everything I can see she's a great friend to have."

At first I thought he was hitting on Lizzy but then dismissed the idea. He seemed far too serious.

"You seem well," I said.

"And God is good. It's been a long haul; I won't deny that. There were times in therapy when returning to the coma looked good, but one day at a time, one step at a time got me back on track. That and a great deal of prayer."

"When we first met, I didn't realize you were a Christian."

"We didn't have much time together. We were interrupted. You might remember the nurse that tracked me down."

"I remember. She didn't look very pleased with you."

He laughed. "There were quite a few nurses who were not pleased with me. I tend to be a bit of a maverick and prefer to make all my own decisions. Medical staff prefer to make decisions for you. Anyway, for me, faith came later."

I looked around the office. The furnishings were rich and stylish, the kind of thing an interior decorator with an unlimited budget might buy. The walls were bright but bare of any artwork. Creative lighting cast streams of undulating illumination off the white surfaces. His desk, small bookshelf, state-of-the-art computer system, and the decor shouted high tech. Only the two sofas and two overstuffed chairs of dark leather hearkened back to pre-tech days.

"From coma to president of a major firm in a year and a half is quite some achievement."

He raised a finger as if correcting a child. "I'm afraid you're mistaken, Ms. Simms. I was president and CEO of this firm before my accident. It's one reason I was still in the hospital instead of being shipped off to some nursing-care facility. In this world, money still talks, and my board of directors did everything they could to take care of me. I'm thankful for that. When I spoke to you last, I wasn't certain I had a home or anything left of my life before the accident. Turns out, I had it all—all except my family."

I asked him to call me Priscilla and apologized for my assumption. Before he could speak again, the door to his office opened and a woman entered carrying a tray of coffee. She placed it on a small table between the two sofas and then left, closing the door behind her.

Sloan removed his feet from the ottoman, rose, poured coffee into the cups, and in a very gentlemen-like manner presented a cup to Lizzy and me. He took his cup and saucer, returned to his chair, took a sip, then set the cup and saucer on the ottoman. The chair in which he sat had a small pouch attached to the left arm from which he removed a remote control and punched a button. Music from Vivaldi's *Four Seasons* filled the spacious room. He raised the volume, then leaned forward.

"I apologize for the additional noise. Working in a high-tech business as I do, I've learned to be very paranoid about unwanted listening devices. Experts sweep my office for electronic bugs at least once a week. This is a highly competitive business, and if I'm not careful others may glean secrets that will cost my investors a great deal of money."

"I don't understand," I said. "If you know there are no listening devices in the office..."

"It's the windows," he replied. "There are a whole host of devices that allow corporate spies to listen to a conversation by picking up the vibration off the windows. In fact, I must ask a favor of you. I need you to turn your cell phone off."

"My cell phone?"

He nodded. "We had an incident not long ago in which one of our executive's cell phone was activated remotely while he was in an important meeting. Everything in that meeting was broadcast to an industrial spy. Technology is a wonderful thing, but it can also be used against us." He paused, then asked, "Do you think I'm paranoid?"

"After all I've seen lately, I wouldn't call anyone paranoid." I decided it was time to get down to business. "I'm still at a loss as to why I'm here. Lizzy told me you had a story to tell."

"I know that your time is short, so I'll give you the *Reader's Digest* version. It was about two years ago when I was in an auto accident. The truth is that I don't remember much about the accident itself. They say that's common. The accident left me in a coma but killed my wife and child, something I didn't know until I came out of the deep sleep. You remember me telling this to you before?"

"Yes, I remember."

"Not a day goes by that I don't miss them, and not an hour goes by that I don't wish they were here. But missing them and wishing for them doesn't change the fact, and I've come to accept that. For our purposes today, it doesn't really matter. All you need to know is what happened while I was in the coma. I lay in a coma for months, and I don't know how it is for other victims but for me was a very difficult time. I saw things. I experienced things. Much of it has faded like a dream does once the morning comes, but some of it will be with me forever."

He looked into his coffee cup as if drawing strength from the dark fluid or as if he would find his next words floating in there.

"I regained consciousness on the very same day that Aster appeared. In fact, I woke up screaming that he was here. You can check with my doctor, Dennis DeGuere, and he'll verify this part. The medical records show that I came to shortly after the earthquake but prior to Aster's arrival. Yet somehow I knew he was here."

"How could you know that?"

"I don't have all the answers, but I know beyond a doubt that he had arrived, and it filled me with terror. They had to restrain me." He pushed back in the chair. "Like I said, most of what I saw while in the coma has disappeared, but I remember enough to recognize Aster. I saw him. I saw him countless times, and every time I did I was terrified."

"What do you mean, you saw him? You saw him while you were in the coma? Like a person dreams?"

"It was in some context. I remember an all-green landscape. The hills in the distance, the ground beneath my feet, even the sky above was some shade of green. I was there alone. To me, it seemed like days passed, and I spent that time searching, searching for anyone to talk to, to relate to, anyone who might give me some insight into where I was and why I was there. I found no one—at least no one like me."

I said nothing but I knew exactly the scene he was describing. I had lived it during my first moments in the bubble. I too saw the all-green landscape with no sign of other life. While it had an element of beauty to it, its emptiness would have been unbearable.

"It was odd," he continued. "It was all very real. I could feel the ground beneath my feet, and when I touched myself, I could feel that, too. All my senses worked. Occasionally I would feel a breeze on my skin and I would hear it move past my ears. Of course, I could see,

242

and my sense of touch worked just fine. But I never grew hungry, never thirsty. I was in a vast wasteland of loneliness—then he appeared.

"It was during one of my forays into the hills, searching for any sign of civilization or any individual, that I came upon a wide chasm. Don't ask how deep the crevice ran—I was never able to see the bottom—but I could see the other side." His gaze grew distant. "The other side was stark and barren, like the desert, with stunted trees and sickly-looking bushes. The sky over there was not like the emerald over my head, but dull gray, like the color of a navy ship. And in that sky hovered Aster's ship, or what we think of as his ship. It hung there in all its many pieces, rotating around that single disc at the center. It looked just like the thing in the sky you videotaped."

The image of the ship I had seen so many times flashed in my mind.

He continued, "That's when I saw him. There were beings on the other side, the same kind of beings you saw with Aster at the UN, the same kind of beings we all saw on our television screens."

He paled.

"They stared at me. They taunted me. They paced up and down their side of the crevice, pointing, shouting, verbally eviscerating me. At first it was just the smaller beings, then came the one we call Aster. He was different than the others—taller, calmer, but no kinder. The things he said…things I will not repeat here or anywhere. I would rather have my tongue cut out than repeat those words. The things he said about Jesus…the things he said about Christians."

I watched tears well up in his eyes, but he continued his tale.

"He said vile things about God and even more vile things about Christ. And when he wasn't mocking them, he mocked me."

I had to ask. "Why did you stay by the crevice? Why not walk away from it?"

"I tried, Priscilla. I did walk away, but here's the thing: it didn't matter how far I walked, how many miles I put between me and the chasm and the evil on the other side—I could still hear them. I heard them hour after hour after hour. I heard them in my head. It was like having a hive of bees living between my ears, bees that never rested, always moving, always crawling, always in frenetic flight."

Tears ran down his cheeks, and the sight of him in his pain made me ache. I wanted to reach out to him, to place a comforting hand on his arm. I looked at Lizzy, who stared unblinkingly at Sloan. Lizzy seldom showed much emotion, but I had known her long enough to know that Sloan's story drove a hot knife into her soul.

"And this went on for all the months you were in the coma?"

He shook his head. "I don't know. I never sensed the passing of time. There was no daytime or nighttime, no sun moving across the sky, no moon to come out at night. Maybe it was the whole time. Maybe it was the last few minutes before I came to. I honestly don't know, but I do know it terrified me more than any dream I've ever had."

Lizzy spoke for the first time in a while. "Do you think it was a dream?"

Again, he slowly shook his head. "No, I think it was a vision, a warning."

I was sure I already knew the answer but I asked anyway. "A warning about what?"

"A warning about Aster, about his real nature…" His voice trailed off, then he took a deep breath. "I don't think the warning was for me, Priscilla—I think it was for you."

"Me? How can that be?"

He looked like a man about to deliver the worst news in the world. "While in my coma, I kept hearing one name over and over. A name uttered by Aster. It was your name…Priscilla. I heard it a hundred thousand times. Then I began to see your image. Never close. Always distant. But I know it was you."

Chapter Twenty-nine

THE CHAIR BENEATH ME CREAKED AS I REPOSITIONED MYSELF. The camera maintained its blinkless gaze.

"I'm sorry for being so fidgety. It's this chair. I've been sitting in it too long, but it doesn't matter. I won't be sitting here much longer. Forgive me if I seem at times incoherent. It's the stress, it's the anxiety, and I suppose it's the uncertainty. I'm trying to be brave, trying to remind myself that things may still turn out all right, that I can actually succeed in what I plan to do. The truth is that most of my brain knows different. For every second of optimism I feel, I'm plagued by a minute of despair.

"I've brought you most of the way now and have only a few more things to share, but they're important things. I must get them out before my camera loses memory or the battery dies.

"I sat in the safety of Allen Sloan's office that afternoon feeling as unsafe as I've ever felt before. What Lizzy had said, added to what I just heard, pulled the carpet from beneath my feet. I wanted to walk out the door and close it behind me, to take the elevator to the first floor, to walk to the lobby and into the warm, open air. I wanted to forget what day it was, what had happened over the last year and a half, and the fear of what would happen next. But I knew that would never happen. Like a train confined to the rails upon which it rides, I was in this to the end. Not by choice. Not by desire. I was a captive of circumstance.

"Allen and Lizzy let me sit in silence for awhile, giving me time to sort through all I'd experienced and all I had just heard. When the gears of my mind refused to turn any longer, I asked a simple question, one I knew would have a profound answer: 'What do we do now?'"

"What do we do now?"

Allen looked at Lizzy, and Lizzy looked at the floor.

I had to ask. "You have a plan in mind, don't you?"

Lizzy answered, "Aster has fooled the world, taken it hostage with his lies, tempted it with promises of good. However, not everyone has been fooled. There are people of faith who would not bow their knee to the creature. Some of us have been getting together secretly, careful of whom we tell, slow to take anyone into confidence.

"It's been very much like the first-century church," Allen said. "In our world, the Western world, most people—and even the Christians—think that the churches have always had an open-door policy, but that hasn't always been true. Certainly the first-century church spread the gospel, baptized believers, taught doctrine, and greeted new Christians with open arms. But in the height of persecution, the church met in secret, and a new person could only attend if sponsored by a known believer. I know it sounds odd, but it was the only way they could protect themselves from spies and infiltrators.

"We've been very careful of whom we've included in this, Priscilla," Lizzy said. "If we hadn't been, then we might now be dead. It doesn't show up on the news because Aster has slowly gained control of how his actions are reported, but we know that many of the faithful have died. Much of this has been in other countries, but our own country has not been spared. We meet in cells, small groups in different cities in different states, and each one has a single individual who is allowed to know about the other groups. The point is, we can't be too careful."

"So you kept all this from me," I said.

She shook her head several times. "No, Priscilla. You cut yourself off from us. You stopped taking my phone calls or answering my letters, but you're right about one thing: there are many who see you as being on the side of the enemy."

"Do they honestly think I had a choice? Do they think I woke up one morning and said to myself, 'My, wouldn't it be wonderful if I could be taken into the employ of some alien from another planet?'"

She sighed, and the expression on her face broke my heart. "There are many who are suspicious of you; this is true. Their suspicions are understandable. Some have lost homes, some have lost the lives of loved ones, and perhaps the most painful of all, some have watched family and friends walk away from the faith. When they see you on television, they think of Aster and the great heresy."

"I no longer feel like I can defend him, especially if everything you say is true, but you have to admit, the others have to admit, that he has brought some good. Soon all of us will live longer and poverty will be a thing of the past. Diseases that take the lives of hundreds of thousands of people will be eradicated. He has done so much for us." Even as the words left my lips, I didn't believe them. I was protesting to save my honor; I was objecting to save face.

Allen looked at me hard. "Priscilla, humanity could have done all of that on its own. The reason we haven't is our world is hamstrung by sin and selfishness. Aster comes along and it looks to everyone like he's giving us a gift, but the gift is something we could have achieved by ourselves."

I bent over and rested my face in my hands, partly because I was tired, mostly because I didn't want to look at the other two. Their words carried the weight of truth. Deep inside of me, something was moving, something not in my organs, not in my mind, but in my soul, and it was hard to experience. I felt as if I were melting. "I don't think I can hear much more."

"Priscilla," Allen began, "I know this is difficult. I know because I've been through it. There's something you need to know, something we need to correct." He rose from his chair, walked across his office, and opened a drawer in his desk. A few seconds later, he was back in the conversation area with a Bible in his hands. He moved through the pages like a man familiar with the book's contents. He sat on the coffee table just a few feet in front of me.

He took a deep breath. "I haven't been a Christian very long, Priscilla. In fact, I became one shortly after I came out of the coma. I was released from the hospital a week later and went to my home. The place had been locked up, but well taken care of, thanks to my board of directors and some very special staff members. The house seemed emptier than it should. Plastic covered all the furniture, and all the foods that could spoil had been removed. And in what had to be a great act of optimism, they left the power turned on. So there I was in an empty house with an empty pantry and, worse, an empty heart."

He seemed to drift off, his mind traveling to a place only he could visit, a place he didn't want to go. "My emotions returned in pieces. When I came out of the coma, I felt overpowering terror but felt nothing when they told me my family had been killed. Maybe it was shock. Maybe it was some kind of mental-emotional defense mechanism. But as time passed, my emotions evened out. What I couldn't feel before came in a tidal wave..."

He broke off, cutting his eyes to the Bible he held, not to read it but to hide the percolating tears.

"I just spent time sitting in the various rooms. By the end of the second day, I spent most of my time alternating between the master bedroom where my wife and I had slept for the previous ten years, and my young son's room. We had had some godly neighbors who took it upon themselves to invite us to church. My wife went, as did my son, and within a few months they were very involved. I was too busy building this place, this edifice to technology, so that people throughout the country could watch whatever program they wanted in high definition. I wish I could have those days back."

I raised my head and looked at Allen. I didn't see a wealthy executive; I saw another wounded spirit. "I can't imagine how horrible that must've been for you."

"Only those who have been through it can understand, but it isn't my desire to gain your sympathy. I have a point in all of this." He returned his gaze to the Bible. "I used to sit for hour upon hour in my son's bedroom, gazing at the baseball pennants mounted to the wall and the posters of famous skateboarders. It took a while before I could start going through his stuff, before I had the courage to begin to remove clothing from his closet, to unpack his dresser drawers, and to put his baseball equipment in a box."

Tears began to roll, but he didn't bother wiping them away. "I found this Bible. The people at the church gave it to him. They even wrote his name on the flyleaf. He was so proud of this Bible. Several times he asked me to read it to him, but I was always too busy."

It took a few moments for him to gather his emotions before he could continue. "At first I would sit on his bed and leaf through the pages, not really reading, but after a week or so I began to read the New Testament. I found Jesus there. I found my faith there. This book has been my constant companion, and I spend several hours a day studying it. There's a passage I want you to read. I want you to read it aloud." He held the Bible out to me, opened to the Book of Galatians. "There in chapter 1, read verses six through nine."

"Galatians 1:6–9?"

"Yes. Aloud, please."

I found the passage, cleared my throat, and began to read. "'I'm amazed that you are so quickly deserting Him who called you by the grace of Christ, for a different gospel; which is really not another; only there are some who are disturbing you and want to distort the gospel of Christ. But even if we, or an angel from heaven, should preach to you a gospel contrary to what we have preached to you, he is to be accursed! As we have said before, so I say again now, if any man is preaching to you a gospel contrary to what you received, he is to be accursed!'"

"Do you understand?" Lizzy asked.

"No, not really."

Allen studied me from his seat on the coffee table, then said, "Aster is not from another planet. He's not an extraterrestrial in the way most of us use the word. He is exactly what Paul the Apostle describes in that passage."

"I still don't get it." I reread the passage. "I understand the part about not listening to another gospel. These verses are saying we shouldn't listen to anyone who brings a message contradictory to that which we already have in the Bible, but even if the messenger is..." It was as though someone turned the light on in my mind, and not just any light—a bright, piercing spotlight. The mysterious, stirring sensation in my soul went into overdrive. "Are you saying that Aster is an angel?"

Allen and Lizzy responded in unison, "Yes."

"But how is that possible?"

"Think about what you're asking, Priscilla," Lizzy said. "How is it possible that an alien from another planet has crossed hundreds of thousands of light-years to visit with us? From the very beginning, the Bible teaches that angels are a created class of beings. God created them for various purposes, and they reside in a different part of our universe—no, let me rephrase that. They reside in a different part of our multiverse. There are over three hundred references to these beings that we routinely call angels. The word *angel* simply means messenger. That's true in the Old Testament Hebrew, and it is true in the New Testament Greek. Which makes more sense to you: an alien traveling across billions of miles of empty space in a spaceship, or creatures moving from one dimension to another?"

"Both seem a stretch." But I didn't believe my own objection. My thoughts ran back to the discussion Lizzy and I had in her truck outside Starbucks. She had been trying to tell me something then.

"Priscilla, you have sat at my Bible study class for several years. Not once in that time have you ever indicated you doubted the scriptural revelation."

"I didn't then, and I don't now. It's just that…there's too much information in my mind, too many competing thoughts, too much emotion."

"Trust me," Allen said, "when I say I understand. It took me months to come to this conclusion, and it's unfair of us to ask you to come to the same conclusion in a matter of moments, but we don't have much choice."

I stood and walked to the back of the sofa, unable to sit down any longer. "So you're telling me that Aster is some form of angel who has come into our realm to mislead us. Further, you want me to believe that his goal is to lead people away from the true faith."

Lizzy turned in her seat so she could face me. "Knowing all that you do, is it so hard to believe?"

"My mind has become so muddled over the last year, it's hard to believe anything."

The expression on Lizzy's face filled me with guilt. "You heard me teach many times, Priscilla, that faith begins in the head and moves to the heart. Our mind is convinced of the truth; with our hearts we act on the truth. What is your heart telling you now?"

"Don't pressure me, Lizzy. I need some time. You don't know what I've been through; you don't know everything I've seen. I have to get my thoughts in order. Maybe it's from all those years spent gathering information and arranging it all in some kind of cohesive story, but I need time."

They let me pace in silence for a few moments. I turned to them and asked, "Just how did you guys team up?"

"You told me about Allen, remember? When you stopped returning my phone calls, I decided to look him up. It didn't take long for us to realize we held the same views."

Allen said, "Lizzy is quite a teacher. She's been helping me understand the Bible at a level I didn't think possible."

"She is a great teacher," I agreed.

"Then why don't you believe her?"

I walked back to the sofa. "I didn't say I didn't believe her. I said I'm confused—overwhelmed. What about this plan you two have cooked up? How do you defeat an angel? Seems to me it would be a lot easier to defeat an alien than some spiritual being masquerading in physical form."

"That's a Christian myth that has plagued the church. Somewhere along the line we got the idea that angels don't have bodies, that they're incorporeal. The Bible shows otherwise. Every place an angel is shown, he is shown as having a body. When Peter is in jail and an angel wakes him, the angel does so by slapping him on the side with his hand. That's a physical act. When Mary and the women see angels at the empty tomb of Christ, they see physical beings. In fact, the Gospels use different terms for them, such as *men*, *young man*, and *angel*. They speak and perform a whole host of other physical acts. Angels are not disembodied spirits. Christians do not become angels when they die. Angels are physical beings that can move from their realm to our realm."

"OK, I stand corrected." I said. "Now let's get back to your plan," I said.

Allen and Lizzy exchanged glances. It was Allen who spoke. "Lizzy has known you for a very long time, but I, on the other hand, have only met you once before and you looked at me like I come from the mental ward. Not that I can blame you. I think it's safe to say that Lizzy trusts you with her life. By revealing this plan to you, I will be doing the same." He stood and stared into my eyes. "I need you to tell me, I need you to promise me, that you will tell no one of what you're about to hear. Can you do that? Can you as a Christian make that kind of promise to me, a fellow believer in Christ?"

I didn't respond at first. Something in his eyes, something in his expression added the weight of the world to the question. Over the years as a reporter, I've learned to read body language and subtle clues in a person's voice to help me know if they are lying or telling the truth. Allen Sloan genuinely believed he was putting his life in my hands. I looked at Lizzy.

"It's your call," she said.

I fixed my eyes upon Allen again and said, "I give you my word."

He nodded and returned to his overstuffed chair, flopping into it like a man who just finished running a marathon in hiking boots. "You had better sit down. This won't take long, but it may be the most difficult thing you've ever had to listen to."

Chapter Thirty

I BECAME CONCERNED ABOUT THE PASSING OF TIME. I had spent too long in Allen Sloan's office, and I had an appointment to keep in the Mojave Desert. Earlier, Lizzy had promised to drive me, but I told her no. I needed the time to think, to mull things over, and to dredge up the courage to do what I must. I had arrived at Allen's office in Lizzy's car. That meant I was without transportation, but Allen came to my rescue by loaning me one of the corporate cars reserved for his key executives.

Five minutes after hearing their plans, I was in a four-door sedan headed up the I-15 freeway on my way to a dry lakebed. It was a three-hour drive, and I used every minute of it to mull over everything I'd heard and everything I had experienced.

Allen had been right. His words carried the impact of a heavyweight boxer. He laid out the plan item by item, step by step. It was logical. It was well thought out. And it was insane. Worse, the plan hinged on me. If I refused to help, then the plan was useless. I had no idea how to defeat an angel, but Allen and Lizzy did, and if they were right, there was a chance the world could return to normal and truth be restored. Agreeing to that was the easy part. The most difficult part was realizing that I probably would never live through the effort.

By the time the terrain had turned from a mix of houses and commercial buildings to the brown tableau of desert with gnarled Joshua trees reaching toward the sky, I had convinced myself that no matter what, I would do what needed to be done.

From I-15 north, I took the 395 past Hesperia and Victorville and continued on to highway 58 headed west. Twenty minutes later,

I pulled into a makeshift parking lot filled with countless cars. The sun was setting, and I was late.

This meeting had been in the works for months, but I had very little to do with the planning. I convinced Aster that I was good at many things, but event planning was not one of them, especially something this monumental. That's where Tim Wacher came in. He was a media genius. I know because he told me so—often. My role remained the same: to be the human influence on the alien named Aster.

Over the months, Aster had met with heads of state, executives from the world's largest businesses and their boards of directors, politicians, and entertainers. A day didn't go by that Aster's face didn't appear on the evening news. By my count, his unusual face had appeared on the cover of every major magazine. No human being was as well known. I was the only one who came close, but my fame didn't rest on what I did but who Aster was. There'd been a time in my life when I wanted fame, when I wanted the big chair behind the big desk at the big network, but that died years ago. Odd—now that I didn't want fame, I had it.

I drove slowly through the overcrowded parking area. Thousands of cars rested in neatly formed rows. There were scores of cars in front of me waiting to be directed by parking attendants to the next available slot. Behind me was a long line of vehicles. I knew where I needed to be, but I had to get through the traffic jam first. Wacher had arranged for staff parking, but now I doubted I would get there before the end of the week. It took thirty minutes for me to reach my destination.

Even before exiting the car, I could hear the joyous noises of tens of thousands of people. The only thing I could liken it to was a rock concert like Woodstock or the infamous "Burning Man." Everything about the gathering went against my grain. I don't mind attending the occasional large party, but this was well outside my comfort zone. I had to force myself to believe that I was walking on a large, dried lakebed in the high desert of Southern California. This was a place where hot-rodders came to test out their vehicles. It was a place campers visited. And at the moment, it was the place where thousands of hopefuls longed for a chance to see Aster up close.

It took me close to fifteen minutes to work my way through the crowds, around vendors hawking little Aster dolls, T-shirts, and homemade DVDs. One shaggy-haired young man was selling a blue T-shirt with the words EVOLVE THE ASTER WAY.

Although the sun was setting, I kept my sunglasses on, not to protect my eyes from the glare but to protect my identity from innumerable strangers. I had also pulled my red hair back and wore a scarf over my head.

Wacher had thought of everything, including a small portable building where staff could meet, separated from the pressing crowds. I worked my way to it and climbed the three steps necessary to reach a small wood deck in front of the entrance door. I turned the handle and entered.

The outside of the building looked plain and drab, but inside it was decorated to the hilt. Chairs and sofas filled much of the space, and to one side was a small kitchen. Along one wall were six small flatscreen televisions, each showing a different area of the meeting grounds.

"You're late." Wacher came over and shook my hand. "We were getting worried. I thought you were riding with Aster. Is he here?"

"No, I decided to drive myself."

Wacher seemed surprised. "Why would you drive for three hours when you could ride in Aster's bubble? I'd give my eyeteeth for a few minutes in that thing. You know you're the only human ever to step foot inside."

"Yeah, I'm aware of that. Who else is here?"

"For the key personnel, you mean? Well, I'm here, you're here, and soon Chris Conlin and Mr. Debatto will be here. Arriving by limo."

"Figures. How much longer do we have?"

Wacher shrugged. "That's not up to me; that's up to your good friend Aster. He arrives when he arrives, but you know that better than I do. Tentatively, we're set to go in about half an hour. The bands are tuning up, and security is trying to move the crowd to the right place. Actually, most of their work is keeping the crowd away from the stage. You thirsty? There's stuff in the fridge. There's some food, too."

"No, thanks. I think better on an empty stomach." Actually, I didn't think my stomach could hold any food. "Listen, I need a favor. I have a couple of friends coming and I promised them a good spot. Any chance you could get them near the action?"

"Your wish is my command. Of course, you need to ask Aster if I can take a spin in his bubble."

"I have asked him about it several times. He keeps saying no."

"It doesn't hurt to be persistent. "

I forced a smile. "I'm not so sure."

I heard the sound of tires on bare ground. It sounded close.

Wacher stepped to the door and opened it. "They're here." He stepped away, leaving the door open. I heard the limo's doors opening and closing, and a few moments later Dave Debatto and Chris Conlin entered. Debatto was dressed casually, wearing a pair of tan slacks and a black golf shirt. Conlin, for reasons known only to himself, given the heat of the desert, wore a gray suit.

"Priscilla!" Debatto said. "Has Aster already arrived?"

I shook my head. "I came by myself this time. I sort of missed my ride."

"Missed your ride?" Conlin said. "How can you miss a ride like that?"

"It's a long story."

Debatto took a seat on the sofa and eyed me for a minute. "There's not a problem, is there?"

I tried not to hesitate. "If there is, Aster hasn't said anything to me about it."

My boss turned to Wacher. "I assume everything is good to go."

"Yes, sir. We're ready to rock 'n' roll. I sent a clearance for a couple of Priscilla's friends."

Debatto raised an eyebrow. "Special friends? You don't have a fiancé or something that I don't know about, do you?"

"There hasn't been much time for things like that lately, sir. These are just some friends I've been putting off for awhile. I'm feeling a tad guilty about not returning phone calls."

"I'm sure your friends understand. They must be very proud of you. You've done things no human ever has, and that makes you unique in the annals of history." He turned to Conlin. "I could use a drink, Chris, how about you? Maybe a beer."

"I'd love one, sir." He seemed pleased at the offer.

"Great. Make mine a lite. I think they're in the refrigerator. They are in the refrigerator, aren't they, Tim?"

"That they are, sir." Wacher grinned at the joke being played on Conlin. "There's some food in there, too, if you want."

Like Wacher, Debatto asked if I wanted anything, and I said no.

"You sure? Chris is already up."

"No, but thanks, anyway."

Colin gave no indication that the joke bothered him. He rose from the sofa and made his way to the refrigerator, extracted two beers, popped their tops, then took one to Debatto. Conlin lifted his can slightly and said, "Cheers."

Debatto took a long draw from the can, swallowed hard, then stifled a belch. A second later he set the can on the coffee table situated in front of the sofa. "Come on, Priscilla, there are some people I want you to meet."

Debatto stood up and moved toward the door. I followed close behind. Outside, streams of people were making their way to the staging area, the place where Aster would make his appearance and walk among the people. The area around the temporary buildings had been cordoned off with a fence, and a half-dozen guards in uniform stood at the perimeter. A few feet away from the steps stood four men. One was tall, in his midthirties, and wore stylish and expensive-looking casual clothing. Perched on his nose was an expensive pair of designer sunglasses. His antithesis stood next to him: a man of average height with long hair, a well-worn T-shirt with the words UFOs ROCK printed across the front, and a pair of jeans that had not seen the washing machine in at least a couple of months. The other two men, like the UFO fan, were young and dressed in a similar fashion. One held a high-end video camera, the kind that costs seventeen thousand dollars; the other held what I knew to be a recording device. I was looking at a video crew.

Debatto jogged down the steps and marched toward the well-dressed man. I stayed close.

"Priscilla, I don't think you've had the pleasure of meeting Ian Robinson. Ian has been consulting with Debatto Media for a number of years now. He's expensive, pushy, arrogant, and always right—well worth his high price. And this is Priscilla Simms."

"I would've known her without the introduction," Ian said with a broad smile. "It is hard to overlook the most famous woman in the world." He extended a hand and I took it. His handshake was firm but gentle and gave the impression of confidence.

"Pleased to meet you, Ian, and I'm not all that special. More of a sidekick, really."

"Oh, I think you're much more than that."

Debatto motioned to the man in the UFO shirt. The man crossed the distance between us in a short jog, but when his eyes fell on me, his jaw dropped.

"Tom, I promised you could meet Priscilla Simms. Priscilla this is Tom Clyn. Young Mr. Clyn has been very useful to us. He's an expert in contemporary UFO lore and a budding documentarian. Over the last eighteen months he has given me and Ian quite an education, haven't you, Tom?"

"I've done my best." We shook hands. His palm was moist and his grip almost desperate, as if he were holding on for his life. I pulled free as subtly as I could. "I've been following your career…I mean, since Aster came. I can't believe I'm really talking to you."

"Um, thank you. You're making a documentary?" I was weary of being the center of attention.

"Yes. Ian set it up, and Mr. Debatto is funding it. I've collected every piece of video ever made of Aster."

"Wow. You must live in a warehouse."

"Mr. Debatto has provided that, too."

"Priscilla," Debatto said, "we're trying to make a video record of everything associated with Aster. It is something he wants, and we're happy to do it for him. As you know, he's met with us quite a few times. He's been very, very helpful."

"Actually, I didn't know that."

"Well, we wanted to play our cards as close to the vest as possible, if you know what I mean. Aster has promised us some very cutting-edge technology that will…well, let's just say it will make the Internet look like last century's technology."

"You've entered into business with him?"

"Of course. Someone has to, and since you were the first person to make contact with him and have been so helpful, he's rewarding us with some very special favors. Later, I'll fill you in on how the proceeds will be shared with you."

"I see. I look forward to that." I knew that conversation would never come. "So you want to include me in the documentary?"

"That's the idea," Debatto said. "And since we have a little time before the big arrival, I felt now would be a good time to get you acquainted with the team. I hope that's all right."

"Of course, Mr. Debatto. I'll be happy to talk to Mr. Clyn."

"Just Tom, please. I'm not very formal."

An understatement.

"Great," Debatto said. "Come on, Ian. There are cold brews inside. Come in and take a load off." The two disappeared into the building.

"How do you want to do this?" I asked Clyn.

"Just a sec." He called his two assistants over. "OK, we don't have much daylight, so I need you two to set up a couple of fill lights. We'll set up just on the other side of the fence. That way we can have the incoming crowd as a backdrop and not have the rent-a-cops walking into the frame. While you do that, I'll bring Ms. Simms up to speed. Sound good?"

They said it did and moved toward a van parked ten yards away.

Clyn started toward the fence. I walked beside him. "You're not wearing a wire, are you?" he asked.

"What?"

"A remote mic or anything."

"What are you talking about?"

He looked at me, and I could see the fear in his face. "Look, man... I don't know....I shouldn't...I can't do this."

"Easy. What's the problem?"

"This could get me killed. For all I know, you may rat me out, but I have to trust someone."

I chuckled to ease the tension. "Killed? Fired maybe, but not killed. What'd you do? Forget the camera?"

"No, no, no. Everything is here. It's just that...you heard what Debatto said about me, right? How I taught him and Ian all about UFOs and stuff."

"Yeah, I heard that."

"Well, he's right, and he paid me good money, too, and since he was paying large coin, I thought I'd do extra research. You know, make yourself so valuable they can't fire you and all that. I mean, it was my first genuine job, my first real opportunity."

"So, what's bothering you? Debatto Media is a huge firm—they can afford to pay large salaries to consultants."

"No, you're not getting it." He stopped and looked around like he heard something—something frightening. "I said I did extra research. I've gone over every inch of videotape, analyzed every second of data, studied the stills and everything else." He lowered his voice. "I don't think Aster is what he says he is."

Lizzy and Allen had already led me to that conclusion. I couldn't help wondering if this was some kind of loyalty test. My paranoia began to break new ground. Trusting strangers was never my strong suit. "What do you think he is?"

"He's otherworldly."

"You think a being that arrives in a spaceship might be otherworldly?" I began to doubt the man's stability.

"No. Look, I don't have much time. For all I know, they're listening to us right now."

"Who?"

"Them. Debatto and his cronies. Aster and his pals. I don't know. Them." He stopped and faced me. "Look, I know I sound paranoid. I *am* paranoid, but this time I have reason."

"I'd like to hear it."

"OK, look. How do I say this quickly? UFO researchers—*good* UFO investigators—gather as much info as possible and from as wide a range of observers as possible. For example, several people see a strange light in the sky. Across town, another group sees the same thing. An investigator talks to both groups and compares their stories."

"Sounds like good research. We do the same in journalism."

"It goes beyond that. Eyewitness testimony is iffy at best. So a good researcher will also talk to radar operators. If a military base is nearby, he makes a call. If there are airports nearby, he makes another call. Even weather radar is useful."

"OK. I'm with you."

He looked over his shoulder. His crew was returning. "OK, I have to bottom line this. Aster's spaceship never ever appears on radar. Of course, I can't get anyone in the military to tell me what their systems and satellites see, but I'll bet my last buck it's the same nothing everyone else sees. And I'm talking superstealth here. I mean, that was my first guess—that his ship absorbed radar waves or something, but I don't think that's it. I've studied the video and enhanced it electronically in every way possible. This ship, that black diamond, doesn't reflect light."

"Tom, it's black."

"That doesn't mean anything. Just because something is black doesn't mean there's never a reflection. I'm not talking about sun glinting off the ship's surface. There are no shadows. The facets always appear the same. A real object wouldn't. In the daylight, the side facing the sun would appear lighter or brighter but never the same as that in the shadows."

"When it first appeared in San Diego, I saw the shadow first."

"Well, of course you did. Light doesn't pass through the ship, so it will cast a shadow."

"I have no idea what you're getting at."

He was becoming more animated and irritated. "I know UFOs. I know more than anybody. It's been my life. Aster is something else, and his ship...I don't think his ship really exists. Have you been inside it?"

"No. I've been in the bubble-thing many times."

"But never the ship?"

"Never."

"That's because it's not there. Ms. Simms...Priscilla, I think you're in danger. I think we're all in danger. If I were you, I'd stay away from Aster, Debatto, and all the others. Something ain't right—ain't right by a long shot."

"What makes you think you can trust me?"

He looked me dead in the eye. "When I said I did extra research, I didn't just mean on Aster and his ship. I've been studying you. I'm no body language expert, but I'm pretty sure he makes you uncomfortable. Seriously uncomfortable. Am I right?

I chose not to answer.

Chapter Thirty-one

CLYN AND I WENT THROUGH THE MOTIONS OF THE INTERVIEW. His two-man crew set up lights, worked the sound recorder, and did everything the videography crew would do. We sat outside, my back to the incoming crowd and Clyn a few feet away. He used a standard interview setup in which I was the only one on camera. He would ask questions, and I would answer them, and if this had been a normal situation he would take the raw material back to his studio and edit it.

Nothing about this felt normal.

Halfway through the taping I noticed two things. First, Allen and Lizzy approached the perimeter fence led by a uniformed security guard. I also noticed Debatto and the man he identified as Ian Robinson standing a short distance away, watching Clyn and me. I sensed they were unhappy.

Once the interview was over, I made my way to my friends, keeping my back to Debatto and Robinson. I didn't know what they had in their minds, but I had a feeling it wasn't good.

"I see you guys made it," I said, painting on a smile. I looked at the security guard and could tell by his expression that he recognized me. I was getting used to that. "Thank you for escorting my friends here. I'll let you get back to your work."

"Yes, ma'am, but..."

"You want an autograph, right?"

He nodded. "If it's not too much to ask. It's for my wife. She thinks you're the greatest." He removed a small notepad from the front pocket of his uniform shirt and handed it and a cheap pen to me. I asked his wife's name and signed my autograph to both of them. He looked like a kid on Christmas, and it should have made me proud but I felt sad for him, and for me. With a wave he walked away.

Then I returned my attention to Allen and Lizzy. "I hope the traffic wasn't bad. It was pretty sick when I drove in." I watched their eyes to see if they spied any activity over my shoulder, but they gave no indication of anyone approaching.

"We didn't drive," Allen said. "We flew in. I own a twin-engine plane. It helps me get around to various offices."

Lizzy smiled. "I was hoping for a great big business jet. I've never flown in a business jet."

"I'm not clear to fly jet-powered craft—not yet anyway." Allen raised his eyes and looked around, then returned his gaze to me. "You OK? You look as tense as a watch spring."

"You saw a guy with long hair doing the interview with me? He took me aside and said that Aster doesn't fit the profile and neither does the ship."

He asked, "What profile?"

"His name is Tom Clyn, and he said he's been researching UFOs for most of his life. He's been investigating Aster's ship. Basically he's saying the same things you've been saying but for different reasons."

"I suppose we shouldn't be surprised that others are picking up on the clues. It doesn't change what we know. We have to do—" Allen looked over my shoulder again. "We're about to have company."

I turned and saw Ian Robinson walking toward me. His body said he was tense, but he wore a smile—a well-practiced smile.

"Priscilla, I wonder if I could have a moment of your time."

"Certainly. But I'd like you to meet my friends—"

"Perhaps another time." He placed a hand on my arm and led me away from the fence, stopping in the center of the cordoned-off area.

"I don't know who taught you your manners, Mr. Robinson, but I'll thank you to take your hand off my arm." My tone remained firm but not angry.

"My apologies. I've been working too long and hard, and I think I've forgotten some of the social graces." He placed his hands behind his back as if trying to assure me that he would not touch me again.

"Mr. Debatto and I couldn't help noticing that you and Tom had a little discussion before the interview."

My stomach tightened. "Don't tell me you find that unusual. It's normal for people to talk—kind of like what were doing right now."

"I think you know what I mean."

"I'm a big girl, Mr. Robinson. I can choose to speak to whomever I wish, and I can do it without clearing it with you."

Robinson's face hardened. "I want to know what he said to you."

"Do you? And what do you think obligates me to answer to you? Last time I looked, I work for Debatto Media, not you."

"Listen, lady, there's too much at stake to be playing around like this. Billions of dollars are on the table, and notice I said billions with a *b*."

I refused to be intimidated. I'd grown weary of living in fear. "Believe it or not, I understand that, and if you're unhappy with my work, I'll just tell Aster that I have to quit because of you. Perhaps you'd like to be with me when I tell them that."

"I don't intimidate, Priscilla."

"You also don't know when you've crossed the line."

"I told you I want to know what Clyn said to you."

"And I told you—"

"Look!" The voice came from behind me.

"He's here!" This time it was a woman's voice, loud and shrill.

Within seconds a cacophony of voices filled the air; hands with extended fingers pointed skyward. Above and moving slowly from the north came the familiar, massive, inverted black diamond. As always, it moved without sound and showed no signs of propulsion. As it approached, it decreased in altitude until it was no more than thirty feet above the ground, so large, so black, so near that people tried to touch it.

I heard people crying, laughing, and gasping, and some literally jumped for joy.

"He's here! He's here!"

I turned to Ian Robinson and said, "Looks like it's showtime. I'm afraid I have work to do." I stepped away from Robinson, and as I did I heard the corporate gasping of the crowd.

I moved through a gate and into the crowd, doing my best to get close to the action. Lizzy and Allen followed.

As thousands turned their faces skyward to look at the black diamond hovering overhead, it began to fragment as it did that first day above the Windom Building in San Diego. The facets of the diamond spread out and once again orbited a flat disk at the center. But then something new happened. Balls of the purest white light descended from the fragments, slowly falling to the earth like a feather falling from some bird overhead. Each ball was the size of a grapefruit, and they came by the thousands.

Twenty feet overhead, they stopped their descent and began to orbit an invisible axis until they formed what looked to me like a spiral galaxy. The tiny spheres began to change color: white to red; red to green; green to blue; and blue to a color I couldn't identify. Soon the light colors began to blend together until a rainbow swarmed overhead.

I expected the crowd to go nuts, but they stood enraptured, faces turned skyward. Several raised hands, reaching for the spheres.

I moved slowly to where Lizzy and Allen stood. Allen suddenly looked pale, fragile, and so light that a stiff breeze might carry him away.

The dancing spheres overhead stopped and once again began a slow descent until they touched the crowd. Some backed away, fearful that they could be hurt by the unknown objects. Many others, however, reached out and gently laid fingers on the glowing balls. Some of those who did touch them squealed with delight at the contact. Everyone tried to lay flesh to light.

"What are those things?" There was a tremor in Allen's voice. "I mean, have you ever seen anything like it before?"

"No, never." My eyes took in every detail, every action, but my brain couldn't process what I saw.

Wacher had created a playbook for this gathering, and, by plan, Aster was supposed to direct his ship to a staging area and appear on a platform created just for this event. But it appeared that Aster had his own playbook because the now world-famous water bubble appeared and began its descent.

"Here he comes!" a few hundred people shouted.

Security guards worked their way through the crowd to a place just beneath the bubble and began to push the crowd back, creating an open area for Aster to land. The people seemed to understand and offered no resistance. As I've seen so many times before, the bubble touched down and disappeared in the blink of an eye.

But this time something was different. Every time I had seen Aster before, he wore a beige linenlike garment. This time he wore a purple robe with gold trim. He was dazzling. The crowd began to cheer and applaud. The sound was deafening.

Aster didn't arrive alone. He seldom did these days, usually arriving with his two companions, the one's he identified as Tanra and Geel. I had never learned to tell them apart and had no interest in doing so now. Both stood near, their hands crossed in front of them.

Those closest to Aster, those in the first four rows that formed a ring about him, reached forward, begging to be touched.

At first, Aster did not move. He stood in the center of the circle gazing at the hundreds who came to see him. Then he slowly moved to the people.

"Aster!" a woman shouted. "Aster, it's my baby. Heal my baby. Please, Aster, heal my baby." A woman forced her way into the open circle, holding an infant in her arms. Tanra and Geel started for her, but Aster raised a hand, stopping them in their tracks.

Aster approached her. She knelt and lowered her head. Extending his long arms, he touched her head, and she jerked as if a bolt of lightning had run down her spine. Then in an act I can scarcely describe, she held out her baby to this creature, this thing, she had never before met. She showed unquestioning trust.

Aster took the child still wrapped in a blue blanket. I felt ill.

The baby wailed but the desperate mother remained on her knees, head bowed.

Aster raised the baby over his head and slowly turned so that all could see. The crowd cheered, and Aster lowered the infant, cradling it in his arms. He touched the baby three times on the forehead and the child stopped his wailing.

"Rise, child. Take your small one. All will be well." Asher spoke his words loud enough to be heard a great distance.

The woman struggled to her feet and took her baby. She slowly moved back to the crowd.

"My leg, Aster. Heal my leg." A man's voice.

"Cancer, cancer. I have cancer—"

"No, me! I'm going blind. Help me, Aster."

It was bedlam—bedlam that fell to silence the moment the tall alien raised his arms. "People, hear me."

I don't know how he did it, what technology was available to him, but his voice carried in an unnatural way. Perhaps he had some way of amplifying his voice, or maybe he could speak louder than any human. In any case, his words rode the air, landing on ears crisp and clear.

"I have come to give you new life. I've come to give you new purpose. I've come to help heal your diseases, to extend your life, to make your future bright in this life and the next."

He continued, "My world is far away, but I will stay with you and heal your nations and meet your needs. We shall work together. We shall achieve together. But I shall need your help. Come, follow me."

"This isn't good," Allen said.

Aster spotted me in the crowd and began to motion for me when he stopped abruptly. His emerald eyes shift from me to Lizzy. He stiffened and lowered his hand. He returned his attention to the crowd. "I've come to bring blessings to you and to all people of this world." He looked up at the ship that hovered over everyone's head. "Feel the rain of blessing."

"We've got to get out of here," Lizzy snapped. "We've got to get out of here right now!"

For the second time that night, someone grabbed my arm. This time I did not pull away. Instinctively, I knew Lizzy sensed something I couldn't. We pushed our way through the crowd—not toward Aster, but away.

"Where are we going? The car? It's in the parking area." I tried to keep my voice down.

"No, not the car," Allen said. "My airplane. It's some distance away, but I hired a driver to bring us the rest of the way in."

I asked, "Will he still be at the car?" We had formed a single file line of three as we tried to push through those attempting to get closer. We were like salmon swimming upstream.

"I doubt it," Allen admitted. "It doesn't matter. I have the keys."

"A hired driver gave you the keys?"

Allen said yes. "He works for me. Besides, a one-hundred-dollar tip works wonders."

I turned to see what was happening behind me. A gentle mist continued to fall from the fragmented spaceship overhead, but then I saw something that froze the marrow in my bones. Row upon row of people were kneeling. The sight of it stopped me midstep.

I heard Lizzy's voice. "Priscilla, we have to go now. I'm serious."

"But—"

"Where do you think you're going?" The familiar voice came from my right. An angry-looking Ian Robinson stepped forward to block my path. "I don't know what's gotten into you, Priscilla, but you're making me very nervous. Shouldn't you be with Aster?"

"If you haven't noticed, he doesn't need a babysitter." I tried to move away, but he stepped in my path and laid his hands on my shoulders. I had grown very weary of his touch.

"I think you're going the wrong way," Robinson said. "It looks like you're trying to leave, and we don't want all the people here to get the wrong idea."

"I don't believe you have the authority to keep me here," I said.

"I may not have the authority, woman, but I certainly have the means."

I started to say something when Robinson spun on his heels and I heard a sickening thud. The well-dressed man dropped to the dirty, dry lakebed.

"Ow, ow, ow! That hurts." Tom Clyn was hopping up and down and shaking his right hand—a hand used to deck Robinson. "You don't know how long I've wanted to do that. The guy's been leeching off me far too long."

I looked at Clyn, then at Lizzy and Allen. Allen stepped close to look at the unconscious Robinson. "I think you just got yourself in a lot of trouble, son. You'd better come with us."

Clyn looked frightened. "Go where?"

"You'd better do as he says," I said. "Everything you told me is right. We have to get out of here."

Lizzy cut in. "We don't have much time. We go, and we go now."

Pushing back through the pressing crowd, we jogged to a Jeep Cherokee parked next to a security car by the temporary building where I'd done the interview. I was breathing hard, and my legs hurt from running on the surface of the lakebed. We wasted no time getting inside. Allen started the vehicle and accelerated west across the open area.

"I don't believe this. I don't believe this," I said on the verge of ranting. "They were bowing to him, like he was some kind of god."

Lizzy looked back at me from her position in the front passenger seat. "Did you recognize the words? They're very similar to what Jesus said."

"Whoa," Clyn said. "Are you saying that Aster is Jesus come again?"

"No—not now, and not ever, but before this evening is through a great many people out there will be saying exactly that."

I asked, "What was that mist? A hallucinogen?"

"Maybe. I'm not certain," Lizzy said. "But it can't be good."

"Is that it?" I said pointing to the windshield. Twenty or thirty yards ahead rested a two-engine, sleek, orange-and-white airplane.

"That's my baby," Allen said.

"Cool," Clyn said. "It looks like that thing can move."

"Two hundred and thirty-eight miles an hour." Despite our situation, Allen sounded proud. "Not bad for an aircraft that's over fifty years old."

Clyn looked like a balloon that just lost its air. "Fifty? You got to be kidding me."

Allen did not ease up on the accelerator as he spoke. "Don't let the years fool you, kid. My father owned it before me. It's the Cessna 310F, and he took great care of it. In his younger days he got hooked on flying by watching the old television program *Sky King*. Naturally, when he earned enough money to buy his own plane, he bought the same type he'd seen on television. After I came out of my...after I got out of the hospital, I decided to have the whole thing refurbished and the engines

270

rebuilt. It has state-of-the-art electronics also. It may be twice as old as you, but I promise it won't disappoint."

Allen pulled the Jeep within five yards of the craft, and we exchanged car for airplane. A few minutes after the propellers had begun to spin, we were airborne. I strained my eyes to see if anyone followed. I couldn't tell. My gut, however, had an opinion.

"Seatbelt, everyone. And just so that you know, much of the airspace around here is controlled by the military, especially Edwards Air Force Base. I won't be taking a straight path. The last thing we need is some jet jockey riding our tail."

I settled into my seat and snapped the lap belt around me. "I don't care what direction you go, as long as it's away from here."

Allen set the pilot controls, Lizzy next to him. Clyn and I sat in the row behind them. The plane could seat six people, so we had room to spare. Once airborne, Lizzy turned and faced me.

"It's time to decide, Priscilla. We've reached the point of no return."

I knew what she meant. Everything rested on my decision. Images of the mother with the baby and Aster's behavior haunted me. The sight of scores of people kneeling as if praying to a god flashed on my mind with strobe-light intensity. I gazed out my window and in the distance saw the massive black pieces of Aster's ship. Were they moving? Approaching?

For the next few moments no one spoke, only the sound of the aircraft's twin engines filling our ears. A year and a half ago, I first saw Aster's spaceship and Aster himself. Now everything had changed. At first I felt honored, lucky, thrilled. Now I felt fear and revulsion. Everything Lizzy had said, all her warnings, echoed by Allen, had been right on the money. I had been foolish not to see it for myself. I knew enough to distinguish between truth and falsehood, between lies and veracity.

My heart ached when I thought how close I had come to rejecting my belief and my faith. The words from the Galatians passage Allen made me read came to the surface of my mind like a cork in the churning sea: "But even if we, or an angel from heaven, should preach to you a gospel contrary to what we have preached to you, he is to be accursed!" Aster might be an angel, but I doubt if he came from heaven.

My eyes met Lizzy's. "We do the plan."

Clyn looked at me. "You guys have a plan? What kind of plan?"

Allen answered for us all. "I don't know where you live, pal, but I'm pretty sure it's not on the way."

"Is your plan going to cause Aster any trouble?"

Allen didn't answer right away, and I didn't know what to say. Clyn came with us of his own free will, but he hadn't signed up for what we were about to do. I had no idea how he would react. "With God's help it will."

"In that case, you can count me in. I don't care where we're going."

The three of us sighed in relief, and then Clyn spoke again. "Um, just where are we going?"

"Minnesota," Allen said. "I hear it's nice this time of year."

Chapter Thirty-two

I CHECKED THE BATTERY IN THE CAMERA, AND IT WAS CLOSE TO DEAD. At best I might have another five minutes of juice left.

"It took over an hour of uninterrupted flight before I began to settle. My fear continued to come in waves, crashing on my soul like a chain of tsunamis. Someplace over Nevada I began to believe that we were not being pursued by Aster or any of his contingency. Of course, it really meant nothing. I knew Aster and the others were tied up with the monstrous gathering in the Mojave and that Aster wasn't about to let such an opportunity go by. But at some point the gathering would end. Aster would enter his spaceship in full view of the multitude of spectators, each probably chanting his name. Then things would change.

"I never knew how, but Aster always seemed able to find me. He appeared in my bathroom while I was bathing; he appeared on whatever street I might be; he found me on the rooftop patio; and without my telling him, he knew which hotel suite was mine. It was as though he had an invisible tracking device somehow attached to me. That should have been a clue that Aster was not a being from some distant planet but a supernatural creature.

"During my self-imposed isolation, I refused to take phone calls from Lizzy and other friends. She and Allen had been meeting, and Lizzy had become confident that there was a limit to Aster's ability to track me. It was her belief that if we could get deep enough underground he would not be able to find me. I argued that the first time I met Aster he had been able to project himself into the cramped confines of the Windom Building basement and rescue Martha, but that didn't change her mind.

"She tried to explain to me the theological implications of multi-dimensional theory, but I understood very little of it. I did get the basic concept. Aster was not a being from another planet; he was a member of a created class of angels. As such, our three physical dimensions and one time dimension did not confine him as it did humans. She said that angels lived in a realm of more dimensions than humans experience, but she wouldn't explain more. She did say that angels have the ability to reduce themselves to our limited number of dimensions.

"'I doubt they enjoy it,' she said. 'Can you imagine what it would be like to move from three spatial dimensions to two? It would be like learning to live on the surface of a piece of paper with the forward and backward dimensions but no upward or downward dimensions. She told me the Bible didn't explain such things but that it gave us enough information to make some biblically based suppositions.

"I took her word for it.

"This conversation took place on the airplane, and it helped fill the time as we flew from Southern California to Minnesota.

"Tom Clyn remarked that many of Lizzy's comments sounded familiar. 'For decades some ufologists have suggested something similar. Several authors supposed that UFOs don't come from other planets but from other dimensions. The whole idea has the UFO community split down the middle. Until recently, I've been on the other side.'

"I couldn't argue with either of them, for what they said fit very well with some of the things I've seen Aster do. For now I was willing to believe it. And as far as hiding underground, well, I didn't have any better ideas.

"We landed at a private airport not far from the Soudan mine. Allen had already arranged for a Ford SUV rental. I can't tell you exactly how long it took to drive from the airport to the mine. Exhaustion blurred it all. Once at the mine opening, he punched a code on a keypad and opened the entry door. From there it was a long elevator ride to the bottom floor. As I mentioned earlier, scientists had converted the Soudan mine into a research facility looking for dark matter in the universe. Aster spoiled the scientists' fun by telling them everything they needed to know. The research grants dried up, and the mine was abandoned."

"You about ready?"

I stopped recording and faced Allen. "Almost. I need just another minute. How are things going with you?"

"I'm nervous. Scared, really. On the positive side, I spent my time talking to the young Mr. Clyn. While you were doing this, I took the opportunity to talk to him about Jesus. He resisted at first but soon began to ask questions. Long story short, there is a new believer in the world."

"That's great! Have you given any thought as to what to do with him now?"

"He wants to go with us. He feels partly responsible and he tells me that since his mother died he has no one else—no girlfriend, very few friends, none close."

"He understands the danger?"

Allen said he did. "I offered to give him some money, rent a car for him, let him go wherever he wants to go, but he refused. He's going with us."

"I'll be ready in one minute." I pushed the RECORD button again. "I said earlier that this is my last will and testament. Being of sound mind, I knowingly and freely bequeath to Maple Street Community Church all my worldly belongings. I would like the gift to be made in the name of Leo Hart. May God bless us and what we do."

I switched off the camera, rose from a chair, and joined the others at the elevator for the long ride to the surface. Before we began our ascent, we paused to pray.

I wondered how many minutes I had left to live.

PART III

Let love of the brethren continue. Do not neglect to show hospitality to strangers, for by this some have entertained angels without knowing it.

—Hebrews 13:1-2

Chapter Thirty-three

THE CONCEPT WAS SIMPLE, BUT PRISCILLA DIDN'T FOOL HERSELF into thinking that what they were about to do would be easy. After exiting the converted mine, they drove to the small town of Iron Mountain. On the outskirts of the town was a two-story, concrete, tilt-up building. A short distance away a dozen antennae pointed at unseen communication satellites in space. Allen parked the SUV, and they slipped from the big vehicle.

"You know, Allen," Priscilla said. "I never did ask how you knew the code to the mine."

"Do you remember Lizzy and I telling you about the many cells of believers dedicated to resisting Aster?"

"Yes."

"One of them is near here, and in that group is one of the directors of the black matter project. He gave me all the info I needed."

"This is your place, too?" Clyn asked.

"We have several sites around the globe. But this one has a special purpose."

"You've said that before," Priscilla said, "but you've never explained."

"Didn't I? Must have slipped my mind."

"More like you thought I had lost *my* mind and might not be trustworthy."

"Lizzy knew you'd come around. Me too. True believers can't walk away from their faith."

"I almost did."

Lizzy stepped in. "I don't think so, Priscilla. Like many people, you were just confused. Truth would win out."

"The truth. Do you think it will be enough?" Clyn wondered.

"The truth is a powerful weapon, Tom. Sooner or later, it wins. In this case, Jesus is our truth. I have every confidence in Him."

"So if Aster shows up, Jesus will keep us from being killed?"

Allen frowned. "No, son, I'm afraid not. He might, but a great many people have died for their faith. We may be no different."

"Oh."

"If you want to turn back, we'll understand. I can give you the car keys."

He thought for a moment. "No thanks. I'm in for good."

As we approached the facility, Allen got around to my question. "This is a lockdown building. That means that it is usually unmanned. We have techs in from time to time, but usually the place is empty. There are two reasons for that. First, the site is seldom used. It's a back-up site should weather or some act of terrorism knock one of our signal gathering sites off-line. A radio signal is sent here, and this station takes over until the other is fixed. Fortunately, we've never had to use it."

"And the second reason?" Priscilla asked.

"The military can lay claim to it. The building has two floors underground. One of them is for military use in the event of a national emergency. It has special capabilities."

"Such as?" Clyn asked.

We reached the only visible door, and Allen punched in a code on a keypad then leaned forward to a black panel.

"Biometrics? A retinal reader?" Clyn said.

"Actually, it reads the pattern of my iris." The lock made a clunking sound as it disengaged. Allen opened the door and let the others in.

"We're headed to the bottom floor," he said. "From there we can do what we came to do. We can access all the DigiTV satellites and a few that aren't our own."

"That's the special capability?" Clyn asked.

"Yes. The military has set up much of it. They want to be able to communicate with as many people as possible in the advent of nuclear or biological war. Homeland Security thinks it's necessary to have a system in place that links all the television satellites together."

"OK," Clyn said. "I know you're planning a broadcast, but just what are you planning on saying?"

Priscilla took a deep breath. "That I unwittingly helped advance the lie, so now I must purposefully advance the truth." The deeper reason she kept to herself: that the world had believed her about Aster before, and therefore she was the only person on the planet who might be believed when she told the truth about him.

"I'll keep an eye out for the bubble." Clyn lowered his voice as if unseen ears might be listening.

Lizzy said, "Don't bother. He doesn't need the bubble. Like his ship, it's an illusion."

"How do you know that?" Clyn asked.

"Because," Priscilla answered, "he appeared without it in my…home."

"Smoke and mirrors," Allen said. "It's all smoke and mirrors. This way."

They moved down a corridor that split the building into two halves. Large Plexiglas dividers allowed them to see banks of electronic equipment stacked in neat rows.

"This facility is operated from a remote site and is monitored twenty-four hours a day. Act as natural as possible. We're being watched on security cameras, but not to worry. I informed everyone who needed to know that I would be giving a tour to some friends. Let's stop here and look through the window. We need to look like we're interested in the system."

Priscilla looked through the clear divider. "So we're alone here?"

"Yes," Allen said. "No one will know anything is wrong until I switch control to this station. We won't have a lot of time, but we should have enough."

Clyn asked, "How many satellites will you be using?"

"DigiTV has four satellites in geosynchronous orbit at 22,200 miles above the earth's surface at 95, 101, 110, and 119 degrees longitude. Two of our competitors have more, but we have the edge on technology. The military system can link them all together."

"That's what we're going to do," Lizzy said.

"Lord willing, that's exactly what we're going to do."

Priscilla thought about the actions they committed themselves to take, and it frightened her. "You know, even if we succeed, our lives will never be the same."

"Because of Aster, no one's lives will be the same anyway," Lizzy countered. "At least this way the truth will be out there."

"And our conscience will be clean...or cleaner."

They started down the corridor again, stopping now and again to play the part of interested tour group.

Priscilla spoke softly. "When it comes to conscience, I'm the only one who needs forgiving. I'm the one who should have seen things sooner."

"Nonsense," Allen said. "People like me helped it all happen. Every broadcast went out over my satellites. And by arrangement with other corporations, Internet signals pass through my satellites, too."

"You were recouping from a coma," Priscilla said.

"Coma?" Clyn seemed stunned.

"It's a long story," Allen replied. "Let's pray I have the opportunity to tell you about it." He started down the hall again. "Next stop, the elevator."

They gathered around the door. Allen stopped for a moment and looked around as if he heard something. "Memorize this number: 022753. It's the override code to everything: security keypads, computer codes, everything."

"What about the iris scanners?" Clyn began to fidget.

"The only one is outside. Don't need them in here. Again, 022753. Everyone got that?"

"Got it," Priscilla said. "Any significance to the number?"

"It's the birth date of my favorite author."

The elevator doors parted.

Priscilla's ears popped.

The air felt thick.

The light turned green.

"I trusted you."

Priscilla spun. Two feet behind her stood an eight-foot-tall being—Aster.

With him were his two companions. None of them looked happy.

Aster extended his hand. His long, extra-jointed fingers caressed her check and fondled her red hair. "As a Bible reader, you may know that some of my kind caused a great deal of trouble in Noah's day, and it

282

all started with women like you. I didn't understand it then, but I'm beginning to see the attraction."

Priscilla slapped his hand away. Fire raced up her arm. It felt like she had struck an oak limb with the back of her hand. Aster's skin darkened several shades, and his emerald eyes became inky black.

Before she could utter a scream, she felt her feet leave the floor. Aster had seized her by the throat, lifted her from the ground, spun and slammed her back into the wall opposite the elevator. She would have screamed but Aster had her throat pinched shut.

She clawed at his arm. She kicked as hard as she could, but Aster was unmoved. Darkness crept into her eyes as lack of air and blood to her brain dragged her closer and closer to unconsciousness.

There was a chiming sound, the odd, unique laugh of Aster. "You can't win. You're puny. You're worthless. You are not worthy to be my pet."

"Hey!" Priscilla caught a glimpse of Clyn charging. He threw a punch that landed on Aster where a human's kidney would be. Aster flinched but showed no pain. Clyn's next sound was a scream as Tanra and Geel attacked. The pummeling was horrific.

As the darkness moved in and Priscilla began to slip into the abyss of unconsciousness, a hand grabbed Aster's arm, clamping on it like a vise. He winced, twisted, then let go of Priscilla.

"Your day is done." Lizzy yanked down, then up, and Aster's legs gave way. He went to the floor as Priscilla had a moment before. Unlike Priscilla, he returned to his feet a second later.

"Stay out of this, seraph. You have no business in this affair." He lunged forward before the last syllable left his mouth, striking Lizzy in the center of her chest with such force that her feet left the ground. Aster's companions sprang from Clyn to Lizzy like hyenas.

"No! Leave her alone." Priscilla struggled to shaky legs.

To Priscilla's surprise, Lizzy seized each creature by the face. They writhed and squealed. Lizzy let go, and the creatures backpedaled. Then she rose.

But it wasn't the Lizzy Priscilla knew. She seemed taller, broader, and her clothing began to tear at the seams.

"I said, stay out of this, seraph. Go back to your God," Aster said.

"I have business with you first."

For the first time in eighteen months, Priscilla saw fear on Aster's face.

"Allen, take Priscilla below."

"No!" Aster bolted forward, putting his full weight into the charge. The force of the impact drove Lizzy back into a wall. The drywall fractured, the overhead ceiling tiles fell. Aster struck her hard on the side of the head. The sound of it sickened Priscilla.

She couldn't let this happen. Still uncertain on her feet, Priscilla mustered as much strength as possible, charged, and jumped on Aster's back. She wrapped her arm around his throat and tried to squeeze, returning the favor. "Leave...her...alone—"

Aster's long arm reached over his shoulder and seized her by the back of her blouse. He jerked with such ferocity that Priscilla lost her grip. She landed hard on her back, the air forced from her lungs. She rolled to her side to see Aster still towering over Lizzy.

Her effort to save Lizzy failed, but it distracted Aster just enough. Lizzy had worked and twisted enough to get a foot beneath her. She pushed up with such force that both she and Aster hit the ceiling. More tiles fell. A fluorescent fixture came loose and swung from the ceiling like a pendulum.

Lizzy was no longer Lizzy. Already a tall woman, she stood a foot taller. Her clothing hung in rags from her broad frame. Like Aster, her features were sharp, her mouth small, and her eyes a deep shade of green.

All of that was startling, but more startling still were the wings on her back. Not a single pair of wings, like those seen in an artist's rendering of angles. Lizzy sported three pairs.

"Whoa!" Clyn said. He struggled to rise. Blood poured from his nose and mouth. Bruises from the beating he had just taken were already forming. Priscilla knew he'd be dead if the others hadn't tried to come to Aster's rescue.

"Stand away, seraph!" Aster's voice was so loud, Priscilla instinctively covered her ears.

"I have stood away too long, cherub. These belong to Creator, not you. I stand with them."

"You choose humans over your own kind?" Aster took a step back.

One pair of Lizzy's wings bent and crossed their tips over her waist; another pair did the same covering her...his...broad chest. The third pair dipped and pointed their tips at Aster. "You ceased being my kind when you began this doomed rebellion."

"Not doomed yet. Someday we will succeed. Those that went before may have failed, but I will not."

"They failed because faith will always win out over the likes of you."

The others had gathered their courage and began an assault on Lizzy. The vicious sound that came from their mouths pierced Priscilla's ears. She could feel the vibration of the sound in her organs, as if the noise were liquefying her from within.

She covered her ears. She cried out in pain.

The sound stopped, and Priscilla looked up in time to see one of the creatures hit the wall opposite the elevator with such force she could hear the wood studs snap. The other creature hit the floor so hard that every bone must have been pulverized—if the being had bones. It didn't move.

Aster started for Lizzy but slowed when Allen threw his full weight into him like an NFL player making the tackle of his life. Aster stumbled an inch to the side, seized Allen by the right shoulder, and twisted. Priscilla heard the bones break and the terrifying scream.

Despite his injuries, Clyn was on Aster before he could let go of Allen. The act was courageous but futile. Aster flung the young man to the side, his back hitting the jamb of the elevator doorway.

She heard a sickening crack.

She heard the air leave Clyn's lungs.

She saw him twitch, jerk, then cease moving. His eyes were open and unmoving.

"No!" She started toward Aster but a thick, powerful hand stopped her.

"Finish your mission," Lizzy said in the same kind of multilayered voice used by Aster.

"But..."

"Do what you've come to do."

"You need help," Priscilla said.

"I have help. Go, now. Help Allen."

Priscilla looked at the elevator, its doors still open. With no one on the next level to call for it, it would remain open.

Aster's skin darkened more. "I will not let her pass."

Lizzy moved with such speed that Priscilla almost missed the assault. Lizzy's wings flew to the side, brushing Priscilla back as her friend advanced like a missile. The impact with Aster would have killed anyone else.

Stunned, Priscilla watched as arms, legs, and wings enveloped Aster.

"Now, Priscilla. Now!"

She sprinted to the elevator, Allen right behind her, his arm hanging useless at his side. They stepped over Clyn's body, and Allen's words about martyrdom rang in her ears: *If a martyr I must be, than a martyr I shall be.*

The elevator doors closed, but not before Priscilla saw the two others rise and attack.

She could hear Lizzy's screams all the way to the basement floor.

Priscilla began to weep.

So did Allen.

Chapter Thirty-four

THE BASEMENT FLOOR WAS BLACK AS A TOMB UNTIL ALLEN MOVED from the elevator. Lights came on automatically.

"We don't have much time. Sit over there." He pointed to a horseshoe desk that reminded Priscilla of a television news studio. Allen moved to a desk with several monitors and a computer. He pressed the computer's POWER button.

Screams, wails, and thuds that sounded like concrete blocks being dropped on the floor filtered into the room. Priscilla covered her ears. "I can't think." She lowered her hands and tears flowed like rivers. "I...we have to go back. We have to help Lizzy...or whoever Lizzy is."

"She's an angel. You heard Aster call her seraph. You saw her wings. She's one of the class of angels known as the seraphim."

"Did you know before?"

"No. Never had a clue. However, I did think she was unusually bright."

The pounding above stopped, and Priscilla found the silence just as frightening.

"I don't know what to say. My mind isn't working. My thoughts—I can't formulate my thoughts."

"You have to," Allen said. "I can't do this. It has to be you. No one will believe me. I'll come across as a crank."

"I don't think I'll come across any better."

"Yes, you will. The world associates you with Aster. They see you as his friend, his advisor. When you tell them the truth, they'll believe it. It's the only chance we have. It's this or nothing."

"I'll...I'll try."

"Computer is up." He reached for the keyboard, then groaned. "Come here. I can't move my other arm. This will go faster with two hands."

Priscilla moved to the computer and sat down. "What do I do?"

"Key in the code."

"The birthday?"

"Right. It's—"

"I remember it. 022753." She typed it in. The computer came alive. A form appeared on the screen. "What now?"

"Put in my name as administrator."

Priscilla did. It took a few moments for the screen to change images. Three icons appeared, one the logo for DigiTV, one the emblem of Homeland Security, and the last the seal of the Department of Defense. "Which one?"

"DOD."

Priscilla moved the mouse and clicked the icon. A loud crash came from the open elevator doors. She snapped her head around. Something had fallen down the shaft and landed on the roof of the elevator cab.

"Quickly," Allen said. "Back to your spot. I can do the rest with the mouse."

Priscilla moved to the horseshoe desk, took a seat, and faced the lifeless camera. "Can you operate the camera?"

"It's automated. No cameraman needed. I just need a few minutes to set up the override and—" Another thud from the elevator, then the sound of destruction as something tore through the roof.

"Hurry. He's coming."

Priscilla leaned to one side to peer around the camera that blocked her view of the elevator doors. Material from the cab's ceiling. Less than a minute later, a body fell into the cab.

Lizzy.

A second later, Aster appeared. He bent, took hold of the unmoving Lizzy, and dragged her into the small studio.

"I know how you humans like a dramatic entrance. The bubble went over well, don't you think?"

"Why can't you leave us alone?" Priscilla asked.

288

"It is not in my nature anymore. Do you not want to know what happened to your friend? Here." He lifted Lizzy's body and tossed it to one side.

It took all of Priscilla's will power not to scream. She looked at Lizzy, who no longer appeared the way Priscilla knew her. That didn't matter. Friendship moved beyond such things. What did matter was that Lizzy was dead.

Aster moved to Priscilla, who remained rooted to her spot behind the desk.

"I see you have been weeping. That brings me such pleasure."

A red light to her side flashed on.

"Where are your buddies?"

As she had seen him do so often, Aster tipped his head to the side. "They did not fare so well. The seraph fought well."

"So now you plan to kill me, too. You're afraid the world will learn about your real nature."

"Oh, they will learn about it in time, but by then it will be too late. And yes, I plan to kill you—slowly. Perhaps I'll pull your organs out one at a time."

"The human race will catch on sooner than you think. You deceived me and many others, but the world will figure it out."

The laughter came. "Humans are sheep. Worse than sheep—sheep provide a useful product to humans, but humans destroy more than they build."

"Not the Christians."

"Yes. The Christians. Creator's Son sacrificed Himself for useless, worthless pets. You are no different from anyone else. Look how easily I fooled you. You are a believer and you saw no evil in me, only good."

He stepped closer and placed a hand under her chin. "You left the gathering too early, Priscilla Simms. They bowed to me." The weird grin appeared. "They worshiped me. Oh, how that must have hurt Creator."

"I will not bow to you. Thousands of Christians will resist you wherever you go."

"No, they won't. Their minds are weak; their knowledge of the spiritual is juvenile. They are just like you. You were so easy to deceive. Humans think they are so advanced with their science and technology. You remain a stupid and backward race."

"I helped start the lie; I intend to bring an end to it."

"You are too late, female. Too late. And you will bow to me before I kill you."

"I'm not as late as you think, Aster." She pointed at the camera. "Say 'cheese.'"

Aster looked at the camera, then at Allen who had slumped in the computer chair. He shrugged his one good shoulder. "While you two were chatting, I sent an e-mail to my chief tech. Everything that happened on the floor upstairs was captured by security cameras and relayed to our central uplink. We'll be broadcasting that to the world, too. I'll say one thing for you: you make great television."

Despite her fear, Priscilla smiled. "How's that for human science and technology?"

For the second time within minutes, Priscilla's back was pressed against the wall, Aster's hand on her throat. This time though, death didn't frighten her. The truth had been told. Her life had meant something.

"Who will save you now?"

From the corner of her eye, she saw Allen rise, then stop. As darkness began to swallow her mind again, she raised a hand and motioned to something behind Aster.

He turned his head, then released Priscilla.

She coughed a few times, then croaked. "Will they do?"

Lining the wall were a dozen beings like Aster, and some like Lizzy, each as tall.

A moment later, Aster disappeared, and a moment after that the line of angels did, too. With the exception of one—a six-winged, majestic creature. It studied Priscilla for a moment, then Allen. It nodded, then moved to Lizzy's body.

Gently, respectfully, the creature picked her up.

Priscilla approached. "She saved our lives. She gave herself so we could finish our mission. I can't believe she's dead."

290

The seraph looked at her as if puzzled, then said. "We do not die. Death is the privilege of humans."

They were gone.

Priscilla slumped to the floor and wept in convulsive sobs. They had succeeded, but at a great price. Allen eased himself to the floor next to her and put his good arm around her—and joined in her weeping.

Epilogue

One year later.

YOU ABOUT READY, HON?"

Priscilla raised her eyes from the Bible she had been reading. "I've been ready for an hour. And they say it's women who are slow."

Allen walked into the room. "You're the one who hogged the shower."

"I was writing my speech."

"In the shower?"

"We've only been married for four months. You still have a lot to learn about me."

He stepped to her and kissed her on the top of the head. "It's a good thing we're close to Columbia University. I don't want to be the one accused of holding up lunch. There will be lunch, right? I mean, they call it a luncheon."

"If not, there's always the school cafeteria."

He paused and looked at himself in the mirror. "Good. I'm hungry."

"You're still trying to make up for all the meals you missed while in a coma."

"That's a cold and cruel thing to say. Accurate, but cold and cruel." His tone changed. "You do know that I am very proud of you."

"I do, and I love you for it. I'm still trying to get used the irony of it all. When Aster came, everyone said I'd get a Pulitzer for shooting his arrival and making the first contact between human and alien. Instead, I'm getting a Pulitzer for my articles on global needs. Go figure."

"You're proving Lizzy's point. We don't need outside help to solve our global problems; we need faith and involvement. You're making a difference."

"But for how long?"

Allen massaged Priscilla's shoulders. "That's not up to us. We do what we can with what we have and let history work itself out."

"I'll give you half an hour to stop that."

"We don't have a half hour. You have to go wow the world one more time."

Priscilla stood. "I wish Lizzy could be here, and Tom Clyn."

"We only knew him for a short time, but I kinda liked him. Paying for his funeral was the least I could do. I just wish he had come to Christ sooner."

"One day in Christ and then a martyr while Debatto and Ian Robinson and the others continue to do what they do. Doesn't seem right."

"Every rose garden has its thorns." He held out his arm. "Come on, let's go. I rented a limo, and I want the world to see me with you."

She kissed him on the cheek, closed her Bible, and took his arm.

"By the way, what passage were you reading?"

"My favorite. It reminds me of Lizzy."

"Don't tell me. Hebrews 13:1–2. Right?"

"Hmm, maybe you have learned a few things about me." She took a breath then recited, 'Let love of the brethren continue. Do not neglect to show hospitality to strangers, for by this some have entertained angels without knowing it.'"

"Unknown angels. That's Lizzy all right."

They walked from the suite.

Outside, Priscilla instinctively looked at the sky. Thankfully, it was clear.

CROSSINGS®
THE BOOK CLUB FOR TODAY'S CHRISTIAN FAMILY

A Letter to Our Readers

Dear Reader:

In order that we might better contribute to your reading enjoyment, we would appreciate your taking a few minutes to respond to the following questions. When completed, please return to the following:

Andrea Doering, Editor-in-Chief
Crossings Book Club
401 Franklin Avenue, Garden City, NY 11530

You can post your review online! Go to www.crossings.com and rate this book.

Title _____ Author _____

1 Did you enjoy reading this book?

❑ Very much. I would like to see more books by this author!

❑ I really liked_____

❑ Moderately. I would have enjoyed it more if_____

2 What influenced your decision to purchase this book? Check all that apply.

❑ Cover
❑ Title
❑ Publicity
❑ Catalog description
❑ Friends
❑ Enjoyed other books by this author
❑ Other _____

3 Please check your age range:

❑ Under 18   ❑ 18-24
❑ 25-34   ❑ 35-45
❑ 46-55   ❑ Over 55

4 How many hours per week do you read? _____

5 How would you rate this book, on a scale from 1 (poor) to 5 (superior)?
_____

Name_____

Occupation_____

Address_____

City_____ State_____ Zip_____